Body Count

Also by William X. Kienzle

William X. Kienzle

Body Count

Andrews and McMeel

A Universal Press Syndicate Company

Kansas City

FOR JAVAN

Credits:
Editorial Director: Donna Martin
Production Editor: Jean Lowe
Book Design: Edward D. King
Jacket Design: George Diggs

ISBN 0-8362-6128-3

Acknowledgments

Gratitude for technical advice to:

Peter Bellanca, president, Bellanca, Beattie and DeLisle, P.C.
Sergeant James Grace, detective, Kalamazoo Police Department
Philip D. Head, vice president, Manufacturers National Bank of
Detroit
Rosemarie Lubienski, C.T.C., Mercury Travel Service, Inc.
James McIntyre, general manager, C.A. Muer Corporation
Rudy Reinhard, C.T.C., World Wide Travel Bureau, Inc.
Father Charles Strelick, J.C.L., pastor, St. John the Evangelist,
Ishpeming
Regis Walling, M.A., archivist, Bishop Baraga Association

Archdiocese of Detroit:
Father Louis Grandpre, M.A., pastor, St. Paul of Tarsus Catholic
Community
Bishop Thomas J. Gumbleton, D.D., J.C.D., auxiliary bishop of
Detroit
Father Robert Morand, chaplain, Wayne County Youth Home
Arnold Rzepecki, A.B., M.S., A.M.L.S., librarian, Sacred Heart
Major Seminary
Monsignor John P. Zenz, S.T.D., moderator of the Curia

Colleges and Universities:
Margaret Auer, director of libraries, University of Detroit Mercy
Ramon Betanzos, Ph.D., professor of humanities, Wayne State
University
Mary E. Hannah, Ph.D., chair of psychology, University of Detroit
Mercy
Father Anthony Kosnik, S.T.D., J.C.B., professor of ethics, Mary-
grove College
Werner Spitz, M.D., professor of forensic pathology, Wayne State
University

Detroit News:
Robert Ankeny, staff writer
Kate DeSmet, religion writer
Tim Kiska, TV writer

Detroit Police Department:
Sergeant Charles Kelley, Firearms Inventory Unit
Sergeant Mary Marcantonio, Office of Executive Deputy Chief
Inspector Barbara Weide, Criminal Investigation Bureau

Hospitals:
Sister Bernadelle Grimm, R.S.M., Samaritan Health Care Center,
    Detroit
Marge Hershey, R.N., Pulmonary Care Unit, Detroit Receiving
    Hospital
Thomas J. Petinga, Jr., D.O., FACEP, director of Emergency Depart-
    ment, St. Joseph Mercy Hospital, Pontiac

Office of Wayne County Prosecuting Attorney:
Loraine Gregory, extradition coordinator
Timothy Kenny, assistant Wayne County prosecuting attorney

With special gratitude to Lynn Lloyd

BIBLIOGRAPHY
Woodward, Kenneth L. *Making Saints.* New York: Simon &
    Schuster, 1990.
Battin, Margaret P. *Ethics in the Sanctuary.* New Haven: Yale Univer-
    sity Press, 1990.
Blaher, Damian Joseph, O.F.M., A.B., J.C.L. *The Ordinary Process in
    Causes of Beatification and Canonization.* Washington, D.C.: Cath-
    olic University of America Press, 1949.
Casey, Genevieve. *Father Clem Kern, Conscience of Detroit.* Marygrove
    College in cooperation with the Fr. Clement H. Kern Founda-
    tion, 1989.

Part
One

1

"BLESS ME, Father, for I have sinned."

She settled into the chair opposite Father Robert Koesler as he recited, "May the Lord be in your heart and on your lips so that you may rightly confess your sins."

"It's been . . . oh . . . maybe a couple of years since my last confession—good Lord, what the hell is that?"

The priest, startled, followed her gaze and found himself staring at a green growth on the table between them. "It's a plant," he explained vaguely.

"You mean it's alive?"

He smiled. "It won't bite you."

"I'm not so sure. It's about the ugliest thing I've ever seen. What is it, do you know?"

"It's a *Gynura*. It's also called a purple passion vine."

"Then how come it's not purple?"

"Well . . ." He was beginning to feel uncomfortable. It was the first time he'd been challenged to defend a plant. ". . . it needs a lot of light to keep its purple. And, as you can see . . ." His explanation drifted off. He gestured toward the tiny stained glass window. A lighted candle and a low-wattage electric bulb were the only other illumination in the small cubicle. He felt the woman was looking at him as if he were mentally deficient.

"It's a wonder it's alive at all . . . it is alive, isn't it?" she pursued.

"Uh-huh."

"If you'll excuse me, Father, why put any kind of plant in a room like this?"

"The new liturgy for the Sacrament of Reconciliation suggests a table, a Bible, a candle, and some sort of plant in the place set aside for face-to-face confession. Speaking of confession: That is why you came, isn't it?"

"Oh, yes . . . sure. I was shopping across Gratiot at the Eastern

Market and I saw your steeple and it was Saturday afternoon. So I thought, why not? And here I am."

So much for his reputation as a sensitive, kindly confessor to rival St. John Vianney, the holy Curé d'Ars. She just happened to be in the neighborhood. "So, here you are. Two years is kind of a long while, don't you think?"

"I suppose." She reflected. "Yeah, it is. Good grief, I can remember the good old days. Once a week. At least once a month."

Koesler could remember the good old days even more vividly than his penitent.

"The good old days!" she continued: "I used to come to confession and say the same old things over and over: 'I quarreled with my husband. Lost patience with the kids. Gossiped.' "

Koesler smiled. "Is that what it's going to be today: Anger? Arguments? Gossip?"

"I wish it were. I got bigger problems than that. Matter of fact, I don't exactly know why I'm here. It was just on the spur of the moment. Maybe I shouldn't have come." She moved as if to leave.

"No; wait." She did. "There must be a reason why you came today," the priest said. "I don't think I've seen you before. Do you live around here?"

"No. Out in the 'burbs. Like I said, I was shopping at the market and—"

"What's the problem?"

"Uh . . . the Church."

"The whole thing?"

"I just can't believe everything the Church teaches. Maybe I've lost my faith. Maybe I'm not a Catholic anymore."

"Like what don't you believe? In God? In Jesus Christ?"

"Oh, no, for Pete's sake, no! Sure I believe in God, in Jesus!"

"Then . . .?"

"Things like birth control, divorce, remarriage, even abortion. To be perfectly frank, Father, I don't think the Church has the slightest clue as to what's going on in the real world."

"Have you prayed over this?"

"Oh, yeah, I read about that in the papers: Some Cardinal in Rome said that if you don't believe what the Church teaches, you should go pray until you do. That seems kind of silly to me."

"Me too."

"You too!" She was startled.

He shifted in his chair so that he more fully faced her. "When I asked if you prayed over this, I meant more in terms of prayerfully forming your conscience."

"You did?"

"I imagine just about every institution, bureaucracy, whatever, would like to dictate what its members believe. It keeps things nice, helps keep them just the way the institution wants. But that's not the way it works for us. I mean, we have an absolute obligation to form our conscience and follow it."

"That does sort of ring a bell," she admitted. "Then what's all this stuff about praying until you agree?"

"Sort of stretching a point, I guess you could say. I must admit it is kind of tricky. You can see where following his conscience got Hitler, for instance. Nevertheless, it holds true: We've got to form our own set of values—what's right and what's wrong. The Church tries to be extremely helpful in assisting us to accomplish this. But no one—not me, not the bishop, not even the Pope—can be a substitute for our own personal responsibility. So you may have a big job ahead of you in settling the questions you raise. You know how the institutional Church feels about artificial birth control, remarriage, and the rest. You'd have to have the strongest, most legitimate defensible reasons to disregard all this.

"On the other hand, if you don't actually believe what you profess to believe, you'd only be kidding yourself. You've got to be straight with yourself and straight with God. We can't fool God. Not in the recesses of our conscience."

The silence was so total the creaks and groans of the ancient church could be heard.

He had given her a lot to think about. Could she trust a guy who kept a plant in a dungeon? Yet what he said seemed to make sense. She was deeper in doubt now than she had been before coming to confession today. But now it seemed a sort of creative doubt. Henceforth, when she took time for silent prayer, at least she would know what it was she was praying about.

If nothing else, the silence reached her. She had to say something. "I don't know what to tell you, Father. I gotta get by myself and think this through."

"Pray it through," he amended.

"Yes, that's right, pray it through. It didn't take you long to say it, but that's a lot to consider. I've felt so . . . uh . . . guilty. It started when the Pope said that the old rules on family planning were right and you couldn't use birth control. I was sure he was wrong. But, then, how could he be? He's infallible!"

"He wasn't being infallible when he said that."

"Okay. But the Cardinal said you had to agree with the Pope whether he was being infallible or not."

"An overstatement, I think."

"Some overstatement! It threw my life into a tailspin . . . my spiritual life, that is."

Another pause. Finally, Koesler asked, "Do you want to go to confession? Do you want to mention some sin of your past life if you're not aware of any sin now? Do you want me to give you absolution?"

Her brow was profoundly knit. "No, no . . . not now. Maybe I'll be back. Would it be okay if I come back that I come to you? I mean, I'm not from your parish."

"It'll be fine if you want to talk to me. When you leave, why don't you take one of the parish bulletins in the vestibule? It'll give you the times when we hear confessions at St. Joe's."

She smiled. "I'll do that."

He blessed her and she left.

It seemed to Father Koesler that he'd been engaged in this sort of activity—demythologizing Church teaching—for an awfully long time now. Since shortly after he'd been ordained thirty-eight years ago.

Then, as now, the most frequent misunderstanding was over birth control. Just before Koesler had been ordained, Pope Pius XII had, in effect, blessed the rhythm method of family planning. Now it seemed archaic. But at the time it was a monumental relief for Catholics, who, until then, had had no acceptable recourse but abstinence.

In his early days of hearing confessions, Koesler had been surprised by the number of penitents who told him that some previous priest had given "permission" to use the rhythm method for a specific number of months. Would Koesler grant an extension?

At that point Koesler had felt forced to explain that it was not the priest's place to treat rhythm as a privilege to be granted, withheld or measured. If advice was sought, priests could advise, but they had no business beyond offering their opinion. And then only if the opinion was requested.

Once again, it was a matter of the individual's conscience being the final authority. And it was the individual's responsibility to shape that conscience.

No one had followed the previous penitent into the confessional. No surprise there. In the "good old days," as the woman had put it, in most parishes there was seldom an interval between penitents. People who confessed once or twice a year did so at Christmas and Easter, and were customarily scolded for not coming more often. It had been, as the woman said, a monthly experience for most, though more often for some.

Slowly—after the Second Vatican Council in the early sixties—things changed. Perhaps the most radical change, as far as confession was concerned, was a transition in the concept of sin. Particularly in the Catholic concept of mortal sin. Upon disturbing reflection, it made little sense to many that God would vacillate between sending one to heaven or hell dependent on a single event—missing Mass of a Sunday, eating a pork chop on Friday.

With one thing and another, the "good old days" seemed gone forever.

It was difficult, from the confines of the confessional, to determine whether or not there was anyone else in the church. "Old St. Joseph's," as it was called more often than not, truly was an elderly edifice. Established in 1856, it had now been declared a historic landmark. In addition to an abundance of Gothic arches, it was overflowing with pictures, windows, and statues depicting God, Jesus, Mary, Joseph of course, and lots of other saints. Over the years in the archdiocese of Detroit, eleven other churches had been dedicated to St. Joseph. But "Old St. Joe's" in downtown Detroit had been the first.

Once it had been a thriving parish with an adjacent Catholic high school for boys, run by the Christian Brothers. But with the shift in population to the suburbs, St. Joe's had become merely a historical as well as an architectural curiosity. Then, with the erection of a series of nearby high-rise apartments and condominiums, "Old St. Joe's" had the potential for a new life.

Father Koesler, after a lengthy pastorate in a suburban parish, had been pastor of St. Joe's just a little more than a year now. And, due in large part to his diligent work, there had been a significant comeback. At least Sunday Mass attendance was healthy and growing.

Koesler's satisfying thoughts about his flourishing flock were interrupted by a woman who entered the confessional and seated herself across from him.

Her appearance was in stark contrast to that of the previous woman. Koesler could not help notice the difference. He knew neither, but this woman was at least vaguely familiar. If he was not mistaken, she had been attending Mass at St. Joe's for the past few months.

But the extreme contrast! What a coincidence that they had appeared, one after the other, on this leisurely Saturday afternoon.

Woman "A" had been dressed appropriately for just what she claimed she had been doing—shopping at the Eastern Market. She had worn faded jeans, sneakers, a sweatshirt several sizes too large, and no makeup.

Woman "B" wore a well-fitted business suit that accentuated her attractive matronly figure. Her hair looked as if it had been "done" recently. Her makeup had been carefully, artfully applied. But her lips, unlike those of Woman "A," were thin, tight, and disapproving.

Koesler waited a moment, then offered, "Peace be with you."

"And also with you," she responded.

Well, at least she was familiar with the updated formula. At this point either the priest or the penitent might have suggested a relevant Scripture reading. But she said nothing, so, in the tentative circumstances, he thought it better not to delay getting to the heart of the matter.

"Bless me, Father, for I have sinned," she said, after a moment. "My last confession was six years ago."

"You recall that it was six years?"

"Yes."

Odd that without hesitation she could pinpoint her last previous confession at six years. Not "about" six years, "approximately" six years, six years "more or less," but "six years" exactly. "Was there something special that happened in your life when you made your last confession?"

She almost smiled. "I left the convent."

Surprised, Koesler asked, "Did you leave the Church too then?"

"No, no, not that . . . at least I kept coming to Sunday Mass pretty faithfully. But—"

"Did you go to confession regularly while you were a nun?"

She shrugged. "I suppose that was the problem." She thought for a moment. "No, maybe it was more the symptom."

Koesler's look was a question.

"I was a convert in my teens . . ." She hesitated. "Do you have time for this?"

He nodded. "I'm in no hurry."

She shifted in the chair and looked away. She was remembering. "My parents had no religion, so they gave me none. Sometime during high school, I felt I was just drifting, especially compared with some of my classmates who had . . . faith. Who were committed to one or another religion. I became interested in Catholicism . . . probably because a close friend was Catholic."

Koesler almost smiled as he recalled the old story of the Catholic girl who wanted her fiancé to convert to her religion. To please her, he started taking instructions—and ended up going to the seminary and becoming a priest. Had this woman's "close friend" been a young man who, wanting to marry her, had gotten her interested in his Catholic religion only to lose out when, tragically for him, she entered the convent and became a nun? Koesler didn't interrupt. It was her story.

"Anyway, I found just about everything I seemed to need in Catholicism. So, as I've already mentioned, I entered the convent. I became a nun.

"You asked if I went to confession regularly when I was a nun." Her smile was bitter. "Every week—to a priest whom we called our regular confessor."

"And," Koesler completed her thought, "four times a year to one who was called your 'extraordinary' confessor."

She glanced at him. "That's right."

Early in his priesthood, Koesler had been assigned as a regular confessor for a group of almost thirty nuns. Thirty nuns confessing every week! In their sinless lives these women had not prepared lesson plans, failed in promptitude, and committed similar crimes. Why a regular confessor? Who knew? There was even a regulation that, for a valid confession, a screen was required to separate the confessor and the penitent nun. Prompting the story of the nun who wanted to go to confession to her pastor in the rectory where there was no established confessional. So the priest held up a fly swatter between them.

"Then," Koesler said, "there came a time when there were no more regular or extraordinary confessors."

She nodded. "Then," she added, "there came a time when the 'community' disappeared. So many of my Sisters left. So few women were entering. So many nuns decided to get into apostolates that had nothing to do with the purpose of our order." She shook her head. "There was nothing left."

"So you left religious life."

"There was nothing to leave."

Koesler knew many former nuns. Most were leading well adjusted, productive lives. Many were married. If anything, this one did not appear to be all that well adjusted. Something was troubling her. What?

"How have you done since leaving?" he asked.

"Materially? Quite well."

"Oh?"

"I'm in estate planning."

Appropriate. The way she came across, she did not appear to be the type who would work well person to person. Better that she juggle figures than do counseling.

"I have no financial worries," she continued. "I've got a comfortable apartment at 1300 Lafayette."

Thirteen hundred Lafayette, among one of the pricier high rises on the edge of downtown, was within walking distance of St. Joe's. Koesler knew it well. "I've rung some doorbells there," he said. "But I haven't run into you."

"You probably called during the day. I'm seldom home until late in the evening. But I've heard of you. I've attended Sunday Mass here over the past couple of months. You seem down to earth. So I decided to try confession."

"You're familiar with the new form? What we call the Sacrament of Reconciliation?"

She smiled, but there was no humor in her eyes. "I saw the signs outside the confessional: private confession on the other side, face-to-face here. I chose this. Yes, of course I'm familiar with it. Vatican II happened some twenty-five years ago. I left the convent only six years ago. Actually, this is one of the very few changes that I came to like. I always thought the screens, the sliding panels, the anonymity was silly."

"That brings up a question: The Council, indeed, took place in the early sixties. What took you so long to leave?"

She seemed overcome by the memory of all those years. "I had a commitment. I was determined to fulfill it. As it turned out, I should have left years earlier. By the time I was forced to decide, there was nothing left. I was skating on water. All the reasons I had chosen Catholicism over the other religions disappeared after that Council. I just wouldn't let myself believe it. I kept telling myself the changes were God's will—that, in time, things would work out. I was wrong. And, in my mistake, I wasted some twenty years of my life—twenty very precious years." She seemed drained.

So that was it. The lady was bitter. Well, in a way, she deserved to be resentful. On the other hand, the wasted time was her own responsibility. No one had barred the convent door, imprisoning her. Although in her circumstances a decision to leave or stay had to be painful, nonetheless it remained her decision to make.

"Isn't it a bit overdrawn," he suggested, "to say that your time in religious life was a complete waste? I'm sure you accomplished lots of things you can be justly proud of. You don't seem the type who would just vegetate all those years—or stand in some corner and pout."

She sat up straight, head erect. "Oh, yes, I accomplished some things. I signed up to teach, and I taught. That's not the point. The point is I wasted my life. The life I should have lived. The things I should have done . . . they're gone. They will never come back."

Koesler reckoned that nothing would be accomplished by trying to find a silver lining in the seemingly impenetrable cloud she had made of her years as a nun. Not now in any case.

He led her through a confession that revealed little beyond her having been a careless Catholic—missing Sunday Mass, neglecting any sort of purposeful spiritual life, and the like. For a penance, he urged her to try to set aside a regular time to read and meditate on the Bible. She expressed sorrow for sin. He absolved her and, seemingly somewhat mellowed, she left.

Strange: consecutive penitents, women of approximately the same age, yet how different from each other. They were almost the embodiment of the present delicate state of the Church, the disparate byproducts of that Second Vatican Council.

For some Catholics, the Council had not come anywhere near to achieving what it had set out to do. Penitent "A" would be one product of that.

For others, the Council had virtually destroyed the Church they loved. Penitent "B" fell into that category. For the rest—the passive majority?—something had happened, they knew not what. But give them a relatively quiet Sunday liturgy without too many demands made of them, and they would go along with most of this foolishness—even the handshake of peace.

Koesler's mental ramblings were cut short by the sound of someone entering the opposite confessional, the one labeled "private confessions."

Actually, the "private confessions" confessional essentially was no different from the ones Catholics had been used to for centuries. Equipped with a kneeler and an armrest fixed to the wall facing the priest, the cubicle had a rectangular opening fitted with a curtain and/or screen and a sliding panel that could be opened and closed by the priest. The purpose of this arrangement was to offer anonymity to the penitent, who waited, in the dark—there was no light fixture—for the priest to open the panel, at which point the penitent was instructed to speak in whispers. Thus unseen and speaking only in a whisper, the penitent's anonymity was virtually guaranteed. Almost all Catholic churches were now well equipped with the "face-to-face" setup as well as some form of the earlier confidential facility.

In Old St. Joe's, one of the former private cubicles had been remodeled and outfitted with the penitent's chair, the table holding the Bible, a candle, and, in this case, the execrable plant.

Koesler could hear the unseen penitent's fumbling footsteps as he felt his way in the dark before dropping to his knees on the low step. Without bothering to turn his head toward the curtain and screen that separated him from the penitent, Koesler slid open the panel.

"Bless me, Father, for I have sinned," came the whisper. "My last confession was about a month ago."

Seems like old times—the whispered voice, the monthly confession.

"I was angry at work a few times. And a couple of times I blew up at my secretary. But she is incompetent. Only I can't fire her. And . . . here's the one that's got me puzzled: My wife says I'm creating a wrong attitude in my son . . . giving him a false set of values."

"Oh?"

"See, one day last week, my son's school showed a movie on Nelson Mandela. The kids who went to the movie were supposed to donate a dollar. The proceeds were to go to the Afro-American Museum. I made sure he had the dollar before I left for work. So when he got home from school, my wife asked him about the movie. He told her that the projector broke down in the middle of the first reel. And, he said, they didn't even give his dollar back. Then my wife bawled him out for being so stingy. She told him how the dollar went to a good cause and he shouldn't even think about getting it back.

"But I didn't know about any of this. So when I got home from work, I asked him how the movie was. And he told me how the projector broke down so he didn't get to see the movie. And then I asked him if they gave him his dollar back."

Father Koesler's shoulders shook with repressed laughter. Gently, he sided with the man's wife, while sympathizing with the penitent's initial reaction to the contribution with no dividend. After issuing a penance, as the penitent recited the prayer of contrition, Koesler absolved him.

After a few moments, Koesler heard the front door of the church clang shut. Which meant that the man who'd just confessed had departed, or that a new penitent had arrived—or both. From inside the confessional, there was no way the priest could tell.

Koesler leaned back in his chair and again became lost in thought. His memory stretched back into the days before the Council.

Twenty-five or thirty or more years ago, Saturday afternoons usually found an unending line of kids streaming in and out of the confessional. All said virtually the same thing: They "just obeyed" their mothers, fathers, aunts, uncles, baby-sitters, garbage collectors—casual strangers, for that matter. Not only were they habitually disobedient, they also committed "adultry" before they knew what it was or what it involved.

Then there was always the kid whose previous confession had been just last week, but in that time, he'd missed Sunday Mass four times.

Don't ask! Interrupt the little ones in their by-rote recitations of memorized sins, and the computers in their little heads would short-circuit, reducing them to impenetrable silence. Then how to get them to finish the list and conclude the confession?

In this, Koesler had proved a quick learner—uncharacteristically. After only a couple of minor disasters with kids stopped dead in their tracks because he sought clarification, he just accepted whatever they said—no matter how contradictory or impossible—issued a penance of a certain number of prayers, and absolved them from their fancied transgressions or peccadillos.

At one time during his early years as a priest, Koesler figured that was how he would die: on a Saturday afternoon, listening to the repetitive confessions of children—from boredom.

But in all likelihood it was not to be. Kids were no longer coming to confession weekly, daily. Adults did not come. Nobody came. Not as they had. The weeks before Christmas and Easter had once been Monday-through-Saturday, dawn-till-night confessions. Now a few hours would take care of the entire load.

Abruptly, the door to the open confessional was flung back. There stood—no, towered—one of the largest men Koesler had ever seen. His body was mountainous. His head was huge. His lips, his mouth, his teeth, raised visions of *Jaws*. His ears were sagging shutters; his bulbous off-centered nose seemed to have been smashed many times over. His eyes seemed to have been put in his face as an afterthought; so small were they that had it not been for their beadiness they would have almost disappeared in the moon-crater face.

Why did he have the feeling he had seen this man before? In a previous parish? At a meeting? In a gathering? The news media, television, the newspapers? The boxing ring? The movies?

The man seemed as startled to see Koesler as Koesler was to see him. "What the hell! What're you doin' here?"

"I'm . . ." Koesler had to think about this one. "I'm hearing confessions."

"Then where's the wall? Where's the goddam window?"

Ah, that was it. "It's on the other side. You came in the wrong door. Go in the other door . . . the one that's marked 'private confessions.'"

The door slammed shut. Koesler could hear him grousing as he barged through the other door; the entire cubicle shook as that too slammed in the behemoth's wake.

Koesler slid the small window open. He could hear the man groping his way toward the kneeler. Koesler could hear it all but could make out nothing in the dark. But of course he had already seen the man. So much for anonymity.

Finally, the man was kneeling—and grunting. Then, after several extended moments of silence, "How do you start this thing again?"

"Bless me, Father . . ." Koesler prompted.

"Bless me, Father . . ." Silence. "Then what?"

". . . for I have sinned."

". . . for I have sinned. Oh, yeah: Bless me, Father, for I have sinned. That's right."

Another silence.

"My last confession . . ."

"My last confession . . .?" the man wondered.

"How long has it been since you went to confession last?"

"Oh. Oh . . . oh . . . I guess my last confession was the first time."

"Your last confession was your first confession? When you were a child?"

"Near as I can figure."

"Not even when you were confirmed?"

"What's that?"

"Confirmation. When a bishop confirms you. You weren't confirmed?"

"I don't think so. I would have remembered that, I guess."

This, thought Koesler, was one of God's neglected children. The man's swarthy cast, together with his features and pronounced accent, suggested a Mediterranean heritage, possibly Sicilian. In Koesler's experience, such people frequently were either extremely religious or total strangers to church. He recalled the man who had stopped in at a Detroit rectory and asked for Monsignor Vizmara, only to be told that monsignor had died five years previously. "Oh, that'sa too bad," the man said, "he was-a my regular confessor."

In any case, something extraordinary must have happened for this man to have come in after all these years. What?

"All right," Koesler said, "it's been a great number of years since you've been to confession. What brings you back?"

"Well, see, I killed a priest."

"You what!?" Koesler suddenly realized that not only had he and his penitent been speaking aloud instead of whispering, but that he himself had just shouted. Koesler was embarrassed. "You what?" he repeated in a whisper.

"I said I killed a priest. You hard of hearing?"

"No. And you should whisper, like I am . . . now."

"Oh."

Silence.

"You killed a priest," Koesler repeated, his tone a mixture of wonderment and near astonishment.

"That's what I did all right." He was not whispering.

"Well . . . why?"

"A contract."

"A contract?"

"Yeah. A contract. Somebody put out a contract on him. They gave it to me. I felt bad about it. I never wasted a priest before."

"You never wasted . . . uh . . . killed a priest before. Does that mean you have killed others—others who were not priests?"

"Oh, yeah. But never a priest. This was my first time." His tone communicated pride in his achievement.

In all his years as a priest, Koesler had heard murder confessed only a couple of times. He considered murder the ultimate crime, if not sin, and he was shocked. But he tried to regain his composure as he forced himself to consider the theological implications of murder.

Obviously, no matter how repentant a murderer might be, there was nothing he could do for his victim. There were other considerations though. *Damnum emergens*—as a result of the murder, were there any ramifications, complications, consequences?

"Did anyone depend on this priest?" Koesler asked in a whisper. "I mean, was he supporting anyone, as far as you know?"

"He wasn't married." The man was definitely not whispering. "At least I don't think he was married. He couldna been married, could he . . . I mean, he was a priest after all!"

"You should whisper," Koesler admonished. "I mean, was he supporting any relative—a mother, sister, something like that? Did anyone rely on him for support—financial support?" The implication being that if anyone suffered as a consequence of this killing, the murderer would incur that responsibility.

"Geez, I don't think so."

"Has any innocent person been accused of the crime?"

"Are you kiddin'? I just did it yesterday. What's with all these questions?"

"I'm trying to cover all the possibilities. For you to be truly sorry for what you did you have to be willing to make reparations for any evil consequences—any bad things that happen because you killed this man, this priest. For instance, if an innocent person were to be accused of this crime—especially if an innocent person were convicted of the crime—you would have to come forward and confess publicly. Would you do that?"

Pause.

"That's a safe enough bet," the man said finally. "If they tagged somebody, I'd sing. But I wouldn't put my last chip on that happening." Pause. Then, "These are crazy questions. I thought you'd want to know who bought it."

"Who bought it? You mean who got killed? Well, it's not absolutely necessary for your confession. But, yes, of course, I'd like very much to know the name."

"Keating."

"Keating? John Keating? The pastor of St. Waldo's?"

"Uh-huh."

"But why? Why would you want to kill Father Keating? No, wait: You don't have to answer that. I just got a bit carried away."

"That's okay. Like I told you, he had a contract on him. He had too many markers he couldn't buy back."

"Markers . . .?"

"Debts. Gambling debts. Everything. Horses, football, basketball, baseball, hockey, numbers . . . you name it, he had a piece of it. Only he wasn't too savvy. He ran up some steep bills. He couldn't make good—so, the contract."

The penitent couldn't see Koesler shaking his head. "This is hard to take," the priest whispered. "Poor Jake . . ."

"There's something else," the penitent said.

Koesler shook himself as if to clear his head. "More?"

"I dunno. Maybe it's a sin the way we stashed him. I dunno. I don't think so. But maybe. I was gonna ask . . ."

"The way you stashed him?"

"I had him buried with Father Kern."

"Kern? Monsignor Clem Kern?"

"Oh, yeah, that's right, he was a whatchamacallit—a monsignor."

"You had Father Keating buried with Clem Kern? I don't understand. Why? How?"

"How? We just went to the cemetery last night, slipped the guard a mickey, dug up Father Kern, opened the coffin, put Keating in with him—Father Kern wasn't all that big, there was room—and planted the box again. It was very smooth. No one would tumble."

"My God! Why would you do a thing like that?"

"Why? Well, see, we're usedta sending messages when we hit somebody. You know, you musta read about 'em. Like when we dump a body in the drink we send the family a dead fish. It tells 'em the guy is sleepin' with the fishes. It's a message. Sometimes a warning . . . you know."

"But why would you bury the poor man with somebody else?"

"Hey! You wouldn't want us to return the body with its hands cut off and stuffed in the guy's mouth. I mean the guy was a priest, for God's sake. We had to treat him with some kinda respec', you know."

Koesler was beginning to wonder if any of this made any kind of sense. "Well, then, why Clem Kern? Why did you bury him with Monsignor Kern?"

"It made sense. I mean Father Kern was the kinda priest the guy shoulda been. Besides, Father Kern always took care-a people who were down on their luck, even priests. And there ain't no doubt about it, this guy Keating had definitely run outta luck. Anyway, I was wonderin' if that might be a sin too . . . I mean buryin' the guy with somebody else? I never did that before. So I never thought about it until after we did it."

Koesler ran his index finger across his brow. Even though the church was pleasantly cool, he was perspiring. "I don't think so. We've got enough to deal with here without spending much time on your cockamamy burial detail."

"My what?"

"Never mind. Let's see . . . you murdered Father Keating. And you mentioned there were others. How many people have you killed, anyway?"

"Oh . . . I dunno. Right off the top I couldn't come up with a figure."

"That many!"

"Not many. But I'd have to think about it a while."

"Well . . . good heavens . . . are you sorry for all these murders?"

"Not really. They were stric'ly business. Hey, that's what I do for a living. You know. It's not natural to be sorry for your job. I mean, a man's gotta have some pride, you know."

"Good Lord! Well, what about other sins?"

"I didn't do nothin'."

"Do you go to Mass on Sundays? Did you ever go to Mass?"

"No. Like I said, I didn't do nothin'."

"I give up. I don't know where you fit in the theology manuals, but you must be confined to the fine print. Well, let's see, you came here to confess killing Father Keating . . ."

". . . and planting him with Father Kern."

"Yes, and burying him with Father Kern . . . that about it?"

"Yeah, that's it."

"Then I guess I'd better give you absolution, though I can't guarantee that it'll take."

"Do your best, Father. That's good enough for me."

"And for your penance . . . wow! I don't suppose you know any prayers?"

"I think I knew the 'Our Father' once. But I ain't sure. Tell you what: How about I go home? I got a record of Sinatra singin' the 'Our Father.' How about if I listen to the record?"

Inspired. "Okay. I'll give you absolution now, but I'm not exactly sure why. Except that's why you came here, and you very definitely are a sinner."

"Ain't I supposed to do somethin'? Seems to me when I went to confession the last time I had to say somethin' while the priest blessed me."

"What a memory! Okay, repeat after me: '*Oh, my God . . .*'"

"Oh, my God . . ."

Maybe that's as far as we ought to go, thought Koesler. But he continued. "'*I am heartily sorry . . .*'"

"I am heartily sorry . . ."

Truth in advertising, thought Koesler. But he continued to lead the man through the traditional Act of Contrition, and then gave him absolution.

The man got up, grunted, then stumbled his way out—leaving the priest somewhat the worse for wear.

Did I do the right thing? Koesler asked himself over and over again. *What would somebody else have done in my shoes?* Undoubtedly some other priest—maybe most priests—would have just told the guy to hit the road. Should the man have been denied absolution? Who could say for sure?

Koesler had been hearing confessions for thirty-eight years. The majority were familiar, repetitious, routine, dull. Once in a great while a confession could be a small miracle in removing an oppressive burden of guilt or as a vehicle for transforming a life. Some few confessions proved unnerving. But this confession—the one he'd just heard—was the oddest ever.

Ostensibly, the man had come for absolution. Was his case so far removed from that of neurotics and psychotics Koesler had absolved in the past—sometimes entire hospital wards of the pitiful people one by one?

In the final analysis—the bottom line, as current culture would have it—this remained a matter between the sinner and God. Koesler believed, firmly, that Jesus gave His disciples the power to forgive sin and that the disciples, in turn, passed on this power to their successors. Koesler could see the wisdom of it. The talking cure. Long before psychotherapy stumbled upon it, God would have known what would comfort and relieve His children. But no matter what power the priest might have as an intermediary, or how important it was that people should forgive each other, God forgave sin.

So it did not much matter whether the murderer was sincere or not in his expressed repentance, his contrition for what he'd done; God would not be tricked. Should a sinner try to fool God, it would be the sinner who played the fool.

Abruptly, Koesler became aware that it had been quite a while since the penitent—the murderer—had left the confessional. He glanced at his ever-present watch: 7:30. He'd been sitting there half an hour overtime, with no penitents on deck. He had fallen behind in his Saturday evening routine. He had to lock the church and return to the rectory.

Hurriedly, he blew out the candle, turned out the light, and stepped from the confessional.

He was pulled up short by the sight of a figure seated in a nearby pew.

The very first thing Koesler noticed was the young man's clerical garb: black suit, black vest, and at the top the roman collar—not the fairly modern and more comfortable narrow white plastic insert, but the full white collar that encircled the neck. Koesler also noticed French cuffs peeking out of the jacket sleeves.

The young man stayed seated, smiling all the while.

Koesler approached him. "Father?"

"Yes, Father."

"Is there something I can do for you?"

"I hope so. There may even be something I can do for you. I'm your new associate."

2

Technically, but far more importantly, in actuality, Father Nick Dunn was not a "new associate" pastor at St. Joseph's parish. He was "in residence."

Father Koesler clearly remembered having received Father Dunn's query letter. Dunn planned to take some psychology courses at the University of Detroit Mercy, a Jesuit institution located near the city's north-central center. Would it be possible, he'd inquired, for him to live at St. Joe's for the duration?

Koesler realized Dunn's contribution to parochial life would be minimal. Help with Masses on weekends could be taken for granted. But little else.

Nevertheless, Koesler promptly assented to the request. Having another priest in the house would be boon enough. In effect, he had forsaken companionship when he'd accepted the celibate life. But St. Joseph's rectory was the embodiment of a hermitage. Though easily adequate for a very large family, the house was home for only one man. And most evenings were so quiet, Koesler could easily imagine raising the drawbridge over the moat.

Quickly recovering from his surprise at finding Father Dunn in church, Koesler took his temporary colleague on a tour while showing him how to lock up the facility. Then the two moved Father Dunn's baggage from his van and got him established in his suite. After which, Father Koesler left him to get settled in.

*   *   *

"Come in," Father Dunn said, answering the knock on his door.

Koesler entered, carrying a bottle and two small glasses. "I thought a spot of port before bed might be in order."

"Absolutely." Dunn turned away from the bureau where he had been stowing clothing.

They sat opposite each other in the spacious study. Each held a glass partly filled with the ruby liquid.

Dunn raised his glass. "To us, Father."

Koesler nodded, smiled, and sipped. "How long since you were ordained, Nick?"

"Three years."

"That gives me about thirty-five years on you. So I could easily be your father . . . even your grandfather. Still, I think it'll work out better if you call me Bob. We are colleagues, after all."

"Suits me fine, Bob."

Koesler looked around the room. "Is this adequate?"

Dunn followed his gaze. In addition to the large study, there was a bedroom not much smaller, plenty of closet space, a lavatory, a queen-size bed, desk, chairs, sofa, basic furnishings. "More than adequate. In my parish in Minnesota, I've got about half this much room."

Koesler nodded. "Sorry about the bathroom being down the hall," he said.

"That's okay. What it lacks in convenience it more than makes up for in size." He sipped the wine. "You seemed surprised to see me . . . in the church, I mean."

"I *was* surprised: I wasn't expecting you until sometime next week."

"Yeah. Well, I was able to get away a little earlier than I figured. So I just came on down."

"Are you all set at U of D? This is kind of late in the term, isn't it? Mid-September? Haven't they started classes?"

"There was no trouble about that. They were very helpful with preregistration. Probably because I'm a priest. Also, I'm not going for credit; I'm just auditing some classes."

"No credits? You aren't going into the counseling business?"

"Not unless I pay for the training. I think the diocese got burned a few times too many. Some of the guys went away, came back with MSWs, quit the priesthood, and went into private practice. So now the policy is to pick up the freight only if the priest audits. Or if he's going for a theology or canonical degree. Not much call for theology majors in business or industry."

Koesler chuckled. "Keep them barefoot and pregnant, eh?"

Dunn nodded. "It doesn't matter to me. I have no plans to leave. I just wanted to increase my skills. I discovered I was counseling people on a pretty regular basis, so I thought I'd better try to learn to do it right. So here I am. Courtesy of the archdiocese of Minneapolis–St. Paul."

Koesler held the port up, seeming to study it in the light. "Yes, here you are. Funny, give or take quite a few years, this could have been a straight player trade."

"Oh?"

"Years ago—good Lord, it must be twenty-five years ago—there was this family that I became friends with. Parishioners. Then the father was transferred to Minneapolis. For quite a few years I spent some vacation time with them. He was transferred a couple more times, then retired. I sort of lost touch with them. Though I do get a Christmas card every year or so. Anyway, for short periods back then, I was a Detroit transplant in Minneapolis. Now here you are a Minneapolis transplant in Detroit."

"That is a coincidence."

"Isn't it? Where's your parish, Nick?"

"Golden Valley . . . you know the place?"

"Sure; one of the neighboring suburbs . . . but not *the* suburb."

Dunn seemed puzzled. Then he brightened. "Edina."

Koesler nodded. "And is downtown Minneapolis still the hub of activity? As I remember it, all the major movies opened downtown. All the major stores were there, and there were skywalks that connected the buildings."

"Still there, all right. You can go pretty nearly everywhere without getting your feet wet."

"Or frozen."

"You were there in winter? Voluntarily?"

"No, but I've heard about it."

"Actually, they do a pretty good job of pushing the snow around and cleaning the streets—even the alleys."

"Impressive. But what else could you expect from those industrious Scandinavians? Those Lutherans are still burying their sins under a blanket of snow."

"It is a pretty Lutheran culture. But, hey, what can you say for a Lutheran town whose three main streets are named after Catholic clergy!"

Koesler tried to remember the street names as Dunn continued. "How is it in Detroit . . . winter, I mean?"

Koesler shook his head. "Don't ask. Just enjoy this September while it lasts. If we get a big snow later, count on getting cabin fever. But then," he reminded himself, "coming from Minnesota, you'd be used to that. However, you're about to experience what's worth the price of admission—fall, and the most breathtaking colors you could imagine."

Koesler became aware that his right knee was quivering. Casually, he slid his hand down his leg and applied pressure on the knee until it stilled. He hoped Dunn had not noticed. Koesler knew the cause of his edginess was that confession of murder he'd heard earlier. He would have preferred to have been alone now. But there was no way of avoiding a courteous welcome for the visiting priest.

If Dunn had noticed the involuntary tremor, he said nothing about it. Koesler was grateful. "The only season I experienced in Minnesota," he continued, "was summer—"

"Oh, summer," Dunn interrupted, "the favorite season of our state bird, the mosquito."

"There's that. But I understand your spring and fall are all played out in a matter of days."

"Hours. They really are over before you know it. Especially fall. One day there are leaves on the trees and the next day there aren't."

"Well, you needn't fear being disappointed in Michigan's fall." Koesler crossed over and topped off Dunn's wine glass, then resumed his seat. "Which leads to a question. I suppose I should have cleared up some details of your stay here when I got your letter. I guess I was just surprised to hear from you out of the blue. And the tone of your letter led me to think that you needed a quick reply. But now that you're here—why?"

"Why?"

"Yes: Why the University of Detroit? And why St. Joseph's? I mean, to begin with, I'm sure the University of Minnesota offers some pretty good psych courses."

"I guess that's true."

"Then . . .?"

"Well, at this stage I suppose I could say something about the value of a Catholic college, especially for one who's going to function in a parochial setting. I could even fall back on the special considerations a priest can expect at a Catholic university. But if I did, you would observe . . ." Dunn's explanation trailed off, opening an opportunity for Koesler to complete the thought.

Which, after a moment, he did. "I would observe that you've got more than one Catholic college in the Twin Cities area."

"Exactly."

Koesler wondered why the other priest continued to avoid a direct answer.

But Father Koesler had lots to learn about Father Dunn. "Then," he probed, "why U of D and why Old St. Joe's?"

"Actually, the order is reversed."

"Oh?" Koesler was tiring of the game.

"I wanted to spend time with you. The University of Detroit was a convenience. I did want some postgrad work in psychology. But, as you suggest, I could easily have gotten that at the University of Minnesota. Or, failing that, at Macalester or Collegeville or the College of St. Thomas, and so forth. Obviously, there is no dearth of Catholic educational opportunities in and around the Twin Cities."

"So?"

"Why St. Joe's? Why you?" Dunn rose and filled his glass once more. "Do you mind?" It was a rhetorical question. "Your reputation, Father—uh . . . Bob."

"My reputation? As . . . what?"

"As a sleuth . . . detective."

Koesler rarely laughed aloud, but he did so now. "My reputation as a . . . *detective?*" He shook his head. "Where in the world did you ever get that idea? You must be reading too much Father Brown!"

"Father Who? Brown? Who's he, another local?"

Koesler was surprised. And a little disappointed. Apparently, the young man had never read or even heard of G. K. Chesterton's fictional priest-detective. "Never mind Father Brown. What gives you the idea that I'm some kind of sleuth?"

"Word gets around. I've read about some of your exploits, mostly through the Catholic News Services in the *Catholic Bulletin*. Even the editor, Bernie Casserly, has written about you. At clerical gatherings, I've heard some priests talk about your . . . what—avocation? I guess I'm surprised that you're surprised."

"Well, I am. But you must be exaggerating. I don't have that reputation even here in my home diocese."

"You're saying you've never worked with the police on a homicide case?"

Koesler shifted uneasily in his chair. "Well, no. But I'm sure you'll learn that that sort of thing is not at all uncommon. As priests, we are, after all, in a helping position. As the years go by, you'll find that you're called upon to aid people in almost every conceivable way. Look what you're doing here: going to a university to pick up some additional skill in counseling. And you're doing it just so you'll be able to help people better."

"But . . ."

"Someday, in all probability, you may very well be called upon to assist the police in some capacity. And when that happens, they're not going to be coming to you because you're a clerical Dick Tracy. It'll more likely be because there's something distinctly Catholic involved. Don't you see? There are times when an investigation involves the medical sphere. In that case, it simply makes sense for the police to get insight from a doctor or a nurse. Or maybe it involves bank fraud. In which case it makes sense to talk to a banker. Or maybe a crime has a very definite Catholic cast. So the police may want some background information from a priest.

"And that, Nick Dunn, is what has happened to me—more than once, I must confess."

Father Dunn thought that over for a few moments. "For the sake of argument, let us grant your premise. Then what do you say to the fact that, by your own admission, you've been called upon 'more than once'?"

"Partly coincidence. But I can see that that explanation is not going to satisfy you. So okay, I have proven of some help to the police in the past—merely to furnish information and insights that almost any priest could have given them. So it is quite natural that they might call on me again—if only because they have become familiar with me. I guess they'd rather deal with someone they've come to know than start all over getting to know some other source. But I assure you, Nick, I am a parish priest of the archdiocese of Detroit. And I have no ambitions to be anything else—any small publicity to the contrary notwithstanding."

Dunn drained his glass and set it on the end table with a gesture of finality. Something else Koesler learned about Father Dunn: a nightcap was not an invitation to empty a bottle; a nightcap was a nightcap.

Dunn regarded Koesler thoughtfully. "You make a convincing case, Bob. And I would be inclined to take you at your word—though, I must confess, I would find that rather disappointing—but for one thing." He paused dramatically. "The confession!"

"The confession?" Koesler feigned ignorance. He suspected he knew where Dunn was headed.

"I overheard that confession this afternoon—the one made by the killer. I couldn't help hearing it; the guy talked so loud."

Koesler set his glass on the table. He was finished even though he had not drained the glass. At this stage, he did not want to risk fuzzy-headedness. He leaned forward.

"Was there anyone else in the church during that confession?"

"Uh-uh. Just me."

"Why are you talking to me about it? You are as bound by the seal of confession as I am."

"I know that. But it goes to offset your argument. Don't get me wrong: I'm not calling you a liar. Not by any means. I'm willing to grant that you don't go looking for homicide cases to work on. Granted, you just want to be a modest, unassuming parish priest. But isn't it funny how these interesting cases come looking for you? And—witness this afternoon—they find you."

"Nick, that wasn't an invitation by the police department. That was the sacrament of reconciliation, the sacrament of penance—con-fession! And, as such, it is protected by the seal."

Dunn spread his hands, palms upward. "Can either of us doubt that a call from the police is just around the corner?"

"I can doubt it. Besides, what difference could it make? My lips are sealed! Anyone—*anyone*—who overhears a confession is bound by the same seal of confession. You know that."

"You don't understand, Bob. Together, we—both of us—know ex-actly who murdered a Detroit priest."

"What's that?"

"You heard his entire confession. I just came in while he was in the middle of confessing. You got the entire story. But I—I!—saw him. I could identify him!"

So Dunn had not been in church when the man had entered what was, for him, the wrong side of the confessional. Thus Dunn didn't know that Koesler had seen the man too.

"This is nonsense, Nick. What difference does it make that I heard his confession in its entirety and you saw him leave the box? Our lips are sealed!"

Dunn pondered that, then smiled broadly. "What a delicious se-cret! The police maybe don't even know the crime's been committed yet, and we know who did it! I feel tingly inside." Indeed, Dunn's eyes were glowing. "Let's check it out."

"What!?"

"I don't know, I just want to make sure."

"What in the world are you talking about?"

"What was that guy's name—Keating, wasn't it? And what parish was that?"

"St. Waldo's." The question was academic; Dunn could easily have looked up the appropriate parish in the Catholic directory.

"Is St. Waldo's in Detroit?"

"Bloomfield Hills."

"Let's call and ask for Father Keating."

"Forget it, Nick. What would it prove if a priest is not in his parish on a Saturday night? Just plain forget it: It's the best favor you could do for yourself and everybody else."

Dunn still had a gleam in his eye. "Ah, but what if a priest is not in his parish on a Sunday morning when all his parishioners come for Mass?"

"Nick, I'm going to bed. And I'm going to bury this special secret deep inside me. And I advise you most strongly to do the same. And I'm as serious as I can be."

Koesler regretted the chill left in Dunn's room after this, their first encounter. He was surprised by it as much as he regretted it.

The dispute—their first—concerned a matter that was of prime im-portance to Koesler: the seal of confession. To him this was one of the most sacred tenets of religion. And in no other expression of religion was it more firmly entrenched than in Catholicism. In all his years as a priest—even as a seminarian—he had never known a priest to violate the seal of confession. Oh, there were a few jokes about it; there were a few jokes about nearly everything. But in actual practice, the seal was inviolate.

He got the impression that Father Dunn did not share that convic-tion. Was it the age gap?

Koesler had lived more than half his life in the pre–Vatican II Church. That span definitely colored his perception of the present post–Vatican II Church.

Dunn belonged to an interesting time frame.

Seminarians who were the immediate product of the postconciliar Church—the late sixties, the seventies—lived in a virtual rebellion against the beliefs and practices of the earlier theology. However, in the eighties, a peculiar rebound occurred in some seminaries, certainly in Detroit, possibly in Minneapolis–St. Paul as well.

With seminaries almost empty of candidates for the priesthood (the legacy of the sixties and seventies?), administrators seemed to be attempting to put as much of the toothpaste as possible back in the tube. The clerical costume, for instance—the cassock, clerical suit, full Mass vestments—returned to acceptable use. But a good portion of what had been discarded and subsequently lost could not be retrieved. It was a strange amalgam. And from this mixture sprang young priests such as Father Nick Dunn.

Koesler was unable to comprehend much of this sometimes bitter rebellion. Nor was he totally familiar with this latest seminary product.

Empirically, there was no compelling reason for Koesler to become an expert in either wave of the postconciliar phenomena. He had developed a theological approach to life that, as far as he was concerned, combined the best of both worlds—pre- and postconciliar. Armed with this comfortable and comforting theology, he was willing to work his small corner of the vineyard until he dropped.

Except for now. Now he would be forced to deal with Father Dunn. But it was getting late. Time enough for that tomorrow.

3

WEEKEND services at St. Joe's comprised a Mass at 5:00 Saturday afternoon, and four additional Masses on Sunday.

Father Koesler got help with this schedule catch-as-catch-can. Mary O'Connor, the parish secretary, spent much of her time during various weeks phoning around in search of the rare surplus priest. Jesuits were always a good bet through the auspices of Sts. Peter and Paul, the nearby Jesuit parish. With the advent of Father Dunn, now, and for at least U of D's first semester, St. Joe's would have the luxury of an extra resident priest.

However, the resident was not a barrel of help his first Sunday. Oh, there was no trouble with his presiding over a couple of Masses. The problem was he had prepared no homily. So Father Koesler had to preach not only at his own two Masses but also at Dunn's. And, as any priest who strove to deliver decent homilies could attest, it wasn't the number of Masses offered but the number of sermons given that wiped one out.

Thus Koesler had spent virtually this entire Sunday morning in church. Searching for a silver lining for this fatiguing cloud, he had ample time to study Father Dunn's characteristics.

A slenderly built man of perhaps five feet nine or ten—some five inches shorter than Koesler—Dunn had a full head of dark blond, carefully groomed hair parted in the middle, set off by a matching mustache. He had a strong voice that probably could project without amplification. He seemed comfortable wearing the full complement of liturgical vestments and—somewhat rare these days—wearing a cassock beneath the vestments. By and large, he seemed the sort of priest Koesler could relate to more easily than the creations of the early postconciliar Church.

With one exception: Father Dunn wanted to be a cop.

Even worse, he seemed determined to grow up to be Father Koesler, whom he perceived as having made police officer before him.

And, judging from last night's conversation, there was no way of convincing him otherwise.

Koesler wondered about that. Everyone he had known in the seminary, of whatever vintage, had wanted to be a priest. And that was it. Oh, here and there one might find a seminarian whose sights were aimed at a monsignorship or, more ambitiously, a bishopric. But those aspirations were still within the parameters of the priesthood.

Where on earth did this desire of Dunn's come from? Certainly there was nothing wrong with wanting to be a police officer. But such a desire had nothing to do with the priesthood—or at least nothing that Koesler could think of. The few times that he had worked with the police had not been comfortable experiences for him. Granted, there was a certain thrill to peeling back the layers of a puzzle to solve a mystery. But he could live without that sort of excitement—easily.

Koesler wanted only to be a priest. How could he bring home this fact to Father Dunn? That young man was digging a shallow grave for his vocational dreams if he couldn't realize he now had everything he needed for an eminently fulfilling life.

Even more troubling to Koesler was the young man's apparent attitude toward the secrecy requisite in the sacrament of confession.

Koesler had been disconcerted by what Dunn seemed to be suggesting last night. That either of them should even consider revealing in any way what both had heard confessed yesterday Koesler found repulsive. And his sentiment had absolutely nothing to do with the man who had confessed the murder of a priest. If anything, Koesler hoped the police would get him. But not with Koesler's help. And not with Dunn's either.

Koesler had heard, and Dunn had overheard, a man confess a sin and, at the same time, confide a secret. That secret, Koesler knew, was sacrosanct. Through the ages, the seal of confession had been challenged by hypothetical as well as factual questions and compelling circumstances. But the seal had to withstand every challenge and remain inviolate or its entire substructure would crumble.

However, Koesler feared that last night's brief discussion over what should be done about the confession of murder was far from concluded. He wished it were, but Dunn gave every indication that he was not convinced. It was this suspicion that late last night had impelled Koesler to consult some of his theology books and further ponder the matter. The more he researched, the more he was convinced his stand was valid.

The essence of the matter was plainly stated in both the old (A.D. 1917) and the new (A.D. 1983) Code of Canon Law.

The most recent statement Koesler found in Canon 983, which stated, in part, "The sacramental seal is inviolable, therefore, it is a crime for a confessor in any way to betray a penitent by word or in any other manner or for any reason." And Canon 984: "Even if every danger of revelation is excluded, a confessor is absolutely forbidden to use knowledge acquired from confession when it might harm the penitent."

Imagine that: The violation of the seal is termed a "crime." And one need not look far to find the punishment for that crime. Canon 1388: "A confessor who directly violates the seal of confession incurs an automatic excommunication reserved to the Apostolic See." And anyone else—as in Father Nick Dunn—who violates this secrecy is "to be punished with a just penalty, not excluding excommunication."

It was Communion time. Koesler washed his hands, almost compulsively.

This, the 1:15 P.M. Mass, was the final liturgy of Sunday. Dunn had also officiated earlier at the 10:30. Koesler, besides preaching at Dunn's Masses, had celebrated the 8:30 and noon Masses. It had been straightway determined that Koesler would continue to offer the Sunday noon Mass as it was in Latin and Latin was Greek to Father Dunn.

After Communion, the Mass was quickly completed. Koesler and Dunn took up positions outside the front threshold to bid the congregation farewell and chat with anyone who wished to bend their ears. Several of the predominantly elderly group briefly greeted and welcomed Dunn. Father Dunn seemed such a nice young man. They hoped he would be with them on a more permanent basis. But they were told at the outset that he would be in residence at St. Joe's only while he was going to school.

Koesler caught sight of the woman who had confessed to him yesterday, the former nun from 1300 Lafayette. This morning she had taken Communion for the first time in the number of months she'd been attending Mass here. She hadn't yet registered as a parishioner. Koesler hoped that would happen. But he was not about to push it.

Soon the flock was gone and the two priests stood quite alone on the sidewalk outside the main doors of the church.

Koesler took the collection basket to the rectory while Dunn closed and locked the church. They met again minutes later in the spacious rectory kitchen. "I hope you don't mind, Nick," Koesler said, "but we don't have a housekeeper on Sundays. There's plenty of food in the fridge, though. So help yourself."

"That's okay. I don't usually have much for breakfast or lunch." Dunn began foraging through the refrigerator.

"Good," Koesler said. "I'll make a pot of coffee."

"Great. By the way, do you have any plans for dinner?"

Koesler usually ate in on Sundays and self-served the entire day unless he accepted an invitation from one or another of his friends. Or, occasionally he dined out with some other priests. Now he realized that his young resident was on his own in a strange city. "Why don't we go out and get something later? There are some nice restaurants in the downtown area, and a few are even open on Sunday."

"Sounds good to me." Dunn had found some sliced lean roast beef and some lettuce. It would make a delicious sandwich. No quarrel there.

Koesler busied himself in and around the sink and the oven. Dunn constructed his sandwich, seated himself at the large dining table, and began paging through the weekend combination *Detroit News and Free Press,* the Siamese twins of a joint operating agreement.

After placing a mug of steaming coffee at both places, Koesler sat down at the table opposite Dunn. He took a few of the back sections of the paper and began paging through them.

Dunn glanced at his coffee. It was still steaming. He'd let it sit a while after adding a smidgen of milk.

After some minutes and several rapidly turned pages, Dunn said, "Oh, by the way, Bob, I took the liberty of phoning St. Waldo's this morning."

Koesler looked up, his brow knitting. "Oh?"

"Uh-huh. Actually twice. I called at about 9:00 and then just after noon."

For no good reason, Koesler found himself annoyed that the calls had been made while he had been out of the rectory offering Mass in church. Dunn's action put him in mind of a willful teenager defying parental rules. "And what did you discover?"

Dunn sensed Koesler's budding displeasure. "Well, the first call reached an answering service. The second time I got through to the rectory by implying that this could be at least a developing emergency. Of course, when whoever it was at the rectory answered the phone—some woman, maybe the secretary or housekeeper—she wasn't at all happy with me."

"I don't blame her."

"Well, people in rectories ought to be available."

"We could argue the point, but what did you find?"

"That Father Keating wasn't there."

Koesler made a brief study of Dunn, who seemed inordinately pleased with his discovery. Which discovery, Koesler concluded, only further indicated that what they had heard yesterday was probably true: The poor man was dead—murdered. "You actually asked for Father Keating?"

"Uh-huh. And from the tone of her voice, I could tell something was wrong."

Koesler was not at all sure of the accuracy of Dunn's instincts. "Tell me, what would you have done if when you asked for Father Keating, she had put him on the line?"

Dunn grinned. "I'd've been pretty surprised. I don't think I would have believed it was the real Father Keating. I would have figured they had somebody pretending to be Keating in the interim."

"Pretending?"

"Sure." Dunn seemed extremely confident. "We don't know what's going on out there at St. Waldo's. Maybe they've gotten word that Keating's been murdered and they're covering it up for the moment."

"And why would they do that?"

"Maybe the police are there. Maybe the police told them not to talk to anybody until they can get the investigation under way."

"Nick, you have an overactive imagination. But now, if you don't mind, I don't want to talk about it. In fact, whether you mind or not, I don't want to talk about it . . . *ever again.*"

Silence. A rather uneasy silence.

Dunn sipped his coffee. The temperature was about right. But the taste!

He must've tasted worse coffee, but couldn't think where. The seminary? Maybe; but, if memory served, even that was not as disagreeable as this stuff. Should he say something to Koesler? No, better not; he wasn't off to all that good a start with the pastor as it was. No use muddying the waters. He wished he had not thought of mud. He gazed into his mug. Did the coffee really resemble mud, or was it just that it tasted so bad that it blighted everything else? He watched Koesler turn the pages of the paper all the while sipping his coffee. Was it possible that he'd prepared two separate brews? Was it possible Koesler had no taste buds?

Meanwhile, Dunn continued to scan the first of the many sections of the paper Koesler had handed him.

He was amazed at the bulk of this Sunday newspaper. It must be as large as the Sunday *New York Times*!

Father Dunn was not far wrong. Had he been in the Detroit area a few years earlier, he would have witnessed one of the last of the great wars between two big-city newspapers. Then, at the conclusion of a battle to blend the management of both papers—allegedly for fiscal survival—the United States Supreme Court ruled that there was no legal reason to prevent the *News* and the *Free Press* from merging their administrative offices while still competing editorially. The resultant product was not altogether acceptable from nearly anyone's point of view. But it did make for a humongous Sunday paper.

Both priests continued to read while exchanging sections of the paper. Suddenly Nick Dunn gasped.

"What is it? What's wrong?"

"I can't believe it! This is too much! It just can't be! I don't believe it!" Dunn wheeled the paper toward Koesler and pointed to a photo.

Koesler studied the picture, wondering what he was supposed to discover.

"Oh, I forgot," Dunn said, "you didn't see him." He tapped his finger on a figure in the photo. "Him! He's the one—the one who went to confession to you yesterday. I'm sure of it!"

Koesler looked more closely at the picture. It hadn't reproduced all that clearly. But, upon scrutiny, there was little doubt: It was he. Once again, Koesler reminded himself that Dunn didn't know that he had seen the man who had mistakenly walked into the open confessional.

The photo ran with a companion story under the heading: "Sons of Italy Honored at Charity Fete." The caption read: "Salvatorean Father Mario Gattari, S.O.S., presents commemorative plaques to brothers Remo and Guido Vespa in appreciation of their outstanding service to the Salvatorean Mission Society."

There was definitely a resemblance between the two, but Koesler was sure Guido was the one who had blundered into the wrong confessional yesterday and eventually confessed killing Father John Keating. If corroboration were needed, Father Dunn's nimble index finger was tapping precisely on Guido's pictured head.

"What I can't figure out," Dunn said, "is why he's getting a plaque. I know Detroit is big on murders, but I didn't know that killers were given prizes! And by a Catholic missionary outfit? Who in hell are the Salvatorean Fathers, anyway?"

"They're . . . they're a . . . uh . . . an . . . Italian missionary group . . ." Koesler spoke in a half-mesmerized state. If anything, he was more surprised and puzzled by this picture than Dunn was. "I think they work in Africa. They've got an office here . . . mostly to solicit vocations."

"But why would they be giving an award to this guy? He's a hit man, isn't he?"

"Donations, funding drives, contributions. If you haven't been exposed to this yet, you will be. There are some Catholic awards—like this one—that are given to the big spenders, or big collectors, that type of VIP. It doesn't matter that the . . . uh . . ."—Koesler glanced again at the paper in search of the name—"the Vespas aren't very practicing Catholics. Shoot, it doesn't matter that Guido Vespa hasn't darkened a church door more than a couple of times in his entire life. The thing is the Vespas must have given a pile of money to the Salvatoreans. Or the Salvatoreans hope this award will prime the pump, as it were, and that the Vespas will give a bundle. It's got very little to do with saints and sinners."

"But"—Dunn was grinning from ear to ear—"we know the whole story! We know the priest has been killed! We know who did it! We even know where the body is buried, for God's sake!"

Koesler regarded the other priest intently for a few moments. "And what do you suggest we do with all this knowledge?"

Dunn thought seriously. "Well," he said finally, "I don't suppose we can just tell anybody—the police . . . the media." He looked at Koesler as if the statement were a question.

Koesler slowly shook his head.

Dunn continued to think. Then, "Wait a minute. You can do something about this even if I can't."

"I can?" Koesler's tone was skeptical.

"Sure. For one thing, I'll bet the cops are going to ask you for help again. Just like you said yesterday, they come up with a case that has a peculiarly Catholic background, they need help with the Catholic angle, and they call on you—tried and true. Except this time you already know which closet the skeletons are in. So you just sort of steer them to the answer. They will be amazed. You will never have been better!"

Koesler shook his head with deliberateness. "You must, you really must have studied the seal of confession in the seminary. And since you're out only three years, it wasn't all that long ago."

"So?"

"So you must know that the confidentiality of information learned through the confessional is inviolable. There are no exceptions."

Dunn shook his head. "What I do know is that there aren't any rules that don't have exceptions. All those absolutes of the pre-Vatican II Church are gone."

Koesler well remembered the long string of absolute rules that he had grown up with, that he'd learned, that he had pretty well observed, for not to observe them was to sin. He remembered them far better than Dunn possibly could. Dunn had heard of the absolutes. Koesler had lived them.

"Yes, I've watched the absolutes crumble . . ." Koesler almost sighed. "It was a cultural shock for most of us old geezers. I doubt you'll ever know what it was like living in those days that stretched back for centuries. I think it was McAfee Brown who wrote that if the Catholic Church ever changed a doctrine radically—say, that birth control was good instead of bad—the official statement would have to begin, 'As the Church has always taught . . .' Simply because we have no way to say 'oops.'"

Dunn chuckled.

"Not being able to say 'sorry' means for one thing that you're dealing with a bunch of absolutes. However"—Koesler's voice took on an uncompromising tone—"the absolute protection of secrecy in the confessional is one of the absolutes that stuck around."

"Come on"—Dunn's tone was cynical—"no exceptions?"

"Okay," Koesler responded after quick reflection, "one exception: If the penitent comes to the confessor afterward—if the penitent takes the initiative—the two of them may discuss what was confessed. No—one more exception: If the penitent releases the priest from the confidentiality. But that, Father Dunn, is that!"

Dunn recognized the implication of Koesler's use of his title, especially since it was Koesler who had suggested they operate on a first-name basis. It took him back to when he was a misbehaving boy and his mother would address him as "Nicholas!"

"To be perfectly frank," Dunn said, "I don't see it. I don't agree. Look, that guy yesterday—what's his name?—Guido Vespa—I heard him use the word 'contract.' This was a contract murder. Now I know I don't have as much experience in this stuff as you do, but I've seen my share of *Godfather* movies. And contract killings are committed by hit men. Men who kill for money, or just because they are employed to kill people.

"Look at the opportunity you've got! You can single-handedly put a hit man out of business, help send him to prison. You'll be saving lives, all the lives that guy would have taken if you hadn't put him away. I think that's ample reason to at least . . . fudge . . . the seal of confession.

"Besides, you wouldn't have to just come out and tell the cops that you heard this in confession. You wouldn't have to even mention the confessional. If they ask you for help . . . you help them. Just sort of steer them in the right direction." He turned his hands palms upward on the table. "Simple?"

Koesler regarded the young man in a moment's silence, then glanced at the still nearly full coffee mug. "Your coffee's cold. Let me get rid of that and pour you a fresh cup—"

"No!" The force of Dunn's reply was enough to halt Koesler's move from his chair. "No," Dunn repeated more composedly. "Don't trouble yourself. I just remembered, I was going to cut back on the stuff." Dunn leaned forward. "Well, what do you think: Doesn't my idea sound great?"

"Your idea . . ." Koesler decided to try a different approach. "There are various kinds of secrets, Nick."

"I know that."

"Just a quick review to make sure we're talking about the same thing, okay?"

Dunn nodded. He did want coffee. But not the hemlock in the pot on the counter.

"Okay." Koesler proceeded: "There is information that by its very nature is confidential. As, for instance, an individual's sexual orientation. Somebody you know is gay but you also know he doesn't want that revealed. Or there's the secret that someone tells you and asks you not to tell. He's depending on you to keep his secret; otherwise he wouldn't reveal it to you.

"Then there's the professional secret—doctor-patient or attorney-client. All of those secrets are precious to the individual who is affected by each of them and so, to varying degrees, that person's desire that such a secret be honored and protected must be honored.

"Anyone who is trusted with any of those secrets may have to weigh the importance of keeping the information to himself against, say, the common good. Possibly the professional secret may be the most crucial of all of them. Is there any time or circumstance when a doctor, say, is obliged to reveal the confidential information about his patient?"

"I suppose. Sure."

"Maybe," Koesler said, "a man with AIDS is sexually promiscuous."

"Of course, the doctor would have to tell. His patient is risking the lives of all those people." Dunn quickly added, "But that's just what I was saying: The doctor has to forget about his professional restraint because of . . . well, exactly what you said: the common good. And you have to steer the police to this hit man or he's going to kill again . . . and again. You'd even be an accessory, no?"

"I don't think so." Koesler rose to pour himself another cup of coffee. If Koesler had taste buds they must have expired, thought Dunn; maybe that's what happens as you grow old: body organs die one by one.

"The difference"—Koesler returned to his chair and his theme— "between the professional secret of the doctor and the confessional secret of the priest is not in the nature of the *secret* but in the person to whom the secret is entrusted."

"Oh, come on now, Bob—you're not going to pull that old cultic-character-of-the-priesthood, are you? Where the priest is somehow superhuman? Priests have come down off the mystic pedestal long ago. Definitely since the Council."

"Well . . ." Koesler smiled. "Yes and no. I know priests are off the pedestal, more or less. And that's both good news and bad. But that's not the point here. The point here is the person to whom the information was given."

"Huh?"

"Look, Nick, I don't want to get too doctrinaire, but I've got to be sure you and I are on the same wavelength. We believe that Jesus is the son of God and so He had the power to forgive sin."

"Don't go too fast, Bob." Dunn's sarcasm was evident.

"I know, I know . . . but be patient; this is going somewhere," Koesler advised.

"Now, we also believe He gave this power to forgive sin to His apostles. He told them that when they forgave sins, the sins were forgiven. But if they would not forgive sins, those sins remained unforgiven. Since there was a dual responsibility—to forgive or deny forgiveness—it seemed appropriate to determine the state of the penitent's conscience and what sins had been committed. And so, there's confession.

"The method of hearing confession developed over the centuries. Probably it was the Celtic monks of the sixth century who incorporated the private confession to a priest with forgiveness without public penance, denunciation, or any public or legal consequences. With that, each person's sins became a private matter.

"A little later on, the confessional booth was introduced in Spain to get rid of some abuses. Whatever. In any case, once you got sins privately confessed and forgiven, along with a private place as the setting, you also got anonymity for the penitent—and unconditional confidentiality. And that was the practice until, in the mid-sixteenth century, the Council of Trent rejected the claim that there *ever* could be an adequate reason for violating the seal of confession. And that's the way it's pretty much been ever since—total, absolute, and unconditional."

Dunn looked askance. " 'Celtic monks'? 'The sixth century'? 'Trent'? You looked those up. You don't have that kind of detail at your fingertips!"

"You're right: I did look it up. Last night after this first came up and we apparently disagreed on an issue that I consider of prime importance.

"Put it this way: I didn't want to lose this argument on some flimsy technicality."

"Have we gotten where you're going yet?" Dunn asked. "I still don't see any compelling reason why the seal can't admit an exception. Everything else does."

"I could take exception to your 'Everything else does,' but for the moment, let's stick to confession.

\ "Now, a gentleman we know as Guido Vespa—thanks to your identification"—Koesler still did not wish to acknowledge that he himself had seen the man—"came to confession yesterday. He confided in me—and, although he didn't know it at the time, to you too—that he had committed murder. He told me this not because I am a doctor, a lawyer, or any other public professional, but because I am a priest. And, in the last analysis, not even because I am a priest. You've heard of the expression *in loco parentis*?"

" 'In the place of the parent,' " Dunn correctly translated. "Somebody who is not the parent of a child is empowered to act as if he or she were the parent—in the place of the parent. But wait a minute—"

Koesler smiled. "You know where I'm going now, don't you? Mr. Vespa told me what was bothering his conscience because—as he was taught to believe—I was taking the place of Jesus. I was taking the place of God. Not *in loco parentis,* but *in loco Dei.* He definitely would not have told me—or you or any other priest—if he had not implicitly believed he was going through a person who was able to forgive his sin. Because that person had received his commission to forgive sin from Jesus, the son of God.

"Me.

"Vespa believed that I have that power because Jesus gave it to the apostles and they passed the power on through their successors. He believes that because that's what we taught him. If he were really wearing his eyes of faith, he would not be confessing to me—he would not even be seeing me. He would believe he was confessing to God. If God wanted to reveal the sin, He could. But I don't believe God ever would.

"And that, in a nutshell, my dear Father Dunn, is why there are no exceptions to the seal. Not because there is a law against revealing a confessed sin. Although there is such a law, both in the old and the new Code of Canon Law—which, by the way, the Church is so firm about that violating the seal is one of only five remaining sins still punishable by excommunication reserved to the Holy See.

"And, yes, I looked that up, too," he added parenthetically.

"But it's not law that makes us keep these secrets inviolate; it's because when we hear confessions, we are eavesdropping. The penitent is not talking to us. The penitent talks to God. And the penitent would not have said a word to us in that setting if he or she had not been led to believe that we were standing in for God. *In loco Dei*.

"And besides all that, the rule of thumb for the confessor is that he do nothing—*nothing*—that would make confession odious, repugnant, offensive to the penitent. That's why, by the way, the priest can't even bring up outside the confessional any sins that have been confessed—unless, that is, the penitent wants to talk about them and brings the subject up spontaneously. The confessional, Nick, is a world set apart. It's a haven for the sinner with God."

Koesler's silence indicated his explication was completed and that he now awaited Dunn's reaction.

There was no reaction.

"Well . . ." Koesler finally prompted.

"I don't know," Dunn said at last. "I'm going to have to think about it. Maybe it's just a reaction to all those unforgiving absolutes of the past—but I've got a problem admitting that anything admits of no exception at all. I'm going to have to think about it. That's the best I can tell you."

"Okay, you think about it. But," Koesler admonished, "while you're thinking, don't do *any*thing. Don't speak to anyone about what you heard—not even to me anymore. Don't do anything that would in any way link the murder of Father Keating to the man we heard confess that sin."

"Okay," Dunn agreed, after some hesitation.

Koesler nodded. "Now I'm going to rest up a bit and get ready for dinner later on. Six all right for you, Nick?"

Dunn nodded.

"Then I'll meet you here." Koesler left the dining area for his room upstairs. He was exhausted, not only from his marathon of sermons this morning, but also from the extensive apologia for the sacrament of confession. As he stretched out on his bed, his last conscious thought was a wish that Guido Vespa had whispered as Koesler had more than once urged. If only Vespa had followed Koesler's direction, Dunn would not have overheard and Koesler would have been spared this argumentation and contention. On the other hand, maybe it was a blessing that he was able to head off this young priest before he violated the seal and would have to go to the Pope himself for absolution.

In the final analysis, Koesler did not need any complication from any other source. It would be plenty hard enough for him to keep this secret. He could not let anyone—including Dunn—know just how hard. All that Dunn said was true enough: Vespa was a career killer, and to keep silence was to leave him free to kill again.

But there were no exceptions. *There were no exceptions.*

And so, on to a troubled nap.

4

INSPECTOR Walter Koznicki, long-time head of the Detroit Police Department's Homicide Division, took the steps. The elevators at 1300 Beaubien were working, but Koznicki felt that he too needed to work.

Koznicki was slightly over six feet tall; his weight at his recent physical examination was 250 pounds. Wanda, his wife, worried about that. He reminded her that he was big-boned. She reminded him that lately his clothes had been more than a little snug. He reminded her that it was natural to put on a bit of weight as one aged. She reminded him that was nonsense and that while his diet seemed about the same as always, he wasn't getting the exercise he needed.

He could not argue that point. He should have been on the street more, but lately he seemed stuck to the chair behind his desk in his office. Wanda was right; he wasn't getting nearly enough exercise. But while he admitted this only to himself, he did resolve to hit the bricks more regularly. Do some of those exercises-while-seated workouts. At all times choose the more physically demanding course. Thus, with the choice of elevator or stairs, use the feet.

By the time Koznicki reached the fifth floor, he was breathing hard. Proof, if he needed any, that he still had a way to go before he was as fit as he should be, as fit as he wanted to be.

As he traversed the hallway, he greeted the few officers on duty this Sunday afternoon. They were surprised to see him. No one could question Koznicki's dedication, but he had long since been convinced that he would not catch all the criminals out there even if he worked around the clock. This conclusion made him a far happier man as well as making his wife a far happier woman.

Koznicki arrived at the squad room and looked in the open door. In the absence of a full or even a partial complement of detectives, there was little to catch the eye other than the drabness and dinginess. It was a place of work and every inch of it stated that fact. Tables and chairs of hard wood and ancient vintage, paint dull and peeling. No suggestion of comfort or frivolity.

Only one person occupied the office expanse. Lieutenant Alonzo Tully looked up as his boss entered. Tully, black, with close-cropped salt-and-pepper hair, was of medium height and build, and as fit as his inspector was out of condition. Much of Tully's trim shape he owed to expenditure of nervous energy.

Normally, it was as natural for Koznicki to be home on a sunny Sunday afternoon as it was for Tully to be at work. Koznicki had not been surprised when he discovered on telephoning Tully's home that Tully was at headquarters. Not for the first time did Koznicki reflect on how fortunate it was that Tully was blessed with a most understanding and patient mate.

Several files lay open on Tully's desk. They represented some of the most intriguing cases his squad was working on. Open-and-shut crimes failed to interest Tully. He loved a mystery, and he felt drawn to the more complex puzzles. The enjoyment he found in his otherwise often macabre work came from unraveling the created maze and catching the bad guy. What the courts did with the perpetrator was the courts' problem. Long ago he had found that the path to mental health lay in not being concerned with whatever was beyond one's control. His responsibility was to catch the perp, which he did as well as or frequently better than anyone else in Homicide. What went on in court was another matter and not his concern.

As he caught sight of Koznicki, Tully did not quite smile. Rather, the lines in his face eased. "Well," he said, "what brings you in today?"

Koznicki lowered himself carefully into a chair opposite Tully, who wondered why the chair did not snap, or at very least cry out for mercy.

"A missing priest," Koznicki replied.

"Oh? I didn't hear about any missing priest."

"Few have." Koznicki touched a handkerchief to his beaded forehead. "He has only been missing since Friday."

"Just . . . missing?"

"So far as we know."

"Why did they bother you? We're not Missing Persons. Besides, has it been seventy-two hours yet?"

"Not quite. But let me begin at the beginning. This priest is Father John Keating, pastor of St. Waldo's of the Hills in Bloomfield Hills. Have you heard of him?"

Tully shook his head slowly. "Haven't heard of him. Haven't heard of the church. But I've certainly heard of Bloomfield Hills."

A fleeting smile from Koznicki. "As it turns out, the fact that it is Bloomfield Hills has everything to do with some departures from standard procedure. St. Waldo's of the Hills may very well be the wealthiest parish in the archdiocese of Detroit."

"I can well imagine."

"So," Koznicki continued, "it is not surprising that among its parishioners can be found some of the most influential people in this area."

Tully was beginning to anticipate Koznicki's direction, and he was not delighted.

"In any case," Koznicki continued, "Father Keating was last seen Friday afternoon. He told the housekeeper he was going to Detroit on business and that he would be home for dinner. That is the last anyone appears to have seen of him."

Tully glanced at his watch. "In another twenty-four hours that will be an excellent case for the Missing Persons Division of the Bloomfield Hills Department—if they've got a Missing Persons."

"You were not listening as attentively as you ordinarily do, Alonzo. St. Waldo's parish contains some of the most influential people in this area."

"Influential enough to get the Bloomfield Hills cops to up the ante to forty-eight hours instead of seventy-two?" Tully was trying to forestall what he reluctantly envisioned as the inevitable.

"Influential enough," Koznicki specified, "to have a missing persons investigation started twenty-four hours early. Influential enough to have the case investigated not only by Bloomfield Hills but Detroit as well."

Tully looked at the array of files on his desk. In a way, he was saying good-bye to them, or at least "till we meet again." Briefly, he thought of trying to talk Koznicki out of this assignment. But then he thought better of it. Walt Koznicki was not the type to speak or act rashly or without careful consideration. He expected his assignments to be carried out, not disputed. Tully knew there was no point in arguing the issue. It was useless to try to change Koznicki's mind.

Too bad. A couple of the cases he'd been studying had been very attractive—compelling, almost.

One was the murder of a man at high noon on Jefferson Avenue directly in front of the Renaissance Center—or, as Detroiters knew it, the Ren Cen.

Lunchtime crowds had filled the streets, yet with plenty of people around, no one had come forward to give witness. The well-dressed attorney had left his downtown office to attend a business luncheon in one of the Ren Cen's many restaurants. He had just crossed Jefferson when suddenly he fell to the sidewalk. No one came to his aid. People walked around and even over him until one of the traffic officers came over to investigate. But it was too late. He was dead, said the medical examiner, before he hit the pavement. Poisoned, the ME pronounced. The vehicle probably something like an umbrella nib or a stick with a pointed tip. The victim would have felt nothing more than a sharp prick. A large crowd, a busy street; he probably didn't pay much attention, or probably disregarded it. Some careless pedestrian—a midday annoyance. As it turned out, it wasn't carelessness, not with a poisoned weapon. Deliberate murder. Murder One. The victim had been identified as, among other things, closely linked to the local Mafia.

The other case beckoning Tully was the murder of a *Detroit News* reporter. He had been killed just outside an inner-city church; apt, since he was the religion writer for the *News*. He was covering a complex, multifaceted story, involving a priest, the parish's pastor, who had gotten married months previously. His marital state had just come to light and the archdiocese was taking steps to oust him from the parish and have him defrocked.

Outraged parishioners had called a meeting at the church. They didn't care whether or not he was married; they did not want to lose their priest. In response, a throng far larger than all the possible members of that parish had gathered. The standing-room-only crowd spilled out onto the street. The leaders of the protest had whipped the multitude into a revival-type frenzy. At the very peak of that passionate response, according to bystanders, shots rang out, which caused the uproar to increase, when no one thought that possible. Several people were hit, the reporter six times. He was dead on arrival at Detroit Receiving Hospital.

Two dead men, neither a platter case. The missing facet of each case was the motive.

There were any number of reasons why animosity toward a lawyer could explode into violence. Frequently, lawyers entered people's lives at one or another crisis period. A harsh divorce settlement. A botched divorce case. The same with reference to a host of similar situations: property settlement, child custody, disability judgment, acrimonious estate matter, and so forth. Among all these possibilities, which one? And why poison? One of those bizarre Mafia statements? It was unusual, and that's what whetted Tully's interest.

And the reporter? Not in Tully's memory had a local newswriter been murdered. As far as he could see, people took out their frustrations with the media by an angry letter to the editor. Or perhaps, at most, a lawsuit. Why would anyone kill a reporter—and a religion writer at that?

For his part, Tully could not quite fathom why the crowd was so unhinged over what was happening to that priest. Tully had only a surface knowledge of organized religion. He was aware that the Catholic clergy were not allowed to marry. In fact, he'd had quite a cram course in the Roman Catholic Church's rules and regulations concerning celibacy. A bizarre case last year had highlighted that Church feature. But—okay—so a priest gets married, he breaks the rule, and, Tully supposed, he's out. Maybe there's an appeal possibility. But it's all there in Church law; why should lay people get all worked up? Were those bullets intended for someone else? Tully thought not. When several rounds all hit the same target, it's not likely the shooter missed what he wanted to hit.

All this Tully could have communicated to Inspector Koznicki in a plea to pursue the cases that were already his. But from long experience, he knew such an appeal was foredoomed. At best, he—or maybe the Bloomfield cops—would find this missing priest in a hurry and Tully could get back to his work.

Could that have been the reason Koznicki was dumping this business on him? Ol' Walt was a crafty guy. He would be well aware that Tully wanted no part of a missing person investigation. And that Tully would do everything in his power to get rid of it. And that the only way to do that would be to solve it or bring it to a successful or otherwise conclusion.

In any event, Tully hoped that some of these intriguing cases would still be waiting for him when he got back to the real world of Homicide.

Tully gathered the files, tapped them neatly together, placed them on the far corner of the desk, and faced Koznicki squarely. For better or worse, Tully was now at Koznicki's disposal.

"Okay," Tully said, "let's start from the top. It might help to know just who this 'influential' person is who got everybody to throw out the rule book."

"Eric Dunstable."

"U.S. Motors?"

"Chairman of the board."

Tully nodded. "That's influential. What's he got to do with it?"

"He's a parishioner at St. Waldo's—make that an *involved* parishioner. He is, in fact, president of the parish council."

Tully reflected on that. "Well, now, Walt, my education on things Catholic hasn't quite got that far. But it does sound impressive."

Only Koznicki's eyes smiled. "A parish council is elected by parishioners. The president, usually, is elected, in turn, by the other council members. Or the council member who gets the most votes becomes the president. Suffice to say that the position—"

"—is an 'influential' position," Tully broke in. "Whatever this guy does is going to be influential, isn't it?"

"So it seems."

"Or he doesn't play."

Koznicki considered a further analysis of the council president's role irrelevant. He moved on. "The housekeeper at St. Waldo's was not overly concerned when Father Keating did not appear for dinner on Friday evening. It seems he is not only somewhat undependable in matters he considers of minor importance—such as a commitment to a meal—but he generally does not bother explaining."

"Sounds like a real sweetheart."

"Undoubtedly he has other virtues," Koznicki said noncommittally. "Apparently, he did not return to the rectory Friday night. He was not there Saturday morning and nothing in his room was disturbed. The bed was not slept in."

"Let me guess: still no concern."

"Correct. But Saturday is another story. As you can well imagine, Alonzo, the weekend is a terribly busy time for priests, what with confession and the Masses."

"Masses?"

"Services. At St. Waldo's there is a Mass late Saturday afternoon, with confessions before and after, and four Masses Sunday morning."

Tully was impressed. "Quite a load for one guy."

It took a moment for Koznicki to realize that Tully thought that the same priest presided at all these Masses. "Oh, no, Alonzo, there is help. I do not know how many priests assist at that parish of a Sunday, but you may rest assured Father Keating does not carry that load alone. I believe he has a full-time assistant and I would assume he has secured another priest—perhaps more than one—to help from time to time. St. Waldo of the Hills is not the sort of parish that would be strapped for help."

"Okay." So far so good, thought Tully. "So the priest wasn't there yesterday—or today."

"Exactly. And this was unprecedented. Father Keating invariably supervised the operation on weekends, settling such questions as which priests would offer which Masses, compiling announcements; in short, making sure everything ran smoothly."

"He didn't call? No word?"

"None. Needless to say, everyone was and is quite concerned. Earlier this afternoon, Mr. Dunstable stepped in."

"Or took charge."

"Probably more accurate. He contacted the Bloomfield Hills Police, and they are already on the case. And then he contacted our mayor."

"Cobb? He found Cobb? On a Sunday?" Tully snorted. "You did say he was influential."

"Mr. Dunstable and the mayor are quite close socially."

Tully shrugged. "I suppose it's about time Dunstable got something in return for all those contributions. One last question, Walt: Why me? I mean, I know no mere question is going to get me out of this one, but just for the record, why me?"

Koznicki treated it as a rhetorical question. "The mayor promised Mr. Dunstable our best detective would head the investigation. And the mayor is aware of your record." There was a note of barely disguised pride in Koznicki's voice over the fact that the mayor recognized Tully's accomplishments.

Koznicki rose slowly. "The mayor contacted the chief, who notified me. I think it best you call in the troops immediately. By the way, the Bloomfield Hills and other suburban police will be assigned to you for the term of this investigation. You will head up this task force."

Koznicki left, knowing he had placed the matter in most competent hands.

The only silver lining Tully could perceive was that as missing persons go, a missing priest is at least a little out of the ordinary. Maybe he would learn something along the way.

In any case, this would, Tully vowed, be one of the briefest searches in the history of missing persons investigations. He would find the errant priest and bring him home safely. Then he would get back to serious business.

5

PAT LENNON sat alone at a small table in a far corner of the cafeteria on the second floor of the *Detroit News*.

She was by no means alone in the cafeteria. A large percentage of those who worked in the *News*'s downtown building began the workday in this spacious dining room. Some hit the cafeteria before their desks. Bleary-eyed, still in their coats, they would straggle in, knowing the day would not get moving until they had their coffee.

Most of them were creatures of habit, sitting at the same table each day, trading gossip with the same people.

That's why Lennon sat alone. Any number of reporters—safe to say all the males—would have been delighted to join her. But her usual companion at this hour was Pringle McPhee, who, this Monday morning, was late.

Pat sipped her coffee with mounting impatience. If Pringle didn't step on it, Pat would go on to the city room without her. Just as she was about to give up, in bounced Pringle. She spotted Pat, smiled and waved to her, then headed for the snail-paced line at the elongated buffet.

Pat watched as Pringle moved along, selecting cold cereal, scrambled eggs, sweet rolls, and coffee. Quite a breakfast, especially for one as trim and slender as Pringle. Pat wondered how she kept her shape without any bridle on that voracious appetite.

Pringle's limp was barely noticeable. Indeed, if one did not know about the problem, one would scarcely be aware of it. As Lennon looked on, she remembered almost subconsciously that night when the car hit Pringle. Now, four years later, Pat could still enumerate Pringle's wounds: bilateral broken legs, a closed head injury, skull fracture, fractured pelvis, fractures of facial bones, abdominal damage, and six broken ribs on the right side.

Pat remembered so well the list of injuries because not only had Pringle been run down in lieu of Pat, Pat had played a vital part in Pringle's rehabilitation.

The rehabilitation had been a remarkable success. Providentially for such a lovely girl, there were no scars. Remaining was only that suggestion of a limp—and a subtle weakening in Pringle's self-confidence.

There was no diminution in her professional confidence. She was a good reporter, steadily getting better, and aware of her worth as a journalist. Her vulnerability lay in her fear of danger. The dread, while understandably natural, bordered on the phobic.

Pringle, in her mid-twenties when she was injured, had defeated death by a hair's breadth. An extraordinarily healthy specimen, she had been able to do practically anything she set out to accomplish. Then came the overwhelming trauma, and the long, agonizing struggle to make the slightest gesture, to think clearly, to walk. Where before she would ski the most forbidding hills, now she hesitated at crossing a busy street.

Because Pat understood all this, she was especially understanding and protective with Pringle. She was a little more than ten years Pringle's senior. The two could have been sisters. Only in comparison with Pringle could Lennon be considered full-figured. They were, simply, two beautiful women.

Pringle sat in her accustomed chair. Pat smiled as she watched her unload her busy tray.

"Anything more on Hal?" Pringle asked.

"Not that I've heard."

Pringle didn't give her eggs a chance to get cold. "What do you think?" she asked between bites. "I mean, it's all so senseless, isn't it?"

They were talking, as was just about everyone, about the killing of Harold Salden, the religion writer for the *Detroit News*.

"Sure it's senseless. I guess it just underscores this crazy society with guns all over the place. And we're right in the middle of it. We're there covering stories that are all about violence. That's what Hal was doing when he was shot: covering a story in a violent atmosphere. It could have happened to any of us."

Pringle dropped a forkful of eggs back onto her plate. Pat glanced at her. Pringle's hand was trembling. Instantly, Lennon regretted her words. It wasn't tactful to mention in Pringle's presence that their profession could be and occasionally was hazardous. Pringle didn't need that.

Quickly, Pat added, "Of course, there's another angle as far as what happened to Hal. Unlike lots of religion writers in the good old days, Hal was a damn good reporter. Good reporters have a tendency to make enemies. You know the old principle: If you have no enemies, you're not doing anything. In that case, then, maybe it wasn't senseless after all."

"What do you mean?" Pringle's concern was evident.

"I mean there are at least a couple of ways of looking at Hal's shooting. It could have been pure chance: He just happened to be standing in the wrong place at the wrong time. Or maybe it was somebody who had a grudge."

"A grudge against Hal? Pat, he was a religion writer! Who'd have any reason to hold a grudge against a religion writer?"

"You forget, he was also a first-rate reporter. And don't think there aren't some very violent people mixed up in so-called religious affairs. There's always the good old Islamic jihad; Allah and Yahweh never did get along. And how about the pro-life and pro-choice people when they confront each other on a street corner? Anger and violence all over the place. *Even* religion? Especially religion! And Hal covered that scene. He must have made some enemies. Any of them could have done it."

This wasn't going well, Pat had to admit. The further she speculated about Hal's murder, the more she was adding to Pringle's nameless fear. This might be an appropriate moment to call a halt to this conversation and get on with the day. She should be at work now anyway. She pushed her chair back from the table.

"Wait," Pringle said, "let me get you some coffee."

It was a longstanding signal. Pringle wanted to talk.

Pat couldn't refuse. "That's okay. You work on your breakfast. I'll get myself some coffee."

When Pat returned to the table, Pringle lost no time in resuming the conversation. "It's a funny thing," she said, "I hadn't thought about it until we started talking about Hal and the religion desk. But you know, if he were alive now, he probably would've gotten my assignment."

Pat looked at her quizzically over the cup rim.

"That's why I was late this morning: Bob gave me this assignment as soon as I hit the city room."

"What story?"

"A missing priest."

"Somebody lost a priest?" Pat could not bring herself to take this seriously, at least not at first blush.

"Yesterday," Pringle explained. "Well, actually Friday, I guess." She fished her notepad out of her purse and flipped it open. "A Father Keating—John Keating. Ever hear of him?"

Pat shook her head.

"He left his parish sometime Friday. Mentioned he was going into Detroit on business, and that's it. That's the last time anyone seems to have seen him."

"He didn't get back for Sunday Masses?" Pat's interest picked up slightly.

"Apparently not. That's significant?"

"You bet."

"God," Pringle sighed, "I wish Hal were here. For lots of reasons, not the least of which is that he'd be covering this story. Short of that, I wish Bob had given it to a Catholic." Her eyes widened. "Say, you're a Catholic, aren't you?"

"Used to be." She half smiled, half grimaced. "Well, I guess I always will be . . . I just don't work at it much."

"Well, this business of not being there for Mass on Sunday: Is that about the same as . . . oh, a minister not showing up for Sunday services?"

"Worse, I'd say. Considerably worse. If it were a Protestant church, I think it would be a considerable inconvenience for the congregation if no one were there to conduct the services. But in the end, they could live with it. Probably somebody would be available to lead them in prayer, sing a hymn or two—wing it. Couldn't do that in a Catholic church."

"Is that the way it is?"

"Seems so to me." Lennon decided she'd had enough coffee; she eased her cup away. "Did Bob tell you anything about the crowd—the congregation? Was there some other priest around to cover for— what's his name?"

"Keating." Pringle looked once more at her notes. "I don't think he mentioned."

"I'd find out about that if I were you."

"Oh?"

"Seems to me a slightly more serious problem if there was no other priest to take the Masses. I can't imagine a priest—especially a pastor—not providing for Sunday Mass if he could help it. If there wasn't any other priest around, then odds are you got a very sick—or dead—absent priest."

"What if all the Masses were taken care of?"

Pat shrugged. "Who knows? An unannounced vacation. Illness, maybe, but probably not as significant. What it comes down to, I think, is that those guys generally are pretty serious about an obligation like this. If a pastor was pretty sure things would be taken care of one way or another, then if it would be a serious inconvenience for him to show up, he might skip it." She thought for a moment. "Wait a minute . . . did you say 'missing' priest?"

"Uh-huh."

"Who says?"

"Who says what?"

"That he's missing." Pat mentally computed the elapsed time. "You said it was Friday when he was last seen in his parish?"

"Uh-huh."

"Friday to Saturday, twenty-four hours. Saturday to Sunday, forty-eight hours. It won't be seventy-two hours until sometime today. If memory serves, the cops don't begin looking for someone as 'missing' until seventy-two hours have gone by. If the cops aren't looking for him, why should you be?"

"But the cops *are* looking for him. Have been since yesterday afternoon."

"How come?"

"Ever hear of Eric Dunstable?"

Lennon whistled softly.

"He's the one," Pringle explained, "who got the cops going on it."

"Eric Dunstable! Wait a sec: What parish are we talking about?"

"St. Waldo of the Hills, Bloomfield Hills."

Pat's chuckle was low and throaty. "St. Waldo of the Wheels. This thing is beginning to come together."

"The Wheels? Does somebody call it Waldo of the Wheels?"

"I've heard it called that now and again. Couldn't tell you exactly why. I suppose it's because the people who live out there are some of the better-known wheelers and dealers in this territory—like Eric Dunstable. Or maybe because they're auto execs who put the world on wheels—like Eric Dunstable. That makes sense . . . I can easily imagine Dunstable getting the Bloomfield cops to bend the rules."

"Not just the Bloomfield Hills police."

"Huh?"

"The Detroit cops too."

"Detroit? Just because he said he was going to Detroit?"

"That's not all," Pringle added. "Not just Detroit Missing Persons; Homicide is investigating too."

"Homicide! My God! That's overkill." Lennon giggled. "Please forgive; I didn't intend the pun."

"That's the part that's got me worried." And indeed, Pringle's face was clouded.

"What's got you worried?" Pat asked supportively.

"Homicide. The fact that Detroit Homicide is in on this. It scares me. I haven't worked on a story that involved homicide since . . ." She did not need to elaborate.

Pat slid her chair closer and touched Pringle's arm. "Don't give it a thought. There aren't that many people with enough clout to get two major police departments involved in a missing persons search—a good twenty-four hours early at that. But if anybody could pull it off, Eric Dunstable certainly qualifies. I can just see him calling in some of his markers from Mayor Cobb. Don't worry: Homicide's there just for show. Just to flaunt Dunstable's belief that he's got pull and the balls to use it."

Pringle smiled. "You think so?"

"Sure. You're gonna have a ball with this story—oops, another involuntary pun." She shook her head and grimaced. "I've got to cut this out before I start work today.

"But you'll see: You'll be fine. Go find the missing priest." She grinned. "By the time you get done, you'll probably be able to give me a refresher course in Catholicism."

6

I_T WAS LATE_ Monday afternoon and Lieutenant Alonzo Tully had not gotten his wish.

Periodically during the day he had imagined the elusive Father Keating simply showing up at St. Waldo's. Those occupying the parish buildings—housekeeper, secretary, janitor, religious education coordinator, teachers and the like—had been forcefully instructed to call either the Bloomfield Hills or Detroit police should anyone spot the priest.

At no point in this so-far brief search had Tully given a damn where Keating had been or what he'd done. As long as the priest stepped forth or somebody located him, all would be well that ended.

Those members of Tully's squad whom he'd called in yesterday afternoon had greeted their new assignment with a variety of reactions. As for Tully's two closest collaborators, Sergeants Angie Moore and Phil Mangiapane, they were poles apart.

Moore greeted the task in much the same spirit as her leader. To both her and Tully, this was a necessary evil brought on by a rich bastard who would settle for nothing less than what he demanded—and by the mayor, a political animal who would exchange his consent for future favors.

Mangiapane, a very practicing Catholic, never could get enough of his religion and its mysteries. And one of those great mysteries, stemming from the sergeant's youth, involved priests—priests and nuns. As a boy, young Philip had wondered: Are they human? Do nuns have legs? Hair? Do any of them ever go to the bathroom?

Fortunately, these sorts of questions seldom concerned him any longer. Still, mysteries did abound. The power that priests had to absolve, to consecrate, to bury, to marry, all these had to be taken on faith—another mystery. Mangiapane did not at all mind taking time from Homicide—even though it was his first love—to search for a lost priest and, along the way, to learn more about these still-mysterious creatures.

Partly to free himself to supervise the investigation as well as to follow his own instincts and leads, partly because they were closest to him on the squad, and partly because they differed in their attitude toward this case, Tully had appointed Moore and Mangiapane coordinators. They now had brought him the results of all efforts to date. To simplify, they had consolidated and summarized the various reports.

"Both our guys and the Bloomfield people have been checking with all the relatives and friends we can find," Moore reported.

"And?" Tully prompted.

"For one thing, there aren't many relatives. Parents, dead. No brothers or sisters. Some distant cousins, and that's about it. And with a couple of them, we had to explain who John Keating was, and then they remembered he was a relative. Those were mostly out-of-towners. The few living in this area at least knew they had a priest relative, but we couldn't find any who saw him on anywhere near a regular basis. We haven't uncovered a relative who would be a reasonable lead. Deadendsville."

"Zoo"—nearly everyone used the nickname from the abbreviated Alonzo—"the thing of it is that priests don't usually end up having many relatives," Mangiapane said. "Especially if they don't have brothers or sisters. They don't get married, so they got no in-laws. So it's not strange that we come up dry."

"Okay, Manj." Tully may not have known much about any of the organized religions, but he was aware that priests had no in-laws unless they had married brothers or sisters, and so they'd have fewer relatives than most. But experience taught that it did not pay to come down too hard on Mangiapane. Criticism tended to inhibit him. And that was not productive.

"There are lots of friends, though, or at least acquaintances," Mangiapane continued. "Funny thing, they're mostly among the elite—the silk stocking crowd."

"Why would that be funny, Manj? That's the neighborhood he operates in, isn't it—Bloomfield Hills? Not too many panhandlers out there."

"Yeah," Mangiapane responded, "but Keating wasn't always out there."

"Oh?"

"We went over his assignments with the secretary. He's been all over the place in a little more than twenty years. Downtown, the core city—before it was 'the core city'—all around the town, some of the suburbs. But he's been in Bloomfield Hills for the past almost ten years.

"The thing is, we can't come up with anyone who could be described as a friend, especially a close friend, anywhere but in Bloomfield Hills."

"That's right, Zoo," Moore added. "We went over the stuff in his office and suite. A few phone and address books but hardly any listing for anyone outside of Bloomfield Hills. Oh, a few in Birmingham, you know, the same neighborhood. But hardly anyone with an address down-to-earth people might live at. Not even the Pointes," she added, and then, with a touch of amusement, "The difference between old and new money."

Moore and Mangiapane glanced at each other. Mangiapane nodded, offering Moore the floor. Moore riffled through several pages of notes. "The single item about which no one seems to have any doubt is that there could be no reason for what's happened. Some—most of his friends were surprised to see us. They didn't know he was missing."

Tully seemed slightly surprised. "These people from the parish?"

"Uh-huh."

"Their pastor misses a whole weekend of services and his parishioners don't know he's not there?"

Mangiapane spoke as one in the know. "All the people who go to Mass on Sunday know is there's a priest there to say the Mass. See, at St. Waldo's, there's an assistant priest and two other priests who come in just to help on weekends. There's a rotation in most places—and that's the way it works at St. Waldo's too."

"Rotation?"

"Yeah, Zoo. Like one week a priest will have a Saturday evening Mass, then next week he'll take early Sunday, then the middle Sunday Mass, then the late Sunday Mass, and then back to a Saturday Mass. But not that many parishioners pay much attention to who's takin' what. All they want's a priest to give the Mass. They just want to take care of their obligation to hear Mass."

"That's it, Zoo," Moore attested. "Even the ones who are aware of what's going on wouldn't think it was alarming if the priest they expected didn't have their particular service. He could be ill. Or for some reason, the priests could have traded schedules."

"What it comes down to, Zoo," Mangiapane said, "is that that's why none of his friends—who are also mainly parishioners—knew anything out of the ordinary might have happened. So they were surprised when we came calling with questions. The only ones who thought something might be wrong were—whatchamajigger—the inner circle: the housekeeper, the secretary—and the assistant priest and the other weekend help of course, because they had to cover for Father Keating."

"So then," Tully concluded, "they were the ones who brought Dunstable in on it."

"Yeah, Zoo. He's the parish council president," Mangiapane added. "The council president, Zoo, is the one who—"

"I know what he does. The inspector filled me in on that yesterday," Tully said. "So, okay, none of the friends or parishioners were on to what was going on. What was their reaction?"

Moore looked up from her notes. "Unanimous, as far as I can see, Zoo. No one could think of any reason why Keating should be among the missing—although some thought he might be taking a vacation. But that had to be a stab in the dark: When you ask them, they immediately admit that's never happened before. Not that he doesn't take a regular vacation. But it's always announced well in advance. And here there's been no such announcement."

"Any grudges, hard feelings?" Tully asked.

Mangiapane smiled. "Not once they found out he was missing."

"That's understandable," Moore said. "If a cop comes to your door, tells you somebody you know is missing, you're not likely to volunteer that you hate the bastard and hope he's dead. But this was different: The general reaction was surprise, surprise that he was missing and surprise that the police were looking for him. If anybody had any hard feelings, they weren't intense enough to pop out spontaneously."

"How about the people he worked with?"

"Guarded," Moore said. "It got to be like pulling teeth. Monosyllabic answers. Little or no information volunteered. We concentrated on the housekeeper, the secretary, and the other priest—the assistant. But we didn't get anywhere."

"The funny thing is," Mangiapane noted, "nobody seems to work for him very long."

"Hmmm?" Tully found that of interest.

"I didn't pay much attention when I found out the assistant priest had been in the parish only six months. That happens. Priests get moved around. Some more than others. But then the secretary said she'd been hired a little less than a year ago. That made me wonder. Then the housekeeper said she'd worked for him just a little more than a year—just before the secretary was hired."

"So the housekeeper overlapped the secretary. She give any reason why the former secretary was let go?"

"I asked her about that," Mangiapane said, "and she said she didn't really know. The housekeeper got along good with the secretary. They'd eat lunch together in the rectory kitchen. Then, all of a sudden—as far as she knew—out of the blue the secretary is given notice and she's gone and a new secretary is hired. And then I asked about her predecessor. She said she didn't get to know her more than just saying good-bye. The two of them passed like ships in the night. But she did find out from a parishioner that the former housekeeper had been there a little more than a year."

Tully scratched the stubble on his chin. "A pattern? Might be worth looking into. Manj, get some of the guys on the former employees. Maybe one or another of them has got some mean words for the boss. How about the priest—the assistant? He's been there the shortest time. Anything there? Do the priests go through that revolving door too?"

"I gotta check that out, Zoo."

"Okay. Did we bump into any pattern—any routines? Keating have any habits that can lead us anywhere?"

Moore shrugged. "I suppose there's mornings." She looked at Mangiapane. "Don't they have services—Mass—every morning? I guess that would tie him up first off."

"It's not like the old days . . ." Mangiapane shook his head. "That's the way it used to be when I was growing up. Waldo's got two priests— which, in the old days, meant there'd be at least two Masses every day. But I wouldn't have bet on that now, so I checked their schedule. They only got one Mass a day. Turns out Father Keating says Mass Tuesday and Thursday mornings. The other priest has Monday, Wednesday, and Friday."

"And Saturday?" Tully asked.

"That's the start of the weekend schedule," Mangiapane said. "There's Mass later in the day on Saturdays, so they don't have one in the morning."

Tully wondered what evil fate dragged him into these cases involving organized religions. He knew little about them and cared even less.

"Well, that clears things up for me, anyway," Moore said. "The housekeeper there told me Keating was away from the rectory a lot, but on a pretty regular basis."

"Regular?" Tully was alert once more.

"Yeah," Moore said. "After Mass on Sunday, Keating would take care of the collection. By that time he'd be pretty beat. He usually left late afternoon and didn't return till Tuesday morning's Mass. Until Manj said Keating didn't take the Monday services, I wondered how he could manage staying away till Tuesday."

"Okay, so he was away from the parish Sunday evening and all of Monday. Anybody know where he went?"

Moore shook her head. "No, but that's not all. Wednesday was his 'day off.'"

"Wednesday!" Tully exhibited surprise. "What happened to Monday?"

Moore laughed. "Apparently, he was away a lot."

"And nobody knew where he went or why? What if there was an emergency?"

"Oh, he always had somebody covering for him," Moore said. "There's the younger priest—the assistant. Or, if he wasn't available, there were the other priests who helped out on weekends. They have other jobs—one teaches at Catholic Central High School, the other is a hospital chaplain—so they're pretty busy. But in a pinch they can take care of the few emergencies that might pop up. And there's also an answering service."

"Sounds like an absentee pastor," Tully said. "Is he ever around? I mean, why did Dunstable stir up all the troops?"

"That's the thing, Zoo," Moore said. "He's around when he's supposed to be. There's the weekend services and Tuesday and Thursday. If there's a meeting—parish council or one of the council's commissions or anything like that—he's pretty reliable. That's the reason the crew got shook up when he wasn't there when he was supposed to be."

It didn't make much sense. Tully could not imagine living in that manner. For him, his job as a police officer consumed almost his every thought. And while he well knew that not everyone by any means matched his dedication to work, he had had the impression that priests, ministers, and rabbis came close to matching him. Especially priests; wasn't that why they didn't get married and have a family—to be totally dedicated to their work?

"Well," Tully said, "in Keating's laid-back schedule, was there anything on the docket for Friday evenings? Saturday mornings? Someplace he should be? Someplace we could look for him?"

"The secretary said that Fridays he spent nearly the whole day working on his sermon for the weekend Masses," Mangiapane said. "So it was a little odd that he took off Friday afternoon. He usually spent Friday nights at the rectory. And he was always around Saturday all day to make sure everything was all set. The housekeeper would have expected him for Friday dinner even if he hadn't told her he'd be back. So everybody got more and more worried as the weekend went by and no Father Keating."

Tully glanced at both officers. "What kind of car did he drive?"

"Lincoln Town Car, '91, black, in tip-top shape," Moore read from her notes.

"The make and plates," Tully said, "we got that on LEIN?"

"Sure thing, Zoo," Mangiapane said. "We got 'em on first thing."

There was silence for a few moments. Tully seemed deep in thought. Finally he spoke.

"Something's missing." He looked at them both again. "A dimension. Like this priest seems to be no more than two dimensions. He's like a shadow. There are all kinds of people who know him—some pretty good. But there's nothing clear-cut about their descriptions."

"I got the same impression, Zoo," Moore said.

"Me too," Mangiapane admitted.

There was another prolonged silence.

"Here's an idea, Zoo," Mangiapane said brightly. "What we seem stuck on is this guy's personality and his lifestyle, but most of all his personality. And we're not getting much help from the people we've questioned."

"What's your point, Manj?"

"Well," the big sergeant spoke hesitantly, "sometimes . . . in the past . . . we, uh . . . we've called in help."

" 'Help'?"

"Experts . . . for advice . . . you know, in areas where we're not familiar. Like . . . the personality of a particular priest. And his lifestyle."

Tully thought he knew where Mangiapane was leading. "Like . . . who?"

"Well, I was thinking . . . Father Koesler. He's been a good resource in the past."

Tully considered for a few moments. Mangiapane remained impassive. Moore looked interested. Finally Tully spoke. "Call in some outside help? I don't plan on this case lasting that long. It'd cost us time to talk him into it, time to get him up to speed, time to brief him."

"We're not exactly breaking any speed records right now, Zoo," Mangiapane said. "Father Koesler could maybe get us a shortcut or two. Finish this thing up and"—Mangiapane knew this would be the clincher—"we could get back to our regular cases."

Tully reflected. "It might work," he said. "It just might work."

*   *   *

It was just a few minutes before 6:00 and dinnertime at St. Joseph's rectory. The aroma of the cooking roast and vegetables drifted through the rectory. Fathers Koesler and Dunn were sipping, Dunn a Beefeater martini, Koesler a bourbon Manhattan. The aroma of the food promised satisfaction, the drinks were relaxing, the weather was ideal. All seemed well.

The two priests were discussing Dunn's first day at the University of Detroit Mercy.

"I've always found," Koesler was saying, "that the worst place to try to find a parking spot was on a college campus until you get a permit to park on the college campus. But of course you've got to park on the college campus in order to apply for the permit. Sort of a catch-22."

Dunn smiled. "I guess you're right. I haven't been on all that many campuses. But U of D seems to have licked that problem—at least temporarily. They give you a day pass that at least gets you to a visitors' lot. After that, I got my sticker and did some registering."

"Really. What are you signed up for?"

Dunn took an index card out of the inside pocket of his jacket. "Let's see; there's Introductory Psychology, Abnormal Psychology, Psychology of Religion, and Death and Dying."

"Isn't that a pretty big bite?"

"No, I don't think so. After all, I'm just auditing, not going for credit. I won't do all the required readings. I'm really interested in the Abnormal, Religion of course, and Death and Dying. Intro to Psych is a prerequisite for all of them. Besides, I'm a holy priest of God and it's a Jesuit school; I'm counting on their being kind.

"By the way, I'm officially a 'special student.' I hope they mean that in a positive way."

"I'm sure they do. Good luck." Koesler raised his glass in salute, then drained the last of the Manhattan. That's the way it used to be, he thought. Then it was no more. The perks accorded men of the cloth seemed to melt away during the sixties and seventies. Now, who knows, maybe it's coming back . . .

The phone rang. Mary O'Connor was gone for the day. And the housekeeper had made it abundantly clear that she was not to be disturbed, especially during the home stretch of meal preparation. Koesler answered the phone. "St. Joseph's."

"Father Koesler?"

He knew the voice. Something inside Koesler quivered. "Yes, this is he."

"This is Lieutenant Tully, Homicide."

Suspicion confirmed. "Yes, Lieutenant."

Dunn looked up, suddenly interested. Of course he could hear only Koesler's end of the conversation.

"We're in the middle of an investigation. Actually, it's a missing persons case at the moment. But there are reasons Homicide has been brought into it. To be brief, do you know a Father John Keating?"

"Yes. Yes, I do." But he was thinking, *Yes, I did*.

"I don't know whether you knew it, but he's been missing since Friday. By now, several police departments are searching for him. But we're coming up short on what makes the man tick. We need to fill in some missing spaces. Would you be willing to help?"

"Really, Lieutenant, I don't know how I could be of help."

Dunn was rapt. Hot damn! I'll bet that's Keating they're calling about. They're following my scenario; they're asking Koesler to help.

"You've helped us in the past, Father. We think you might be able to help us now. How about it?" When Koesler did not reply immediately, Tully added, almost offhandedly, "If you have any doubts, I could ask Walt Koznicki to call."

Oh, God! That's the last thing in the world I want. It would take tremendous concentration and carefulness not to let anything from that confession escape his safekeeping even with just Lieutenant Tully looking over his shoulder. How much more difficult it would be with an old friend like the inspector. "I don't know, Lieutenant . . ." Koesler's tone was apologetic. "I'm awfully busy and pressed just now."

Tully's sigh was deep. "I can't force you to help us. But the longer this priest is missing, the greater the probability that we're not going to find him."

Silence.

"He *is* a priest," Tully emphasized.

Briefly, Koesler considered the number of times he had responded to a request for assistance from the police. At no time had there been a greater ostensible reason for him to cooperate than in this instance. Outside of an intolerable secret such as he was now guarding, there was no adequate reason for his not providing all the help and direction possible. But there was no way he could tell the police, or anyone, why he was reluctant about getting involved. There was no way out of this. He had to get involved. Maybe he'd find a way to help without touching on the secret. It would be an extremely narrow line to walk. He breathed a quick prayer for guidance. "All right, Lieutenant, I'll do what I can."

"Fine. I'll be right over—"

"Wait!" Koesler's tone was forceful. "Not now. Not tonight. I have several extremely important appointments. I simply cannot break into that schedule. I simply can't."

Though disappointed, Tully would not be choosy—and he knew it. "First thing tomorrow then?"

"Yes."

"Eight all right?"

"Fine."

"I'll see you then." Tully hung up.

The housekeeper's voice came from the dining room. "Dinner, Fathers."

Koesler left his now empty glass on an end table. Dunn carried his unfinished martini with him. "It happened, didn't it?" Dunn was elated. "You got called into the Keating case. He's officially . . . what—not dead?"

"Missing."

"And they want you to help find him. Delicious."

"Look, could we forget this for now? I do have some important appointments this evening, and I'd like to try to enjoy supper without courting indigestion. Who knows, maybe they'll find Father Keating before tomorrow morning."

"Let us pray."

"Okay. Bless us, O Lord, and these Thy gifts which we are about to receive from Thy bounty, through Christ, Our Lord."

"Amen."

"Amen indeed."

7

FOR A MONDAY night, the crowd wasn't bad. The Fast Lane actually was filled with customers. In that sense, it wasn't a bad crowd. But there was no line of people waiting to get in.

Pat Lennon and Pringle McPhee arrived around 9:00 P.M., which, for that establishment, was the shank of the evening.

They'd met for dinner after work. They'd been doing that with some frequency lately. After dinner, Pringle had suggested they visit The Fast Lane. The club, in a downtown section known as Bricktown, had been open only a few months and she hadn't been there yet. Pat was not eager to go; she'd been there once and didn't much care for it. But Pringle's suggestion was more an appeal. So Pat agreed, with the proviso that they keep their visit brief.

The sound assaulted them as they opened the door. Pringle smiled. It was her sort of place. Pat winced and acknowledged to herself that they were doomed to shout for pretty much the rest of the evening.

They were faced with a choice: upstairs or downstairs?

"What's down?" Pringle asked loudly.

"Pool tables. Adult—very adult—video games," Pat answered just as loudly.

"And up?"

"Dancing. The club."

"Then it's up." Pringle took the stairs, followed by Pat.

It was just a few steps to the first—actually the second—level, the dance floor. Pringle's mouth dropped open as she beheld the surreal scene.

The building was rectangular with two rectangular tiers above the dance floor. Looking up into the high recesses of the vaulted ceiling, Pringle could imagine herself in a bullring, the Colosseum, or an ancient opera house . . . though it was safe to say no concert hall had ever heard a sound like this.

The noise level was several times louder than a screeching jet. The dance floor was almost choking with gyrating bodies, all amazingly there of their own volition. Except for those who were dancing so close they were almost on the other side of each other, it was difficult to tell who was whose partner. From the two upper levels, spectators enjoyed a more encompassing view. And they were enjoying the view; otherwise why would so many be crowded against the railings taking in the action below?

In a reserved spot in the uppermost tier sat a very kinetic disc jockey. He not only played the tapes, he controlled the volume, the fluctuating glitter and flash, the strobes, and the video projectors that threw much-larger-than-life images of the dancers onto the gigantic screens—not unlike those in sports palaces that endlessly repeat instant replays.

Pat and Pringle took the stairs. Arriving at the second tier, they discovered why so many of the patrons were clustered at the inner railings. All the alcoves were occupied by couples, threesomes, and quartets in various stages of assignation. Here and there fronting the outer walls were black granite-and-marble bars with soft, cushy stools. These were pretty well occupied, although there was an occasional empty stool.

Not only was it impossible not to be overwhelmed by the music, they could feel it. The entire floor throbbed to the tempo that spread concussively into and through their bodies.

The scene was not much short of a full-blown bacchanal.

Pringle squeezed her way to a bar and got drinks for herself and Pat. They found a spot near one of the corners where they could watch most of the action—on the floor, at the bars, along the railings, and, if one considered sex a spectator sport, in the alcoves.

"I had no idea!" Pringle almost had to shout to be heard above the din.

"They don't leave much to the imagination," Pat yelled back.

As they took in the action, it was easy to spot singles mingling in the crowd. It was hard not to pity them. Most were desperate for someone—anyone—who would value them. And most would fail to find that certain someone here.

What with the haze—there were only nominal smoke-free areas in the club—and the kaleidoscopic lighting, identifying specific dancers was challenging. But even in this maze, Pringle thought she spotted someone she knew, someone everyone knew. "Isn't that . . .?"

Pat tried following Pringle's line of vision. "Isn't that . . . who?"

"You know . . ." Pringle was uncertain. "The gossip columnist? With the *Suburban Reporter*?"

"Where?"

"There. Don't you see?" Pringle was now pointing. "Dancing . . . there, near the far corner . . . see?"

Even though the two of them were almost shouting, they also had to face each other and mouth their words exaggeratedly in order to communicate through the clangor and resonance.

Gradually, Pat's vision did manage to cut through the smoke and the strobe flashes. "Very good, Pringle. It is indeed, Sally Dean."

"No, no . . ." Pringle shook her head. "Lacy DeVere."

Pat grinned. "I knew her when she was Sally Dean."

"Really?" Pringle turned to look at the subject in question and then back to face Pat. "She changed her name? I didn't know that."

"Pringle, she—" Pat stopped and jerked her head toward a just-vacated alcove. She and Pringle made a beeline for the space and settled into the chairs. They were as grateful for the quasi haven from the noise as they were for the seats. Now at least they could carry on a conversation without immediate threat to their vocal cords. "Pringle, she changed just about everything. Her name—legally; her hips—liposuction; her breasts—implants; her nose—plastic surgery; her hair coloring—her hairdresser knows; and several husbands—divorce."

"Wow! I would have guessed the hair—that's a most unlikely shade. But I didn't know the rest."

"We worked together—no, at the same time—at the *Free Press*. A long time ago, maybe ten years. She was Sally Dean then, a staff writer—and not a very good one either."

"I knew you'd been at the Freep," Pringle said, "but . . . Sally Dean? I never heard of her."

"Don't feel bad. Not many people remember the name. I'll never know how she got past the personnel director. Ordinarily he was one of the best in judging prospective employees, but he sure blew that one. Or maybe," she added, "he was away on vacation."

"She was that bad?"

"Walking proof that a good copy editor really can make a silk purse out of a sow's ear. She couldn't spell. She had no concept of grammar. She paid no attention to detail. She put streets on the wrong side of town. She misidentified people in her stories."

Pringle's eyes widened. "How did she ever make it through probation?"

"She slept well."

"She—? Oh, I get it."

"Seemed like her only talent. It was unerring the way she could pick out whose star was rising at the paper. Then she'd practically throw the poor boob into bed and almost literally rape him."

Pringle giggled. "Poetic license?"

"Only a little. But not grossly exaggerated."

"Well, what happened to her? I mean at the Freep?"

Pat half smiled at the memory. "She picked the right guy, as usual, but he moved."

"Moved?"

"Moved on. He's in Hollywood now. He writes for TV mostly."

"She couldn't go with him?"

"Uh-uh. He didn't need a waif then and he needs one even less now. Like the song from *Pajama Game* says, 'He's living in the Taj Mahal/In every room a different doll.'"

"And at the Freep?"

"Karma at last. When the winner she picked left town, the guy who took his place near the top of the totem pole was someone she had royally screwed—and I don't mean sexually."

"Aha! A variation on the Golden Rule: Be nice to people on the way up; you're likely to meet the same people on the way down."

"Exactly. It was a foregone conclusion; he made life so miserable for her, she had no alternative. Somehow—and I've never been able to figure out how—she walked away with a fat severance check."

They rested their voices for a few moments and sipped their drinks. Pringle got up and moved to the railing to watch the action. Having again spotted Lacy DeVere, née Sally Dean, she could scarcely take her eyes off her. Pat sat and sipped. After a couple of minutes Pringle returned to the alcove.

"I still don't get it," she said at length. "According to your story, when she left the *Free Press,* she was at the bottom of the heap. Now she's got practically a new body and one of the most feared word processors in Detroit. I mean, how did she get from there to here?"

Pat shrugged. "You can't keep a bad apple down. As far as her body is concerned, as some astute observer once remarked, Lacy doesn't get a new wardrobe; she just gets reupholstered."

Pat was thoughtful for a moment. "Actually, I'm one of the few who knows where she went after the Freep. For some incomprehensible reason, she confided in me—and I have no idea how many others—just before she left the paper and this town. She got a job—if you can believe this—teaching journalism at Mankato College in Minnesota. With that cachet in her suitcase, she got a few honest jobs and began the overhaul and repair of her body. Her ultimate aim was just what she's accomplished: to return and become a force to be reckoned with."

"But to really get even, wouldn't she have to be back with the Freep . . . or the *News?*"

"Don't sell the *Reporter* short. Especially since the JOA, the *Suburban Reporter* has become a pretty popular and potent vehicle with a growing circulation. Personally, I don't think she's done settling the score. But God knows what she's got in mind—uh-oh." Pat nodded toward the far end of the railing along the stairs. "That's what comes of talking about her. The ESP is working: She must have spotted us. Here she comes."

"That's okay," Pringle said. "Now that you've filled me in on her background, she's not nearly as intimidating."

"Good. But don't let down your guard for an instant. Just remember: The first ten priorities in Lacy DeVere's life are the things she wants. And she'll do anything and use anybody to get them. So watch it."

For a fleeting instant Pat considered bailing out. She would never be in the mood to mingle socially with Lacy DeVere. But actually, the urge to beat a hasty retreat was more for Pringle's sake. Pat glanced at Pringle, who had stood and moved to the railing with a smile of anticipation. Pat rose to join Pringle. This did not bode well. Why was she put in mind of the unsuspecting doe in the sights of the hunter?

As she approached them, Lacy resembled a powerboat sweeping aside from its path all lesser obstacles, in this case, people.

When she reached them, Lacy dove directly at Pat, embraced her, and kissed the air. "Pat," she enthused, "how good to see you again."

"Hi, Lacy." Pat's tone was noncommittal, several degrees less enthused than Lacy's.

"It's been too long," Lacy said. "Where've you been keeping yourself?"

"Working. Writing."

"Of course you have. I read you just about every day. As usual, your stuff is good and, more often than not, on page one."

It was obvious that this last remark was a fishing maneuver for a reciprocal compliment. But Pat withheld comment.

"And who's your lovely friend here?" Lacy pursued.

"Lacy DeVere, meet Pringle McPhee."

"Pringle McPhee! At last! I've wanted to meet you but our paths haven't crossed till now."

"You know who I am?"

"Of course I do. I've read your byline in the *News* frequently. Everybody says you're the next Pat Lennon."

"Lacy," Pat said, "there's no need for a new Pat Lennon. I'm not retiring. And I'm not writing my autobiography—or my obit."

"Of course you're not, dear," Lacy said with mock affection. "It's just that Pringle here is going to be knocking you off the front page one of these days."

"Oh, no!" Pringle protested.

"Page one is big, Lacy—no ads. There's plenty of room for lots of bylines," Pat said.

"Well, of course there is, sweetie." Lacy regarded Pat head-on. One of them had thrown down a gauntlet and the other had picked it up. It didn't really matter which had done what; the battle was joined.

"Besides," Lacy continued to address Pat, "there have been rumors lately that your work has begun to slip a bit. I mean, ever since your lover boy . . . your significant other—my glory! what do they call paramours these days?—anyway, ever since good old Joe Cox slipped the tether and ran off to Chicago." The touché was implicit.

Pringle gasped. It was common knowledge that Joe Cox had been lured from the *Detroit Free Press* to the *Chicago Tribune* by an offer he found impossible to refuse—especially in the face of the hodgepodge that the JOA had made of Detroit's newspapers. It was also common knowledge that Cox and Lennon had been living together for more than ten years. Common knowledge, that is, mostly to the local media people. Readers of both metropolitan dailies knew only that Cox and Lennon were the premiere reporters on their respective papers, and that Cox had moved on.

But now, that information was grist for Detroit's foremost gossip columnist.

Pringle went livid. "Pat's work hasn't slipped one bit. She's as sharp as she ever was. And that means she's the best. And besides, you're insinuating that she and Joe have broken up. That's not only untrue, it's malicious!"

Only by a stretch of the imagination could Lacy's smile be described as sincere. "Whether Pat's stuff is as good as it ever was is in the eyes of the reader. And an informal *Reporter* poll says she's slipping."

"And when you publish the results—as I'm sure you're about to," Pat said, "I suppose you'll qualify it as 'unscientific.'"

"What's science got to do with anything?" Lacy was still smiling. "As for absence making the heart grow fonder, my sources tell me Mr. Cox's testosterone has gone berserk. He's at Chicago's Playboy mansion more often than Hugh Hefner."

"That's a lie!" As she took a threatening step toward Lacy, Pringle stumbled.

"Careful, sweetie," said Lacy, "you don't want to depend too much on that gimpy leg."

Pringle gasped again. "How did you—?"

"It's my business to know . . . and to tell. That car that ran you down did a lot of damage, didn't it? Any scars left, my dear—to discourage pouring that beautiful body into a bikini?"

Pringle's lips were a thin line. "No scars, Sally Dean! How about you? Some stretch marks? Some remnants of the stitches?"

Lacy threw back her head, laughing uproariously. "Ancient history, sweetie! I see Pat's filled you in. Well, once upon a time there was a Sally Dean. But she is no more. Once I was on the bottom, struggling. Now I'm on top. Like some of the saints who started out not all that good, then turned their act around and got to be perfect at what they did."

She laughed again. "Yes, dear Pringle, there are those who would like to dig up old Sally Dean. But most of them are too busy worrying about what Lacy DeVere knows about *them*. And what Lacy DeVere is going to write about them.

"All's fair, Pringle, dear. And by all, I mean everything."

Pringle was strongly tempted to throw the dregs of her drink in the woman's face. Pat, sensing Pringle's impulse, shook her head "no." Lacy too perceived what had almost happened.

She wagged her finger close to Pringle's face. "Don't even think about it, sister. You've got to learn to look one step ahead. You need to stay on the good side of me. Otherwise I'll destroy you. Not right away. When you least expect it. Now, that'll give your phobias a chance to work overtime."

Again, Pringle was caught with her mouth hanging open. How does she know . . .? How can she know . . .?

Sensing the unspoken sentiment, Lacy repeated, "It's my business to know. And it's my business to tell."

"Come on, Pringle," Pat said, "let's get out of here."

As they turned to leave, Lacy called after them, "Oh, and Pat dear, let's do lunch someday soon."

"Maybe," Pat said over her shoulder. "Then we'll see who eats what."

Outside The Fast Lane, everything was refreshing. They'd left behind the smoke and the noise and, above all, Lacy DeVere.

Although Pat Lennon lived in a nearby high rise, she would not consider walking these streets at this hour. She would have taken a cab; however, Pringle's car was only a few steps away.

When they arrived at the car, after having paid the parking attendant, Pat noticed Pringle scanning both the front and rear seats before entering. Sound procedure, but in Pringle's case it was, along with her growing list of obsessions, one more manifestation of her frame of mind.

They drove the few blocks to Pat's apartment building in silence.

Before leaving the car, Pat turned and asked, "You okay?"

"A little shook up. This is the first time I ever met anybody I could so thoroughly dislike so quickly. But there's not much she can do to me, as far as I can see. She seemed to be aiming mostly at you. So I guess I ought to turn the question around: You okay?"

Pat smiled and nodded. "It'll take much more than Lacy DeVere to reach me."

"But that poll she was talking about—"

"Remember, Pringle, and don't ever forget: Lacy DeVere is out for number one, first and foremost and always. If she can make a point, she won't let anything as insignificant as a mere lie inhibit her."

"So?"

"So I seriously doubt that the 'poll' ever saw the light of day. You poll readers on features, comics, columnists. You don't poll readers for their opinions on reporters. Most readers don't know whose byline is on what. Pringle, you and I don't get our pictures in the paper. We do our job, but nobody knows who we are. That 'poll' was one of Lacy's less spectacular inventions, okay?"

"I suppose. But what about what she said about Joe?"

Pat's smile was tight. "Probably nothing but an educated guess. I don't think Joe will ever run out of wild oats. It's one of the reasons we never married—not by any means a major reason, but a reason nonetheless."

"You and Joe are okay, then?"

"I guess. We get together once or twice a month. But this commuting between Detroit and Chicago gets tiring after a while. I'll be honest: It hurt like crazy when he left. Now it's not so bad. I even kind of enjoy the peace and quiet. I never thought I would. But now it would be tough to go back to living with someone again."

As Pat stepped out of the car, she stopped and turned back to Pringle. "Just remember: Lacy DeVere looks out for number one exclusively. If you get in her way, you gotta know you're at very least in for a head-on collision."

8

FATHER KOESLER was used to surprises. They happened to him often enough.

Last night he had been juggling a series of appointments, along with an unusual number of phone calls. So many, indeed, that he'd asked Father Dunn to take the phone and see if the busy pastor couldn't return the calls later.

One of those calls he returned was from one Marlene Pietrangelo.

He had no idea who this Mrs. Pietrangelo was until she identified herself as the penitent who had visited him last Saturday evening in the confessional. They had discussed in general terms the Church teachings and positions with which she disagreed. Although she hadn't been to confession in two years, she'd declined confessing at that time. So instead of the Sacrament of Reconciliation, they'd had a chat. It was not definite, but she had mentioned that she might return. Koesler was surprised she'd called so soon.

She had, she said, a problem she hadn't specifically brought up on Saturday. She wanted to see him now. Accent on the *now*.

Koesler had an appointment with Lieutenant Tully the next morning. But there was something in her voice, an urgency that couldn't be ignored. This might well be a fish that wanted to take the bait and might well lose the appetite if not hooked now.

Fortunately, she was able to be at St. Joseph's at 7:00 Tuesday morning. One more indication of her earnestness: a willingness to travel from a northern suburb to downtown Detroit at that early hour.

She arrived at precisely 7:00. He tried to lead her directly to the heart of the matter, which turned out to be that she was in a second marriage without having had the first annulled.

Another surprise.

Koesler mentally reexamined their conversation of Saturday. It had been there, but well concealed. Among the positions of the teaching

Church with which she disagreed were birth control, divorce, remarriage, and abortion. As it turned out, the only one of these she had not acted on was abortion. What had appeared at the time as a theoretical difference of opinion was actually a conflict between practice and an apparent law.

Some nonthreatening questions elicited the fact that hers would not be a complicated case. Her first marriage—to another Catholic—had been by civil ceremony and never ratified by a Catholic priest. Both that marriage and the subsequent divorce had taken place without benefit of clergy. Yet she had assumed that when Catholics married—by any legal means—the union was recognized as valid by the Church. And that was why she and Mr. Pietrangelo had therefore also been married by a judge: Their erroneous understanding was that it was impossible for them to be married "in the Church."

Koesler was happy to explain that this was one of life's most easily rectified problems.

For an annulment of her first marriage, all that was needed were recent copies of the original couple's baptismal records, on which there would be no notation of marriage—a clear indication that they had not had an ecclesiastically recognized wedding. For a valid marriage, a Catholic couple needs a priest and two witnesses at their exchange of consent. The marriage license signed by the justice would show that a priest did not perform the marriage. The "clean" baptismal certificate would indicate they never had a priest convalidate their union. A fact to which they would of course attest. And, voila! Perfect grounds for the simplest of annulments.

Only one further consideration. The Pietrangelos were having difficult financial times; could they afford the process?

Again Koesler was able to deliver good news. In the matter of annulments, more often than not there was no happy news. So he was particularly pleased that this woman had a case that would require only the simplest and least complicated procedures in the annulment field. And it would not cost her a penny.

He was uncertain how many dioceses footed the bill for Tribunal fees, but he hoped they all followed Detroit's example. Here, the local Church court simply charged nothing for cases that remained on the local level. About the only matter that had to be sent to Rome was the Privilege of the Faith case, which involved not a declaration of nullity, but a dissolution of a nonsacramental marriage in favor of one between two Catholics. While a Privilege of the Faith case was extremely complex—having to prove that a baptism never happened—and quite expensive, the Detroit Tribunal absorbed the cost. The sole procedure not covered by this policy was an appeal; anyone wishing to appeal a decision was on his or her own financially.

By assuring Mrs. Pietrangelo that she had an excellent chance to have her marriage convalidated and further assuring her that the process would be free of charge, Koesler had made her day. And because she was extremely happy about all this, so was Koesler. Almost.

There was still the matter of having to "help" Lieutenant Tully solve a mystery, the solution to which Koesler already knew. Boxed in as he was by the sacred seal of confession, he was skating on the thinnest of ice. He had never been in a situation precisely like this in his entire life. He would have to be more alert and guarded than he had ever been.

Certainly more astute than he'd been with Marlene Pietrangelo. She was by no means the first person who had fooled him by disguising her actual motive behind a smoke screen. A few pointed questions would have brought out the fact that it was her marital state that troubled her, not some hypothetical disagreement with Catholic morality.

Koesler was in the process of psyching himself up to cope with the unpredictable questions and unintentional pitfalls that Tully would throw at him, when the doorbell rang. With a prayer to the Holy Spirit for guidance, Koesler went to let Tully in.

But Tully remained on the porch. "I wonder if you can go with me to St. Waldo's. We can talk on the way. And there's something I'd like you to do for me when we get there. Can you go now?"

"Well, sure . . . just wait till I get my coat and hat."

Tully was wearing neither hat nor coat. He considered this to be a fine September day. Cool, yet not cold. But to every man his distinct metabolism.

Once in the car and on their way, Tully asked, "What time do you have to be back?"

"Oh, there's no hurry. I don't have an appointment until 7:00 this evening."

"Then you don't have any daily service?"

"Mass? Yes, as a matter of fact. At noon. But Father Dunn agreed to take it."

"You've got an assistant?" Tully was given to think priests were an endangered species. But then he'd asked Koesler aboard for the very reason that he knew very little about this subject.

"No, no." Koesler shook his head, almost dislodging his hat. They didn't make cars for tall men wearing hats. "I doubt St. Joseph's will ever have an associate pastor again."

Tully put that bit of trivia in his computerlike memory. They aren't called assistants. They're associate pastors.

"There's a young priest from Minnesota come to live with me while he studies at U of D. Fortunately, he doesn't have classes on Tuesdays until late afternoon." Under no circumstances was Koesler going to volunteer the information that Dunn had selected Old St. Joe's for his headquarters because he wanted to grow up to be an amateur detective. In that direction lay a can of worms.

"Oh, well, now, there's an assist—an associate at St. Waldo's," Tully said.

Koesler smiled. "St. Waldo's is in a class by itself. It may be the wealthiest parish in the archdiocese. There are quite a number of Catholic families in the parish boundaries. They are used to prompt service and I guess they get it." He paused. "But maybe I'm being too simplistic. They've got an associate and dependable weekend help not so much because the parishioners are wealthy but because there are so many Catholics there." Another pause. "Of course they don't have a school . . . oh, forget it, Lieutenant: They have an associate because the Cardinal sent them one."

Tully nodded. Actually, Koesler's fumbling stream of consciousness revealed more about parish structure and Church politics than the priest was aware of. Tully also noted that Koesler invariably called him Lieutenant. Which reminded him that even though Walt Koznicki and Koesler were good friends, they always addressed each other by their respective titles. If that was the case, thought Tully, it was a cinch that he and Koesler would never be on a first-name basis. He could live with that.

"When I talked to you last night," Tully said, "I asked if you knew Father Keating. But I didn't establish how well you know him."

It was a statement, not a question. But Koesler answered anyway. "Pretty well. Jake Keating was just a few years younger than I—"

"Was? Why past tense?"

Tully was quick. Koesler already knew that, but he wasn't prepared for the question. "I don't know, Lieutenant. I guess because I was thinking back to when we were teenagers. And I guess because he's missing . . . that plus the fact that the Homicide Department is investigating. But you're right, and thank God you are. Okay, well, Jake is a few years younger than I. We were in the seminary together for something like nine years. And then, of course, we were together off and on since then. So, all in all, our relationship goes back almost forty years."

"That long!"

"In total years, yes. But we were never what might be called good friends. We are friendly, but not particularly close. Especially these past few years."

"Past few years?"

Koesler wondered if Tully was consciously using a psychological ploy of the reflective mirror.

"Maybe about ten years," Koesler said. "Just about from the time he became pastor of St. Waldo's."

"Is that usual? That a couple of priests would part company because one of them became a pastor?"

Koesler scratched his chin. "Hard to say. I was a pastor before Jake became one. But we still saw each other socially occasionally. Waldo's just sort of swallowed Jake. That sometimes happens; the demands on a priest's time can vary from one assignment to another."

"Tell me about him, starting from when you knew him in the seminary. I want to get to know this guy, what makes him tick . . . what might contribute to whatever has happened to him."

Koesler thought a moment. This seemed a safe area. But he'd still have to be cautious. Tully, as he had just demonstrated, was incredibly perceptive.

"Well, Jake came from a decidedly upper-middle-class family," Koesler began. "Most of us Catholic kids who crowded into the seminary in those days—the forties—came from lower-middle- to middle-class homes. Jake's family was definitely on a level well above most, if not just about all of us. His dad was an executive at General Motors, and the family lived in St. Mary's of Redford parish on the west side—Grand River near Southfield."

Tully nodded. He knew that neighborhood well. It had changed. There were no GM execs living there anymore.

"It's hard to explain what the seminary was like. You sort of had to be there," Koesler continued. "We were all in it together. We were all governed by the same rules and standards. We were all expected to achieve set levels in academics and . . . well . . . it sounds pretentious to say it, but holiness."

He was silent for a moment, remembering.

"Anyway, any differences in our backgrounds quickly disappeared. We were just kids in a special kind of high school, college, and finally, theologate. We were being educated—prepared for a very specific kind of life that called for a facility with Latin as well as English, a strong foundation in the liberal arts, and a proficiency in moral and dogmatic theology, liturgy, Church law, and sacred Scripture.

"What I'm getting at, Lieutenant, is that in a youthful circle where everybody was socially equal, Jake Keating stood out. I don't think it was anything he consciously did or said or the way he related to the rest of us. The rest of us could imagine what it was like to belong to a posh athletic club, a pricey spa. But Jake's father did belong to such clubs. And Jake would take a few of us along from time to time."

Koesler's narration led him further down memory lane. He silently recalled a time when Jake Keating took Bob Koesler along for a family dinner at the then exclusive Detroit Boat Club on Belle Isle. There were Mr. and Mrs. Keating, Jake—an only child—and a wide-eyed Bob Koesler. They were seated in the elegant and fully occupied dining room. Kocsler briefly took in the ambience, the likes of which he'd experienced before only in the movies. Then his interest fell upon the other diners. They all seemed to be talking to one another. But they weren't making much noise. Nothing at all like what went on in the seminary refectory with a noise level that challenged even the students' youthful hearing.

Next, Koesler had noticed the bread plate, containing the sole item of food on the table. Nurtured in the prime maxim of seminary dining—he that doth not grab doth not eat—he ripped the heel from the loaf of bread and began eating it rapidly. He slowed to a dead stop when he caught the expressions of the others at table. Mr. and Mrs. Keating were looking at him as if he were Oliver Twist. Jake was smiling broadly. It wasn't a malicious smile, just amused. Then Jake mouthed words so precisely no lip-reader was needed: *Do what I do.* That direction was a godsend as Jake led Bobby through the courses using the proper silverware and exercising appropriate restraint.

"So," Tully interrupted Koesler's daydream, "Keating seemed a lead-pipe cinch to end up in a place like St. Waldo's?"

"Hmm?" Koesler came back to the present. "Oh, no, that's not what I was getting at. I'm just trying to do what you asked: give you an idea of what made John Keating a special person. The one thing— just one, but maybe a very important one—that set him off from the rest of us, is that he came from considerably more wealth than the rest of us.

"For instance, one of the other seminarians who lived in St. Mary's of Redford told me something that fits in here. He was talking about his confirmation—that's a religious ceremony for Catholics, usually when they're quite young. Anyway, even though he hardly knew the man, he chose Jake's father as his sponsor at confirmation—because he thought he would get an expensive gift."

Tully smiled. "Did he?"

"Uh-huh. A hundred dollars—which, in those days, was an awful lot of money.

"Keep in mind, Lieutenant," Koesler added, "that outside of just a few incidents like that, Jake was no different from the rest of us. He was one of the guys. We played together, prayed together, studied together, pulled pranks on each other. So, on a day-to-day basis, there was no special awareness that . . ."

". . . that John Keating could buy and sell the rest of you guys?"

Koesler could not improve the phrasing. "There's maybe one more incident that may kind of shed a bit more light on this. When we were ordained priests, there were two items we were expected to provide for ourselves: a chalice and a car."

"A what and a car?"

Koesler chuckled. "The chalice is the cup that's used for Mass. It came with a circular plate—a paten—and the inner surface of both was supposed to be gold-plated. It was an expensive item but not nearly as expensive as the car, of course. A few—only a very few—of the fellas were able to do summer work and save enough to buy these things themselves. But for the vast majority of us, our folks stretched their budgets to the breaking point to get these things for us."

"Everybody had to come up with those?" Tully recalled the finan- cial pinch felt by both himself and his parents when he was in his early twenties. No chance in hell that he and/or his family could have come up with a used, let alone a *new* car—let alone a gold cup.

"No, no; those things weren't a prerequisite for ordination. Espe- cially the chalice. There wasn't a parish that didn't have chalices that could be used by anyone who didn't have his own. But, traditionally, each new priest was supposed to have his own.

"You could get along without a car too. But that would be tricky. We had to be mobile—sick calls, Communion calls, meetings, a thousand things that required transportation. You could borrow someone else's car, but that was awkward at best. Of course this didn't come as a surprise, either. We and our families saw this coming years before we needed these things, so there was a lot of dedicated saving going on for a lot of years.

"And that's how it was. Now you'd suppose that the young Father John Keating would have a state-of-the-art chalice and car. Chalices began at a couple hundred bucks. After that, the sky was the limit. The cup could be entirely gold-plated, maybe set with precious gems. I suppose I remember this so clearly because all of us took special interest in what Jake would get from his parents.

"Anyway, his chalice was very nice—ornamental, but not vastly different from the rest of ours. The diamond from his mother's engagement ring was embedded in the base of his chalice. Not an uncommon thing. And his car—that was very interesting. His dad—a G.M. executive, remember—got him a new Olds. The rest of us were deliriously happy with the lowest-priced Fords, Chevys, or Plymouths. But Jake got an Olds.

"The important thing about this story—in case you're wondering, Lieutenant—is that Jake's dad could easily have come up with a top-of-the-line Caddie. But Mr. Keating had some very firm opinions about how a priest ought to live: not in poverty, but not lavishly either.

"There were those of us who felt that Jake didn't agree with this philosophy at all. And if we were correct, if that was true, then Jake must have been extremely disappointed when his father died and his mother followed her husband a year later."

"They didn't leave him anything?"

"Oh, nothing that drastic. But not all that far from drastic by Jake's lights. Rumor had it that they left him about twenty percent of their estate—enough for him to live comfortably. But not by any means luxuriously. They did it not because they didn't love him, but because they did."

"Okay, I think I got it." They were nearing St. Waldo's and Tully had plans for Koesler once they reached the parish. "Just one more thing: How would you describe his lifestyle all these years he's been a priest?"

Koesler whistled softly. "That's a big order. Let's see . . . I don't see much difference from when he was a seminarian. He was a good companion. I was with him—and, of course, a bunch of other priests—on three or four summer vacations in Florida."

"*Summer* in Florida?"

"Summer in Florida," Koesler insisted. "In those days, at least, the associate pastors took their golfing vacations in the summer. It was the pastors who generally went down there in season. Anyway, I was also with him on a few minivacations to see some Broadway shows in New York."

"Sounds nice."

"It was." Koesler saw no need to apologize for an occasional vacation. "At all times, Jake Keating was one of the boys. With one plus: Vacation with Jake meant a complimentary G.M. car—a courtesy car, courtesy of all the contacts Jake had made through his father's job."

"He must have been a desirable companion."

"He was. Oh, not just because he could get free transportation. He was . . . as I said, one of the guys. He would have been welcome with or without the car. He just was no stranger to money." Koesler leaned forward slightly. "I think you turn left at the next street."

"I know. I've been here before. The investigation didn't start today, Father."

"Oh, of course." After a moment, Koesler added, "One last anecdote to kind of spell out his attitude. It was one of Jake's favorite stories. His first assignment was at St. Robert Bellarmine. The pastor there was scrupulous about accounting for parish money. Jake, the pastor, and a few trusted women would spend much of Sundays and Mondays counting the collection. If they were a penny off, they had to start the whole thing over. Almost everyone I know would have gone crazy there. But not Jake. He was right at home with that procedure.

"Then, after five years at Bellarmine, he was sent to St. Martin's, on the east side. His first Sunday there, there was a double collection. The ushers took up the regular collection at the regular time. Then after Communion there was a second collection for the Pope. It's called Peter's Pence. Well, Jake had the last Mass that Sunday morning. When he got down to the rectory basement, he couldn't believe his eyes. The pastor and the women who helped him had opened all the envelopes, and all the money—from the regular collection as well as Peter's Pence—was all together in one pile in the middle of the table. Then the pastor sliced into one small corner of the pile and pushed a small part of the collection to one side and said, 'I think the Pope should get this much.' It took Jake several days to get over the shock."

Tully didn't quite see the point of the story, but he chuckled anyway.

The point was blunted because that anecdote was only roughly half of what Koesler had originally intended to tell Tully. Which was how Jake and the much older pastor had become friends and the results of that friendship. While the pastor took a somewhat casual approach to a double collection, he was far more meticulous about his own assets. He had, over the years, amassed an enviable portfolio of blue-ribbon stocks. And he had encouraged Jake to follow his example.

And Jake had, indeed, begun to invest. But he was too stubborn to listen to what turned out to be the pastor's excellent advice. And Jake had lost a bundle.

Halfway through his relation of the collection incident, Koesler had decided not to tell the remainder of the story: The conclusion would have implied that Keating was a gambler—and a not very successful one at that.

Too close—much too close to that unexposable secret. Koesler couldn't chance connecting the two. The story was innocent enough. But if the police had followed Koesler's lead, they could have walked right into the information Keating's killer had revealed. The killer would have concluded that Koesler had violated the seal of confession. And that simply would not do. It would not do at all.

As Tully pulled up in front of the rectory, Koesler beheld one of the busier scenes he had ever seen at a Catholic church on a weekday.

There were people all over the place, on the sidewalks, in the driveways, talking on car radios, walking across lawns clearly posted "Keep Off the Grass." Many wore police uniforms. But the uniforms definitely were not uniform. Koesler could not read the sleeve patches from this distance but they appeared to identify different municipalities. He was impressed with the scope of this investigation.

Tully turned the ignition off but made no move to leave the car, so neither did Koesler.

Without turning to Koesler, Tully said, "You did a good job filling me in on our missing priest. Now I'd like you to help in another way."

"If I can."

"So far, the interrogation of the parish personnel has left a lot to be desired. These people are plenty uptight—at least with the police. I think they may open up a bit with a priest—you. Are you aware, for instance, that people don't seem to stay employed here for very long stretches?"

"Now that you mention it," Koesler paused a moment in thought, "now that you mention it, I was vaguely aware that the associate pastors moved in and out of here with some frequency. I wouldn't have any occasion to know about people like the housekeeper, secretary, or janitor. The priest assignments are usually listed in our Catholic paper. So I'd read about the associates' moves. What those frequent moves mean is something else again. What with the drastic shortage of priests, there's a bit more movement of priests than there used to be. So it could be quite naturally understandable. Or it could mean some friction with the pastor. I suppose that would more likely be the case if the other personnel move in and out a lot."

Tully nodded. "I think it's a problem with the pastor. I think they expect him back any minute and they're afraid if they bad-mouth him to us—even if it's the truth—it might get back to him and they'd be looking for another job. There's a good chance they'll be more willing to talk freely to a priest than to a cop."

Koesler agreed. "I think that might be especially true of the associate pastor. One priest to another. But I must confess I don't know who's here."

Tully took a notepad from the inside pocket of his jacket and began looking for the associate's name. While he did not find it odd that Koesler could not have known where all of Detroit's priests were living, Tully would have been somewhat surprised had he realized how little the older priests knew about younger priests. "Father Mitchell—Father Fred Mitchell."

Koesler smiled. "Now that's a lucky break. I do happen to know Fred. That will make this a bit easier."

"Then," Tully said, "let's have at 'im."

"Lead on," said Koesler as he unfolded from the car.

9

"Uh-oh," Tully said with feeling.

Koesler turned sharply to face the officer. But Tully was looking past him toward the rectory.

Following Tully's line of vision, Koesler about-faced to see a woman heading determinedly toward them. His first impression was of a mannequin whose paint had not quite dried. She wore a gray business suit, but no hat. As she cantered, a double string of pearls bounced against her ample bosom. There was something wrong, not necessarily with her figure. But her headlong dash seemed entirely out of character.

As she drew closer, Koesler realized what had made him think of wet paint: Her lips were well overglazed with bright red, and she was wearing far too much rouge, eyeliner, and mascara. An overcharged mannequin whose paint had not dried.

Koesler breathed a sigh when the woman zeroed in on Tully. "Zoo!" she half gushed, half shrieked, "you're in charge here, or so they say. And they won't let me in the rectory!"

"Who won't?" Tully was ambivalent about his nickname. Normally he was unconcerned as to what people called him. Almost the sole exception was this woman. He shuddered inwardly anytime she waxed familiar.

"The cops! *Your* cops!"

"Maybe they don't want to be disturbed."

"Who?"

"The people who live in the rectory."

"The priests?"

"Well . . ."

"You're kidding! They're supposed to be available all the time. Where do they get off not wanting to be disturbed?!" She seemed to notice for the first time that Tully was not alone. "And whom have we here?" Her face was only inches from Koesler's. That made him uncomfortable.

"Lacy DeVere," Tully said, "meet Father Koesler."

She had her notebook out and was scribbling in it. "Is that K-e-s-s-l-e-r?"

"K-o-e-s-l-e-r," Koesler corrected.

"Who are you?" Lacy asked. "I mean, what are you doing here? Did the archdiocese send you? Are you the new pastor?"

"Hold on," Tully said. "We're just consulting with Father. He's providing us with a little background information."

"That's it," Koesler said. "I'm a consulting adult." No sooner were the words out of his mouth than he regretted them.

A peculiar expression crossed Lacy's face. "Just what we needed—a priest who does one-liners. Okay, then, Father Koesler, why you? How did you get to be the sourceperson?"

"Well," Koesler said, "if it comes to that, who are you?"

"Lacy's got a column in the *Suburban Reporter*. She's only been back in Detroit about a year." Tully turned back to Lacy. "Father Koesler's helped us before. He's helping us again."

"A priest-detective? Father Brown lives again?"

"We're investigating a missing priest, Lacy," Tully said.

Lacy's attention was once again focused completely on Tully. "Is he dead?"

"Who?"

"The missing priest—Keating."

"Lacy! Right now it's a missing persons case."

"Then what's Detroit Homicide doing on it? Out in Bloomfield Hills?"

"Just cooperating with the 'burb departments."

Lacy did not look convinced. "Maybe, maybe not. But if I don't get in that rectory to ask some questions, I'm going to see that somebody's ass gets burned."

"I'll see what I can do about it, Lacy." Tully motioned Koesler on toward the rectory.

When the two reached the front door, Tully leaned close to the uniformed officer standing guard. "See that lady with the paint job?"

"Yes, sir." The officer hooked his thumbs under his belt.

"She doesn't get in here even if she has the Pope with her."

"Yes, sir!" He had tangled with her earlier, and based on that skirmish alone he had hoped that someone would make his life easier by countermanding the order excluding media people from the rectory.

Now he knew that if that woman got by him, he'd be sweeping out the police barns. At this moment, it was difficult to decide which would be worse: fighting her off or cleaning up after the horses.

Tully and Koesler were met at the door by a very nervous, impressed, and—once Tully had shown her his badge—deferential housekeeper, who led them into a large, rather cluttered room. There, seated in an overstuffed leather office chair behind a king-sized desk, was a young man wearing an open-necked brown shirt, under an orange cardigan.

"Hello, Fred," said Koesler.

The young man's eyes widened. He smiled broadly. "Bob! Fancy meeting you here. How many times have I invited you over? And now that you've finally come, the pastor isn't here."

Tully realized that he had a lot to absorb here. He had seldom been in a house whose furnishings and decor were as opulent, almost to the point of garishness, as this rectory. The one and only priest he knew to any extent was Father Koesler, who lived a Spartan existence. Tully had assumed that all priests lived more or less at that level. Evidently not Father Keating. Then there was the associate priest—for that surely was who "Fred" was. Not only completely out of uniform, but joking about the pastor's unaccountable absence. Interesting. "We haven't met," Tully said.

"I'm sorry," Koesler apologized. "Father Fred Mitchell, this is Lieutenant Tully. He's in charge of the Police Department's investigation of Father Keating's disappearance."

Tully and Mitchell nodded at each other. Mitchell made no move to stand. Nor did he invite his visitors to sit. So Tully took the initiative and the chair closest to the desk. Koesler, noting that he now stood alone, also seated himself.

There was a moment's silence while Tully continued to take in the details of the room. Mitchell studied Tully. Koesler was uncertain just what he should do. Then Mitchell spoke. "This case should be solved any minute, now that you're on it, Bob."

Koesler reddened. "The lieutenant asked me to come along. I'm trying to help him get some insight into Jake's life."

"Good luck," Mitchell said.

"What is this room?" Tully asked. "A study?"

"*His* study." Mitchell emphasized the possessive.

"*His?*" Tully repeated the emphasis.

"Definitely," Mitchell said. "I'm not allowed in here. Far as I know, none of my predecessors was allowed in. No one comes in without an invitation. Leave your money at the door."

"When the cat's away . . .?" Koesler smiled.

"Exactly," Mitchell said. "This mouse is going to play in the master's den." He pushed the chair back, drew his legs up, and deposited his feet on a desk top that undoubtedly had never before experienced shoes.

Koesler had never lived in a rectory where any room was declared off-limits to any priest, resident or visitor. He knew such rectories had existed, but he was surprised to find one in this day when there were so few available clergy that priests could pretty well pick and choose where they would live and serve.

Such arbitrary and arrogant exercise of authority had to be one reason why Keating couldn't keep an associate pastor more than a comparatively short time. At a different period—not all that long ago—priests simply went where they were sent and remained until they were ordered elsewhere. A system that generated a number of pastors who were notorious as tyrants.

But, no more.

Koesler knew that Jake Keating would not return to St. Waldo's. Perhaps, he thought, depending on who would take Keating's place, Fred Mitchell just might set a new record for longevity here.

Tully had been studying a painting hanging on the wall facing the pastor's chair. He inclined his head. "Who's that?"

"The master," Mitchell responded.

"The pastor? Father Keating?" Tully was surprised. The portrait had been expertly executed by some gifted artist. It showed a man in a clerical collar and a black suit whose folds suggested soft and expensive silk. The man was leaning forward. His jet black hair flowed in gentle waves. The face was sharply masculine—handsome in the same sense that Humphrey Bogart could have been considered handsome.

"That's something, eh?" Mitchell said. "The old man sits here—as often as he's here—and eyeballs himself."

Koesler did not appreciate having Keating, several years his junior, being referred to as "the old man." "Come on, Fred, it's not unique that someone has a picture of himself in his own office."

"A portrait? In oil? With professional lighting? Painted by Alfredo Pomponi? That's not exactly a framed Polaroid!"

Tully thought of all the pictures of cops on the walls of the various corridors at headquarters. Most of Detroit's top brass were there. So Koesler's point that it was not unusual to find pictures of individuals exhibited where they work seemed valid. But . . . an expensive portrait? The only one Tully could recall was of the mayor, and it hung in Maynard Cobb's office. Maybe there was something to be said for arrogance. The more Tully learned about Father John Keating, the less likable he appeared.

"You don't like him very much." Tully's inflection made it a question.

"It shows?" Mitchell said sarcastically.

"Look," said Tully, "it doesn't make any difference to me whether you get along with him or not. We've got to find him. The sooner the better. Up till now, so my officers tell me, nobody here—housekeeper, secretary, janitor, everybody—including you—none of you have knocked yourselves out being cooperative."

"That's probably true," Mitchell said. "But what you've got to understand, Lieutenant, is that nobody who works for our pastor likes him. Oh, maybe at first, but he doesn't wear well at all. Not with employees. Only nobody but me is going to come right out and say it. Keating will return and you can bet your bottom dollar he'll find out what people have said about him. For Nancy and Mary and Sam and the rest of them, that means if they tell you the truth they'll be unemployed. Me? I won't be unemployed. I'll just be shipped to another parish. And that will be fine with me."

"Then why didn't you say all this to the other officers?"

"I wasn't all that keen on finding him. But now, I understand: It's your job. So ask away and I'll try to be helpful."

"Okay." Tully took out his notepad and pen. "After all you've just said, this may seem silly, but did Father Keating have any enemies?"

Mitchell snorted. "All right. I get your drift: By 'enemies,' you mean anyone who would—like—kill him."

It was evident that, even taking into account the way Mitchell felt, he was unwilling seriously to consider Keating dead, let alone murdered.

Tully nodded. That is what he had in mind.

"No," Mitchell said, "I wouldn't say that. Not to my knowledge anyway. On the one hand, he certainly has left a trail of unhappy people in his wake. All the people he has fired over the years—for no serious cause, as far as I know. Then there are the priests who have been assigned here, and left as soon as they decently could. But I can't think that any of these people could hate him enough to . . . do that."

"How about parishioners?"

"No way! Especially not parishioners. He got along famously with them. To give the devil his due he was a forceful preacher. I mean by that . . . uh . . . pro forma. He had a great voice, partially seasoned by large quantities of very good scotch. But a great voice anyway. He knew when to dish out hellfire and brimstone, I think they used to call it—and when to assure everyone that all was well."

"But," Tully said, "it doesn't seem he was here much. Gone part of Sunday, all day Monday and Wednesday. They put up with that kind of part-time service here?"

Mitchell chuckled. "These people out here know what the score is. They're not only wealthy, they're well informed. They know that someday—and not that far down the road—there will be priestless parishes. And while Waldo's is not going to be among the first of those, this place will take its turn—eventually. They've got a pastor they like; they want to hold on to him.

"And don't let that 'out of town' schedule fool you. If a parishioner wants to see him, it doesn't matter when, Keating will meet Monday, Wednesday, whenever. If somebody's in the hospital or there's a death in the family—Keating's there."

"That sounds more like it," Tully said. "There had to be something to balance this picture."

"I don't want to spoil this image of pastoral service," Mitchell said, "but to be perfectly honest, there's a fringe benefit to all Keating's availability: He lives his parishioners' lifestyle."

"Oh?"

"I mean tickets to plays, the opera, ballgames; tickets to events that are sold out, tickets when there aren't any tickets. Trips in company planes. Trips around the world. Trips to play golf with Palmer, Trevino. Vacations with the incredibly rich and brain-dead."

No wonder, thought Koesler, that the gang hadn't seen Keating on any of their rather modest outings lately—not to mention days off. But why hasn't Mitchell mentioned Keating's gambling? Is it possible that Keating could have hidden a vice for which he'd been murdered from a priest who lived with him?

"Then," Tully said, "if you can't think of anyone who would or could physically harm him, how about the man himself? As far as you know, has he had any personal problems? Blackouts? Serious forgetfulness? Has his health been okay?"

"Keating? Healthy as a horse, far as I know. And where would he go? He's found the promised land right here."

"You mentioned scotch. Not a drinking problem?"

"Amazing! Built up a tolerance, I guess. Doesn't seem to affect him . . . not seriously, at any rate."

"Okay, Father. Anything else you want to say?"

"No, I don't think so. Just that if he's off on a wingding, I hope he doesn't hurry back just for my sake."

Tully rose. He handed Mitchell a card. "If you think of anything else—anything at all—call me at this number. If I'm not there, they'll know how to reach me."

As Tully and Koesler reached the door of the den, they were met by the substantial figure of Sergeant Mangiapane. "Zoo, we just got done tossing Father Keating's room."

"And?"

"Nothing—oh, hi, Father Koesler."

"Hello," Koesler said. Now what was his name? Something Italian . . .

"Nothing, Manj? Nothing that would give us any idea where he might have gone?"

Manj. Manj. Of course: Mangiapane. *But don't tell me there were no betting slips! Nothing that would tip the police that the guy had to be a compulsive gambler?*

"No," Mangiapane repeated. "We did come up with a private phone and address book. A lot of entries. We're gonna check 'em out. But as far as we were able to tell, Father Keating was planning on coming back here Friday night. All his clothes are here—pretty expensive stuff—his shaving gear; everything's in place. We went up to the attic. All his luggage is there, neat as you please."

Of course he intended to return Friday night, Koesler thought. And he would have if he hadn't met up with Mr. Vespa. It was so frustrating not being able even to hint at what the police should be looking for. Nothing he could do but count on the police finding out what had happened to him on their own. Koesler believed they could do it. *But how in the world would they ever find the body?*

"Okay," Tully said, "check out his address book. It's about the only lead we've got right now."

They became aware of a commotion just outside the front door. Two distinct voices, a man and a woman, shouting at each other. The woman's voice was the clearer. And she was using language she never learned, or should never have learned, from Mother. Then another male voice joined in.

The door opened narrowly and a uniformed officer—the one to whom Tully had spoken on the way in—squeezed through. No doubt about it, he was harried.

"What the hell is going on out there?" Tully demanded.

"It's that crazy bi—" He spotted Koesler's clericals. "It's that crazy lady, Lieutenant—the one you told me to keep out."

"And?"

"She found out that another reporter is in here. Somebody from the *News* —McPhee. She's in the kitchen interviewing some of the help. Somehow she got invited in the back door. Anyway, that crazy lady just heard about it and is . . . well . . ." He gestured toward the door through which Lacy's purple prose continued to penetrate.

"What's with her?" Tully wanted to know.

"Hogan spelled me for a little while. I'm going right out soon as I pull myself together. It'll probably take the both of us . . ."

"Unless one of you shoots her," Mangiapane contributed.

Somehow, no one found that humorous.

"Come on," Tully said to Koesler, "let's get out the back way."

As they started toward the kitchen, they were met by Angie Moore. "Father Koesler: Good to see you again."

"Yes, indeed." *Who was she?* Koesler met so very many people.

"Zoo," Moore said, "they found the car."

"Keating's."

"Uh-huh."

"Let's go."

The flow of their departure was temporarily interrupted when they reached the kitchen to find Pringle McPhee in conversation with the housekeeper and the secretary, who started guiltily as if caught with their hands in the cookie jar.

Tully scowled, angry that his cordon had been breached. But after a moment's thought he not only could see no actual harm done, but also see the humor in it. Though he refused all comment in response to Pringle's questions, there was the hint of a smile on his face as he, Koesler, and Moore exited, leaving Father Mitchell to play press secretary.

Meanwhile, Lacy DeVere continued to assault the battlements. To no avail.

10

KOESLER was riding in Tully's car. Moore and Mangiapane were following in another. Tully had explained to Koesler that when they arrived at Keating's car, which had been found parked on a well-maintained residential street in northwest Detroit, there would be a complete complement of Detroit police specialists performing their specialties.

"I don't know how you—the police, I mean—did it," Koesler said. "There must be abandoned cars all over the city. Finding Father Keating's car—and this quickly—well, it's almost like finding the proverbial needle in the haystack."

"It's not that mysterious," Tully said. "As soon as we got into this as a missing persons case, we—actually the Bloomfield Hills police—put out a statewide broadcast on the car and the license plate number along with putting it in LEIN."

"Excuse me," Koesler interrupted. "LEIN—is that an acronym?"

"Yeah . . . Law Enforcement Information Network. Once the data is fed into LEIN, it's accessible to all law enforcement agencies in Michigan. So, in theory at least, you've got every kind of cop in the state keeping an eye out for that car. The way it works in practice is that at any given time there are lots of missing cars listed in LEIN. And when a Michigan cop, state police, FBI, whatever, sees a car being operated in a suspicious manner, or one that is parked too long or in a questionable place, they check and see if it's listed in LEIN.

"That's what happened here. A private citizen reported this car had been parked in his neighborhood. That neighborhood is a better-than-average location, so a current Lincoln Town Car is not out of place. But this car has been standing there for the past four days. They checked it out with the CAT section—that's Commercial Auto Theft—but it hadn't been reported as stolen. Then an ABAN officer—that's Abandoned Auto officer—checked it through LEIN—and there we have it. Keating's car. So, no miracles. Just standard police work . . . well, here we are."

Here they were, indeed. Tully had not adequately prepared Koesler for the scene. Not only was there a bumper crop of cops around and in the car, but a large number of curious bystanders were trying to get a good look at what was going on. Some of the onlookers were being questioned by police; others were being interviewed by TV, radio, and print reporters.

Tully's car—followed by that of Mangiapane and Moore—was waved into the inner circle.

"This is it, Zoo," a lieutenant from ABAN said with a hint of pride. Then he noticed Father Koesler, the sole civilian in this coterie of cops. "What's he doing here?"

"He's with me. Be nice. Let him look, but not touch."

"Got any prints?"

"Lots. All over the car—except for the steering wheel. Wiped clean."

"Interesting."

"And guess what, Zoo: Guess who lives on this street, just three doors down from here?"

Tully merely looked at the officer.

"Carl 'Double C' Costello."

"Now that is interesting." Tully thought for a moment. "Carl's a little long in the tooth now, isn't he? I thought he was out of the business. I haven't heard his name mentioned in years."

"Me neither. But it is a coincidence, isn't it? I mean, the priest's car found just a few yards from the front door of the Mafia. Maybe Costello ain't what he was. But maybe he put his hand back in—one for old time's sake?

"Or, maybe it's just a coincidence."

"Coincidences don't have any explanation; that's what makes 'em coincidences. I think I'll just take a short walk and check this one out."

Then Tully remembered: He had Koesler in tow. What to do with him? Leave him here to feel like a fifth wheel? Or take him along? They were too pressingly involved in this investigation to break off and take him home. Tully felt responsible since it was he who had involved Koesler in the first place. Besides, if Costello was anything, odds were that he had to be Catholic.

Tully stepped close to Koesler and spoke softly. "Father, have you ever met a Mafia don?"

"Once." Koesler shuddered. The memory was not one of his favorites.

Tully didn't pursue the subject. "Well, let's go meet another one. Then we'll take you home."

Home would be most welcome. Images of the *Godfather* movies with their dark, disturbing, threatening interiors, the potential for grave bodily harm, even death, as a constant backdrop alternated in Koesler's mind with the memory of the time when he, Koesler, with a recorder taped to his body, had been ushered into the presence of a Mafia don who was prepared to add Koesler's blood to that already on his hands. And who would have, had not the police burst in.

Then another even more disquieting thought: Guido Vespa! What if Guido Vespa were there? If Koesler showed up on his doorstep with the police he would be certain that Koesler had violated the seal. Would Vespa strike out at them? At him? The man had killed before; he'd told Koesler that in confession. He would have even more reason for violence now, thinking he had been betrayed, than he had when he was merely paid to kill.

This, Koesler concluded, was far and away above any call of duty.

But for the life of him—maybe literally!—he couldn't think of any plausible way out of it. Maybe he was overreacting; after all, there must be any number of residences in Detroit inhabited by Mafia members. Why should this one, as opposed to all the others, be the one that housed Guido Vespa? Koesler shook his head as he followed the lieutenant. His imagination must be getting the better of him! But where there was Father Keating's car, could Father Keating's killer be far behind?

Tully, Mangiapane, Moore, and Koesler mounted the steps to the front porch. Koesler carefully looked the house over. This house, at least, bore no resemblance to Marlon Brando's *Godfather* mansion.

That was reassuring.

While the movie's mansion seemed never to quit with its security features, ample parking space, spacious yards, and gigantic size, this seemed a modest home, especially in comparison.

Here was a large, two-story, but quite conventional house. Well kept up in a well-kept up neighborhood. It was homey, with the lived-in quality that suggested that many generations had grown up and moved on. Koesler hoped everything inside would be as quiet and peaceful as the outside.

Tully rang the doorbell. The little group waited in silence.

It seemed longer, but it was only a few seconds until the door opened. A dark-browed young man stood just inside the screen door, which he made no move to open. He wore Sansabelt slacks and a T-shirt that emphasized an expansive torso and muscular arms. Without moving his head, his eyes scanned the four visitors. "So?"

Tully showed his badge and identified himself, as well as his companions. The young man seemed unimpressed. "So?" he repeated.

"Mr. Costello," Tully said, "Carl Costello in?"

"I'll go see." The door was resoundingly closed.

Tully looked around, evaluating their surroundings. He noticed Koesler's inquiring expression. Tully smiled. "Don't let it bother you. That's Remo . . . Remo Vespa. We all know each other pretty good. Remo likes to pretend he's never met any of us. The old man's his grandfather and he's probably home. Remo will make us wait a little while, just to show he's in charge. Or so he'd like us to believe. When push comes to shove—and it has more than once—we have to let him know who's really in charge. Meantime, he likes to play this little game.

"It's probably the most innocent thing he does," Tully added.

Oh, my God! Remo Vespa! Of course; the Sunday paper that pictured Remo and Guido Vespa. *Oh, my God! What now?* The last, and only, time Koesler had seen Remo Vespa was in that photo. And then Koesler had not been focusing on Remo but on his brother Guido—Guido the Confessor.

Koesler gave serious consideration to offering his regrets and trying to find a cab.

In the midst of his inner debate, the door reopened.

Remo was there again, but he was standing behind another man.

"Carl, long time no see," Tully said.

At one time Carl Costello must have been a very large man. His face was heavily lined. His oval head was crowned with wispy white hair. His glasses were bottle-bottom thick, magnifying the tired-looking eyes behind them. His rumpled trousers were topped by an unbuttoned sweater over an open-collar shirt. He held himself barely erect.

Costello looked at Tully for several long seconds as if to focus on a blurry image. "So what is it, Lieutenant, you gonna read me my rights?" He began to chuckle deep down in his chest. The chuckle quickly became a cough so violent it worried Koesler.

When the coughing finally stopped, Tully said, "No, Carl . . . not yet, anyway. Just some questions. You gonna invite us in?"

Costello did not appear eager to reply. He peered at the group on the porch one by one, studying each unhurriedly as he had studied Tully earlier. Then he got to Koesler. Costello pulled up short. "Hey, you a father? You a Catholic priest?"

For the first time in his life Koesler was reluctant to identify himself. He had no idea what would follow the admission that he was, indeed, a priest. Was the whole family in on the killing of Father Keating? Probably. Did the whole family know that Guido had confessed the murder to him? Probably not.

"Wassamatter," Costello said good-naturedly, "you forget if you're a father or not?"

Koesler reddened. "No . . . of course not. Yes, I'm a priest, a Catholic priest. Father Koesler."

"You should watch the company you keep, Father." Costello chuckled again, and again it developed into a coughing spasm. He turned his head slightly to address his grandson standing behind him. "Wassamatter with you, anyway, sonny? You see a father on the porch and you don't invite him in? What are you—a Catholic or what?"

"Sorry, Gampa. I woulda done that, but the father came in this package deal. I didn't think you'd want the heat in here."

"We got better hospitality than that, Sonny." He turned back to the group. "Come on in, fellas . . . and good lady. Though I must tell you, Lieutenant, if you hadn't had the father along, you woulda had to have some paper with you to get in. But . . ." It was a verbal shrug. ". . . what the hell; it's a short life."

Tully entered first. But Costello stood back waiting for Koesler to cross the threshold. "You bless my home with your presence, Father.

"Hey," his voice raised only slightly, "Momma: Come see who come to visit us."

As Mangiapane and Moore entered, with Sonny bringing up the rear, from somewhere in the back of the house, probably the kitchen, since she was drying her hands on an apron, came a gray-haired woman. Though she might have been of a certain age, she was still quite attractive; she had held on to her youthful figure remarkably.

"Father," Costello announced, "here is my wife, Vita. Vita, see who this is. It's . . . uh . . . Father . . . uh . . ."

"Koesler," the priest supplied. He caught the surprise in her eyes. Evidently this home did not get a lot of priest visitors.

"Welcome, Father," she said. "You bless our home with your presence." She walked quickly to Koesler, took his hand with both of hers, and kissed it. Instinctively he started to pull away, thought better of it, and left his hand in Vita's clasp.

Koesler had almost forgotten that once that had been a time-honored custom. Long ago, when newly ordained priests blessed people, the faithful would kiss the hands that so recently had been anointed with holy oil. Even then, Koesler had felt squeamish about the practice.

Then, also in those early days, sometimes the elderly ailing people would kiss his hands when he brought them Communion.

He wondered about what he had seen and heard just now. Somehow, though he knew it was far too facile, Koesler expected all Italians—as well as Poles, Irish, and Hispanics—to be Catholic. But he never would have expected to be greeted so warmly and with such faith by the Mafia or their family. He was reminded of how comfortable and at home Jesus always seemed to be in the presence of outcasts and those whom society branded as hopeless sinners. He resolved to meditate on this later when he could be alone in prayer.

For the moment, despite the cordial welcome, he had to be on his guard. There was still the secret to protect.

Vita Costello, after a few more words of welcome for Koesler—and an invitation to dinner, which the priest graciously declined—returned to the rear of the house whence emanated appetizing aromas of marinara and meatballs.

Carl Costello led the way into a spacious living room, which looked as if it had been furnished in the twenties and thereafter left untouched. The elderly gentleman moved with deliberation to a chair that appeared to be both comfortable and his. Behind the chair Remo stood almost at attention. He might have been a guardian angel or a sentry.

Koesler and Tully each picked an easy chair; Moore sat on the couch. Mangiapane remained standing behind the couch, mirroring Remo's angel-or-sentry stance.

Costello held up his left hand, with the index and middle fingers extended. For a moment Koesler wondered why the don was giving the peace sign. But Remo quickly lit a cigarette and placed it between the upraised fingers. Koesler now knew the source of Costello's cough.

"Now, gentle lady and gentlemen," Costello began, "in what way can we be of service to you?"

Innocent or guilty of whatever, Carl Costello was cool. He might easily, thought Koesler, have been a conscientious citizen eager to help the police in any possible way.

"Carl," Tully said, "you heard we got a missing priest in Detroit?"

"Bloomfield Hills, I heard, Lieutenant." Costello was almost apologetic.

Tully nodded. "He lives in Bloomfield Hills. He's a Detroit priest."

"It was on the radio and TV, is how I know," Costello said. "I don't get around in those circles too much anymore."

"The last anyone saw of him—that we've talked to—he was heading for Detroit. That was Friday afternoon last. No one's heard from him since."

"Is that so!" Costello said. Impossible to tell whether the expression was sincere or sardonic. "Perhaps he will return soon."

"It's been four days, Carl. That's a long time to be missing."

"It is indeed. But there is always hope. Sonny, why don't you drop over by church tonight and have a Mass said for . . ." Costello looked to each of his four visitors for assistance.

The long pause proved too much for Koesler. "John Keating," he said, "Father John Keating."

Costello nodded good-naturedly toward the priest. "Thank you, Father.

"Sonny, write that down: Father John Keating—wait: Father, maybe you would say the Mass."

Koesler felt most uncomfortable. If he consented, Costello would offer him money. Which he would refuse. He—most Detroit priests—no longer accepted Mass stipends. Costello would insist; there would be explanations. All very inappropriate.

"I'm sorry, Mr. Costello," Koesler said. "Our parish is booked solid for weeks with Mass intentions. I am praying for him though." All of that was true. However, the prayers were for the repose of Keating's soul.

"I understand, Father," Costello said. He turned his head. "Sonny, go to Holy Family. They can't be so busy. Have the Mass said."

"Right, Gampa." Remo was writing down the name.

"Carl," Tully spoke pointedly, "get serious."

How serious can I get, Costello's gesture implied.

"You know anything about the missing priest?"

"Me! I live in Bloomfield Hills? I should know this priest?"

"He's worked other parishes, some in Detroit, even Little Italy. You could know him from lots of places."

"Anybody could know him from lots of places, Lieutenant. Come on, why me?"

Tully's storied patience was wearing thin. "Carl, guess whose car that is out there that's attracting all that attention?"

Costello leaned forward and craned for a better view of the bustle practically outside his front window. "Well, now, Lieutenant, I learned to add. The kind, you know, where two plus two equals four. I'd guess that since you been asking me all these questions about a missing priest named Father Keating, which I've never seen in my life, and since the car in question is parked almost in front of my house, I would guess that that car belongs to the missing priest, Father Keating." Costello looked at Tully with the wide-eyed innocence of a schoolchild who hopes his answer is the right one. "How'm I doin'?"

"Until we came in your house and started questioning you, you weren't curious about what all those police officers were doing with that car?"

"I seen cops before."

"You didn't see that car before today?"

"I didn't say that."

"You did see the car before today."

"I didn't say that either."

"One of your neighbors has been watching it for four days. That's why he called the cops and reported a suspicious vehicle."

"He done good."

"And you?"

"I mind my own business. There's a law against that?"

"You want us to believe there's no connection between you and that car? That it's just a coincidence that a car owned by a person who's been missing four days ends up practically in front of your house?"

"I don't care what you believe."

The conversation was getting a bit intense. It was Costello who tried to defuse it. With a tone of calm reason, he said, "Look, Lieutenant, what is this? We both know I've been around the block a few times. If I done anything to this priest—and God forbid I did!—I'm gonna have his car parked in front of my house? Like I hang a red flag from the car's antenna? Be reasonable, Lieutenant. Gimmee credit for being more than a dumb school kid!"

"Maybe one of your family left it there."

"And I didn't check into it?"

"You didn't notice the car until today."

"I didn't say that. Besides, Lieutenant, why would I have anything to do with a missing priest?"

"Maybe one of your family had something to do with it. Maybe Guido. Maybe Remo. Sonny here doesn't look too clean."

Remo stiffened. Costello checked him with a gesture.

Yes, yes, yes, Koesler thought. *Guido! Go after Guido.*

"Look, Lieutenant," Costello said, "nobody here had anything to do with your missing priest. Ain't there supposed to be a motive for this kind of thing? Why would we mess with a priest? Especially a priest from Bloomfield Hills?"

"That's what we want to find out, Carl. Why? Somebody want him iced bad enough to hire a hit? Unpaid bills? Lots of possibilities."

Yes, yes, yes, Koesler thought. *Gambling debts.* Why isn't this ESP working? It was Guido and it was gambling debts. *Can't you hear my thoughts, Lieutenant Tully? Can't you read my mind?*

"You been reading too many detective stories, Lieutenant. Whoever put that car there probably had a grudge or something. We didn't have nothin' to do with it."

"You didn't have anything to do with the car. You didn't have anything to do with the priest."

"What I said."

"Then you won't mind if we look around your house, eh, Carl? You got nothin' to hide."

For the first time, Costello's demeanor became deadly serious. "For that, Lieutenant, you gotta have some paper."

Tully rose. Koesler and Moore followed suit. "We'll be back."

The four found themselves out on the sidewalk. Only a few of the gawkers turned to look at them, and those spared only a momentary glance. The police checking out the abandoned car were far more interesting.

"Anyone's rump get hit by that door?" Mangiapane asked.

Moore laughed. "We did get ushered out rather firmly," she agreed.

But Tully was all business. "Manj, stay here. Make sure that we question everybody in every house on this block. Neighboring blocks too. We ought to be able to find somebody who saw something out of place—anything odd. That car didn't just grow there.

"Angie, get a warrant. I want our people to go through every inch of that place. Somebody there is in on this. Maybe not the whole family. But someone.

"I'll take the father home. I want to check with Organized Crime, see what they've got on this family. OC ought to have the latest sheet on Costello. I got a hunch if I let OC know what's going on, they might be able to put some pressure on the family."

On their return trip downtown, Tully was the only one to speak. He made a single statement. "In the beginning, I thought this whole investigation was a waste of time. At least the time of Detroit Homicide. But now that it looks like the Costello family could be in this thing . . . well . . . it's down to: Is Keating in hiding somewhere, or has he been wasted?"

And Father Koesler agonized that it was impossible for him to give Tully the answer.

11

It WAS ALMOST 6:00 in the evening when Lieutenant Tully dropped off Father Koesler before St. Joseph's rectory with, for Tully, profuse thanks for the priest's help and time throughout the day.

As Koesler turned from the departing car he was momentarily awed, not for the first time, by the massiveness, the fortresslike character of St. Joe's rectory and church in the last clear light of day. He could hear, in his imagination, "A Mighty Fortress is Our God." One of his favorite hymns.

There were no lights visible in the rectory. Not surprising; both the housekeeper and Mary O'Connor would be gone for the day. It would be deathly quiet now for at least another hour, when his appointments and meetings would begin. Perhaps he could squeeze in a nap before the evening busyness began. Offered his druthers, he would have preferred a nap to dinner. He was that tired.

Then he remembered. Nick Dunn. He had no idea where his visiting priest might be now, but Dunn's presence would have to be taken into account. It struck Koesler that this was just a little bit like being married in that he had someone else to consider instead of scheduling for himself alone.

He entered the dining room to find Dunn doing some sort of paperwork at the dining table. "Oh, there you are," the younger priest said brightly.

"Here, indeed, I am. Have you eaten?" Koesler hoped that Dunn had finished dinner. Therein lay a chance that he might sneak in that nap.

"No, it's in the oven. All I have to do is heat it. I was hoping we could talk over supper."

Damn, there went the nap! "Okay. But we'll have to shake a leg. I've got an appointment in about an hour."

"Plenty of time. Shall I fix us a drink?"

"Thanks. But make mine light. Plenty of water. I've got a busy evening ahead."

Dunn began heating dinner, prepared the drinks, and joined Koesler at the dining table.

Koesler tasted his drink. It was very light—scotch and water with a heavy emphasis on the water. It occurred to him that he hadn't expected to see Dunn this evening. "Don't you have a class at this hour? On the Mercy campus?"

"I cut it."

"You cut your first appearance? What's the course?"

"Psychology of Religion. How much psychology can there be to religion?"

"Plenty. I thought these papers all over the table were your notes from class."

Dunn shook his head. "They're notes, okay, but not from class. We'll get to them shortly. First, how did your day go?"

That explained it: Dunn was so obsessed with the police investigation that he had cut class and postponed dinner in order to eat with Koesler—all just to learn what had happened.

Very well, then. But he would skip over his early morning meeting with Mrs. Pietrangelo. That wouldn't interest Dunn.

On to the cops and robbers.

Koesler recounted the course of the investigation: the drive out to St. Waldo's; a résumé of what he'd told Tully of Koesler's contacts with Keating through the seminary and priesthood; Fred Mitchell's description of Life With Father, as Keating's associate.

Koesler skipped the bit about Lacy DeVere's frustrated attempt to gain entry to the rectory and Pringle McPhee's success. Next, he told of the drive to the far east side, describing in some detail the meeting with Mr. and Mrs. Costello and Remo Vespa.

Toward the conclusion of Koesler's narrative, Dunn, who had been hanging on to every word, served the reheated dinner of spaghetti and meatballs. While it tasted good, Koesler surmised that Mrs. Costello's meal was even better. If his olfactory sense could be trusted, that is what the Costellos, and likely the Vespas, were eating, probably at this very moment.

Koesler wiped sauce from his lips. "And that," he concluded, "pretty much brings us up to date."

"Hmmm," Dunn commented, after the manner of Bulldog Drummond, "and Guido Vespa wasn't there."

Koesler looked at him with some asperity. "You're not going to get back into that confession again, are you?"

"Now, I know you're not thrilled to talk about it. But between us, we're not violating the seal. We're talking about a confession we both heard. Actually, I think we're talking about whether there is some way we could help the police without breaking the seal of confession. Isn't it something like a consultation between doctors? I know the weight of the secrets is not equal—the professional versus the sacramental secret. But the doctors are not violating the patient's right to privacy. They are professionals trying to help the patient . . . no?"

Koesler had to admit to himself that there was merit to Dunn's argument. They were doing nothing to make Vespa's confession odious or difficult for him. As long as they kept their remarks between the two of them, there seemed to be no violation of the seal. It was just that in Koesler's many years as a priest, he had never discussed in any way any confession with anyone. It was the unique character of this situation that pushed Koesler toward reticence.

"Okay," he said finally, with some reluctance, "but let's tread very gingerly. We're on dangerous ground."

"Fair enough," Dunn agreed. "Didn't Guido's name come up at all?"

"Yes, it did, at one point. There was even the mention of gambling." Koesler smiled. "I gave ESP my best shot, but it didn't seem to work.

"Now, can we get around to all those papers you pushed aside here?"

It was Dunn's turn to smile. "They represent a busy day for me. A morning spent at the Detroit main library and, once I convinced a sympathetic managing editor at the *News* of my need, an afternoon going through the *News* library."

Koesler sighed. "If only you got that wrapped up in your studies . . ."

"I will. I will. All in due time. First things first."

Being a detective is not your first—or second or third—priority, thought Koesler. But he let the admonition pass unspoken. It would have accomplished little or nothing. "So then, what was the object of all this research?"

"The Mafia, or, more properly, La Cosa Nostra. Know much about it?"

Koesler gestured toward the stack of notes. "Not as much as you do now, I'll bet. Shoot!"

Dunn began assembling the notes. "It may come as no surprise to you that the Mafia is only a shadow of its former self."

"I didn't know that."

Dunn looked at Koesler to try to discern whether he was joking. Apparently not.

"Well, then," Dunn proceeded, "it will come as a surprise to you: Almost everybody involved in the war against the Mafia seems to agree that La Cosa Nostra is declining. They're not quite in agreement as to the reason. However, there's a guy named . . ." Dunn consulted his notes. ". . . Blakey, from Notre Dame, who was chief developer of something called the Racketeer Influenced and Corrupt Organization Act that worked pretty good in court. He's quoted here in a *New York Times* article: 'It was sort of like George Kennan's containment policy of the Soviet Union. We tried it, and by God it worked.' "

"Just what is this . . . act?" Koesler checked his watch. He didn't want to be late, especially since Dunn's information could be delivered anytime.

"It was . . ." Dunn searched for the pertinent note. "Ah . . . here . . . it was a courtroom tool that allowed the Justice Department and the FBI to concentrate on enterprises rather than individuals. And that helped them remove the highest leaders of the Mafia by means of convictions and long prison sentences. So that now, this one guy says, 'Outside of New York and Chicago, the Mafia is an anachronism.'

"Now here is an interesting part. A couple of experts say that certain changes in society contributed to the Mafia's decline. One: white flight from big cities lessened the Mafia's political influence and also lessened the protection they used to get from the police and their political machines. That's got to be true in Detroit . . . no?"

"Sure it is," Koesler said. "I can remember the big Italian parishes, the heavily Italian neighborhoods. All gone now. Dispersed throughout the suburbs. I was surprised to find the Costellos still living in Detroit."

"We're going to get to that," Dunn promised. "But here's another change: As the leaders were convicted almost wholesale, the ones who took over were less competent than their predecessors.

"And another: When the Mafia loyalties disintegrated, some of the members broke the code of silence and became informers.

"And finally: Rival crime groups sprang up. Some of them Asian, Colombian, and black Americans. These new groups pretty well control crime in the inner cities, where the Mafia's power used to be.

"Now, get this one, Bob: There's a Mafia defector who said his crew could no longer find reliable assassins in its own ranks and they were forced to issue outside contracts. Now that's going to have something to do with our Guido Vespa."

"But how—?"

"Let me finish." Dunn checked his own watch. He wanted very much to complete his presentation before Koesler was forced to leave for his appointment.

It occurred to Koesler that during Dunn's rather carefully planned presentation, the young priest had served this entire warmed-over meal while he, Koesler, had done little but eat and first talk and then listen. Dunn had even served the drinks. Koesler had contributed nothing to the dining experience. It didn't seem fair. "I'll fix us some coffee."

"No!" Dunn realized he'd been more emphatic than the occasion warranted. But the prospect of having to endure another unique Koesler brew was more than innocent humanity should have to suffer. "I mean, I've had quite a lot of coffee today. None for me, thanks."

"Okay, okay." Koesler thought the vehement response a bit excessive. Perhaps Dunn was simply keyed up over all he'd accomplished this day. "I'll get some for myself, if you don't mind."

Dunn wondered about the lining of Koesler's stomach. How, he puzzled, could Koesler tolerate that acid? Maybe it was in the same category as the ugly baby who everyone except the parents knew was homely.

Dunn raised his voice as Koesler went into the kitchen to blend freeze-dried coffee with hot water to somehow produce hemlock. "When you get back in here," Dunn called, "I'd like you to look at this chart that I got photostated at the *News*. It shows the makeup of the Mafia in Detroit some thirty years ago. They've got it arranged like a family tree."

"Oh, I vaguely remember that. When it was first published, I couldn't figure out how the law enforcement agencies could do that without a trial. It seemed to be a denial of 'innocent until proven guilty.' I couldn't figure how the police could get away with that, unless it was factual and the people identified there simply didn't want to go to court with—what?—a defamation of character or libel suit."

"The interesting thing," Dunn said, "is that back then there were six families that ran the Mafia in Detroit. And Carl 'Double C' Costello was the boss of one of those families."

"The gentleman we visited today," Koesler said. "I guess I wasn't paying much attention back then . . . that or I've just forgotten." He returned with his coffee—black.

Funny, thought Dunn, it smells all right.

"Look here . . ." Dunn turned the chart toward Koesler. He pointed to two pictures side by side far down the list. One was Remo Vespa; the other was Guido Vespa. They were in the category of "soldiers." In the accompanying article, they were further identified as "made men" and "buttons." Meaning they had been solemnly inducted into La Cosa Nostra and, in addition, they were assassins— "hit men."

"They look like choirboys in these pictures," Dunn observed.

"They probably were," Koesler replied. It was quite beyond him how members of the Mafia families squared the kinds of things they did, particularly vicious crimes, with an easy familiarity with religion. But he was aware, in some imperfect way, that the inception of the Mafia concept had little to do with its eventual development.

"See this article?" Dunn pushed another photostated news story toward Koesler. "It talks about how the mob made its money from labor racketeering, gambling, loan-sharking, extortion, prostitution, smuggling, and narcotics trafficking. And see this story?" Dunn moved another sheet toward Koesler. "It says that in Michigan, the mob's major activities are illegal bookmaking, labor racketeering, and loan-sharking." Dunn looked at Koesler expectantly. When Koesler did not respond, Dunn said with an emphatic Dont'-you-get-it? tone: "Illegal bookmaking! Don't you see, Bob? *Illegal* bookmaking!"

Obviously, Koesler was not getting it.

"The cause of Keating's murder, Bob! Guido Vespa said it was because of Keating's bad debts. And the Mafia is into illegal bookmaking!"

"I fail to see . . ."

In all honesty, Dunn was not a little disappointed with his hero. Koesler was the fairly famous amateur detective. He should be ahead of this game. Instead he failed to see . . .

And then it dawned on Dunn: He hadn't given Koesler the whole picture. "Wait: There's one more thing I haven't told you. Remember, the article said that some thirty years ago there had been six families in the Detroit area? Now there is only one that's still functioning. And it's not the Costello family." Again he looked expectantly at Koesler.

It was embarrassing. Obviously, Dunn expected him to be arriving at a correct answer to this puzzle. But if there were such an answer, it certainly had escaped Koesler's observation.

Dunn gave up. He'd have to spell it out. "The way I see it," he began, "Keating liked to gamble. No—more: He was a *compulsive* gambler. But apparently none of his close friends was aware of that, else one or more of them would have told the police during this investigation. And nobody has . . . am I right?"

"Far as I know."

"But according to our very best source—the man who executed him—Keating bets on just about everything. Now if Keating's close friends don't know about this, Keating is guarding the secret carefully. To use a metaphor that Keating would have loved, he's playing his cards very close to the vest. Which means . . .?"

"Which means he probably isn't doing much or any of this gambling in legitimate areas. Else," Koesler took Dunn's cue, "the people he chums with would be aware of what was going on. And if his friends were alert to his compulsive gambling, while they probably wouldn't have interfered—no one criticizes 'Father'—they surely would have mentioned it when Keating turned up missing. He's a 'missing person' under such circumstances that anyone who knew of his reckless gambling would have suspected the connection. And would have told the police."

"Exactly," Dunn agreed. "So if Keating is not gambling in Monaco or any of the other legitimate hangouts, he might be putting down bets with *illegal* bookmakers—the Mafia. Because that's one of the remaining rackets of the local Mafia. And if he *is* placing his bets through the Mafia, there's only one family left to handle his business. There's only one of the six originals left."

"But the one remaining family, you said, was not Costello's. So how does Guido Vespa figure into this if—wait a minute . . ." Koesler fingered through Dunn's notes and photostats until he found the one he was looking for. He read it aloud: " 'A high-ranking Mafia defector bitterly said that his crew could no longer find reliable assassins in its own ranks and had to take outside contracts.' "

"So . . ." Koesler allowed the conjunction to stand alone as he weighed the present state of the question. "So . . ." he repeated, "according to your theory, Keating bet outrageously on just about everything. We have Vespa's word on that. He ended up head over heels in debt because he couldn't cover his losses. Again, Vespa's word. Plus, it occurred to me today while I was with Lieutenant Tully, that the one incident I personally know of when Jake Keating played a hunch was with stocks and bonds, and he lost a pile . . . although compared with what he apparently got into recently, the stocks and bonds gamble was innocence itself."

"You didn't tell Tully that," Dunn wondered.

"Almost. I was saved by prayer, I guess. That was too close to the confessional secret. Anyway," Koesler continued, "according to your theory—if I'm following you correctly—since there is no indication that this gambling was going on aboveboard, so to speak, it may be presumed that Keating's bets, as well as his debts, were with the Mafia.

"And, from what is conventionally known about the Mafia, they do not stand still when someone tries to take advantage of them. So the Mafia, unable to get its money back, exacts retribution in the form of a contract to kill Father Keating." Koesler shuddered. "This whole thing gets so ugly."

But Dunn, whose theory this basically was, continued with what he believed to be the correct scenario. "We already have, courtesy of the newspaper clipping, the complaint of 'a high-ranking Mafia figure' that nowadays they can't depend on their own families to execute a contract. They have to use outside resources.

"So here's Keating, hopelessly in debt to the one remaining Detroit family. And this family, apparently—probably because they can't trust this to anyone in their own organization—gives the contract to Guido Vespa. And he was, we know from that ancient Mafia chart—maybe still is—a button man.

"So," Dunn concluded, "Guido Vespa is offered and accepts the contract, kills John Keating, and later—because he's never before murdered a priest, and because of his Catholic upbringing, however vague that may have been—he confesses the sin to you, and is overheard by me." There was a look of irrepressible self-congratulation on Dunn's smiling face.

The two priests regarded each other in silence. At length, Koesler looked at his watch. Not much time before he would have to leave. "So . . .?"

"So . . . what?" Dunn replied.

"My question precisely," Koesler said. "So what? Even if everything happened just the way you have constructed this chain of events, what difference does it make? The basis of this story is still Guido Vespa's confession. Neither of us would have the slightest notion of what might have happened to Jake Keating if Vespa had not told us of his role in the disappearance. And *that* neither of us can disclose to anyone under any circumstances. If either of us were to go to the police and say that the Mafia put out a contract on Father Keating because he couldn't pay his gambling debts, and the guy you're looking for, the hit man in this case, is Guido Vespa, the police certainly would ask, 'How do you know?' And we would—we could—say nothing. There's no proof of any of this except a confession that is completely out of bounds. So: So what?"

Dunn gave every indication that he had not considered the implications of his scenario. Now he did so. The seconds were ticking away; Koesler would soon have to leave.

"Well," Dunn said finally, "you yourself said that this afternoon you tried to communicate with the police through ESP. And you were only trying to get them interested in Keating's gambling habits and make Guido Vespa the focus of their investigation.

"Okay, so it didn't work. But ESP can work; it has worked. Now that we have the whole story, why don't we try in a concerted way to get through to the cops with that extrasensory perception? That lieutenant will undoubtedly be talking to you again. You never know, there may be some way of communication, something we can't anticipate right now. But something may occur. The Holy Spirit . . ."

"Nice, Nick," Koesler said. "I'm the last one who would question the power of ESP, especially when it's fortified by prayer. 'More things are accomplished by prayer than this world dreams of.' But . . . but . . . do we have the whole story?"

Dunn seemed perplexed. "Of course we do!"

"Then," Koesler said, "what about the car?"

"What car?"

"Jake Keating's car. If Guido Vespa murdered Keating, what was Jack's car doing parked outside the Costello house? Would a murderer take an easily traceable car and leave it where the police could make an obvious connection between victim and killer?"

Dunn scratched his chin. "That is a puzzle. I don't know—wait, didn't you say that when you got to Costello's house there were a lot of police technicians around the car?"

"Right."

"And that one of them was working on fingerprints?"

"Uh-huh."

"And he said there were no prints on the steering wheel?"

Koesler nodded.

"That means," Dunn continued, "that Keating certainly didn't drive the car to that spot. Why would he wipe his own prints off the wheel?"

"True."

"Well . . . what we do know is that Guido Vespa killed Keating. Why would Vespa leave the car in front of his grandfather's home?" Dunn paused. "I don't think he could or would have done that." He thought for another moment. "Wait: Guido wasn't at the Costello home today; Remo was."

"That's right."

"I'll bet Guido hasn't been there since Friday. And if that's the case," Dunn was animated once more, "somebody else is involved. Like it says in the Bible, 'An enemy hath done this.' Somebody who knew what Guido had done, some enemy of Guido's, moved Keating's car to that neighborhood and left it there. If this person knew that Guido wasn't going to be there, and if this person knew that Guido alone—and nobody else in his family—knew about this contract—then what a beautiful way to get revenge! The Costellos, the Vespas, whatever, would have no idea where that car came from. They would have no reason to get rid of it. It wasn't any business of theirs. But the cops will find it eventually and they'll be able to trace it to its owner easily. And the Costellos and Vespas are in big trouble."

Dunn seemed to expect applause.

Koesler thought it over. "It certainly sounds plausible. Next time I get a chance, I'll try to find out if Guido was at the house anytime since Friday."

The doorbell rang.

"That would be my appointment," Koesler said. "I'd better go let them in."

"Them?"

"A couple. She's a Catholic. He's thinking of converting."

Dunn looked puzzled.

"Something wrong?" Koesler hesitated at the doorway.

"Something else just occurred to me. I guess I'm playing devil's advocate to my own theory. I know you've got to get the door, but could you give me another minute before you start in with them?"

"Sure. I'll be right back."

And he was. "So?"

"It's money," Dunn said.

"You need some?" Koesler was joking, or so he hoped.

"No . . . no. Keating. From what you've told me, he had plenty of money. Of all the problems he had in his lifetime, money had to be the least of them . . . no? Then why couldn't he pay off his losses? Especially since the alternative was death."

"It's true, Nick, he did grow up with money. And he always had some special perks—like his contacts in the auto industry. But his parents left him merely comfortable, not wealthy. He didn't have much more ready cash than the average priest. If he vacationed well, it was because some of his parishioners adopted him into their lifestyle."

"No, I could well imagine that, if he gambled as compulsively as Guido Vespa said, he could well have been in over his head."

"Okay then, how about his parish? Maybe the wealthiest parish in this diocese, no?"

"Sure it is. But . . . steal from the parish to pay off the Mafia? Oh, I don't think so."

"I suppose the diocese would find out one way or the other in an audit."

"Well, there's not going to be an audit. Not for a long while, anyway."

"Oh . . ." Dunn looked surprised. "Why not?"

"The diocese doesn't audit until there's a change in pastors. Take it from one who moved from one parish to another about a year ago.

The diocese sent its auditors to my former parish as well as to this one."

"Okay, but we know Keating isn't going to come back. What about that?"

"We belong to a select few who know that, Nick. To the diocese, the parish isn't vacant. They just don't know where the pastor is. Trust me. There was a similar case a while back where a pastor had to go away for a long period of treatment. They merely appointed an administrator for the interim. Undoubtedly that's what they'll do now."

Koesler turned to leave, hesitated, then turned back. "Besides, in response to your *advocatus diaboli,* there's a parish council along with a finance committee that keeps a steady hand on parochial money. And you can be sure that with the sort of successful businessmen they have in that parish, the finances would be carefully watched.

"And finally, Nick, if he had used money from St. Waldo's coffers and paid his debts, he'd be alive today."

Dunn brightened. "So my theory stays intact!"

Koesler smiled grimly. "Your theory stays intact."

Koesler walked down the hall toward the office where the couple awaited. As he walked, he could not shake the nagging thoughts surrounding the case of the missing Father Keating.

Something about this case troubled him. Something besides the confessional technicalities quandary. Something that had been pulling at the corners of his consciousness from the very beginning. One thing was certain: Whatever it was, it had nothing to do with either Nick Dunn's scenario or his own doubts.

Actually, he thought, Dunn had done an excellent job of putting clues together to build a credible theory on what was behind the disappearance of Jake Keating. Except that Koesler had no real expectation that either he or Dunn would find any legitimate avenue to share what they knew and what they speculated. In all likelihood, it would all be buried in that completely isolated field protected by the sacred seal of confession.

Nonetheless, Koesler wondered what it was beyond that that troubled him.

12

IT WAS ONLY an informal, casual understanding, nothing signed in blood or a legal contract. But Pat Lennon and Pringle McPhee met in the News cafeteria most mornings before getting down to work. No hard feelings if one, the other, or both didn't show up.

By pure coincidence both arrived at the food counter simultaneously this morning. They greeted each other as enthusiastically as possible for the early hour. As the two moved down the line, most of the men in the cafeteria watched them, some surreptitiously, others openly. Each of the women was used to drawing male attention. Of the two, Pat was the more experienced in handling such attention.

They seated themselves at their usual table in their usual corner. Like many workers they were creatures of habit.

As usual, Pringle had selected a generous breakfast while Pat had coffee and toast.

"I meant to tell you," Pringle said, "that really was a great obit you wrote for Hal Salden."

"Well, thanks." It was somewhat unusual to receive praise for writing an obituary. But in this case it had been a labor of love; Pat really had respected and liked Salden. She was pleased that Pringle had appreciated her effort.

"I especially liked the way you brought out his professionalism," Pringle said. "He was a really good reporter. He was always interesting and even fun to read."

Pat smiled as she spread a thin layer of marmalade on her unbuttered toast. "Yeah. I think religion writers today have a lot to live down. Most of today's writers are genuine professionals. But a while back . . . well, there were some pretty weird characters covering religion. Let's just say a lot of them didn't do religion any favors. But today's crop is by and large professional. And Hal was among the best of them. He respected his field, and it showed. He would have been really good at whatever beat. But religion was lucky to get him."

"I agree. And I think you brought that out in the obit. Are the cops any closer to getting his killer?"

"I don't think so."

"You're on that story too, aren't you?" Pringle was eating a bit more rapidly than usual.

"Uh-huh. It's curious. They haven't got any suspects yet. But most of all, they haven't got any motive. From what some of the witnesses say, it seems that the weapon was an automatic of some kind. There were two other people wounded, but Hal took the most rounds by far. It was like the gunman was not all that expert, but for all of that, Hal is dead."

"But why?" Pringle wondered. "It isn't all that rare for a reporter to be injured in the line of duty. But usually it's just an accident—being at the wrong place at the wrong time. So why aim at a reporter? You don't like the news he's reporting? That's literally killing the messenger!"

"Hold on, Pringle. The cops haven't decided yet that Hal was the intended victim. I think the current theory is that the gunman is a psycho. If that is the case, they don't know whether the guy was sore because the priest was forced to give up his parish, or mad because the priest got married. Or it was just some kook who saw an angry crowd and it was dark and he decided he could get away with some random shooting. All we know is that he got Hal and we're the poorer for that."

"Yeah," Pringle agreed, "what a waste!"

"While we're passing out bouquets, that was a nice job you did on that missing priest. You left the Freep in the dust. They just carried the news story yesterday. And you got an insider look. From now on, Pringle, it's your story."

Pringle finished the last of her pancakes. Pat speculated that Pringle could eat so much and still stay slender because she ate so rapidly: She neither chewed nor digested her food—it just passed right through her.

Pringle touched the paper napkin to her lips. She had only coffee left. Over that she would dawdle. "I kind of lucked into it—I was lucky to have been late. When I got to the rectory, I could see that Haggerty from the Freep and DeVere from the *Reporter* were trying every which way to get in. But the cops wouldn't let them. Either the cops had orders or were cooperating with the priest's wishes; whatever, they weren't going to let anybody in.

"I found out the TV and radio people had been there and gone. They just did some standups in front of the church and left.

"I watched Haggerty and DeVere for a while. They were funny, especially Lacy." She giggled. "I kept thinking of what you said and I could imagine her offering to sleep with every cop on duty there. Anyway, whatever she tried, it didn't work—and she was furious.

"That was when I decided if the front door was closed to visitors maybe the back door might open. I was lucky again. It turned out the housekeeper was very upset with all that was going on. Haggerty had already tried to get in the back way, but she wouldn't let him in. Orders. Turned out Lacy didn't even think to try it."

"Amazing!" Pat shook her head. "So how'd you get in?"

"I asked for a glass of water. Told her I wasn't feeling too well. Which was not far from true. On that alone, she let me in. Later, when it came out I was a reporter, it didn't seem to matter. She wasn't about to throw me out. We were getting along too well by then. She really wanted to talk—girl talk—but she also gave me some priceless background. Later, the secretary came in. Again some hesitation. But in the end she was pretty cooperative."

"How'd you get those quotes from the priest?"

"That was where Father Mitchell was showing the police out of the rectory via the back door. When the cop, Lieutenant Tully, spotted me in the kitchen he was pretty upset. Then, after he thought it over, I think he was amused that I got in and Lacy was screaming her lungs out at the front door. He wouldn't talk to me, but, on the other hand, he didn't stop the others from talking. Besides, I'd already got the essence of the story from the two women. Mitchell's comments were sort of the frosting on the cake. So that was pretty much it."

Pat was smiling, picturing Lacy DeVere stalled on the front porch, too damn blockheaded to use her imagination and try to find some other way of getting in. All of DeVere's brashness got her diddly squat. Pringle's journalistic flair got her the story.

"I wonder," Pat said, "what, if anything, DeVere went with?"

"Well, I'll be—" Pringle said, "I didn't even look. I picked up a copy of the *Reporter* this morning and I didn't even look to see if she's in there." Pringle spread the *Reporter* on the table and began paging through it. "Here it is." She smoothed the paper flat and scanned the column. "You know, that's not a very flattering picture of Lacy."

"That's okay," Pat said. "If people can't recognize her from her picture, it just saves her from being identified and hit over the head by her many dissatisfied customers." Pause. "Anything about St. Waldo's and the missing Father Keating?"

"Here it is." Pringle read aloud:

" 'Poor St. Waldo of the Wheels remains pastorless as of this writing. What could keep the high-stepping Father Jake Keating away from his benefice where he has the Midas touch? Nothing! shouts his superrich flock. So the powers that be suspect foul play. They've got no less than four police departments investigating the disappearance, including Detroit's Homicide Division. While our Big City vies with D.C. for the title of Murder Capital of the U.S.A., Detroit's finest are doing double duty in lieu of a moat keeping reporters from doing their job. Hey, fellas, go find the priest . . . if it's not too late. Does the presence of Homicide give us any hints? Processional song for Waldo of the Wheels this Sunday: "Sometimes I Feel Like a Shepherdless Sheep." ' "

"Wow!" Pringle exclaimed. "That's tasteless. I mean, that's really tasteless."

"Vintage DeVere," Pat said. "Actually much better than DeVere is capable of. The *Reporter* must've hired a damn good copy editor."

"How about this?" Pringle said, as she continued to read DeVere's column. " 'Is Detroit's Mayor Maynard A. Cobb finally going to tie the knot? Inside that armor-plated, bulletproof limo—whose occupants can see you but you can't see them—there's been a torrid affair going on. And Hizzoner just fresh from losing a paternity suit! Probably a good move on his part making an honest woman of his paramour, before he becomes the new Father of our Country.' " Pringle chuckled.

"Yes, indeed," Pat said, "a superior copy editor." She finished her coffee.

"Uh-oh . . ." Pringle was distressed. "Oh, Pat . . ." She turned the paper toward Pat, index finger indicating the pertinent paragraph. It was the item immediately following the one about Mayor Cobb.

" 'And,' " Pat read, " 'speaking of making honest women of paramours with benefit of clergy, is there any truth to the rumors that Detroit Homicide detective Alonzo (Zoo) Tully and the Detroit *News*'s Pat Lennon are a Thing? If so, it's going to be news to Tully's live-in-lover, Alice, not to mention Lennon's significant other, Joe

Cox, now off to the Chicago newspaper wars.'" Pat winced. "Two for the price of one, eh?" She looked up from the paper to meet Pringle's pained expression.

"Pat . . .?" Pringle's inflection made it a question.

Pat smiled. "Don't let it reach you, Pringle. She was out to get me. Remember the other night at The Fast Lane? When she claimed she had a survey that showed my reportorial skills were slipping? And I told you not to hold your breath till she published that—because there wasn't any such survey? But one way or another she was trying to get me. I had no doubt about that. Well, here's her best shot. I just feel sorry for Tully. He doesn't need that. Neither does Alice."

"Why Tully?"

"Didn't you say that when you were in St. Waldo's rectory, Tully walked past you in the kitchen on his way out?"

Pringle nodded.

"And that DeVere was having kittens out front trying to get into the rectory?"

Again Pringle nodded.

"Well, that's probably it. Tully was supposed to get her in there and he didn't. So, two for the price of one. I told you to watch out for her. When she's got you in her sights, she'll pull the trigger."

"But you . . . and Tully? That's crazy!"

Pat shook her head. "Yes and no." She was thoughtful for a moment, remembering. "When you got hit by that car a few years back . . . well, something almost happened between Tully and me. Tully's Alice was very, very ill. And Joe was off doing a fluff story on the Mackinac boat race—and he really ticked me off because we had to cancel our vacation for him to take the assignment." She looked fully at Pringle. "Zoo and I were both vulnerable at the time. Like I said, something almost happened. But it didn't."

"Then how . . . what about this column?"

"There may have been talk at the time. I don't know for sure, but I wouldn't bet against it. Anyway, DeVere wasn't anyplace near this town when all that was happening. She must've nosed around, gotten some conjecture. That's all she ever needs."

"But the column . . . it's a lie and it's libelous! Won't you—or Tully—sue her?"

"We probably should. But we won't. It takes so much time and costs so much financially and in emotional drain, it's just not worth it. But this is a good example of how creeps like DeVere operate. She deals in half-truths so much she wouldn't recognize the whole truth if it bit her.

"Take that piece about the missing priest: She has no idea what happened to him or where he is. Detroit Homicide is on the case. The word *homicide* is enough for her, so—he's dead. Simple as that. Then she gets in a cheap shot at the wealthy parishioners and is sufficiently sarcastic and just plain nasty to get people sniggering and joining her fun and—most important—quoting her. They'll probably have a chorus or two of 'Sometimes I Feel Like a Shepherdless Sheep' at The Fast Lane.

"And the piece about the mayor? I'll bet she hasn't the slightest idea what's going on in his life. Maybe one night she spotted Cobb and a woman get into his car. And he's got the blacked-out windows. Take over, imagination!

"And if you happen to become a victim, you'd better grin and bear it. The alternative is madness. But the same thing that happened before could happen again."

"You mean—?"

"Yeah—she screwed a bunch of people when she was working her way up the Freep ladder on her back—and the same ones thumbed their noses at her as she slid back down and out. It could just happen again."

"Let us pray," Pringle intoned.

They both laughed. They needed that.

13

IT WAS SEVERAL hours after the end of his shift, but—not unusual—
Lieutenant Tully was still at work. Frequently he worked late or arrived early or both. What was odd was that he was not working on a
homicide—his life's obsession; rather, he was trying to close an obsti-
nate missing persons investigation. He had gathered all the material
his team had uncovered and brought it into the office of his immediate superior, Inspector Walter Koznicki. The two were going through
it together for what Tully fervently hoped would be the final time.

Tully knew that Koznicki would be under continuing pressure to
keep this investigation going—pressure from the chief, the mayor, and
. . . what's his name . . . Dunstable. That was the direction from
which this missing persons case had emerged. And if the investigation
were to be abandoned, each man would have to convince the next
man, in reverse order. So it would be a tad more difficult to convince
Koznicki it was over. Koznicki himself would see the light easily. But
the inspector would have to anticipate objections from the chief, he in
turn from the mayor, and so on.

Still it was important to close the book on this case and move on to
more appropriate investigations. So Tully dove in.

"I must admit, Walt," Tully arranged the notes and documents so
the inspector could view them in some sort of order, "when we started
on this thing, I didn't think we had any business getting . . . involved."

"You made that eminently clear, Alonzo." Koznicki almost smiled.
"And now . . .?"

"Now I have to admit that Keating not only started out for Detroit
a week ago, he got here—certainly his car did—and he may not have
left Detroit."

"You think, then . . .?"

"There's no reason in the world for him to be a missing person of
his own free will. As far as we could determine, he had everything in

the world to live for. He was head of the wealthiest parish in the Detroit diocese. Have you ever been in the priest's house there?"

Koznicki shook his head as he continued to scan the documents while listening to Tully.

"I've been in ritzier homes," Tully said, "but not many. I didn't think priests lived that high. He didn't get any more money in salary than any other priest, but he plugged into the lifestyle of the richest people in the Bloomfield Hills area. Vacations in the Caribbean, Vail, you name it—around the world, literally. Why would anyone want to leave that?"

Koznicki thought for a moment. "You may have touched on a possible reason, Alonzo. I agree with everything you have said thus far. In many ways, Father Keating has been living an enviable life. But, generally, I believe you are correct in your belief that priests do not live such a luxurious lifestyle. So, is that not the material from which conflict is made?"

"I don't—"

"What I mean, Alonzo, is that I can imagine a priest who lives that well experiencing . . . what might be called a crisis of conscience." Koznicki selected one of the documents and indicated an item on it. "From your own notation, Alonzo. I believe this is part of your conversation with Father Koesler, when Father tells you of the bequest left Father Keating by his parents. Instead of being as generous to their only child as they might, they left the bulk of their estate to various charities and only enough to their son so that, with prudent care or management, he would be fairly comfortable for life—but not really wealthy.

"That indicates to me that the parents, though very well off themselves, felt that the vocation their son chose should bear some witness to the life of Christ. Catholics sometimes refer to their priests as 'other Christs.' "

"God knows, Walt, I don't know much about religion. But the word poverty doesn't come to mind when I think of that priest's house—or the neighborhood, for that matter."

"Exactly, Alonzo. Thus the conceivable conflict. It was not that he was schooled or trained to live lavishly. True, his parents were wealthy, but they definitely communicated moderation, particularly in their bequest. According to Father Koesler again," Koznicki adjusted his bifocals, "Father Keating's seminary experience was indistinguishable from the others. He was comfortable with the benefits that money can bring. But he was 'one of the boys.' And in his earlier days in the priesthood he continued to be 'one of the boys,' joining his fellow priests in modest vacations and trips. It was not until he was assigned to St. Waldo's that he began to lose touch with his confreres. As you have pointed out, in recent years he seems to have changed, living on a considerably higher scale than most other priests.

"Put it all together, Alonzo, and I believe we come up with a considerably different picture than that of a priest enjoying the life of Riley. On the surface he could easily be described as having the best of all possible worlds. But I believe it very possible that inwardly he may have felt very deeply that he might be betraying his vocational commitment. While seemingly not disturbed, he may have been very touched inwardly. He might even have been extremely distressed—depressed even. Did your investigation turn up any suggestion that he might be suffering from clinical depression—even a hint of something of that order? Was he seeing a psychotherapist of any sort?"

Tully had in no way anticipated Koznicki's line of thought and inquiry. Nor did he agree with the inspector's hypothesis. But he gave Koznicki's questions some thought.

"I don't know that anyone can answer that question, Walt," he said, finally. "Seems Keating was away and unaccounted for a good bit of the time. Where he was, what he did when he was away from the parish, has to be anybody's guess. He could just as easily have been seeing a shrink anywhere from once in a while to regularly. But if he was, he kept it real quiet. There were no notations on his calendar of any such appointments, although there were recorded appointments with his regular GP and his dentist."

"And what did his doctor have to say?"

"Reluctant at first, naturally. But when we convinced him, he opened up. Even so, he still didn't say much. Keating was in good shape for his age; a bit overweight, but he handled it well. There was no mention at all of any emotional problem, or any referral to a shrink. But, like I say, anything was possible in all the time he was away. And there was nothing, now that I think of it, on any of his check stubs that showed a payment to any shrink. Though God knows he had enough accounts. I can't say we even found all of them. The guy is simply hard to pin down. He may have been torn up inside, but he sure as hell didn't show it on the outside. Everybody we talked to painted a picture of somebody who really enjoyed life—had everything to live for."

"So . . .?"

"The bottom line is, we haven't found him—dead or alive. And we really tried. I can't think of another missing person who's had as many cops looking for him. The 'burb cops did a very professional job. Together we talked to just about everybody who might have an informed opinion. Nada! It was like everybody could think of hundreds of people who might just walk away from things, but not Keating. Not Keating."

"And the Costello family?"

Tully scratched his five o'clock shadow. "That is where I changed my mind on the necessity of our getting involved in looking for him. I didn't buy the possibility that he might be dead until I heard that his car had been found in that neighborhood."

"And what of the fact that the car was found just outside the Costello home? Why would they leave such a clue?"

"Another answer I haven't got. Of course, the families are notorious for sending messages: the dead fish, the genitals in the mouth, that sort of thing. The car seemed dumb—too dumb not to mean something. Mangiapane came up with the theory they were thumbing their nose at us: Here's his car. Right at our front door. Let's see you make a case of it. We'll hand you the clue on a platter. But you'll never pin it on us. And you'll never find the damn body either. Moore thinks it's possible some other family left the car there. A retaliation. A feud payback. Whatever. But I sort of like Manj's idea."

"You do not believe he is alive then?"

Tully shook his head somberly. There was a sense of pessimism. "It could be anything. He might have been depressed, like you said. In which case—maybe suicide. He might have amnesia. In that case, he's probably wandering around somewhere, and he'll probably come back some day. But I don't think so. I think he was iced. The mob—somebody in organized crime. Though OC couldn't come up with anything. And we went through Costello's home from A to Z. Nothing.

"One thing for pretty sure though: If the mob hit him, we'll probably never find the body. We might have his car, but I'll bet they did something inventive with the body.

"The thing that beats me is—why? If the mob hit him, you can bet it wasn't an accident. He was into them for something. But what? Racketeering? I doubt it. Narcotics?" Tully shook his head. "No indication whatever. Loan-sharking? Again, no indication. Gambling? Always a possibility. You never know you got the bug till you're in front of a one-armed bandit with a roll of quarters. But—no gambling slips. No personal checks to any notoriously shady character. Just . . . nothing."

"An individual who, for whatever reason, took out a contract on him?" Koznicki suggested.

Tully seemed to be studying the desk. He did not raise his head. "Anything's possible. But at the moment, that's no better than a guess. There were people who didn't care for him—especially people who worked for or with him. But there's no hard evidence for that or for any kind of conspiracy. If anybody is guilty of any crime against Keating, it's well hidden."

"Your conclusion?" Koznicki asked, though he knew the answer.

"It's over, Walt. We've done everything we could, at least for right now. We've been everywhere we could go. We've checked everything we could. Who knows, something may crop up later—though I can't think what. But, you never know. Anyway we're at a dead end for now, unless we get some more clues or tips."

"Are the suburban police in agreement?"

"Uh-huh. They're ready to close it as an unsolved missing person. There's no place to put it but in 'open homicide' with all the others. They're—we're—ready and willing to open it up if there are any further developments. But for now . . ." Tully raised both hands, palms up, in a gesture of futility.

"Very well," Koznicki said. "I will relay this decision to the chief."

"He's not gonna like it."

Koznicki nodded in unhappy agreement. "Nor will the mayor. But I am satisfied we have done all that could be done. We can consider the matter closed—at least for the moment . . . at least for you."

Tully gave a sigh of relief. He was convinced he had done his best. But it was beyond doubt a dead end. The police had no alternative at this point but to go back over all the ground they'd just covered. And they could have done that forever. But the prospects of a breakthrough were practically nil.

Koznicki gathered up the documents and reports, put them in a folder, and the folder in his desk drawer. "Another day's work done," he announced. The two men left the room together.

On the elevator Tully asked about the two homicide cases that had particularly interested him before he had been drawn into the Keating investigation.

Ordinarily, Tully would have been up on their status. It was his practice to take an interest in everything that was going on in the division. But the search for the missing priest had occupied all of Tully's attention, mostly because of his efforts to resolve it and get on with more appropriate matters.

Given Tully's indisputable interest in the total homicide case load, which was common knowledge, Koznicki was a bit surprised that the detective could be unaware of what was going on in other investigations. But it was a gratifying surprise—indicating the total dedication he had given to the Keating case.

"We have someone in custody," Koznicki explained, "in the case of the lawyer who was killed. Actually, it was odd that it took so long for an identification given that the attack occurred at noon on a crowded downtown street. But the crowd was part of the problem."

"Yeah," Tully agreed, "that noontime crowd crossing Jefferson near the Ren Cen can be overwhelming. Like you could pick up your feet and be carried across Jefferson."

"That was the precise problem," Koznicki said. "The killer got directly behind the victim and stabbed him with a poisoned-tip umbrella. But there were so many packed together, a lot of them wearing coats and carrying umbrellas. There was a promise of rain, and it was overcast. We had to interview an unlikely number of witnesses before we could filter through to the likely suspect. Many of the prime witnesses were, of course, reluctant to acknowledge that they'd seen anything—"

"Don't tell me," Tully interrupted, "they were all going to the john at just the time of the killing."

Koznicki chuckled. "Something like that. In any case, the identification we did come up with led to the husband, or I should say former husband, of one of the lawyer's clients. A divorce case. Messy. And expensive."

Tully chewed his lip. "That was more of a platter case than I expected." He was now grateful he had not been involved in that case.

He had not anticipated that it would be handed to the police on a silver platter, but it evidently had: The most likely suspect apparently was guilty. However, it hadn't been signed, sealed, and delivered yet. Tully would keep an eye open for developments in the case of the lawyer killed in broad daylight.

"As to the other case," Koznicki said, "there has been very little progress on the *News* reporter's death. Once again, the initial problem lies with the witnesses. There were many potential eyewitnesses, but this time it happened in the dark of night, again in a crowd with many qualifying circumstances. At this point, the investigation does not seem promising."

They left 1300 Beaubien, Police Headquarters, and stood for a moment on the broad sidewalk. Koznicki looked out of the corner of his eye. He could almost see the wheels moving in Tully's head. "Are you interested, Alonzo?" he asked almost needlessly.

Tully smiled. "Oh, I guess, maybe. I think I'll just go back upstairs and run through that file." He turned and hustled back up the stairs. Of course he couldn't wait to get started. Here was a mystery that, unlike the Keating case, had an obtainable answer. Somebody had killed a *Detroit News* reporter. All Tully had to do was find out who-dunit. And more often than not that was how Tully solved cases. They might never find Father John Keating—dead or alive. But, by God, Tully was going hunting for whoever had killed the reporter.

Part
Two

14

Earlier in the twentieth century, Detroit's theater district—such as it was—was located bordering along Woodward not far from the river on streets such as Larned, Congress, Fort, and Lafayette. Many of those legitimate stages later became movie houses. All were now long gone.

Now, later in the twentieth century, the theater district—such as it is—of downtown Detroit lies above Grand Circus Park, about a mile north of where it once was. And the streets surrounding this district can be dangerous.

It was just after 10:00 on a balmy September evening when the show at the Fox Theater let out. A generally satisfied audience spilled out onto Woodward Avenue, which had the distinction of being M-1, the first highway in Michigan.

Most of the patrons had parked in the large adjoining lot. But Father Koesler, in a tribute to frugality, had parked in the underground garage beneath Grand Circus Park, which, even though evening rates had been drastically reduced to attract customers, was nearly empty. The garage was only a block or so south of the Fox, but a lot could happen in that short distance. And if anything did happen, chances were it would not be pleasant.

The four priest friends who had attended tonight's performance had come in two cars. Father McNiff had chauffeured Fathers Marvin and Mulroney and had parked in the Fox lot. Indeed, of all those in attendance this night, Koesler seemed the only one to have parked any distance from the theater. Since the four had agreed to meet at Carl's Chop House for an after-theater meal, Frank Marvin volunteered to go with Koesler so he would not be alone. Thus the two set off, walking briskly down Woodward.

It was eerie.

The area just outside the theater was brightly lit and swarming with happy, chatting people. Two steps from that scene and it was like a set from a wartime movie. There were streetlights, but it was nowhere near as illumined as the overlit Fox marquee. And there were no people. The impression that the infrequent pedestrian had quickly passed into some sort of no-man's-land was due in large part to the contrast between a small zone comprising noisy people packed together like sardines and a desolate street—all within a few feet of each other.

The two priests could not help but be aware of their isolation.

"Is it worth it?" Father Marvin asked.

"What?" Father Koesler returned.

"The five or so bucks you save by parking in the garage."

"A penny saved, et cetera," Koesler said flippantly. But he didn't feel that insouciant. As nonchalantly as possible he glanced over his shoulder to see who, if anyone, was behind them as they walked. There was no one in front of them as far as the eye could see.

But there was someone behind them.

A lone young man, possibly a teenager, in jeans and T-shirt. Somewhat lightly clothed, even for this mild weather. Definitely not part of the theater crowd. A casual pedestrian headed . . . where? Home? A rendezvous? Nowhere in particular?

Koesler did not want to alarm Marvin. But he certainly wanted to stay alert to this potential threat.

They walked in silence a few more steps. Koesler again glanced over his shoulder. The young man maintained his course in their wake. He stayed about eight to ten yards behind them, matching their pace. But something was added now: a car, old, weatherworn, so dirty it was difficult to tell how many passengers were in it.

Koesler did not wish to turn around and confront the young man or his companions, which very likely the occupants of the car were. The car was creeping down Woodward at the same slow speed as the priests and their shadow.

"Bob," Marvin said softly, "somebody seems to be following us."

"Oh?" So Marvin had also noticed this small procession. Koesler did not want either himself or Marvin to panic, but there was an unmistakable sense of serious danger here.

Of course it was possible the young man was simply out for a walk on an inviting evening. He might have been keeping a date.

And if Koesler flapped his arms, he might fly. No, that steady pace kept both by the pedestrian and the suspicious car boded no harmless explanation.

The fact that their quarry were priests apparently carried no weight with these predators. It was as if two animals had allowed themselves to be cut off from the herd and were now being stalked by wolves.

Koesler felt they would be lucky to be merely robbed. Yet he saw no alternative to playing this out and seeing what would happen. Though he was extremely apprehensive, he tried to act casual for his own sake as well as Marvin's.

The two priests reached the corner of Adams and Woodward. Across the street was Grand Circus Park, beneath which was the parking garage, and safety—if they could reach it.

Ordinarily, they would have crossed with the light at the corner. But Koesler opted for a shortcut. He nudged Marvin to jaywalk toward the center of the Adams block and the ramp leading down to the garage.

They turned sharply to the right. Koesler glanced back. The young man also turned right. Now there was no doubt: He was following them. Whatever was going to happen would happen in just a few moments.

But something else was happening. The car did not turn right. It continued south on Woodward. That unexpected event was followed by another. The young man veered off and followed in the direction of the car.

Surprised, both Koesler and Marvin stopped to see what was going on.

They saw a marked blue and white Detroit police car, which had unobtrusively pulled up behind the other car. The officer had turned on neither siren nor flashing lights. But the police car had been spied by the driver of the car following the priests. And when the young man noticed his companions veering off, he also abandoned the chase.

For a brief instant Koesler thought the single officer in the car might give them a ticket for jaywalking. He would have welcomed one considering what the policeman had saved them from. But the blue and white simply glided by, the officer therein neither smiling nor showing any sign of concern. Probably he too was glad nothing had happened.

The two priests hurried to Koesler's car. Koesler paid the dollar parking fee, then drove up the exit ramp. Both men looked in every direction. They were not being cautious of other traffic as much as making sure their potential muggers were nowhere in sight. Coast clear, they headed in the direction of the restaurant.

Well on their way, Marvin spoke. "Thank God for the Detroit police!" It was said with fervor and sincerity. Thereafter, neither spoke.

McNiff and Mulroney had arrived at the restaurant only moments before Koesler and Marvin. It was late in the evening and this was one of the few eateries still open and offering everything from a snack to a full dinner. There were three main dining rooms, only one designated as nonsmoking. At this hour, that meant little; heavy smoke hung almost motionless everywhere.

Most of the tables were empty; the quartet was seated almost immediately. It took several moments for their eyes to become accustomed to the soft lighting and the smoke. When they were able to see more clearly, McNiff immediately observed, "You guys look like you saw a ghost!"

"Damn right!" Marvin answered. "The 'ghosts' almost were us!"

There followed a graphic, detailed, and somewhat embellished narration of their memorable if brief stroll down Woodward. As he told the story, Marvin grew progressively more animated as well as more resentful of Koesler's penny-pinching style that almost got both of them murdered.

Following this, there was general agreement—Koesler dissenting—on the danger of Detroit streets, especially after dark.

Responding to one of Koesler's attempts to diffuse so sweeping an indictment of the city, McNiff countered, "What about that *News* reporter, Salden? What does that say about your safe streets? Here's a guy just trying to do his job. And the job is covering religion, for God's sake! And he gets killed!"

"Not too good an example, Pat." Mulroney, it was generally acknowledged, was well read and well informed on current affairs. "According to reports I've read, whoever shot Salden wasn't firing at random."

"No?" When challenged, McNiff tended to react defensively.

"No," Mulroney responded calmly. "It seems that all the shots—or all the shots that can be accounted for—hit Salden. The other people who were wounded were hit by bullets that went right through Salden."

Marvin shuddered. "Do you mind? Koesler and I just went through an experience where we might have been used for target practice. I'd just as soon not talk about how bullets go through bodies."

Koesler seconded the motion. He was no more eager than Marvin to converse about murder. "There's tonight's play."

"Yeah . . . doesn't it make you feel good to know that one of the brethren wrote it?" McNiff said.

With that, their waitress arrived, looking the worse for wear. She appeared quite elderly. Her white stockings hung loosely from swollen legs and ankles. Her wispy white hair was frazzled. One could be forgiven for wondering why she continued working this late at night, if indeed at all. One could only assume she really needed the money.

"Get you something to drink?" Putting her weight on her left leg, she listed to port.

McNiff ordered a manhattan, the others beer. The waitress shuffled off.

"Yeah," Marvin picked up McNiff's observation, "imagine a Detroit priest getting a play he wrote staged at the Fox!"

"He deserved the break," Koesler said. "*A Consequence of Heritage* is a good play. Humor, conflict, a gentle touch, even a bit of tragedy. And did you notice in the program notes that Cliff mentioned how even though his play is about a Polish family, it could be understood as being indicative of any ethnic group?"

"I'd agree," Mulroney said. "The tendency is to think of it as a slice of Polish life, because that's the way it's presented. But, with minor changes, it could portray almost any ethnic group. And even at that I wonder if it has to be ethnic."

The waitress returned with their drinks. "Ready to order?" She shifted her weight to her right foot and listed to starboard.

"How's the soup?" Mulroney asked.

"Like water. It was better earlier. Don't order it now."

The four were surprised at her candor. They all grinned.

"Okay," Mulroney said, "I'll have the deluxe hamburger, well done."

"You don't want it well done," she replied. "It'll be like shoe leather. Get it medium."

"Uh . . ." Mulroney was not sure how to respond. ". . . but I . . . well, okay, if you say so."

"And," she added, "don't get it deluxe. By this time the French fries are greasy. Get cottage fries. And don't get them on individual orders; get an order for the whole table."

By now, the priests were laughing heartily.

Their laughter did not seem to affect their waitress one way or the other. But she pretty well managed to order dinner for all of them, one by one.

After she left, Koesler returned to the topic at hand. "Getting back to Mo's question about whether the play had to be ethnic; I think it not only had to be ethnic, but also a slice of the past. I mean, the kind of home life Ruskowski is portraying seems to me to be typical of what we had in the thirties and early forties, but certainly not sustained after World War II."

"No, no." McNiff stirred the ice in his drink with his index finger. "I've seen lots of families like that."

"Lately? Come on!" Koesler said. "There were only two sets in the entire play. The principal set was the home. A living room took up almost the whole stage with one upstairs bedroom where Grandma just lay in bed with her back to the audience waiting to die. Her granddaughter comes home and has to put on a nun's veil to visit Grandma who hasn't been told that the girl left the convent years ago. And the other set was the grandson's room in a rectory. How many families do you know of today with two kids, one a nun, at least previously, the other a priest?"

"Okay," McNiff conceded, "maybe not a priest and a nun, not anymore. But that wasn't the point. The fact that the kids had religious vocations was incidental to the point of the play. It was this close-knit family that depended on each other. And that's not uncommon anytime."

"I didn't think they depended on each other so much as they devoured each other," Marvin said.

"Now, pay attention," Koesler admonished McNiff. "Frank used to review plays for the *Detroit Catholic*."

McNiff, grinning, drew a large imaginary circle, then mimed someone dealing playing cards.

Marvin laughed. "Okay, I get it: big deal!" He nodded. "Maybe so. But remember Grandma up on the shelf: Everyone and everything eventually had to revolve around that still, silent figure. That signified the unhealthy relationship that bound that family together. There wasn't much free choice going on there."

"Yeah," Koesler agreed, "Grandma was the central character of that play. She was the patron saint of that family. That is, she was the saint until she spoke her last words—which were also her first words in the play."

"There goes the ethnic thing again," Marvin said. "She cried out much the same as Christ did on the cross. But her last words were in Polish. Which the mother first translated as 'Father, into Thy hands I commend my spirit.' But to her priest son, she admitted that Grandma's last words were, 'Shit! I don't want to die!' And there went her sanctity."

"Oh, I don't know," Koesler said through his laughter, "like the priest grandson said in the play—minus the vulgarity—that's about what Christ said through his torment and death: 'I don't want to die.'"

"Even including the vulgarity," Marvin said, "there's no reason why that should argue against her cause for sanctity. It doesn't seem to be hurting Clem Kern."

Koesler choked on his beer.

No one reacted immediately, but as the choking continued, McNiff began to pound Koesler on the back, perhaps more vigorously than necessary.

Koesler waved him away as the breathing passage cleared.

It wasn't news to Koesler that Monsignor Clem Kern had been nominated for sainthood. When his cause had been initiated years earlier, it had been big news, and played as such by the media. But that was a long while ago. And at the time, Koesler had subconsciously packed the item away in the recesses of his awareness. After all, wasn't the aphorism something to the effect that one should be slow with unqualified praise after the manner of the Church, which didn't canonize people until some three hundred years after their death? Since Monsignor Kern had been dead not even twenty years, Koesler had given the cause little thought. Even when Guido Vespa confessed the bizarre entombment of Father Keating with Clem Kern, Koesler hadn't adverted to the ongoing cause for sainthood.

"You okay?" McNiff wondered.

"I'll be all right," Koesler wheezed. "Just went down the wrong way."

"Clem Kern wasn't vulgar!" McNiff turned back to Marvin.

Marvin grinned. "He could be earthy when the occasion demanded."

"Besides," McNiff said, "what chance has old Clem got? A parish priest from Detroit? Now, if he'd been a martyr . . ."

"Not so," said the resourceful Mulroney. "It's not all that out of the question . . . at least not today."

Their salads arrived. There were no further drink orders, and their lugubrious waitress departed.

"For the last thousand years," Mulroney continued, "Popes have been doing the canonizing all by themselves. Officially, since A.D. 1234—an easy date to remember. But the point is, in all this time there have been less than three hundred saints named."

"So?" McNiff said.

"So," Mulroney replied, "in 1988 alone the present Pope named 122 saints. So he likes saints; that's obvious. He can and he does make lots of them. As a matter of fact, he kind of prods the Congregation for the Causes of Saints to keep the machinery going. As we all know, just from watching TV, the Pope gets around. For centuries, the Popes were the self-proclaimed 'prisoners of the Vatican.' Well, Paul VI got around pretty good. But he was a stay-at-home compared with our current guy. And, usually, when he visits a country, he likes to make one or more of the natives a saint.

"Say, for instance, he were to come to the States again—"

"Spare me," Marvin interjected. "Have we finished paying for his last visit yet?"

That brought an appreciative laugh.

"Seriously," Mulroney continued, "if he came back to the States, he'd probably want to name a saint or two. Why not good old Clem Kern?"

"Because, for one thing, Solanus Casey is ahead of him," Marvin observed.

"Well," Mulroney said, "a doubleheader then. Casey and Kern."

"Both from Detroit? You've gotta be kidding!" Marvin said.

"Not Kern!" McNiff said authoritatively.

"Why not?" Marvin wanted to know.

"He's just not the stuff saints are made of," McNiff insisted. "Okay, so he was good with bums. Better than I could be, I'll admit. But giving bums a meal ticket just ain't the way to become a holy saint."

"Pat, you're not putting down the works of mercy!" Koesler by now was recovered from the shock of being reminded that Clem Kern, who was sharing a room with Jake Keating, was by no means completely forgotten.

"What?" McNiff reacted.

"Give food to the hungry, drink to the thirsty, shelter to the homeless; visit the sick, the imprisoned; bury the dead," Koesler enumerated. "Those are the things that Clem did best and, according to Christ, that's how you get into heaven. Or, absent all these things, how you get into hell."

"Besides," Marvin added, "Clem wouldn't let anybody refer to them as bums. They were 'gentlemen of the road.' At least that's what Clem insisted on calling them."

Somehow, everyone seemed to be zeroing in on McNiff. Which is how most of these priestly outings usually ended.

"Frank's right," Mulroney said. "Clem didn't just give his 'gentlemen of the road' a good word and a pat on the back. He had an arrangement with some of the local motels to house the gentlemen and send the bill to him."

It was cottage industry time for Clem Kern memories. The harvest of stories had begun. Koesler approved. Monsignor Kern had been so much an embodiment of the Gospel message that it was helpful to remember his goodness. It was, indeed, the memory of this compassion that had motivated Guido Vespa to provide Clem with a companion into eternity. *If only these guys knew what I know!*

But of course they never would.

"Remember," Marvin said, "when Clem figured that though there were lots of places to send recovering alcoholics in the AA plan, there weren't many places for just plain drunks? So he began the process of buying a flophouse in the neighborhood. Some of the small-time merchants in the area objected. So they went to court. And the judge asked Clem, 'Does anybody in your facility have a history of venereal disease?'

"Clem thinks about that for a while. Then, in that droll drawl of his, he says to the judge, 'Well, Your Honor, I don't believe we include that question on any form we asked the people to fill out. But I suppose in any facility that takes care of a large number of men, you could probably find some history of venereal disease. Perhaps in the Detroit Athletic Club, for instance.'

"And the judge says, 'Father Kern, *I* am a member of the Detroit Athletic Club.' And Clem says, 'Yes . . .'"

"Then there was the time," Mulroney jumped in, "when there was a Playboy Club in Detroit and the bunnies went on strike against the club. In the next day's papers, there was Clem Kern, clerical suit and all, bundled up against the cold, walking the picket line and carrying a strike sign right along with the bunnies."

"Now," McNiff objected, "you can't think it's a sign of high virtue to be picketing for the rights of naked"—he always pronounced it "nekid"—"women to wait on tables!"

"He wasn't campaigning for nudity, Pat," Koesler said. "The girls claimed they weren't getting a fair share of the tips. Clem was campaigning for justice."

"Justice!" McNiff snorted. "That's not what the people think. They think he's just parading with naked women."

Everyone but McNiff was laughing.

"First of all," Koesler corrected, "they weren't 'nekid.' It was the middle of winter and everybody was pretty well covered up. And everybody knows Clem was virtually the patron saint of labor. My God, he was practically the chaplain of the Teamsters."

"Weren't you tied up in the middle of that once?" Marvin asked.

Koesler smiled. "Happened while I was at the *Detroit Catholic*. Our one janitor, who also drove a truck, joined the Teamsters. All of a sudden I found myself bargaining with the Teamsters.

"Now, I've got nothing against the Teamsters, but the *Detroit Catholic* newspaper versus the Teamsters was David and Goliath all over again. Except that we didn't even have a sling or a stone. So, in a sort of desperation, I called Clem and asked if he could intercede for us. He asked who I was bargaining with and I told him the guy's name. And Clem said, 'Oh, I know Claire very well. He always has me say Mass daily when he's negotiating.'

"So I asked Clem how many Masses he was going to say for the Teamsters so I could say the same number against them."

Even McNiff joined in the laughter.

"Needless to say," Koesler concluded, "Clem didn't ask them to call off the hounds and we didn't win that one."

The waitress brought their entrees. She more or less plopped the plates before each of them. It was not an encouraging presentation. However, having taken on faith the presumption that she had saved them from watery soup, leatherish meat, and greasy potatoes, her absence of charm did not foreordain a diminished tip.

As they began eating, Marvin said, "He didn't take his monsignorship seriously. That alone should argue for his heroic virtue."

That brought a smile to everyone.

"I'll say," Koesler added. "At his own installation ceremony, he arrived at the cathedral late, and he was wearing borrowed monsignorial robes."

"I don't get it," McNiff complained. "All these qualities that you guys seem to think were cute as well as virtuous, were flaws in character. Sure he was late for his own investiture. But he was late for everything. He was late all the time. He smoked too much. And he was a terrible driver. In fact, that's what killed him: a traffic accident."

"Well, you're right about one thing, Pat," Mulroney said, "you *don't* get it. Sure he died as a result of a traffic accident. But no one else was injured. How typical of Clem Kern; he wouldn't hurt anyone else for the world. Remember the time the con artist hit him up until Clem gave him some money? Another priest who had witnessed the guy's performance—which was so implausible even the visiting priest could see through it—couldn't figure why a priest as streetwise as Clem would fall for something so transparent. And Clem just lit up a cigarette and grinned and said, 'I didn't want him to think he was losing his touch.'

"See, he didn't even want to hurt a con man.

"The point is, Pat," Mulroney continued, "that people like Clem Kern seem to be just what this Pope is looking for. And if the Pope is looking for something specifically, you can bet the Congregation for the Causes of Saints is looking for the same thing. And what the Pope wants—along with the traditional martyrs and the like—are individuals that ordinary people can identify with. And Clem Kern, with his smoking, his tardiness, and his lousy driving habits was a person a lot of people could identify with.

"Then, on top of that, you've got a guy who practically invented the corporal works of mercy. After his wake, at his funeral—altogether attended by some twenty-five thousand people, all of whom considered themselves personal friends of Clem—Frank Angelo, late of the *Detroit Free Press,* said that Clem Kern made Detroit a sweeter place to be. What could be a better tribute! Personally, I think he's going to make it!"

They ate in silence for a while.

"Wait a minute . . ." Marvin had evidently experienced a sudden doubt; his fork was suspended between plate and mouth. "I haven't got any solid evidence or proof—only hearsay—but, isn't it kind of expensive? I mean, the whole process. I've heard that there are a lot of expenses. I can't pin it down right now, but I know I've heard somebody say that. In fact, if memory serves, that is supposedly why so many religious order priests and nuns have been canonized and so few diocesan priests make sainthood. The religious orders can commit funds from their conglomerate treasure—which in large orders like the Franciscans or the Dominicans or the like can be a considerable fortune.

"But diocesan priests have—what?—a relatively small territory like Detroit or Chicago or even New York or L.A., where money is always tight. Isn't that so? And if it is, what chance has Clem Kern got? I can't see this archdiocese throwing a whole bunch of money at a process of canonization. For Pete's sake, the outcome isn't even certain. And on top of everything else, Clem Kern managed to stay rock bottom poor. Does anybody know? Is this expense thing true?"

There was no immediate response. Finally, Koesler said, "I don't really know. But I've heard the same thing."

Mulroney, making ready to address the question, laid his fork on the plate. "It's true. It is expensive by almost anyone's measure. In Rome, the talk is it's in the ballpark of fifty to a hundred thousand dollars. And that doesn't even take into consideration the significant cost of the celebration at the end of the whole process.

"But, to come up with an actual figure, you might be interested in another American, Mother Elizabeth Seton. The final tab on her canonization, from initiation to conclusion—including the whole formal process, renting fifteen thousand chairs from the Vatican, printing the souvenir programs; tickets, flowers, an official painting, and so forth—the bottom line was in excess of $250,000. And if you think that's breathtaking, Katharine Drexel's bill was $333,250!"

McNiff couldn't help himself; he whistled, softly, but enough to turn several heads at nearby tables. "Where would we ever get that kind of money!"

"Not from the archdiocese of Detroit!" Koesler said without fear of correction.

"No," Mulroney agreed, "not from the archdiocese. Not in a million years. But—and I'm not sure whether to be surprised or not—but it is coming in. Some in dribs and drabs—nickels and dimes from the 'gentlemen of the road.' And some thousands of dollars from the better-heeled downtown executives and firms—the very people Clem used to hit up for the cash that flowed from them through Clem to the poor.

"No, money, oddly enough, may not be as big a problem as we might think. If you recall, money was never a significant problem for Clem: He never had any. But it never was a problem. Example: One day a woman came to him with a seven-hundred-dollar gas bill that she couldn't pay. Clem didn't have a penny. But he told her to go home and he would take care of it. A little later that same day, some people from Grosse Pointe gave him a check for $750. And that's the way it went for him. He was indifferent about money personally. But he always got it and he always gave it away."

"Just a second . . ." McNiff was gesticulating with his fork. Happily there was no food on it. "Has it dawned on any of you that Mo has one hell of a lot of familiarity with the process of canonization and Clem Kern's chance for it?"

"Yeah," Marvin agreed. "We know you come up with an awful lot of arcane information, but this is out of the ordinary even for you. I mean, knowing how many saints have been canonized in the past thousand years, the A.D. 1234 date when Popes took over, how many saints were named by the present Pope in a given year, and—save the mark—how much it cost to make Drexel and Seton saints . . . did you bone up on this just for tonight's conversation? And how in hell could you know we were going to get going on Clem and sainthood?"

"Wait a minute, wait a minute," Koesler interjected. "It was Mulroney who got us started talking about Clem. We were discussing the play we saw tonight and Mo shifted the conversation." Koesler beamed as if he had won a contest.

Marvin shook his head in disbelief. "Even then . . ."

Mulroney smiled. "Both charges are true. I did steer the conversation and I did hit the books, but not just for tonight's get-together."

"So what's up?" McNiff wanted to know.

Mulroney couldn't help showing pride. "I'm part of the process. I was named about six months ago but it wasn't to be announced until now—or, rather, next week. But I wanted to tell you guys before it hit the news. Just keep it to yourselves until the beginning of next week when the announcement's made."

"No kidding! No kidding!" McNiff seemed unable to get over the news. "I can't believe it. I never thought I'd know somebody who worked on a canonization. What happens next—you go to Rome? Are you the devil's advocate?"

Mulroney laughed. "No, I don't go to Rome. And I'm not *advocatus diaboli*. As a matter of fact, along with a lot of other streamlining, they did away with the devil's advocate." Although, thought Mulroney, from all that had been said during this dinner, McNiff easily could qualify for the position naturally. "What they've got now, instead of lawyers, postulators, and devil's advocates, is a relator, who gets a lot of help composing what is in effect a biography of the individual—the servant of God—containing the good as well as the bad. The relator picks a collaborator to actually write the document, called a *positio*.

"The collaborator's usually from the same diocese as the candidate and is supposed to be trained in the historical-critical method and also in updated theology. And . . ." Mulroney paused. ". . . the collaborator in the case of Monsignor Clement Kern is Father James Mulroney." He finished with a vocal flourish.

"No kidding!" McNiff was very impressed. "You're a . . . a . . ."

"Collaborator," Mulroney supplied.

"Sounds like a role out of World War II," Koesler said. "Are you going to be involved in some sort of war crimes trial after the canonization?"

Mulroney chuckled. "Only if Clem doesn't make it."

McNiff was so impressed he seemed to have forgotten all about his dinner, which was only half-eaten. "You've been a collaborator for months? What have you been doing? Do you get to talk to the Pope?"

Mulroney kept smiling. He'd anticipated that McNiff would be most bedazzled by the news. "No, I don't get to talk to the Pope. Maybe someday but not yet. And what have I been doing? Just going about my job very, very quietly. We've got to gather everything we can find that Clem wrote. That's important to the process. We've got to put together anecdotes, like the ones you guys were telling tonight. Thank you very much."

"Don't you have to find some miracles that you can attribute to Clem?" McNiff asked.

"Getting all that money donated might be one of them," Marvin said. The others found this humorous.

"I don't care what you guys think," McNiff said. "This is exciting. Imagine: Having a priest we all knew so well become a saint!

"But Mo, how come you're going to be public with your job now? What's the occasion?"

"Actually, we have no choice. We've got to make what we're doing public. It's the next step in the process. We have no alternative. It's at this stage that we are bound by the rules to make certain of his identity. We've got to make certain that, when we get done with this business, we've got the right person."

"You mean . . ."

"That's right," Mulroney completed Marvin's thought, "we're going to exhume the body."

"Bob! Bob! Are you all right?" McNiff began once again pounding Koesler's back.

Once again a liquid had gone down the wrong way and Koesler had begun to choke. In a few moments his struggle for air seemed successful; his wheezing subsided.

"Be careful, Bob," Marvin admonished, "your food is not supposed to kill you. At least not that suddenly."

"Anyway," Mulroney continued, "the bottom line is that I'm going to be able to invite just a few people to witness the exhumation and the ritual surrounding it. It may very probably be a once-in-a-lifetime opportunity. So how about it? You guys game?"

Marvin and McNiff accepted enthusiastically. Koesler, tears streaming down his cheeks from the choking fit, was able only to nod. *Just try to keep me away from that one! If you think the money pouring in is a miracle, wait till you see who, uninvited, is sharing Clem's final resting place.*

15

THIS WAS where it had all started. The cataclysm known as the Detroit Riot of 1967 began in a building just a few doors north of St. Agnes Catholic Church.

At that time, Zoo Tully had lived in this neighborhood. He recalled the event very clearly. He remembered how the police had reacted to the rioting. Some were able to relate and more were incapable of relating to the black community that inhabited the fringes of the New Center area, which encompassed the golden-domed Fisher Building and General Motors headquarters, as well as bordering on Harper Hospital and the Cultural Center. That experience had cemented his resolve to join the police force and make a difference.

Now Zoo Tully and Phil Mangiapane were standing on the sidewalk outside St. Agnes Church on Twelfth Street, now better known as Rosa Parks Boulevard.

The street was all but deserted. But Tully could well imagine what it had been like when, a little more than a week ago, a riotous situation had occurred right here. Though much less far-reaching than the '67 conflagration, still it had been a riotous scene nonetheless.

"This is where the guy was standing, Zoo . . . right here." Mangiapane indicated the spot. He had done yeoman's work in catching up with the department's investigation to date. And coming off the time spent looking for Father Keating, there was a lot of catching up to be done.

"The church was packed," Mangiapane continued. "Of course there isn't a hell of a lot of room in there. So the crowd spilled out down the steps and onto the sidewalk here. It was sort of a semicircle with the biggest part of the crowd right here—right in front of the center doors. They had a loudspeaker rigged so the crowd could hear what was going on inside. It was in the middle of all this that Salden bought it."

Tully was struggling to pay attention. He had decided to start from scratch with his investigation of the killing of Harold Salden, religion writer for the *Detroit News*. Familiarizing himself with work already accomplished by Homicide detectives would provide him with a shortcut. Mangiapane and several other members of Tully's squad had absorbed all they could of the progress of the investigation so far. If anything, the officers were a bit surprised that Tully was not already far ahead of them, but then they marveled too that he was not putting in his usual twelve to sixteen hour days.

The reason Tully had not been devoting himself as usual was the same reason he was having difficulty concentrating on Mangiapane's briefing: trouble at home.

Neither Tully nor Alice normally bothered reading Lacy DeVere's column. But when a co-worker had twitted her on the subject, Alice had checked the column and read the item linking Tully with Pat Lennon.

She was not amused.

Initially, Tully couldn't blame Alice. It was a shot out of the blue and it had hit her hard. He agreed that she deserved an explanation. So he had explained—or tried to. He and Lennon had worked on the same case; he to solve a killing, she to write what proved to be an exclusive story. Their parallel efforts had thrown them together. Probably they had been seen together. But, nothing had happened. Where DeVere had come up with that outrageous tidbit was anybody's guess. Nonetheless, it was pure fantasy. Under ordinary circumstances he would have mentioned it to Alice as part of their normal everyday conversation pertaining to what each was doing at work. But Alice had been so ill at the time that normal conversation had become a rarity. And since there had been nothing to it, after Alice had recovered it had simply slipped his mind.

All of which was true, but not totally believably true. Their relationship was scarred by Alice's lingering doubt and Tully's impatience with that doubt.

At long last, Alice said that she believed him. But it didn't take a psychic to detect the incredulity.

The situation was affecting his work, and that was intolerable. His work came first. That was a given. He was growing angry with Alice's suspicions. It was blossoming into a full-blown dilemma for him.

He put extra effort into absorbing what Mangiapane was telling him. "What was the beef again?" he asked. "The meeting was . . .?"

This would be the second time Mangiapane explained the reason for the meeting. He was becoming concerned. "See, Zoo, this priest, the pastor of St. Agnes, announced the Sunday before that he was leaving the priesthood to get married."

"Sounds simple enough. Why the problem?"

"The people who go to church here got really upset. For one thing, there's a pretty good chance that the archdiocese can't or won't send a replacement. Which means they'd probably close the parish. See, they're running out of priests. And the ones they got don't want to take a core-city parish. So the parishioners called the meeting. But then a whole bunch of outsiders showed up, and that's when the trouble started."

"Outsiders?"

"Some of them belong to an organization that wants priests to be able to get married, and the rest are real conservative right-wingers."

The Catholic Church! Tully couldn't seem to get away from it. If this continued, one of these days he would probably become a Catholic by default. "With a crowd like that, weren't there any cops here?"

"Yeah. They even beefed up the personnel when things started getting nasty. But all the action was inside the church. Those two groups got here early, so they were pretty much all inside. The people outside, on the street, were mostly parishioners who got here late, and some gawkers who were attracted by the loudspeakers and the crowd. Salden got here just about on time but everything was jammed. I guess he was trying to get in when he got it."

"Trying? Maybe that's what happened: He pushed some hopheaded trigger-happy dude. It doesn't take much anymore."

Mangiapane shook his head. "Six rounds, all in Salden. The two people who got wounded were hit by slugs that went through him. I suppose it could have been spur-of-the-moment, but it looks premeditated. Some of the people around him said he was just part of the crowd trying to get as close as he could. But he wasn't physical about it at all."

"Okay. I like it better that way. Let's say he was the intended victim. Then, why?"

"Up for grabs, Zoo." Mangiapane consulted his notepad. "No problem that anybody could uncover with his wife. They were close. She broke down when she was informed. She's in St. John's Hospital now, recovering."

"Hmmm. No girlfriend?"

"Not that we can find."

"Who'd want to shoot a reporter? Talk about killing the messenger! And a religion writer at that. Who gets mad at religion writers?"

"The people who were here for that meeting were pretty worked up, Zoo."

Tully considered that for a moment. "Yeah, that's right, isn't it? Any kind of make on the perp?"

Mangiapane smiled. "Everybody went to the bathroom."

Tully smiled, but more grimly. Either because they were afraid or did not want to become involved, lots of witnesses routinely offered unlikely excuses for seeing, hearing, and saying nothing. It was as if, at the crucial moment, the witness insisted he or she was somewhere—anywhere—else. The bathroom would do.

"The few who would talk had pretty contradictory stories. It was a man. It was a woman. He was tall. She was small. About the only points of agreement were that the perp was adult, with a long black coat that could easily conceal the weapon, and a dark hat pulled low over the face."

Tully rubbed his chin. "Sounds like the perp came to do business. Somebody who didn't plan on shooting wouldn't have covered up so completely. No reason to unless you know beforehand that you're going to off somebody."

Mangiapane nodded agreement. "As soon as the shooting started, everybody out here on the street hit the deck. The people inside could hear the shots, but they weren't sure right off what it was. Then within seconds everybody knew what had happened, and—pandemonium. In that time, the perp faded away. It was dark—no moon—and the streetlights here are few and far between. Besides, most of 'em weren't working."

"As usual," Tully commented.

"Right. So when the dust settled, everybody out here got up except three—two wounded and one dead."

"A make on the weapon?"

Mangiapane glanced again at his notes. "MP5-KA4." He was impressed.

So was Tully. A nine-millimeter machine pistol, he reflected. Able to be adjusted to fire either semiautomatically, as a full automatic, or in bursts of three rounds. A very powerful weapon.

"There seemed to be some agreement," Mangiapane said, "that the shooting was *bam-bam-bam, bam-bam-bam*. So he probably geared it to fire in three-round bursts. They were fully jacketed, military-style bullets."

No wonder a couple of others got it, Tully thought. Bullets like that don't deform when they hit, so they tend to go through things—people. Probably had to buy both pistol and bullets somewhere out on the street. That might prove to be a break, out on the street where so many breaks originate. Follow the gun. Trace it, and when you find the last guy who sold it, you find the perp.

Tully verbalized his thoughts. "Probably bought from one of our gunrunners. On the street, at any rate. Manj, see if any of our guys are out there looking for whoever sold it. If they're not on the street, get 'em looking. Get some uniforms on it. Call in some markers. This is the best lead we've got so far."

"Okay, Zoo. Where you gonna be, just in case?"

"For starters, I think I'll go down to the *News*. See if I can pick up something from the paper."

*   *   *

Tully easily could have swung onto the Lodge and sped his return downtown. But he wanted a few minutes to himself for thinking. So he turned down the one-way Fourteenth Street. In any case, when possible he preferred traveling the streets of his city rather than the freeways. State Police patrolled the expressways quite adequately. The streets were his, and he knew them like he knew his own body.

Damn that DeVere broad! His life had been in such a comfortable rut. Alice was well and their life together very satisfying. Work, as usual, was challenging and fulfilling. Since these were the only two areas of his existence that mattered to him, all was well. Until that bitch dredged up that nonexistent affair between him and Pat Lennon.

To be honest, Pat had entered his life at a time when he was in a state of depression. Alice had been suffering from a prolonged and indeterminate illness. In effect, he had found her depression infectious. For the first time in their relationship, he'd found it painful to go home to her. Enter Pat Lennon.

Their paths had crossed in a singles bar. Not technically, but in reality each had cheated in going to that bar. Technically, neither was married. But both Tully and Lennon had "life companions." Except that Tully's was ill and Lennon's had needlessly abandoned her at a critical time.

In truth, something very probably would have happened had Pat not been the morally stronger of the two. Not that she would have shied from an affair with him had there been no extenuating factors. Pat had sensed that he was committed to Alice but that he was physically hungry—not for just anyone, but the "right" woman. And she had refused to compromise his situation.

While that may have been commendable, now, thanks to DeVere, they had the name without the game.

And damn Alice too, while he was at it! Why in hell didn't she have more faith in him? He had never been unfaithful to her. The only time he'd even come close was with Lennon. But the fact remained, he had not strayed.

Still, what if this situation were reversed? What if some gossip columnist had written something implicating Alice and someone else? He found it difficult to imagine. But, what if? If she denied it, would he believe her? Would he believe in her even without a denial?

As it happened, the situation had never arisen. To his knowledge, Alice had never been involved with anyone besides him . . . at least not since their relationship had begun. But . . . what if she had? What if, at very least, someone implied that Alice was interested in seeing someone else? What if she were seen dining . . . or in a car . . . with another man? Would Tully still trust her? Implicitly.

Tully had to smile, at least briefly. He simply couldn't even imagine Alice two-timing him. And if someone were to suggest that she was, he would just refuse to believe it.

Then why in hell couldn't she react to scurrilous innuendo against him in the same way? Wasn't there something in the Bible about do unto others? Or was it, in the jargon of the streets of Detroit, do unto others, then split!

Ah, the streets of Detroit. They had their own language. You had to be savvy enough, alert enough, experienced enough to understand that language.

This guy walking up Fourteenth, the upper torso like Rambo, spindly legs can barely support him, yet a definite swagger to his walk: He's a graduate of Jacktown—Jackson State Prison. He went in there a ninety-eight-pound weakling. He got treated like a toy. Then he started pumping iron. He was really motivated. Eventually, he could break most of his tormentors in two. Mostly, he no longer looked like a fragile boy. He was big. He was powerful. And he had developed the joint swagger.

And he's walking very purposefully. He is definitely going somewhere. He is going to a dope house. If he leaves that house scratching his head, he hasn't scored. He's got to figure out where to go next to find some crack or whatever. If he leaves the house striding securely, he's got his fix. He's got something to do.

Tully shook the image from his mind. This wasn't what he wanted to consider on his way downtown. Damn that DeVere broad! She had proved to be a distraction. Intolerable!

Back to Salden. Was it a random shoot? So common on the streets of so many big cities. So terribly common on Detroit streets. Because somebody wants a classy jacket, a stylish pair of shoes. A drug turf war. A case of mistaken identity. For no good goddam reason at all.

The possibility of senseless murder was a brooding presence almost all the time. Guns were so available. Anyone who owned only one was a virtual pauper. And guns, compared with just about any other weapon, were so surgical. Not the mess that comes with a knife, a hammer, an ice pick, hands around a throat, you name it. Especially with the powerful guns of today, just ride by without stopping and spray a house. Kill everybody in sight, even those out of sight.

And that, of course, was it: The nine-millimeter machine pistol became a weapon of choice if one wished to hit a great number of people indiscriminately. Set the control for automatic fire and spray the crowd. That's the ticket for terrorism or for a spaced-out crazy.

But what if you have a machine pistol, capable of mass destruction, but you pump two bursts, six rounds, into one back? You've got to want that one person very dead. Especially if you use jacketed military bullets. In that case, you not only want the guy very dead, you don't particularly care if somebody else buys it too.

And that is precisely what happened with Salden. Two bursts, six rounds pumped into his back. The killer doesn't specifically want to hit anybody else. If he had wanted to bring down some others, he could easily have sprayed the crowd. No, he wanted Salden. He wanted him so badly he simply didn't care what happened to the slugs after they did the job on Salden. It was as simple as that.

But that's where the simplicity stopped.

Who would want to kill a reporter? A religion writer? And why?

This is what called to him like a siren song. No platter this. A real whodunit. Tully could hardly wait to find the answers. And the answers, he strongly felt, began at the *Detroit News*.

16

THE LOBBY OF THE *Detroit News* always reminded Tully of a high-security mausoleum. The softly lit grayish granite interior suggested little joy and offered little comfort. Behind a no-nonsense counter reigned a receptionist whose prime task seemed to be keeping visitors confined to the lobby unless an employee appointment was confirmed and the employee came to escort the visitor, who was given an identification tag that must be visibly worn at all times in the building.

The only relief from this solemn interior was a series of exhibits from recent *News* triumphs and/or scoops and a souvenir counter.

Tully considered briefly several methods of gaining entree to the newsroom. He could of course show his police identification. However, that did not always carry the clout here that it did with most institutions. And he was not in the mood to play games with the receptionist.

Discarding the confrontational approach, he considered whom he might call on to give him access to what he wanted to investigate.

This thought process took only seconds. Without breaking stride, he approached the receptionist and asked for Robert Ankenazy, one of the features editors and an acquaintance. He did not even bother showing his badge. That would only have complicated what promised to be a simple procedure.

Did Tully have an appointment? He did not, but he was sure Ankenazy would see him. Privately, he hoped only that the editor was in.

Tully spent a few minutes moving from exhibit to exhibit, paying no attention to what was framed on the walls. He was thinking only of what he wished to learn from Salden's working place.

Ankenazy greeted Tully with curiosity more than warmth. The receptionist handed Tully an ID tag. She gave no indication she knew he was a police officer. That was fine.

Once in the elevator, Tully explained his presence, and asked about

Salden's relationship with his co-workers. Ankenazy gave every indication that he had already given considerable thought to this question. But he knew of nothing untoward. To the best of his knowledge, no one in any way coveted Salden's job. Indeed, no one on the staff had or approached having Salden's qualifications for the position of religion writer. In fact, it was going to take considerable time to find a replacement. And when the replacement was found, it would be a while before he or she could come close to approaching Salden's competence.

"So," Ankenazy said as they stood just inside the hall-like structure that was the features department, "what do you want, Zoo?"

"I want to sit at his desk, dig through the drawers, see what he was working on."

"Done!" Ankenazy led the way through the partially staffed room. Many of the staff writers were out on assignments. Those who were there, and neither on the phone nor typing into their CRTs, looked up as Ankenazy and Tully walked through. Tully knew he was being studied. He concluded that reporters were inquisitive. So were cops.

Ankenazy indicated the empty desk that had once been used by Hal Salden. By no means was it the only desk not in use. But because it had last been used by a man who'd been slain, it seemed more a monument than a work site.

Nonetheless, Tully adjusted the chair and sat down. He looked around the room. He wanted to see what Salden saw everyday at work. Who did he see when he looked up from his desk?

Ankenazy identified those who worked at nearby desks, none of whom were presently in the office. None of whom, as far as Ankenazy knew, had any but the most cordial relationship with Salden.

"There was no—or very little—competition for bylines with Hal," Ankenazy explained. "The religion beat is special. Only occasionally is a religion story of general interest. Then you're liable to see a regular staffer covering the story. Regularly, the religion writer ends up covering sectarian news that isn't of much general interest. But that wasn't the case with Hal. He was first a damn good reporter and only secondly was he assigned to the religion beat. That plus the fact that he was able to turn a story that might otherwise be buried on an inside 'religion' page into page-one news. What I mean to say is that Hal was considered one of our most respected writers. And that, coming from his peers, for a guy on the religion desk, is some kind of testimonial."

Tully thought that a significant statement—almost a tribute. He filed it away for future reference.

He started going through the drawers, the single most striking aspect of which was their near emptiness. A small ruler, a gadget for measuring something—probably photos—surprisingly little paper, paper clips and rubber bands that looked as if they'd been there for decades—and a little black book. Just what Tully was looking for—or so he hoped.

He paged through the book. Phone numbers, addresses. From its appearance, Tully guessed the book and its contents were ancient and outdated. This didn't seem to be what he was seeking.

Ankenazy sensed this. "What exactly are you looking for, Zoo?"

"This desk doesn't look like it's even been used in this century. Is this just as it was when Salden was working at it?"

"Uh-huh. Some cops were here right after . . . right after Hal died. But they didn't take anything."

"Didn't he keep any notes? Things he was working on?"

"Sure. That'd be in his basket."

"His what?"

"The CRT there. The word processor. If he had anything going currently, if he just wanted to leave himself some message or reminder, it would more than likely be in there."

Tully stared at the silent screen. "Well, okay. How do I find out what, if anything, is in there?"

"His immediate editor—I'm not the guy—would have his password to get access to the basket. But he's not here just now. Wait a minute; maybe this'll work. Pat!"

She had just entered the room. Tully recognized her instantly, though he hadn't see her in nearly three years.

She approached Ankenazy, a slight smile on her lips. Then she caught sight of Tully and the smile froze.

Pat was obviously completely surprised. It was one of those rare times when she had no comment whatsoever.

Tully tried to gauge the situation. Was this some sort of sick gag? Coming on the heels of the DeVere column, he wondered if someone was putting him on. If so, Pat Lennon was not in on the game. Her surprise seemed most genuine. Either that or she deserved an Oscar.

Ankenazy? Again, he gave no indication that this was a setup on his part.

Perhaps it was a coincidence. Odd; he'd been so obsessed with the gossipy item, his memory so filled with Lennon—and now, here she was.

"Pat's worked with Hal in the past." Ankenazy completely over-looked any sort of introduction; for whatever reason he obviously felt none was necessary. "She'd be as good as anybody to help, or answer questions. I've got some stuff to get organized. So, if it's okay with you . . ."

Tully had expected to be shuttled off to someone else. He had dropped in without an appointment and could not have counted on Ankenazy's being available or even being in. But Pat Lennon? Coincidence? Miracle? Or, always possible, some sort of joke?

"You got a few minutes, Pat?" Ankenazy asked.

"Sure."

"Lieutenant Tully here is investigating Hal's death. He gets carte blanche on any of our resources—library, files, whatever." Excusing himself, Ankenazy left them.

"Well, Lieutenant, what can I do for you?" So she was going to be formal. Maybe, under the circumstances, not a bad idea. However, he wouldn't match her with Miss or Ms. Even without their previous association he would have gone immediately to a first-name basis.

"I want to get inside Salden's head," Tully said, without preamble. "I'm pretty certain this was not a random shoot. Somebody wanted him out. Any ideas, Pat?"

"About who killed him?" She folded her arms and shook her head. "He was a nice guy. What can I say? Sometimes he was kind of hard on this or that religious leader. But—not like that. I can't imagine any of them . . . no." She shook her head again.

From what little he knew of them, Tully thought she might be selling religious leaders a bit short. He could well imagine some threat-ened religious figure getting violent. Who knows; the investigation might turn up something along that line. And if such a thread were to be uncovered, Tully would be ready to follow it up.

"Maybe it'd help if I knew something more about him," Tully said. He remained seated at Salden's desk.

Lennon shifted her weight to her left side and leaned against the desk. The position accentuated the lovely curve from her narrow waist over the full hip to her knee. Tully appreciated the view, one of nature's masterpieces.

"I'll try to give you a thumbnailer."

"As detailed as possible, please."

"Okay," Pat agreed, "something more than a thumbnailer." She pulled up a chair and sat down. "Hal started as a copy boy, right at the bottom, some twenty years ago, long before I got here. He worked his way up to the sports desk and covered most of the local teams. Before his next move, he was the main writer on the Tigers. Then he moved to the city desk. Again he specialized in the local angle—city hall, the council, the mayor, Lansing. He was really very good at everything he did. The next move logically would have been his own column. It's what many of us would like. But he turned it down—to just about everybody's surprise—and asked for the religion beat.

"Of course, in a way, he did get his column, because a personal column sort of goes well with that territory. But the way he covered religion was the same as he covered everything else—thoroughly and professionally. It sure as hell enhanced the value of religious news. It wasn't the Saturday throwaway anymore. I worked with him quite a bit from time to time and I was always proud to be associated with him."

"Sports, the local scene, and religion," Tully summed up. "And no enemies?"

"Some," Lennon admitted. "But if they were at all fair, they had to grant that Hal was objective and evenhanded. Anyway, if you're going to do a job as a reporter, you make enemies. We all do. But we don't expect them to get violent, and 99-plus percent of the time they don't.

"So there's a bit more than a thumbnailer on Hal. Not much of a eulogy. And I feel his loss lots more than I'm expressing. But . . . there you are."

Tully was caught off guard. He had detected no strong emotion in her review of Salden's career. And there was no sign of misty eyes. But he believed her. She probably had been deeply moved by Salden's death. She had to be damn good at controlling her emotions.

"Okay, thanks," Tully said. "One last thing: I was trying to find out what he might have been working on, some of his notes. But . . ." He indicated the partially open desk drawers.

"The notepads?" She smiled. "Those are mostly history. We do take notes, of course, but we usually transfer them to our baskets." She gestured toward the CRT. "That's the basket."

"Ankenazy mentioned that. But it's just a blank screen."

Lennon got up. "If you'll let me in there, I'll see if I can't remember his password."

The desk, the chair, the CRT did not offer much room to maneuver. As Tully stood and tried to trade places with Lennon, they brushed against each other. Lennon's body probably was no softer than any other well-proportioned woman's, but it did indeed seem so. And there was a fragrance that was more than the subtle dab of perfume with which Pat routinely started her day. It was her scent, and it was so distinct he could remember being conscious of it even years back.

Lennon was afraid she might be blushing—something she couldn't remember having done since high school.

It was all so awkward. Three years ago, they had parted friends. Lennon had been aware that Tully's companion had recovered her health, and Tully had to have known that Joe Cox had returned repentant and forgiven. Lennon and Tully's relationship had been a classic friendship wherein either would respond to a need of the other. It was just that over these past few years, such a need had not arisen.

Both Lennon and Tully, though neither expressed it, would have enjoyed this fleeting collaboration had it not been for Lacy DeVere's column item. And though neither expressed it, both felt like telling Lacy DeVere to go to hell.

"Lemmee see now," Lennon said, "I think I remember Hal's password." She tapped the keys and spelled out, HOLY FATHER.

Nothing happened.

She shrugged, tried again, and typed, HOLY SMOKE.

The screen lit up.

"He was a joker," Tully observed.

"He had a sense of humor," Lennon amended. "I'll rummage through here. I've done it before when working with Hal, though not often. If you think he had a peculiar sense of humor, wait'll you try to figure out his unique shorthand. We're inside his mind now. But I haven't the slightest idea of what we're going to find." She tapped more keys.

"I knew there'd be something under 'miracles.' It was one of his favorite slugs. The only other person in the media that I know of who shares Hal's fascination with offbeat religious phenomena is Nelson

Kane over at the *Free Press*. The two of them used to get together from time to time, usually at the Anchor Bar, and try to top each other.

"That's what this story is. Hal told me about it when it came in over the wire. It involves a teenage girl who is allegedly possessed by the devil . . . not that original a story. The essence of it wasn't weird enough all by itself to attract Hal's interest, except for one detail: The girl allegedly had a habit of levitating. She would drift off her bed and float to the ceiling. For that reason, the priest appointed to exorcise her had to be very tall—so he could get her down from the ceiling.

"I can almost hear Hal topping Kane's image-of-Christ-in-the-hot-dog-bun story with the king-size exorcist. He would have had such fun with that one."

Pat was smiling at the idea of the two old war-horse buddies shamelessly pulling each other's leg.

Then she brought herself back to the present. "But that's not what you're looking for."

"It tells me something about Salden, so that's good. But I am looking for something he might have been working on that would cause somebody to want to kill him."

"Right." Lennon continued to feel uncomfortable rummaging through Salden's basket. As if she were invading his privacy. But she was more than eager to help find his killer. She tapped more keys.

"Here's one," she said. "Granted I'm not sure I can read all these shorthand notes accurately. But this one looks like some sexism popping up at St. Andrew Episcopal Church in Rochester. As I recall, that church just recently got its first female priest, who also happened to be called to be its rector. That was a lot for some parishioners to swallow. I think this is the one Hal had in mind with this notation."

"A conflict," Tully said. "If he was working on this story, he put himself in the middle of some pretty strong feelings . . . no?"

"Probably."

"A guess might be—especially since the story was under the . . . whatchamacallit of 'sexism'—"

"Slug."

"Yeah, the slug . . . of 'sexism'—that he would have been in a position to defend the woman priest."

"He would be. Yes. He wouldn't treat the story with his opinion showing. But he could slant it in his column. That is, if I'm right that this is the story he's referring to in this note."

"So those who oppose her becoming rector would be angry to damn mad. They might have no reasonable outlet for their anger at, say, their bishop or priests. So maybe they direct it at a reporter?"

"Could be," Lennon admitted. "But, see here—at the end of this note—there's a 'K' standing all alone. I don't know what that means. But it meant something to Hal, or he wouldn't have added it to the note."

"Well, we'll put that on the back burner. Anything else in there?"

Pat began tapping keys as the information in the CRT kept marching across the screen. Nothing appeared to Pat to be of any consequence. Then she stopped typing and seemed to be studying the screen.

"Something?" Tully asked.

"I don't know. There's an emphasis line and an exclamation mark here. Very unlike Hal."

Tully studied the screen, not really knowing what he should be looking for—or at. "Whatta we got?"

"Just some words: 'shells, just shells! look into . . . trace down! could be key!' Then again, off to the side there, another 'K.' But I still don't know what that might mean."

"Hmmm . . ." Tully tried to decipher. Something was knocking at the back of his consciousness. "Wait a minute. Didn't you say Salden used to work on the sports page?"

"Yeah. A long time ago."

"But it was part and parcel of him, wasn't it? You said he was completely committed to whatever he was working on . . . right?"

"Yes."

"There's a symbol in baseball for a strikeout: the letter 'K.' That's what this might be? That he struck out on these stories?"

"Could be. That would be just like Hal: mixing metaphors, so to speak. But that leaves us with nothing but the oversize exorcist. And that definitely is not what you were looking for."

Tully thought for a moment. "Anything else come to mind, Pat?"

Lennon ransacked her mind. "Noooo . . ." She drew out the "no" to an elongated syllable. "There's the story about the missing priest. It's Pringle McPhee's story at the moment. It would have been Hal's. But that's the horse before the cart: Hal was murdered before the priest turned up missing."

"That's it?"

Lennon hesitated. "I . . . uh . . . might just as well ask you: How did that DeVere column go over with your Alice?"

Tully winced all but imperceptibly. "Not so hot. I'll know better if ever she starts talkin' again. And your Joe Cox?"

"He's out of town." She did not care to add, "probably permanently."

"It would be interesting to know how he'd react to it. He's always been the one with the roving eye. I wonder how he'd feel if the shoe were on the other foot—even if it wasn't true."

Tully made to leave. "Seems like you and I got the name without the game."

"Yeah," Pat agreed. "It's a lucky thing you're the one who packs the gun. I think I'd shoot her."

For the first time this morning, Tully smiled broadly. It was an engaging smile. "I think you'd have to get in line, Pat. Thanks for your time."

"Sorry I couldn't be more help."

He left. Lennon, rocking gently in Salden's chair, watched as he walked away. All his mannerisms reflected his personality. The way he walked, his speech patterns, his bearing, his rare smile, all spoke of a person brimming with self-confidence. It was not the posturing of a braggart. It was the quiet statement of a dependable, mature adult.

Take that, Joe Cox!

Tully turned the corner and was gone. Lennon thought of what he'd said: The name without the game. *The name without the game.*

Interesting.

17

THE BOX containing the mortal remains of Monsignor Clement Kern had been unearthed. Evidently that was enough for that day. The grand opening of the casket had been postponed.

Meanwhile, the unopened casket rested on a bier in the nave of the church just outside the sanctuary. And the church, quite naturally, was that of The Most Holy Trinity in old Corktown where Clem Kern had been assigned for thirty-four years.

Tradition has it that when the Lodge Freeway was constructed, linking Detroit's northern extremities to downtown, the highway was supposed to go right through the site of Trinity Church. This prospect made Cardinal Edward Mooney, then archbishop of Detroit, a happy man. Trinity long had been a financial loser and a drain on archdiocesan funds. Mooney was said to have been ecstatic over the proposed demolition of the building. Some thought the Cardinal himself would come and bless the bulldozer that would do the deed.

Then, according to the story, a city councilperson, who would live in infamy in Mooney's heart, spoke up to save the little parish that had been there when the Irish immigrants circled their wagons around it and later when the poorest of the poor had huddled within it for warmth, shelter, and sustenance. The courageous councilperson won out. And now, when motorists tool down the Lodge, they relive that administrative fiat as they head directly toward the little old church, only to veer off eastward at the very last moment. Trinity survived, to be transformed by the selfless ministry of Clem Kern into a monument for the ages.

It was now the third day since the casket had been removed from the earth of Holy Sepulcher Cemetery. It was the day as well as the hour when the casket would be opened.

The prime purpose for this otherwise ghoulish enterprise was to establish, insofar as it was possible, that the body of the man who might one day be venerated as a true saint actually was the body of the Servant of God in question.

There was another reason. There was always the possibility that in the process, the exhumers just might stumble upon another miracle. In the past, there had been some marvelous discoveries at this stage in the process of canonization. Sometimes the body was found in a remarkable—miraculous?—state of preservation.

St. Catherine of Siena as well St. Clare of Assisi were cases in point. Enshrined within altars in their respective hometowns, they looked as good as new after centuries of inanimation—or so it is said.

Then there's the blood of St. Januarius, which liquifies each year on the anniversary of his death, until last year. Still, not a bad track record.

And, among many surprisingly preserved saints, there's the case of St. Francis Xavier. He died on a small island off the coast of China. His associate buried him on the spot, taking the trouble to throw quicklime over the body. Later, after scraping away the soil and lime, Francis's body was discovered to be remarkably lifelike, even supple. He was to be entombed in the wall of the cathedral in Goa. Workers found the hole in the wall not quite deep enough. So they simply forced the body into the space, breaking the neck in the process. Francis Xavier's body is still on display. It is, by now, quite mummified. But, considering all that was inflicted upon the poor remains, he's holding his own.

Such incidents provide the special excitement and promise inherent in a canonical exhumation. One never knows in what condition one is going to find the Servant of God.

Of course, modern methods of embalming, the better-made caskets and vaults can muddy the matter. In today's world, is a well-preserved body a sign of God's favor to the deceased? Could it be a miracle, or could it be the miracle of modern technology?

Whatever.

Still there was the undeniable thrill of anticipation. What would Clem Kern look like these many years since his death and burial? Those strong of stomach, at least, wanted to know. It didn't much matter in the final analysis whether he had been preserved or not. If he were well preserved, in all probability it would not be accepted as miraculous. Clem would have to come up with something clearly spectacular on his own. However, in the eyes of many of his old buddies, it would be good to see him again.

However, not all of his buddies could be present for the viewing, not by any means. The viewers were there by invitation only. And there weren't many of them. There were, of course, representatives of the mortuary industry. There were heads of archdiocesan commissions and committees. There were a few who were invited but for squeamish reasons had declined. There was Cardinal Mark Boyle, who, as the local bishop, had authored the original petition to Rome to start this case. Finally, there was Father Mulroney, and his three friends, Fathers Marvin, McNiff, and Koesler.

As the "relator's collaborator," Mulroney was pretty much running this paraliturgical event. He had led an appropriate hymn and offered some appropriate prayers. He had held a copy of some of these specially prepared prayers for Cardinal Boyle to read aloud. The Cardinal had spread some sweet-smelling incense over the burning coals in the thurible. He had walked around the casket, sprinkling it with holy water. He had retraced his steps around the casket, swinging the thurible back and forth, filling the small church with the aroma of incense. Some of those present, Koesler included, rather hoped that the aroma might modify whatever smell there might come from the casket once it was opened after years in the ground.

In fact, the process of raising the lid was going on right now. Inspired by the preceding elaborate ceremony, the morticians were taking their sweet time in getting the lid off. They were sort of winging their own paraliturgy in an area wherein none had been composed by anyone.

An unmistakable air of expectancy permeated the small group.

Wayne County's medical examiner had not been invited. He might have been the only one to whom this was old hat. The morticians present had some slight experience with exhumations, though never in the case of one who might be named a saint. As to the rest, emotions ranged from dread to morbid interest.

The only one who felt completely ambivalent was Father Koesler. He was pleased that Clem Kern was finally being given the sort of respect and attention that rightfully should be his. On the other hand, he was apprehensive about what he knew would be found in that casket.

Meanwhile, the morticians continued to fiddle with the fasteners that needed to be loosened before the entire lid could be removed.

"If they ever get that damn thing off, I don't think we'll be able to see what's left of Clem for all this smoke," Father Marvin said in a stage whisper.

"Don't get me wrong," McNiff stage-whispered in return, "but I don't see what's taking them so long." He turned to Father Mulroney, and, still whispering, said, "I really am glad you invited us for this ceremony, although we won't be able to tell our grandchildren about it. But how long is this supposed to go on?"

Mulroney smiled. "It shouldn't be much longer," he whispered. The four priest friends were standing close enough together to communicate through whispering without unduly disturbing the others. "I wonder what everybody will think when they find that Clem is not alone in there?"

Koesler's eyes popped. He could not believe his ears. "What did you say?" He forgot to whisper, momentarily drawing the attention of the others. Koesler made an apologetic gesture, then repeated the question, this time in the approved stage whisper. "What did you say?"

"I said," Mulroney whispered, "I wonder how many here know that Clem is not alone in there?"

How could Mulroney know?! It couldn't have been through the confessional, or Mulroney would not be bandying the information about so casually. Hadn't Guido made his crime a sacrosanct secret only to Koesler? If Mulroney knew, and if he could be so offhandedly candid about it, why hadn't he told the police long ago? God knows everyone in Detroit who read papers or listened to radio or television knew the police were looking for Father Keating. Koesler clearly was bewildered.

His wondering was brought to a sharp conclusion by a flurry at the casket. Evidently, the morticians had finally undone all the fasteners. But now, they found the casket lid either too cumbersome or too unwieldy for two men to lift. As Father Mulroney stepped forward to help out, he asked his friends to lend a hand.

Marvin and McNiff joined Mulroney immediately. Under ordinary circumstances, Koesler would have helped too. But by now he was not only frozen in place, he had squeezed his eyes shut. Why had he come?! Yet how could he have stayed away?

Until Mulroney said something just a few seconds ago about how Monsignor Kern was not alone in the casket, Koesler had assumed that he and Father Dunn—and, of course Guido Vespa, plus whoever had helped him insert Keating—were the only ones who knew about Father Keating and what would be his penultimate resting place.

Eyes closed, Koesler was unable to gauge the sounds made by the bystanders. However, he had expected a considerably more shocked reaction. He did clearly hear McNiff say, "What the hell is this?" Still, that was hardly the response Koesler had expected from the sight of two cadavers in the same coffin. He opened his eyes.

At first he could see nothing. His eyes had been shut so tightly that upon opening them the light momentarily blinded him. In addition, smoke from the incense continued to pour from the thurible. It was several moments before he was able to focus.

No doubt about it: There was the body of Monsignor Clement Kern.

And nobody else.

And the explanation of Mulroney's allusion to Clem's not being alone as well as McNiff's surprised "What the hell is this?": In the casket, at about the level of Clem Kern's hip, was an unopened bottle of Courvoisier, that extremely pricey cognac. Its position in the casket indicated that someone had slid it in just as the lid was lowered. Apparently, it was meant to accompany the monsignor into eternity. And apparently, Father Mulroney was among the few who knew about it.

But—the essential concern—Koesler carefully counted the bodies. There was one. One body.

Could there be a false bottom? What if Guido and friends had planted Keating beneath Kern somehow? That outside possibility was torpedoed when the morticians removed almost all the padding from the casket, probably searching for any particle of Clem's clothing, or of his body, which might someday become a treasured relic.

As a result of the morticians' digging about, it was clear that, one, there was room in the casket for a couple of—if somewhat cramped—bodies, and two, the body count remained at one.

Unable to grasp the significance of this turn of events, Koesler absently studied the one body available.

It didn't seem that Clem was going to be a self-performing miracle. There was no doubt the remains were that of Clem Kern. All the contours were there. But Clem, in life a small person, had shriveled still more. What skin that could be seen—head, neck, and hands—was dark and discolored. The eyes and cheeks were sunken. There seemed to be some sort of fungus growing there. The body was leathery, seemingly mummified. Someone touched a vestment; it disintegrated. Someone else touched a finger; the nail simply dropped off.

That was enough for Koesler.

He moved away from the casket. It was an easy directional change; everyone else seemed to be closing in on the coffin to see what they might see. So, that quickly, Koesler was alone.

How to put this together? There was no doubt about Guido Vespa's confession. Koesler had not dreamed it. If there were any doubt—and he was not hesitant to doubt himself—there was the testimony of Father Dunn.

Guido had freely and spontaneously confessed not only the murder of Father Keating but the peculiar disposal of Keating's body.

But the body wasn't here. It wasn't anywhere in the casket. Could Guido have gotten the wrong casket? If so, whose? Why would he lie about a thing like that? Why would he lie in confession? To what purpose? The confession was reserved between the priest—himself—Guido Vespa, and God. Dunn's involvement was purely accidental. Between Koesler, Vespa, and God, what would be the point of such a detail if it were a lie? Who was Vespa trying to kid?

Or could it be possible . . . could someone have removed Keating's body? Undoubtedly Vespa had help in digging up that casket. One of his henchmen? Now there was a distinct possibility. One or more of Vespa's sidekicks returns to the cemetery, digs up the casket once again, and takes Keating's body. Where? Why? To blackmail Vespa? Perhaps someone who found out that Church authorities were going to exhume Clem's body. Certainly within the past week or so that was no secret. As the time neared, the media were active in publicizing the event. If one of Vespa's henchmen stole Keating's body, as it were, could he—would he—blackmail Vespa?

Ees a puzzlement, as the King of Siam was wont to say.

There was no point in Koesler's remaining in the church. He wasn't about to force himself to view the body again. In fact, he couldn't understand why the others seemed so fascinated with what was left of Clem Kern.

Nor was there any particular problem with Koesler's leaving. No one appeared to be paying any attention to him whatsoever. So he simply circumvented the crowd and walked out the first door he came to.

There he found a group of clamorous media people who had been barred from the ceremony. Father Mulroney considered the sun-guns, the cameras, the gaggle of newspeople extraneous to the solemnity of this event. They had been promised entree only after the ritual was finished. So, actually, the media people could have entered now, but Mulroney and the others inside had forgotten all about them.

To the media, Koesler was fresh meat; they descended on him in a feeding frenzy.

He was caught off guard. He, too, had forgotten their presence in the outer darkness where there was little weeping but a lot of gnashing of teeth. Questions poured in from every side.

Had he seen the body? Was it miraculously preserved? Was there anything unusual about Monsignor Kern, other than that he was dead? (One had to allow for that sort of question in any media interview.) Were any of those who viewed the body especially moved by the sight? Did anyone faint? Get sick? Of what did the ritual consist? *When could they get into the church and do their goddam job? Didn't anyone in the Catholic Church ever hear of a deadline?*

As far as Koesler could judge, just about every conceivable question had been thrust at him except, Was Father John Keating's body in the coffin with Clem Kern? That was Koesler's question, and he wasn't sharing that with anybody.

Wait. There was one with whom he would be forced to share that question. And that person was waiting most impatiently at St. Joseph's rectory, listening to every newscast. Fruitlessly hoping to learn what or who was sharing Clem Kern's space.

Father Koesler needed to get back to the rectory right away.

*   *   *

Father Nick Dunn was as stunned as Koesler had been to learn that Monsignor Kern was as alone in his casket as he had ever been.

Koesler explained his hypotheses to the other priest: one, that Guido Vespa had lied about depositing the body, or two, that someone had removed Keating's remains sometime after Vespa had interred them with Kern.

After considerable thought, conversation, and cups of coffee—made by Dunn—both priests agreed: Either Guido had lied about this detail—and neither priest could think of any reason for that—or, and more likely, someone, probably someone from the reburial squad, had stolen the body. And why? It had to be some form of blackmail. Possibly the blackmail had its roots in some arcane Mafia tradition. Maybe it had something to do with the contract.

Maybe—and this was Dunn's hypothesis—the contract called for Keating to be buried with Kern. And that, after killing Keating, is exactly what Vespa and his gang had done. Then comes the news that Kern is going to be disinterred. So somebody, not necessarily from Vespa's gang, but somebody who knows the two priests are buried together, steals Keating's body, thus violating the terms of the contract. Now the one who has the body is in control and is in position to blackmail Vespa.

It sounded good. But Koesler was still uneasy over discussing someone's confession with a third party. He realized that some of his feeling was the result of a perhaps overly cautious approach to the seal of confession. After all, neither priest had done anything whatsoever to disturb Vespa's privacy. Both priests had heard the confession and neither priest had revealed the secret of that confession to anyone in any way. Still, it was a foreign feeling to Koesler to share any confessional secret with anyone but God.

Koesler felt it necessary to remind Dunn that they were still dealing with the sacred seal. But in the unlikely event that Vespa had lied about where he buried Jake Keating, even that lie was included as an inviolable secret. Dunn agreed.

At that moment, the phone rang.

Dunn, since he happened to be seated near the phone, answered. "St. Joseph's." He listened briefly, eyes widening. In apparent amazement, he handed the phone to Koesler. "It's for you. I'm not sure, but I think it's Guido Vespa."

"Father Koesler?"

The voice over the phone sounded like that which Koesler had heard through the grill of the confessional. In neither instance was there a whisper. There was the same throaty quality and a strong hint of an Italian-American accent.

"This is Father Koesler."

"This is Guido Vespa. Was you there in the church today when they—whaddyacallit—opened the thing, the coffin?"

"I was there."

"Then you know."

"I know, but I don't understand."

"Yeah. I gotta see you."

"You want to see me? Can you come here, to St. Joseph's, to the rectory?"

"That wouldn't be so hot, Father."

"All right. Then where? When?"

"You know where the Eastern Market is?"

"Sure. Of course. I can walk there easily from here."

"Yeah. Okay. I'll meet you at the southeast corner at 11:30."

"Tonight?"

"Yeah."

Koesler was quite familiar with the locale. At that time of night it would be dark and deserted. The only likely illumination would come from the sparsely placed overhead streetlights—if they were working. He was wary of meeting in such a desolate spot. "Why don't we meet in a more public place? Maybe a restaurant?"

"No. I don't wanna have any people around. And you can't bring nobody. But we gotta meet."

Once again Koesler hesitated. Practical judgment dictated that he refuse the invitation and insist that if they were to meet at all, it would have to be in a much more public place. But experience told him that Guido Vespa would remain adamant and insist on the market for their rendezvous.

Two circumstances influenced Koesler to acquiesce to Guido's insistence. Quite naturally he was more than curious about Vespa's explanation of what had happened. Secondly, Vespa sounded as though he was desperate to talk to the priest to whom he had confessed. The second reason won the inner argument; Koesler could not bring himself to turn down a soul in need. "All right. I'll meet you there."

"Alone."

"I'll be alone."

"Thanks, Father." Vespa broke the connection.

"He wants to meet you tonight?" Dunn had of course heard only Koesler's end of the conversation.

Koesler nodded.

"I'll go with you." Dunn considered that a rather fearless offer.

"Not if you don't want to abort this meeting. The gentleman was quite insistent that I come alone."

"But that—"

"Alone!"

"You'll tell me about it?"

"I certainly hope I have that opportunity."

18

THE DISTANCE from St. Joe's to the market was only a few blocks—albeit long blocks. Father Koesler was sure he could walk there in less than half an hour. Nonetheless, he gave himself a full half hour, leaving the rectory at 11:00 P.M. Koesler also left behind him an anxious Nick Dunn.

Dunn was left at the rectory to "mind the store." Hardly a daunting task since nothing much ever occurred at this hour of night. Of course there was always the possibility of an emergency sick call or a sudden death in one of the condos or apartments. But usually that involved an EMS ambulance and the services of a hospital chaplain.

Father Dunn was left behind because there was no room for him in this enterprise by edict of none but Guido Vespa.

Koesler's thoughts ranged all over creation as he walked briskly up Gratiot toward the market area. He was quite alone on the sidewalk. The few vehicles on the street sped by in a wink.

This sort of isolation engendered apprehension as he skirted one shadowy doorway after another. Anyone could pop out from any doorway, ahead of him or behind. Koesler knew that his clerical collar was little deterrent to a mugger desperate for whatever could buy some crack cocaine to send him into a far more pleasant fantasyland.

Forget the muggers, he thought. My God! He was going to meet a murderer. A man who had, among many other victims, indeed killed a priest! Sometimes, thought Koesler, this soul-in-need philosophy could get a practitioner in trouble. And this, very definitely, qualified as one of those times.

Father Koesler's recent past was overflowing with too many questions and too few answers.

It had been a simple Saturday afternoon. The usual sporadic confessions. Then—Guido. Why had Vespa wandered into St. Joe's for his second-ever confession? Why had he blundered into the "open" side of the confessional? With that simple error, Koesler had seen the penitent. A fifty-fifty chance. If Vespa had only entered the other side, he would have been nothing more than a voice, a whisper. Well, no; he wouldn't have been a whisper. Koesler had tried, without any success, to get Vespa to speak sotto voce.

Then another turn of bad luck having Father Dunn happen in just then. Just in time to overhear Vespa's confession.

In the final analysis, it didn't matter all that much that he had seen Vespa, since Dunn also saw him. And then Dunn identified him from that fortuitous picture in the next day's paper.

That Koesler had been dragged into the investigation of the missing Father Keating was not so much a matter of happenstance. By now, Koesler was almost accustomed to having his precious routine interrupted by a homicide investigation that bore a heavily Catholic aspect. Like the swallows returning to Capistrano or the buzzards to Hinckley, it had become an annual event.

But this was the first time he had known who did it before the investigation even began. With but a couple of exceptions, it was the only time he had been sacramentally prevented from participating fully in the case.

What a strange affair . . . capped by the missing body! And now, in all probability, he was about to find out what had really happened to Father Keating's body. Would he be able to use productively the information he was about to learn? Probably not. Unless Vespa were to free him from the secrecy of Vespa's own confession—which seemed highly unlikely—everything would still be bound by that earlier confession.

So . . . this evening would be entirely devoted to the service of one needy soul.

With this thought, Koesler arrived at the marketplace.

The only establishment open at this hour in this part of town was the Roma Café, too far distant to shed any light here. Otherwise the marketplace was deserted.

During the season, farmers brought their fresh produce, plants, and flowers to the market. During business hours trade in the outdoor market was brisk. Now the area resembled a stage set: an uncompleted cluster of buildings with ancient roofs and no walls, which had been deserted and abandoned. Papers, driven by a slight breeze, drifted along the pavements and walkways. Creatures were stirring, but only to feed on the scraps left behind when the farmers departed.

Only a few streetlights were functioning. They did little beyond casting unreal shadows. Even though Koesler's eyes had adapted to the darkness, he could not see very clearly.

"You been waitin' long, Father?"

This was the third time he had heard the voice. In the confessional, over the phone a few hours ago, and now.

Guido Vespa.

Koesler about-faced abruptly. At first, he could make out only the outline of the other man. But from that outline, he could tell the man was easily as tall as himself and considerably heftier. As Vespa stepped closer, his face moved in and out of the unreliable light.

Koesler was at a loss to know how Vespa had arrived. The priest had neither seen nor heard any vehicle entering the market area. And it was quiet enough to have heard such a sound clearly. Vespa must have parked away from the scene, possibly on Gratiot.

"I said, You been waitin' long, Father?"

"What? Oh, no. Just a few minutes, I guess."

"It's just 11:30," Vespa said.

Koesler looked at his watch. He was able to tell the time only because of the luminous dial. "So it is. Just 11:30. Well, let's get down to business, Mr. Vespa."

"Guido," Vespa suggested. Then, "You was there," he said flatly. "You know."

"Guido then," Koesler replied. "Yes, I was at Trinity Church today when they opened the coffin."

"How'd he look?"

"Huh? Who?"

"Father Kern." Typically, Vespa used the title Kern had preferred: Father.

"He looked okay, I guess . . . I mean for having been dead and buried for so long."

"That's good. He was an up-front guy."

"I agree. But that's neither here nor there. There was only one body. The undertakers took out all the lining. There was no false bottom. The body of Father Keating simply was not there. So . . .?"

"That's part of what I gotta tell you," Vespa said. "I made that up . . . the part about putting Keating in with Father Kern."

Koesler was once again surprised. Both he and Dunn had been banking on the alternate scenario that had someone exhuming Keating's body after Vespa and company had paired Keating and Kern. So Vespa, by his own admission, had lied about Keating's disposition.

"But . . . why?"

"I shouldna done it. I always do somethin' stupid like that. Never leave well enough alone. I was tryna be cute. It seemed like a nice touch. I mean, Father Kern woulda helped a guy like Keating. He was always doin' that kinda thing. Now I got a problem. If I hadn't told you what I told you, this whole thing wouldna blew up. When I told you I planted Keating with Father Kern, I didn't have any idea they was gonna dig up Father Kern. If I'da known that, I'da never made that thing up."

"When do the lies stop, Guido? Did you even have a contract?"

"Oh, yeah. I had a contract okay. I'm not makin' anything up anymore. This is straight. I even told—well, never mind, it was the person who gave me the contract that I told I was gonna see you tonight. I'm gettin' everything straight. You can put what I'm tellin' you tonight in the book. I swear on my mother's grave."

"Okay, Guido, I believe you. What is the truth, the whole truth, and nothing but the truth?"

"Hey, that's just like in court. Okay. Get this, Father: That wasn't no confession I made to you."

There were several moments of silence as Vespa let this information sink in, and Koesler, for his part, digested this strange statement.

"It was no confession?"

"No. I used to go to confession once in a while. A long time ago. Once in a while, but not much. That wasn't my second confession after the one I did before First Communion. It wasn't no confession at all. It was part of the contract. Honest to God, Father, it was part of the contract. And that ain't all—"

It happened quickly and suddenly, but there was an indefinable rhythm, even choreography, to it. The shots thundered in this cavernous space. As if the huge man were weightless, Vespa's body jerked up and seemed to hang in midair for a split second.

Almost simultaneously, actually a split second later, Koesler was spun around. He pitched to the pavement as if he had been slam-dunked.

The pain in his shoulder permeated his body. He clenched his teeth as he winced. His mind clouded over. Fearing loss of consciousness, he bent every power of his brain to fight off the darkness.

The longer he remained conscious the more clearly he felt the agonizing pain in his shoulder. Still, he fought the looming unconsciousness that threatened to engulf him.

He was able to move his head. So he could see the hulk of Vespa lying facedown a few feet away. "Guido? Guido!"

No response. Koesler was unable to tell if there was much blood draining from either of them. Maybe Vespa was merely unconscious. Koesler prayed through the waves of pain and nausea that that was so.

He heard a siren in the distance. He fervently hoped it was coming for them. There was no other possible way he could think of to get out of this mess. Neither he nor Vespa could help themselves, let alone each other.

The siren continued to grow louder. At least it was coming in their direction. With the run of luck he was having, he half expected the sound to continue to increase until it passed them and then diminish in the distance as it answered some other emergency.

But it didn't. The volume crescendoed until the blue and white screeched to a stop near the two fallen men. The driver headed for Vespa, his partner to Koesler. The priest thought he heard the driver say, "He's gone!"

He managed to ask, "How did you . . .?" Then he found it difficult to speak.

"Someone heard shots and called 911." The policeman turned to his partner. "Get EMS." Koesler sank back into grayness.

*   *   *

As the ambulance sped toward Receiving Hospital, he felt his clothing being cut away. Somebody had applied a pressure bandage to stanch the flow of blood.

Koesler hoped they would give him something for the pain. They did not. Their only concern at the moment was to stop the bleeding and get him to the hospital as quickly as possible.

Someone asked him who the president of the United States was. The question actually had him stumped for a moment. He gave brief thought to, as a joke, giving them the name of Cardinal Mark Boyle. Boyle at one time had been president of the United States Conference of Bishops.

Fortunately, Koesler rejected this momentary temptation to frivolity. The ambulance crew was in no mood, and the mistaken identification would have clouded the diagnosis.

Once they reached the hospital, the flurry of professional activity amplified.

Koesler, the center of all this attention, could only wish this whole thing hadn't happened. He had an impression of himself as a piece of meat whose various cuts were being processed. Somebody had taken his blood pressure. He tried to hear what the count was, but so many people were talking simultaneously he couldn't isolate on any of them.

Several X rays were taken of his shoulder area. He wouldn't have known that so clearly but that several consecutive times the cubicle he occupied was cleared of all personnel.

Finally, a doctor—bearded, young, olive-complexioned—appeared directly in Koesler's vision. "Father, there's a bullet in your shoulder. It's got to come out. Other than that, you seem to be in good shape. A few bruises, but the bullet is our concern."

This was followed by injections, a peaceful, floating feeling, and finally, mercifully, unconsciousness.

19

FATHER KOESLER sensed that he had awakened more than once through the night. But this time his head was just a little clearer.

He looked around. No doubt about it, this was a hospital room. And, he observed gratefully, a private room. The times he had awakened earlier it was difficult to know whether he was dreaming. The dull, throbbing pain in his shoulder argued in favor of reality.

But this was the morning of a bleak, overcast day. His brain was beginning to function with some clarity. He remembered—or thought he remembered—a nurse explaining that if he experienced pain, he should push the button on his contraption just to the left of his bed. That would feed a measured dose of painkiller into him. He pushed the button.

Next, he tried to put the events of last evening together. It was not easy. Nothing even remotely similar had ever happened to him before.

Okay. He met Guido Vespa at the Eastern Market. Koesler remembered how dark it had been and how poorly lit the area was. It had been the first time he and Guido had been together when both of them were standing. They were roughly the same height, but Vespa was much heavier. All of this together probably explained why Koesler would not have seen the gunman. It was dark, and everything was in shadows. Koesler would most likely have not seen anyone approaching to the rear of Vespa due to Vespa's bulk. Additionally, he had been paying such close attention to Vespa's incredible story that it would have taken an almost deliberate effort of a third party to be noticed by Koesler.

And that brought him to the crux of the matter: Vespa's message.

Could he take seriously Vespa's claim that he had invented the detail of burying Father Keating with Monsignor Kern? Koesler believed he had to take the man seriously. For one thing, there hadn't been an extra body in the coffin. But also—and Koesler now felt this to be so—last night Vespa was not kidding. It was almost as if he somehow realized that something was about to happen. In effect, it was a death-bed confession that became an actual confession at the point of death.

If that were true, then the heart of what he said also fell into the realm of a deathbed confession. And that was that he had had no intention whatsoever of making a sacramental confession on that memorable Saturday afternoon. It had been—what did Vespa say?—part of the contract. It was what theologians term "simulation." It appeared to be the real thing, but it was sham. On the other side of the confessional, it would be as if the priest were to pretend to absolve but did not. Or like a priest pretending to consecrate the bread and wine at Mass but withholding the intention to consecrate.

Thus, Vespa's confession was no confession at all. So, Koesler—and, for that matter, Dunn—was not bound by the seal of confession.

The remaining question was a very large Why? Vespa had explained last night that his pretending to make a confession was part of the contract to kill Keating. But why did the contract carry that provision?

As his thinking became more and more lucid, almost everything that came to mind ended in a question mark.

Why did Vespa fake a confession? Why would anyone stipulate to that as part of a contract? What had happened to Guido Vespa? Could he have survived last night's shooting? Did whoever fired that gun intend to kill Koesler? Lots of questions, very few—or no—answers.

Koesler was not feeling at all well. His right arm lay across his waist in a sling and the arm was bound tightly to his body by a bandage around his chest. The pain was less sharp than it had been, but he did not want to press the morphine button again. In fact, he felt somewhat nauseated.

He located the nurse's call button and pressed it. Within seconds the door opened. But instead of a nurse, Inspector Koznicki and Lieutenant Tully entered. Koesler's expression telegraphed his surprise.

Koznicki smiled warmly. "We were waiting for you to wake up."

Koesler returned the smile, though it was modified by his discomfort. "I guess I'm glad to see you. But I really need the nurse just now."

With some confusion the two officers abruptly left the room, to be immediately replaced by a nurse. As soon as she heard his symptoms, she left, to return at once with an injection that quickly calmed his stomach.

Almost apologetically, the two men returned.

"You gave us a scare and a surprise," Koznicki said. "The last thing I expected to hear last night was that you had been shot in the company of Guido Vespa in Eastern Market close to midnight."

Koesler nodded slowly. "How is Guido? Did he make it?"

Koznicki shook his head. "He was dead at the scene. But you, how are you feeling?"

"I've been lots better. I guess I was shot. That's a first. I haven't seen the doctor yet." It occurred to Koesler that the officers probably had seen his doctor. "How am I?" he added.

Koznicki smiled. "You will be all right. You sustained a shoulder wound from a bullet that seems to have passed through Guido Vespa and lodged in you. The surgeon says that your rotator cuff has been virtually destroyed—a combination of the wound and the fall you took after being shot. But everyone assures us that with a strong program of physical therapy, you should be almost as good as new."

As Koznicki explained this, Koesler looked from one officer to the other. Koznicki was a policeman. But in this instance, he was first and foremost a good and close friend to Koesler. Tully, on the other hand, was in all instances a cop. And he was evidencing an eagerness to get some relevant facts. At this point, there seemed to be an implicit agreement among the three men that it was time to get down to business. Unspoken were Koesler's acquiescence to be interrogated and Koznicki's permission for Tully to interrogate.

"To begin then, Father," Tully said, "what were you doing there with Vespa?"

"He called earlier last night and asked that I meet him there. It's kind of a long story—one I couldn't tell you before, and one I can tell you now." Koesler began with Vespa's confession that Saturday afternoon. The mere mention of the confession brought a startled look to Koznicki's face. It bespoke his astonishment that Father Koesler would reveal what had been told him under the sacramental seal.

Koesler of course anticipated this reaction. Koznicki worried over the sacramental breach. Tully was more concerned with the legal implications of the confession.

So Koesler explained—several times, from different angles to make sure his freedom to talk now was completely understood—how the sacramental seal had been reduced to no more than a professional secret at best. From Vespa's spontaneous revelation and the manner in which the explanation was made, it was clear that he had wanted Koesler to understand. Even if it were a professional secret, the need to solve Keating's murder mandated Koesler's complete candor in revealing his information to the police.

That explained, the three settled down to analyze the information.

Koesler proved far more easily convinced that Vespa's claim to have double-buried Keating was poetic license. The officers, particularly Tully, decided to put that on the back burner to be resolved later, perhaps at the closing of the case.

Of more immediate interest was a contract that called not only for a murder but also for the confession—albeit simulated—of that killing to Father Koesler.

While Koesler was at a loss to understand it, neither of the police seemed to have any problem with it. "It was meant to silence you," Koznicki stated.

"This began as a missing persons investigation," Tully said. "It turned into a suspected homicide case. The important thing is that the central character was a priest."

"In the past," Koznicki continued, "you have been generous enough to give your time and insider's knowledge to investigations such as this. Sometimes you have happened to be on the scene. More often we have asked for your cooperation and participation."

"And that," Tully said, "is actually exactly what happened here. We were called in on the missing priest case, and I called you. Whoever gave Vespa that contract knew our past association well enough to guess that we'd call on you. And we did. But you couldn't give us much help, could you?"

"Well, no," Koesler admitted. "I couldn't do much of anything. I was mindful all the time that I couldn't do anything that might compromise the seal."

"Clever, was it not?" Koznicki said. "Whoever commissioned Vespa guessed correctly all the way along, and removed you from any active participation in this case by having Vespa make that bogus confession."

"I'm curious," Tully said. "What did you think when the investigation turned to Carl Costello—Vespa's grandfather?"

It was Koesler's turn to smile. "I was rooting for you—silently, but rooting anyway. In the beginning, I couldn't refuse your request that I act as a sort of technical adviser. I've never begged off in the past. If I were to have just flat out turned you down, I was afraid that in itself would be suspicious. It might have led to a lot of questions, questions that could have had no answers."

"That is a distinct possibility," Koznicki said.

"So," Koesler continued, "I decided I would help as much as I could without relying on anything at all from that confession. It was a very narrow boundary. I knew that going in, but I had no idea it would be as difficult as it proved. At one time, Lieutenant, I referred to Father Keating in the past tense—and you called me on it."

"I remember. But it seemed a natural slip, especially since Homicide was investigating."

"As long as you were asking for background information on the various characters—Keating and his associate priest—we were on neutral ground," Koesler said.

"Looking back on it," Tully said, "you weren't your usual self. You did seem to be holding back. But of course that's hindsight."

"Well, I'd like to get in on it now," Koesler said. "You are going to reopen the investigation, aren't you?"

"Absolutely," Koznicki said. "We have the murder of Guido Vespa to solve. And thanks to the information you have now given us, we will reopen the investigation regarding Father Keating. In all probability, whoever issued the contract to Vespa in turn murdered Vespa and will be sought for conspiracy in the death of Father Keating."

The two officers rose to leave. But before leaving, Tully said, "As far as getting back into this investigation, you'd better not count on that. You've got some recovering to do."

"But—"

"Tell you what we'll do," Tully said. "We'll try to keep you updated on our progress. We owe you that much."

"And," Koznicki added, "it may seem quiet in this room. But outside, in the corridor, there are lots of newspeople who are champing at the bit to get to you. And they will as soon as the doctors give permission."

"What's keeping them out there now?" Koesler asked.

"I've got a couple of uniforms on duty," Tully said. "And we'll keep one, at least, on duty around the clock. Whoever killed Vespa may have wanted you dead too. May have thought when you fell he'd got you both. In that case, he might try to get at you again. As long as you're in this room, we can provide protection. So take it easy. And by the time you're released, we may have this thing wrapped up."

"The media," Koesler said, "what should I tell them? Or what shouldn't I tell them?"

"Good question," Tully said. They had not anticipated the confessional material. He looked to Koznicki. After a moment's thought, the inspector spoke. "It would be better if you did not mention the confession. Perhaps you should state only that Vespa called last night and asked you to meet him. Say that he made mention of the contract and then someone you could not see fired the shots.

"In other words, tell the truth, but not all the truth. There may never be a necessity to mention the false confession. It is enough that we know that you are not bound by the seal. It would cloud the matter if you had to explain this over and over again to the newspeople."

Koznicki then promised that he would return soon for a visit, and the two officers said goodbye. Koesler could hear the clamor in the hallway as the door opened and they left his room.

The conversation had distracted Koesler from the pain. Now he was all too aware of it again. It was not as sharp as it had been. That was encouraging; he wanted to use the morphine as sparingly as possible.

There were so many things to think about. He was certain his mind would be too occupied with ancillary questions to pay much attention to this dulled pain.

His first thought was of Nick Dunn. Even so, Koesler considered it a belated reflection. After all, Dunn was in this as deeply as he. They had both been privy to the same confession. They had both been keeping the same secret. The difference was that Koesler had been shot and Dunn had not.

Of course in the balance of things, Koesler had only been wounded, whereas Vespa had been killed.

Vespa. Vespa and his simulated confession. I should have tumbled right off the bat . . . or at least lots earlier in this game. There was something rotten about this right from the start.

The confessional stalls were clearly marked. A child could have told the difference between the side that allowed a face-to-face visit and the side that provided anonymity. Why had Vespa entered the open side? It guaranteed Koesler's seeing and recognizing a penitent who, having announced that this was his first confession since childhood, would naturally choose the screen. But before he entered the screened-off side, he had to be seen so that Koesler would know whose secret he was keeping.

Then why hadn't he been able to quiet Vespa down? Why had
Vespa insisted on talking so loudly? So loudly that he could easily be
heard by anyone in the otherwise quiet church. Did he know the
church was not empty? Did he know that Father Dunn was out there?
No, how could Dunn have been there; he hadn't known that Koesler
had seen Vespa. He must've come in afterward. Or, had he . . .? Was
Vespa's loud voice for Dunn's benefit?

So convenient that Dunn should arrive at just that crucial moment.

What did Koesler know about Dunn anyway? Nothing official,
that's for sure. A letter from a Minneapolis priest requesting residence at St. Joe's while studying at U of D Mercy. Was he really a
priest from Minneapolis? Was he really a priest? Was he in on this
somehow?

The door opened. The media people were getting louder. The door
had been opened by a police officer, probably the one guarding his
door. "There's a Father Dunn here to see you, Father."

So this is how it was going to work. Koesler had never before had a
secretary who packed a gun. He felt safer. "Show Father Dunn in, by
all means."

Again the babel in the corridor as the door was opened, the cop
leaving, the priest entering.

Nick Dunn was the soul of concern. How sincere was this concern? Had Dunn known all that was going to happen ahead of time?
Was he as surprised as Guido Vespa when the contractor decided to
end the deal with a gun?

"How are you?" Dunn asked. "God," he continued, without waiting for a reply, "what a shock! I was waiting up for you. I couldn't
figure out what was keeping you. Then the call from the hospital! I
came right away. Do you remember: I gave you the Sacrament of the
Sick. Do you remember?"

If Dunn was in on this, it was an award-winning performance.
"Now that you mention it," Koesler said, "I do seem to recall your
being here."

"They let me into the recovery room after they operated. You were
unconscious. But I was here in this room with you afterward. Do you
remember? I kept falling asleep. You told me to go home before I fell
off the chair and hurt myself."

"I said that?"

"Actually, you were kind of funny. At one time when you woke up and I was falling asleep, you said, 'Can you not watch one hour with me?' "

"I said that?"

Dunn nodded.

"Well, thanks for the vigil, anyway—even if I don't remember it all that clearly."

"So how are you? How do you feel?"

"I've been better—lots better. But speaking of home, how's everything at the parish?"

"Bob, you haven't been gone that long. But don't worry, I'll take care of everything that needs taking care of. What the hell, I can stick around the rectory and take seriously that reading list the university handed out. Don't worry, it's not that big a deal. What's the prognosis? How long're you going to be here?"

"Haven't seen the doctor yet. But I've seen the police and I've got something very important to tell you."

Koesler related what Vespa had said about the nature of the confession they had both heard. The story was punctuated with "no kiddings" and "I'll be damneds" from Dunn. All the while Koesler wondered how much of this was really news to him.

Nick Dunn seemed to digest this new information as quickly as Koesler could dish it out. Dunn asked many questions regarding the simulated confession and proposed some theories to attempt to explain the weird incident. But no matter who proposed the hypothesis, Koesler or Dunn, it could be no more than speculation—at least on Koesler's part. Was it an attempt at silencing Koesler—and Dunn—or was it Vespa's invention, like the disproved double burial?

"So," Dunn concluded, "we were released from the seal by Vespa, only to be silenced again by the police."

"That's the way it looks. And, speaking of an investigation, *we* never had one."

"What?"

"Well, not an investigation as such, but any kind of check into your background."

"Huh?" Dunn appeared bewildered.

"I don't want to seem less than a gracious host . . . but what do I really know about you? Somebody sent me a letter from Minneapolis requesting residence while he studied at a local university. I never checked into it. Outside of your showing up here, I have no idea who you really are."

"Well, hell, you could always look me up in the Kenedy Directory, Bob." A testy note crept into Dunn's voice.

"And what would I find?" Koesler too was getting irritable. "I would be surprised if I didn't find a listing for a Nicholas Dunn assigned to a Golden Valley parish in the Minneapolis–St. Paul diocese."

Dunn spread his hands. "So?"

"So how do I know that it's you?"

"Huh?"

"If I were going to impersonate a priest, I sure as hell would make sure I picked a name and an identity that existed in the Catholic Directory. It wouldn't make sense not to; it's too easy to check."

"And another thing," Koesler continued, though Dunn made a futile attempt to say something, "when we first met on that Saturday afternoon, you made a number of mistakes."

"Mistakes? What—?"

"You said you were my new associate. And you're not, of course; you're 'in residence' here. If you were an associate, you'd have faculties to function in this archdiocese and all you'd need would be my delegation. But we had to get you faculties." Koesler's attitude seemed to say he'd made a very telling point.

"Bob," Dunn was defensive, "I didn't mean that in the technical canonical sense. I just meant that I was here not only just to live but to help out . . . to be your associate. I didn't think you'd—besides," he broke off, "that was a long time ago. What the hell are you getting at?"

"And that's not all . . ." A note of triumph crept into Koesler's voice. "You said that the three main drags in Minneapolis were named after priests. That would be Marquette, Hennepin, and Nicolet. Well, Marquette and Hennepin were priests, but not Nicolet. He was a French explorer." Another point scored.

Dunn seemed genuinely embarrassed. "I knew Nicolet wasn't a priest. It was just a slip of the tongue, nothing more. You can remember that conversation in such detail? My God, what a memory!"

"And wasn't it a convenient accident, such a coincidence, that you just happened to show up at the exact moment Guido Vespa was going to confession plenty loudly enough for you to hear everything he said? You didn't arrive in church just a few moments earlier when Vespa entered the wrong side of the confessional and I saw him?"

"You saw him? You knew who he was! I didn't know that!"

"Sure, you got there conveniently after he'd entered the other side of the confessional so you wouldn't appear to know that I'd seen him. But you saw him when he left the confessional. So you could pretend you were the only one of us who knew who he was. That gave you a dominant role to play. You could recognize him in the picture in the paper the next morning. I couldn't have shut you out of this case if I'd wanted to. And the paper . . . did you know in advance that his picture was going to run in the paper?"

Dunn was reduced to just looking at Koesler. Dunn's mouth hung open. Then, slowly, a smile began to form. Gradually, it became a grin. "I'll be damned," Dunn said, "you suspect me!" His head tossed. "I love it!"

Dunn's reaction served to push Koesler into a somewhat defensive posture. "Well . . ." he drew out the word, "a coincidence is a coincidence because there's no rational explanation for remarkable similarities. Once you can build that missing explanation, the chance of coincidence begins to vanish. There were a whole bunch of coincidences surrounding your arrival. It's only natural to try to shoot them down with a reasonable explanation."

"And you think," Dunn was obviously beginning to enjoy this, "you think that I was in on this thing. That maybe I'm not who I seem to be. That maybe I'm not even a priest?"

The ease with which Dunn was voicing what Koesler had merely implied was beginning to unnerve Koesler.

"If what you suggest were true," Dunn said, "what would I have to gain from all this?"

"I haven't the slightest idea of what anybody had to gain from all this. As far as I know, the earlier part of Vespa's story is true: John Keating piled up some astronomical gambling debts. I can believe that. That a contract was put out for his murder and that Vespa did the killing. That Vespa's fake confession, to keep me out of the picture, was part of the contract. But there are other people in this case. And we don't know who they are. Somebody put out the contract. Somebody shot Vespa and me because Vespa told me that the confession was a fake. Maybe the two 'somebodies' are the same person.

"What I'm getting at is there's room for lots more people in this case. Maybe all those coincidences were not really coincidences. In which case, you made your entrance at the perfect time to play a part in this matter. And if that is true, I don't know what part you may be playing or what you have to gain. Only that your presence in this is more than a little suspicious."

Dunn was still smiling. Koesler wondered if Dunn was not underplaying all this too much. Where he might have reacted with anger, he was reacting with good humor. The latter was proving more effective. Was it all a very good act?

"At this point," said Dunn, "I could move out. But I don't want to leave Detroit. I really want those courses at U of D. And especially with the priest shortage, I could get a residence in almost any parish. But one of the reasons I asked to stay with you is because I wanted to see how you operate, particularly when, as you put it, you get dragged into these police investigations.

"Well, I'm getting a better picture than even I counted on.

"So here's what I'll do: If you don't want to throw me out right now, I'll prove to your satisfaction that I am the real Father Nicholas Dunn from Minneapolis. And that I'm still in good standing with the diocese and the Church. Then, if you want to suspect that a real priest could get mixed up in this, I'll do what I can to put your suspicions to rest.

"How about it?"

Koesler's immediate thought was that a "real priest" was already mixed up in this—Jake Keating. But he didn't mention that. Instead, he said, "Okay, let's take it from there. You continue on at St. Joe's. But I don't think it's asking too much for some documentation on your status."

"Done then. And no hard feelings?" Dunn extended his hand.

Koesler became aware that he wasn't going to be using his right hand for a while. He reached out his left hand. "No, no hard feelings. Sincere apologies if my suspicions prove groundless."

There was a perfunctory knock and a white-jacketed man entered the room. An identification card hung from his breast pocket; a stethoscope dangled from around his neck. There were introductions all around. Father Dunn then left, promising to see to the routine services at St. Joe's until Koesler could resume his duties.

"You've attracted quite a mob out there," the doctor commented.

"The media people? I'm not looking forward to that."

"I'll limit their time with you. Think you can go about fifteen minutes?"

"Yeah, I think so. How bad is it . . . my shoulder, I mean?"

The doctor shook his head and pursed his lips. He was a fine-looking specimen. His full head of salt-and-pepper hair was styled. His features seemed chiseled from impressive granite. From Koesler's position in bed, the doctor seemed about seven feet tall. Probably he was a six-footer. He put Koesler in mind of God. Or, rather, someone who thought he was God.

"The slug came out nicely," the doctor said. "There wasn't much I could do about the shoulder. The rotator cuff is, for all purposes, gone. There's a hole like this," he cupped his hands to form a large O. "I debrided it . . ."

"You what?"

"I . . . gave it a haircut. Cut away the damaged tissue. I made sure the bleeding was stopped, and closed you up. Want to see?"

Koesler was about to pass on the show-and-tell portion of this program when the doctor folded the hospital gown away from the shoulder and with one fluid motion pulled the bandage away from the skin.

Koesler was grateful he was not terribly hirsute. At least there was no hair pulled out by the roots. He turned his head to study the area. It was what was left of his shoulder as colorized by Ted Turner. There were glorious reds, purples, and oranges against a white background.

He was surprised there did not appear to be any stitches. "I'm stapled!"

The doctor chuckled. "It's been a long time since I've heard them referred to as staples."

"What then?"

"Clamps. But you're just as correct; they're staples. In a couple of weeks, I'll take them out. Meanwhile, they'll hold you together."

"What happens next? I don't know how much use I've got of my arm. It's strapped to my body."

"What comes next is you'll start on physical therapy. They'll move your arm. Then, little by little, you'll move your arm. Then you'll begin working with weights."

"That bad!"

"That bad. But if you continue your exercises you'll regain most of your strength. But you'll have to be very faithful to those exercises . . . do them religiously. As it were," he added quasi-humorously.

"Doctor, I normally sleep on my right side. How's that going to work—I mean, with the arm?"

"Don't even think of it."

"That bad!"

"That bad. You about ready for the onslaught of the media?"

"I guess."

The doctor opened the door and stepped back.

In they came. Though there weren't nearly as many as Koesler expected, actually there were a representative number. As the door to his room had repeatedly opened and closed, the intermittent clamor had sounded as if it were coming from a considerable mob.

TV, radio, and the print media were represented. Koesler recognized most of them, though he knew hardly any of them. One he did recognize and know was Pat Lennon of the *News*. He'd met her in the very beginning, on the occasion of the first homicide case in which he'd been involved, as well as on subsequent investigations. He knew that she was perhaps the premiere reporter in the city. Thus he wondered at her presence here. Because this incident involved him so deeply, he could not imagine that it was important enough to attract someone with Pat Lennon's credentials.

Koesler had not grasped the fact that the shooting of a mobster and a priest together was, by far, the top story of the day. It would make the national and even the international media.

Limited as he was by his own knowledge of the case, as well as by the boundaries suggested by Inspector Koznicki, Koesler had relatively little information for these reporters. Only that he'd been called to that meeting with Vespa last night and before he'd said—or heard—very much at all, the two of them had been shot.

No, Koesler had not known Vespa previously. No, since Vespa had had so little time before the shooting, Koesler did not know much of the reason for this meeting. No, he had no idea who had fired the shots.

There were many more questions coming from every quarter, but none of Koesler's answers were much more specific or helpful than these.

The news groups left the room in their usual order. TV first, then radio, finally print.

Last to leave was Pat Lennon. She lingered a moment. "You'll have to forgive my buddies. They've got deadlines. I do too—but I just wanted to say I'm awfully sorry this happened to you."

"That's very kind of you. Thank you." Koesler was aware that the media commonly gave the impression they cared for nothing but the story. He was also aware that in most cases the men and women of the media cared very deeply about the people and events that needed to be reported on. He was moved by Lennon's expression of concern.

Now that he was alone again, he realized he was tired to the point of exhaustion. And the pain was making itself felt again. Probably it had been there all along, but he'd been distracted by all the visitors— the police, Nick Dunn, the doctor, and the reporters. Whatever. The pain seemed to be denying him the sleep he desperately needed. With some reluctance, mixed with gratitude for its availability, he depressed the morphine button once again.

While waiting for it to take effect, he thought about his situation.

His involvement in this whole thing had begun when somebody considered him some sort of supersleuth. Nothing could be further from reality. Anyway, this somebody was determined to have Jake Keating executed, probably over unpaid gambling debts. This somebody didn't want him—Father Koesler—to contribute anything to the inevitable investigation. Thus the bizarre plan of the fake confession.

Well, the somebody was correct in that he *had* been called upon to take part in the investigation. And as far as contributing to any resolution of the case, he might just as well have been bound, gagged, and blindfolded. But if he hadn't been silenced by what he had thought to be the seal of confession, what might he have contributed? There was no way of telling; it was a condition contrary to fact.

If only that somebody had not had that wild misconception as to his detection talents, if only he had refused to meet Guido Vespa at Eastern Market . . . he wouldn't be lying in a hospital bed in a sea of pain with a destroyed rotator cuff.

The good news, he thought, as he began to drift, was that it was over. Once the police caught whoever had hired Guido, the case would be wrapped up. They might never find Jake Keating's body. But one thing for sure, Koesler wasn't going to help them find it.

Part
Three

20

IT WAS GOOD to be home. If one had to be in pain, there was a lot to be said for the comfort and familiarity of home. If all that could be done for one in the hospital was to medicate against pain, that could be accomplished as well at the rectory.

The hospital agreed. So, on the third day—biblical?—he rose from his hospital bed and returned to the rectory.

Before leaving Receiving Hospital, Koesler had attended his first physical rehabilitation session, and discovered how very little spontaneous motion he had in his right arm. The therapist assured him that if he was faithful to the exercises, he would recover at least some of his former mobility and strength. Perhaps more than a little. But it was going to be a long haul.

Mary O'Connor, parish secretary, had been most solicitous, as had many of the parishioners. He had to assure them over and over that he was not ill, just injured. And that he was fully capable of getting around, laboring awkwardly through a one-arm Mass, and signing checks—as long as he moved the paper. He couldn't move his arm.

Father Dunn was doing his best to see to the routine needs of the parish, attend as many classes at the university as possible, fulfill his reading assignments, and put to rest as many of Koesler's doubts and suspicions as possible.

He had helped Koesler make phone calls to the Minneapolis Chancery as well as to several priests, all of whom attested to Dunn's identity. Yes, Father Dunn had been granted a leave of absence. Yes, he was a classmate. Yes, he had told one and all that he was going to take up residence at St. Joseph's parish in downtown Detroit. Yes, that certainly sounded like Nick Dunn's voice on the telephone extension.

In addition, Dunn had asked his Chancery to send him a *celebret*—a document stating that he was a priest in good standing. It was something he might have brought with him to Detroit. But he'd had no inkling that he would become a suspect in a murder investigation.

The relationship of Koesler and Dunn had altered somewhat. Koesler was uncomfortable having Dunn around. Koesler had intimated—if not made an outright accusation—that Dunn might be up to his ears in a murder conspiracy. Hardly the mark of a gracious host. Dunn, for his part, seemed to be in high good humor as he sought to allay the pastor's fears. Dunn was the soul of cooperation in finding ways of establishing his identity and being completely open to any of Koesler's suggestions along that line. Thus whatever tension existed seemed to stem from Koesler. It made him uncomfortable.

Koesler had just taken a pill for pain when he heard the front doorbell.

Dunn had already left for one of his morning classes at the university. Koesler could hear the click-clack of Mary O'Connor's shoes on the hardwood floor. They had an understanding that since Koesler had no appointments on his calendar for this, his first morning back, Mary would screen all phone calls and visitors and pass along to Koesler only what might be termed emergencies or urgent business. Otherwise, on his behalf, she expressed his thanks for good wishes and gratitude for prayers.

Mary appeared at the study door. "There are three people here you might want to see: Mr. and Mrs. Costello and Mr. Vespa." Her concern was evident.

"Yes, yes, you're right. Please show them in, Mary. And could you get us some coffee? I'd do it, but things are still a bit awkward," he added, indicating his right arm still encased in a tight sling that was suspended over his cassock.

Mary nodded and went first to admit the visitors, then to the kitchen, murmuring a grateful prayer that Father Koesler had given up making coffee for the duration. Everyone would be better off for it.

The three visitors entered the study. Mrs. Costello went to Koesler immediately, took his left hand, and, before he could demur, kissed it. Her sympathy was obviously sincere. Carl Costello nodded, then took a chair across from Koesler, who was seated behind his desk. He had not attempted to stand. Remo Vespa stationed himself in front of the door.

Costello inquired into the state of Koesler's health. Koesler explained the injury and quoted the rehab technician's assurance of at least partial recovery with fidelity to exercise. Amenities completed, Costello addressed the reason for the visit.

"You have done us a great favor. A significant favor." Costello regarded Koesler intently.

"It was really nothing. All it took was a phone call."

"No, no, Father," Mrs. Costello insisted. "Guido and Remo are like our own children. And to think that after all these years, Guido should be buried Catholic! What can we say? What can we do?"

Koesler smiled at her. "I know your pastor. He tends to interpret Church law rather strictly. I thought he could use my input."

Quite naturally, since the shooting, Koesler was sensitive to the memory of Guido Vespa. After all, they had not only been shot at the same time but even with one of the same bullets.

With Guido dead, Koesler had wondered about the funeral. How he would be buried probably wouldn't have mattered to Guido one way or the other. But Koesler sensed it would matter a great deal to the grandparents, particularly to Guido's grandmother. Both Mr. and Mrs. Costello had demonstrated a deep reverence for Koesler's priesthood the one time they had met.

Although, given Carl Costello's earlier active membership in the mob, Koesler was unsure of his sincerity. But there seemed no doubt that Mrs. Costello really meant it. For her sake, if for no other reason, Koesler had decided to get involved in Guido's funeral.

Once he had determined which was the Costellos' parish, a few judicious inquiries revealed, to no surprise, that Mrs. Costello attended Mass regularly, Carl showed up on important occasions, but neither Guido nor Remo had darkened the doorway since their youth. That part of Guido's make-believe confession appeared to be accurate.

The pastor was Koesler's elder by nearly ten years. Now on the verge of retirement, Father Tintoreto lived by yesterday's rules. With no one around to testify that Guido had even absentmindedly genuflected within anyone's memory, Mario Tintoreto would surely refuse a Catholic funeral. On several occasions when priests gathered, Koesler had heard Tintoreto boast of threatening his recalcitrants with being "buried like a dog." It seemed to be, particularly with Italians, the ultimate ultimatum. If the denial of Christian burial did not reach them, Tintoreto thought nothing would.

For the pastor and for his parishioners, then, refusing to bury the dead had to be taken seriously. It was imperative there be no exceptions to the rule. Thus the Costellos had no hope for Guido. In Tintoreto's favored phrase, Guido would be consigned to the earth like an animal.

Enter Father Koesler with his phone call to Father Tintoreto, during which Koesler testified to not only having seen Guido in St. Joseph's Church just a few weeks ago, but, imagine this: The backslider had actually made a confession! Koesler neglected to describe what sort of confession.

Mario Tintoreto had been stunned. Indeed he could not recall ever having been so dumbfounded. But he could not doubt the word of a fellow priest no matter how much he wanted to. And he did want to.

As far as Koesler was concerned, funerals were more for the consolation of the bereaved than for the benefit of the one who had already entered eternal life. He had thought no more about it until the appearance of the Costellos this morning and their expansive expressions of gratitude. For Remo, this was a matter of no importance. For Vita Costello, it was a miracle. For the Double C, it was a puzzle.

For as long as he could remember, Carl Costello had kept careful tabs on who owed whom what. He was scrupulous about the balance sheet. He assumed everyone else conducted life's affairs in the same manner. He had no idea why Koesler had intervened on Guido's behalf, thereby bestowing a tremendous favor on Mrs. Costello. The truth was, the Double C owed for a significant favor. The question was: What did Koesler want?

Koesler believed he read all this in Costello's manner, in his eyes.

"You have done us a great favor, Father." There was a pronounced wheeze in Costello's voice, perhaps from too much smoking, or a throat injury. "It is much more than a phone call. As far as I know," he gestured to include not only everyone in the room but everyone in the whole world, "no one asked you to do us this goodness. You did it all on your own." Costello did not articulate the word "Why?" but it hung in the air.

"If it has helped you in your time of loss," Koesler said, "that's good enough."

But Costello was not about to let the matter rest. "That meeting—when he was killed, you were wounded—what was that about? I don't understand why he would call you. Talking to a priest, that was not something Guido did."

"He didn't tell you anything about it?"

Costello shook his head. "Nothing." He looked Koesler full in the face. "Father, I know you would not lie, not even to effect a good thing like Guido's Catholic burial . . . but did he really confess to you?"

Mary O'Connor almost did not make it into the room with the tray holding the coffee. Remo was leaning back against the door as she pushed against it from the other side. Mary's slight weight made little impression against his heft. Finally, she coughed loudly enough to be heard. Remo stepped away from the door and Mary almost fell into the room.

It was a humorous exchange, but Koesler would not laugh until much, much later—in retrospect.

A slightly embarrassed and self-conscious Mary O'Connor served the coffee and departed.

Koesler turned back to Costello, and, fixing him with an intent look, said, "Yes, your grandson went to confession to me . . . sort of."

Costello was clearly confused. " 'Sort of'?"

"Carl, Mrs. Costello, Remo . . . you already know more about this matter than the news media does. You know about my call to Father Tintoreto. My agreement with him was that when the media asks how Guido qualified for a Church burial service, he is to tell them only that he was given evidence that Guido had attended church recently. And that's all he's going to say. The media will press for more detail. But that's all they're going to get."

Costello chuckled. "Father Tintoreto will enjoy that. He likes being in charge."

"An exception was made for you three, the most immediate family Guido had. There was no disagreement on that point. You deserved to know. Now I'm going to tell you something only the police know." Koesler, for the sake of expedience, chose to omit Dunn from those who knew about the bogus confession.

First, Koesler needed to explain insofar as it was feasible why it was permissible to tell them the details of Guido's confession-that-wasn't-a-confession. As he began the explanation, he noted a look of surprise on Costello's face similar to that which Koznicki had exhibited in the same circumstances.

After Koesler's third time through, when, by their expressions, it seemed his small audience comprehended and was satisfied, Koesler said again, "Now, I've just told you something only the police know. And it's extremely important that no one else know . . . you understand?"

The three looked at each other. Costello spoke. "We have observed *omerta* many times. We know well how to keep a confidence."

"Good," Koesler said. "Now, I need to know: What do you make of it?"

"The contract? The confession?" Costello asked.

"The contract first."

"It's been years," Costello said, "since anyone in our 'family' accepted a contract. Our understanding was that we were out of that business. I would have to guess that if there was an offer and Guido accepted it, the contract would have to have come from the outside."

"The outside?"

"No 'family' would be involved. It would have to be from someone with no relationship with any of the families. Someone who knew of our past and counted on Guido to accept it."

"It's possible then?"

There was sadness in Costello's eyes. "I don't like to think of Guido betraying our trust. But yes, it is possible. Very possible. Whoever offered the contract would have to have a sweet pot . . ."

"A lot of money?" Koesler interrupted to clarify.

Costello nodded decisively. "A lot of money. If someone still active in a 'family' heard about it, it could have cost Guido his life." Thinking on that, he added, "It did cost him his life."

"But not," Koesler said, "at the hands of anyone in a 'family.'"

"Not from what you've said," Costello agreed. "It was most likely by the one who gave Guido the contract."

"Then what about the confession? What about its being part of the contract?" Koesler asked.

Costello reflected for a few moments. Then, "It's not uncommon for contracts to have other conditions attached to them. I've never heard of confession to be one of those conditions."

"As I told you, the police think it was to keep me from freely participating in the ensuing investigation."

Costello nodded. "And it was on the money. That's why you were with the cops when they came to my house . . . right?"

"Yes. If the theory is correct, the contractor assumed, from my past involvement, that the police would ask for my help. And the guilty party didn't want to chance my helping the police. So—and I guess we'd have to say he was clever—he had the one who killed Father Keating confess to me that he had done it, and in doing so, he sealed my lips.

"But, moving on: Do you think Guido could have done it? Killed a priest, I mean?"

"Guido told you it was because of gambling debts?"

Koesler nodded.

Costello shrugged. "The debts would have to be out of sight. But, yeah, sure: It's like you're doin' business with somebody and you don't like the business he's in. But it's business . . . so, you go along."

"He'd kill a priest?!"

Costello nodded. "And go to confession too. If that's what the contract called for."

"Okay," Koesler said. "Now we come to the last part. The bit about burying Father Keating with Monsignor Kern."

Remo snorted and was about to laugh when a glance from Costello silenced him. Koesler had virtually forgotten there was anyone else in the room.

"That's what turned this whole thing around," Koesler said. "The matter was completely closed until they exhumed Monsignor Kern's body. The police had discontinued their investigation into Father Keating's disappearance. My lips were sealed permanently. Then came the matter of identifying Monsignor's remains. And Father Keating's body was nowhere in sight. I guess at that point, I was pretty sure Guido had lied to me. And I thought, if he lied about that, then about how much more?

"Anyway, at that point, Guido decided he'd better come clean. So first he told the guy who gave him the contract. Does that make any sense?"

"It would have been the honorable thing to do," Costello said.

Somehow, in Koesler's eyes, "honor" didn't seem to have much of a role in this case.

"He was going to break a very important provision in the contract," Costello explained. "One of the principal stipulations of the contract was to keep you on ice by confessing. Now Guido was gonna violate that part of the contract by telling you the confession was a fake. He had to tell the guy. It was the honorable thing to do."

There goes that word again, thought Koesler. "But nobody would have known about any of this if he hadn't added that bit about the burial. Why would he do a thing like that?"

"Why would Guido do a thing like that?" Costello closed his eyes tightly as if shutting out past memories. "Because that was part of Guido's style. He always went too far. He thought it was clever. He did foolish things. Other times he bragged so much he made up stuff just to be a big guy.

"In the old days, he'd go out to make a collection. Then he'd come home with the money and tell us he broke the guy's fingers for making us wait. He'd be a big guy, hot stuff. 'The Enforcer!' Then we'd find out he hadn't done it: He got the money okay but he didn't do anything to the guy. He'd learn a little. But what he learned was to brag about things we couldn't check out—at least things he thought we couldn't check out."

"So," Koesler concluded, "in light of his past boasting, it makes perfect sense that Guido would lie to me for no other reason than that he wanted to add a sensational but fictitious touch. Sort of like his signature?"

"Sort of like his signature," Costello agreed. "Yeah, it got so he couldn't help himself. If he didn't think that what he had to do was very imaginative, he'd make up something. Just to impress people. I don't know where the priest's body is. Maybe only Guido knew. Now, nobody'll know." He shook his head. "I told Guido a hunnert times he had to quit doin' that. He wouldn't listen. Now . . ."

There was silence for several moments.

"Is that all you wanted to know, Father?" Costello asked finally.

"Yes. You've cleared up a lot for me. I couldn't figure out why he volunteered that bizarre story. I thank you very much for explaining it for me."

"It is for us to be grateful to you. You went out of your way to get Guido a Catholic burial. We appreciate that, especially Mama. Like I said, we are in your debt. Anytime you want somethin', you come to me. Hear? You come to me."

For the life of him, Koesler could not envision a time when he would need any favor that Costello could provide. But one never knew. The future was unpredictable. Koesler rose and accompanied the trio to the front door.

After they left, Koesler reviewed the visit.

There certainly was no doubt who headed that family. Remo was around only to serve and protect Carl Costello. And, after the initial greetings, Mrs. Costello had been so still it was almost as if she had not even been present. So in charge had Costello been, Koesler wondered that the Double C had let Guido get away with his penchant for weird exaggeration. Such a futile vice. It was almost guaranteed to get him in trouble. And in this instance, it certainly had. Koesler could only ascribe Costello's forbearance to the Indulgent Grandpa Syndrome.

Koesler returned to his office and slumped down in his chair.

At least it was over. Too seldom in life did all the loose ends get tied up in a neat, tidy fashion. When it did happen, it brought a sense of satisfaction. And he was sure that, at least as far as he was concerned, the matter of the missing priest was concluded.

Jake Keating, despite having grown up in a wealthy family, had proven himself a poor gambler when he lost all that money in stocks and bonds. What few people ever knew was that he also was a compulsive gambler. Put the two together—an unlucky and compulsive gambler—and you have the making of a peck of trouble—or tragedy.

So, inevitably, Jake got in over his head. Koesler could imagine the bookies or whoever Jake dealt with being at first amused that "Father" lived to gamble and that, in addition, he proved to be a patsy. Then the amusement fading as Father ran up staggering debts. Undoubtedly there were threats. Finally, Don Whoever, the head man, hired Guido Vespa to kill Keating. It certainly would be an outstanding lesson throughout the gambling world that the bookies were deadly serious about collecting what was owed: Even a priest, even the pastor of Detroit's wealthiest parish, was not untouchable.

If Guido had let it rest there, the gambling community—and they alone—would know what had happened to Jake Keating. The police had written it off as an unsolved case. Koesler and Dunn would have shared a memorable experience they could share with no one else.

But Guido had to add his distinctive touch to the plot. It was one of those exaggerations of his that would satisfy some inner compulsion and, at the same time, be safe, since no one would ever check it out.

Except that Guido didn't anticipate the exhumation of Jake Keating's purported resting-in-peace partner, Monsignor Clem Kern.

Guido then decided he had to pick up the pieces of his fumbled plot. He would tell Koesler that the confession had not been genuine, that it had been part of the contract. Then, in some strange way, he felt duty-bound to inform the contractor that he was going to really confess what had really happened—though not sacramentally.

Either Guido told the contractor where the meeting was to take place or he was followed. In any case, Guido was killed and Koesler had come closer to death than he'd ever been.

Thank God the police had no further need of him. There wasn't anything he could any longer assist with. The case had gone well beyond his field of expertise. The police were looking for the gamblers to whom Keating had been so deeply in debt. Koesler would, naturally, continue his interest in the case, but from the sidelines.

And just as well. The dull discomfort his wound was imposing made it difficult to concentrate on anything for very long. And the helplessness of his right arm was fairly frightening, as well as discouraging. He tried to put his faith in the therapist who promised that, with fidelity to exercise, things would improve.

He promised himself that he would be faithful. A little prayer wouldn't hurt either.

At least the police wouldn't need him anymore.

21

FATHER KOESLER continued sitting at his desk. He had corrected the slump and was now sitting upright. He eased his arm out of the sling, and with his left hand carefully placed his right forearm on the desk top. He tried to raise the injured arm unaided, but simply could not. He tried to slide it around the desk top and was able to accomplish that. He tried to take heart in this small feat. Every little bit, he thought.

Again he heard the doorbell. He hoped Mary could take care of whoever it was. His long visit with the Costellos had tired him. That was another problem: a lack of stamina.

He heard Mary's heels clicking toward his office, and his heart sank a little. Mary was well capable of handling most parish matters on her own. She would not subject him to visitors unless it was necessary. She was about to announce the arrival of someone she thought genuinely needed to meet with him.

Speculation ended as she appeared at the door and announced, rather sadly, he thought: "Lieutenant Tully to see you."

Koesler nodded, thanked her, and waited for the lieutenant's appearance.

Koesler had not seen or heard from Tully since that first day in the hospital. Tully's companion at that time, Inspector Koznicki, had been back to look in on him a couple of times. It was possible that Tully was here for the same innocuous reason. But Koesler doubted it. Wincing all the way, he tucked his arm back into its sling.

"Still sore, eh?" Tully said, as he took the chair lately occupied by Carl Costello.

"Yeah," Koesler said through clenched teeth.

"Have you thought any more about the other night . . . the shooting?"

How about that, thought Koesler; not even a "How are you?"

"No, Lieutenant. In fact, I've sort of tried not to think about it. Although this arm kind of reminds me of it."

"Well, try to remember it now," Tully virtually commanded. "Can you remember seeing anyone at all in that area . . . besides Vespa, of course?"

"How come now, Lieutenant? Why didn't you ask me in the hospital?"

"Couple of reasons. You were in real bad shape the morning after. And since then, some other things have surfaced that make it important for you to try to remember all you can."

Koesler obediently tried to picture that night. "No, I didn't notice anyone. I got there first, so I was looking for Guido Vespa. Since I was actually looking for him, I surely would have been aware if I'd seen anyone else. But even when he got there, I didn't see him until he addressed me."

"Did he come up from the rear?"

"Uh . . . yes."

"Which way were you facing?"

"Lemmee see . . . away from the river, so . . . north."

"The guy who shot Vespa and you: He wasn't more than a few feet away. You didn't see anyone, anything?"

Koesler tried especially hard to remember. As he used to do while trying to meditate in the seminary, he made an imaginary composition of place. He concentrated until that meeting came alive in his memory. It was so dark in that marketplace. There were no lights in any of the nearby structures. Few street lights were working. Even though his eyes had become accustomed to the dark, he could barely make out anything. He could hardly see Vespa. He saw Vespa's outline. He couldn't discern any of Vespa's features. But he clearly recognized Vespa's voice.

"Lieutenant, I barely saw Vespa. In fact, I couldn't swear I actually did see him, it was so dark. I did recognize the voice though."

"So you didn't see anybody come up behind him while you were talking? Think carefully."

"I am. I am." Koesler tried to remember something he couldn't remember. There was a theory that one could remember forgotten or suppressed details through hypnosis. However, he was not under hypnosis. He doubted it was even possible for him to be hypnotized. "No, I'm quite sure I didn't see anybody else. You say the killer was only a few feet from us?"

Tully nodded.

"Boy! I don't know why I didn't see *something*. I think I may have been straining to pay close—singular—attention to Guido. It was as if I needed glasses to hear. I couldn't make out his features, just his form, and the voice. I remember sort of leaning toward him to make certain I caught every word."

"Did you know there is a tunnel undernearth the market?"

"There is?" Koesler was astonished. "Imagine living my whole life in this city and not knowing about a tunnel under the market!"

"It's possible the killer used the tunnel. But, let's go on. The moment of the shooting—what about that?"

Koesler was too courteous to call an end to this interrogation. The last thing he wanted to remember was that moment that not only took a life but changed his future by, in effect, disabling him. But he dutifully thought back. "The noise was overwhelming. Everything happened so fast I'm having a difficult time trying to get it to go in slow motion. There was the noise, and Guido seemed to . . . uh . . . levitate for a second. Then, it was as if someone hit me in the shoulder, very hard, like with a baseball bat. I never fell so fast or so hard in my life. Or if I did, I was a lot younger and in lots better shape."

"Okay," Tully said, "now this is important: What about the sound of the gun?"

"I told you: It was loud—ear-shattering."

"No, I mean the way the gun was fired—the cadence. Do you have any idea how many shots were fired?"

"Wait a minute." Koesler thought. "Six . . . yes, six."

"How do you know?"

"They came in bursts of three. Two bursts. Like, bang-bang-bang, very close together. Then another bang-bang-bang."

Tully wore one of his rare smiles. "That ties it."

"What?"

"Father, you remember the shooting death of that religion writer for the *News*?"

"Sure, of course: Hal Salden."

"Interestingly enough, you and Vespa were shot with the same gun that killed Salden."

"No! How did you . . .?"

"A hunch. I was investigating the Salden case, so I was familiar with the weapon and the type of bullet used. It was the same as the one used on you and Vespa. The distance was roughly the same, just a few feet away. A couple of bystanders were hit by slugs that passed through Salden. And you, of course, were hit by one of the slugs that went through Vespa. That kind of gun and ammunition is not all that common. And, finally, what started me thinking about a possible connection was religion."

"Religion?!"

"He was a religion writer and you're a priest. Probably no one thing got my attention, but when you put them all together. . . . The killer even set the machine pistol to fire in bursts of three in both shootings."

Koesler scratched his head. "Boy! Isn't that incredible? The same person in both shootings."

"The same gun," Tully corrected. "And we're going on the theory that the gunman was the same too."

"But why? I mean, what does that do to the premise that whoever shot Guido was the same person who gave him the contract?"

"Really messes it up. But we can't wish it away. It's reality. There has to be some connection between Vespa and Salden."

"Could Hal Salden have found out about the threat to Father Keating's life? That could explain the need to kill Salden."

"Maybe. If that's true, that might be the reason Salden was killed several days before Keating disappeared. If Salden learned about the contract, or even suspected it, he could have warned Keating and the guy wouldn't have walked into what must've been a trap.

"Keating drove into the city. Maybe the bookies arranged the meeting. Maybe they told him they were gonna work out something where he could pay it off. It seems pretty sure the guy walked into it blind. He couldn't've had any idea they were gonna kill him or he'd never have gone. If Salden got wind of it, he could've screwed the whole deal by warning Keating.

"But, as of now," Tully summed up, "that's all guesswork. We gotta get the facts. What really happened with Salden and why?" Tully looked searchingly at Koesler. "I know you're not feeling too great just now. But every bit of time that goes by means we have less and less chance of breaking this thing. So, would you mind going with me to the *News*? I want you to look at something. Maybe it'll mean more to you than it did to me."

"Oh, Lieutenant, I don't think—"

"It's what's in Salden's CRT—his notes. Remember? That's the out-side connection: You're a priest and he was the religion writer."

They had him again! He also realized that during the Costello visit and now during this conversation with Tully, his injury hadn't both-ered him noticeably. It probably helped to be distracted. Trying to help the police might be just what the doctor ordered.

Koesler agreed to go, asking for a few minutes to make sure all the day's pastoral matters were covered.

22

PAT LENNON arrived in the city room a little late and breathless. This was shaping up as a day of frustration if not downright disaster.

She'd had an appointment with the city councilman who was the swing vote on whether the mayor would get his long-awaited wish for his private airplane. First, the guy was more than an hour late for the appointment. Then he claimed he hadn't yet made up his mind. The vote was scheduled for this afternoon. If he had come through, as he had promised, she would have had a dandy page-one scoop. The guy knew damn well what his vote would be, she was sure of that. He was just too chicken to tell her.

Added to that, she was not feeling at all well. She had awakened—a bit late—with a migraine. Groggily, she had neglected immediate medication, and now the monster was evading her control.

Added to that, Joe Cox had called last night. He stated—he did not ask or say, he stated—that he would be coming to see her this weekend.

It wasn't that she'd had anything scheduled. But where did he get off issuing ultimatums like a victorious general! During the disagreeable conversation, he only thinly disguised the fact that he had read the item in DeVere's column, which undoubtedly a "friend" had sent him.

Lennon, in no uncertain terms, told Cox that if he insisted on coming there would be no one- nor, for that matter, two-night stand. And he could stay elsewhere, since he would not be welcome at what had been their downtown apartment.

In all, she was already in a mood most foul when she became aware that something was amiss. Someone was in the city room who shouldn't be. And that someone was where she shouldn't have been.

Lacy DeVere was seated at the late Hal Salden's desk, studying his CRT.

In the wild, when a predator falls upon her prey, she is instantly all over the victim, who has no avenue for escape. The only element lacking when Lennon descended on DeVere was the victim's exit. Throughout the city room, fingers paused above keys, heads turned, and mouths hung open as Lennon used every strong word she'd learned during her outstanding reportorial career.

Taken by surprise, DeVere, who in turn possessed a most colorful vocabulary, was on the defensive. She lurched to her feet, managed to grab her briefcase, and began backing out of the room. Unrelentingly, Lennon, eyes blazing, continued to advance, until, eschewing an elevator that was too removed, Lacy almost tumbled down the marble staircase.

Lennon marched back through the city room. Some of the personnel chuckled, some sat in shocked silence, others felt like hiding under their desks; one or two essayed applause, which was quickly aborted when Pat swiveled her head to glare at them.

She plunked herself down at her desk and, after a few moments, began to snicker. It was as if her rampage had purged her.

Hesitantly, Pringle McPhee sat down at a neighboring desk.

Lennon turned to her. "What's on your mind, Pringle?"

McPhee couldn't have been more thankful that Lennon had regained her composure. Especially in light of what she had to say. "Uh . . . Pat . . . I'm the one responsible for DeVere's being up here."

Lennon looked at her with increased interest. "No kidding! Whatever made you do a thing like that?"

Pringle bit her lip. "I don't know exactly. She intimidates me, I guess. When the call came from the security desk that DeVere wanted to see me, I was just curious. So I met her in the lobby and she seemed real friendly. She said she wanted to check a couple of things through Hal's computer. It was in connection with a tribute to Hal she was putting together."

Lennon's disbelief was evident. "DeVere doing a tribute! Even for someone who's dead? Not very likely."

"Well, she could have been."

"More like she wanted to steal some ideas or some leads. Why do you let her get to you?"

Pringle's embarrassment was still plain. "Because she is what you said about her—selfish, not very talented, but really cruel. That's where the intimidation comes in. I know she can hurt me and . . . well . . . I'm afraid of her."

"Pringle, what can she do to you? You lead a pretty straight life. Hell, by today's standards you're practically a Camp Fire girl."

"There was that time . . . with the car . . . you know, the attempted murder. She knows . . ." Her voice trailed off.

"Pringle, you didn't attempt murder, for God's sake! You were the victim!"

"I know, I know. But I'm still afraid . . . of certain things. DeVere knows. I feel so vulnerable with her."

Pringle reminded Pat of a frightened deer. She felt like cuddling her. But this was neither the time nor the place. She also felt angry, very angry, at DeVere. "So you let the bitch up here. Well, it can't be all that bad. How long was she fiddling in Hal's basket?"

"Oh, no more than ten or fifteen minutes at most."

"You didn't give her Hal's password, did you?"

"How could I? I don't even know it."

Pat smiled as she leaned over and patted Pringle's arm. "I don't think she could have stumbled on it in that little time. Besides, I was feeling pretty rotten. I needed an outlet for some king-size frustrations. I didn't even know I needed to explode until I did. DeVere was made to order. So . . ." Pat smiled. ". . . all's well that ends well—" She broke off as she spotted her editor leading two visitors in her direction.

Pat felt a flutter of excitement; one of the visitors was Zoo Tully. The other was Father Robert Koesler.

In her job, Pat had met quite a few Detroit-area clergymen. But she knew none better than Father Koesler. Several stories she had covered either revolved around him or events he had been involved in. Only a few days ago, she'd interviewed him in the hospital. So she was well aware of his injury and how it had come about.

Introductions were unnecessary, as Pringle had encountered Tully and Koesler at St. Waldo's.

Bob Ankenazy got to the point without preamble. "Pat, these two gentlemen need access to Hal Salden's basket. You got in there the other day. Got time to help them now?"

"Sure," Pat said. "Hal's basket is getting to be a popular place."

"Popular?" Tully's interest was evident.

"The DeVere . . . uh . . . woman was poking around in there a few minutes ago," Pat said. "I threw her out!"

Tully nodded. "Good for you." No law against it, but odd that DeVere would be interested in Salden's notes. He would preserve the incident in his mental file.

Ankenazy went back about his business as Lennon led Tully and Koesler to Salden's desk. "How're you getting along, Father?" Pat asked as they neared the desk.

"It's okay. Hurts a bit."

I'll bet, thought Pat. Something here must be pretty damn important to drag a wounded priest away from needed rest and recuperation. Her never-quiet reporter's instinct went into high gear.

When Tully had been investigating the missing priest, Pringle had told her, Koesler had been in tow. Not that that combo was unique. In the past few years, when there had been a strong Catholic element in a homicide investigation, Tully and Koesler had become a version of Disney's Spin and Marty.

But that was over and done with. The police had abandoned the search for Father Keating. As far as the authorities were concerned, Keating undoubtedly had been murdered. But they couldn't find the body and they had no suspects.

That was how things lay when Tully had been here a few days ago. He'd been working on the murder of Hal Salden. And Father Koesler had been nowhere in sight.

Then Koesler was shot—along with Guido Vespa, the once and maybe again mobster. Koesler was there because Vespa had asked the priest to meet him. At least that's what Koesler had said in the hospital interview. Why? Who knows? According to Koesler, they were shot before Vespa got very far in explaining himself.

So then what? The cops should be out looking for whoever shot Vespa.

Instead, Tully's back to search Hal's basket. Why? They hadn't found that much in it. Tully couldn't have forgotten what he'd seen. He wanted Koesler to take a look. Why?

Hal Salden was a religion writer. Koesler's a priest. Could that be the connection? Not very strong. If that were the connection, why wouldn't Tully have brought Koesler with him the first time? Afterthought? Maybe.

Nothing else came to mind immediately. But it was an interesting puzzle. Definitely worth looking into.

Pat sat at the keyboard, the two men looking over her shoulder. She punched out HOLY SMOKE and the screen lit up. She waited for a reaction, but none came. Well, Tully had seen Hal's little joke before. But Koesler made no comment. Serious business.

She punched up the "miracle" story of the allegedly possessed girl whose levitation was supposed to be curtailed by assigning a tall priest to get her down from the ceiling.

"Do anything for you?" Tully asked. Lennon knew the question was intended for Koesler.

"Outside of the fact that I don't believe it, no, it doesn't do anything for me," Koesler replied.

Lennon moved on to the story of the Rochester Episcopal parish that had gotten its first female priest.

"What about this one?" Tully asked.

Koesler perused and pondered. "It would be a good story for Hal," he said thoughtfully. "There's lots of drama and conflict in women's rights—or the lack of them—in the Church. This is an internal matter with the Episcopal Church, but I can understand the problem. Allowing the Mass to be offered in English, letting lay people distribute Communion, the greeting of peace—things like these generated an awful lot of bad feelings and anger in the Catholic Church some twenty-five years ago. And a lot of that is still going on. And none of that approaches having a female priest, let alone a female rector. I happen to believe it's the right way to go. But I can understand how some parishioners would react. The problem is, in which direction would their anger be focused? Would they be angry at the people who hired her? Ordained her? Or at the Church that made it possible? Or at the woman herself? Or the reporter who made their discomfort and pain so public? Would they kill the messenger?"

"Kill the messenger?" Lennon repeated softly. "Hal would be the messenger. But . . . I don't think so."

"In any case," Koesler said, "I don't see any connection."

Connection? What connection? Lennon moved her prior theory—that there was some sort of link between the shootings of Salden and Vespa—from the back to the front burner of her mind.

Tully interrupted her thoughts. "Go on to the third item we were looking at the other day, Pat."

Again, Koesler studied the words on the screen. "To tell the truth," he said finally, "I don't see what these have to do with anything. 'Shells! look into . . . trace down! could be key!' " He looked at Lennon. "Does anybody know what this means?"

"I'm the one who thought this might be significant in some way," she admitted. "I was wondering about Hal's using all those exclamation marks."

"It's legitimate punctuation," Koesler observed.

"Uh-huh," Lennon agreed, "except that Hal Salden scarcely ever used an exclamation mark. There are people who use two or three of them after some statement they think is superimportant. That bugs the hell out of me. Then there are those who almost never use one. Hal belonged to that group. And look there: ten words and three exclamation points. It's just odd. But I haven't the slightest idea what the message means."

"Shell Oil comes to mind," Koesler said. "But I've got no clue why a religion writer might be interested in Shell Oil." Pause. "Wait a minute: There's a 'K' at the end. Could that stand for Keating? Father John Keating?"

Without response, Lennon flipped back to the St. Andrew's item, and pointed to the solitary "K" at the bottom of that listing.

"I hadn't noticed that," Koesler said. "Two references to Keating in two different unconnected items? That doesn't make any sense, does it?"

"We noticed the 'K's too," Tully said. "Seems that Salden used to be a sportswriter."

"Ah . . ." Koesler caught on immediately. ". . . and the 'K' stands for strikeout. Which is what I just did."

"It's okay, Father," Tully said. "Not every hunch pays off. This was sort of a wild guess—that Salden's notes might have rung a bell for you. It doesn't look like that's gonna happen. Sorry. Why don't I get you back to the rectory and you can get some rest?"

Koesler agreed. But privately he had to admit he'd felt better in this city room than he had in the rectory. Distraction was proving to be a pretty effective anodyne. He resolved to keep his mind focused on anything but his misery.

Lennon watched thoughtfully as the two men left the room. There had to be some sort of connection between the shootings of Salden and Vespa. But what? Why had Tully brought Koesler—a wounded priest—into the Salden killing?

In any case, whatever Tully had hoped Koesler would find in Salden's notes the priest had not found. So now what? Does Tully give up on trying to establish some sort of link between the shootings? Now that her interest has been aroused, should Pat Lennon give up trying to find out what the police are doing?

Fat chance.

23

IF MEMORY served, Lieutenant Tully usually arrived at work unusually early. That was why Father Koesler dialed Homicide at 7:00 A.M.

Koesler, in a steadfast effort to keep his mind active, thus distracting himself from discomfort, hadn't needed to look far. He kept rehashing the murder of Father Keating. Which, somehow, had spawned the murders of Hal Salden and Guido Vespa, as well as the wounding of innocent bystanders at St. Agnes—and, of course, himself. In truth, he had not come to any conclusion, but he had come upon another possible avenue of inquiry. Thus the early-morning call to Tully.

Koesler was both in luck and correct: The lieutenant was in.

"I've been thinking about yesterday, Lieutenant," Koesler opened. "You took me to the *News* and introduced me to Hal Salden's notes. The one about the exorcism was just an amusingly odd story with a religious twist. Something like the now-outdated photos of nuns on roller coasters.

"The one about the Episcopal parish and its woman rector might, if one stretched his imagination far enough, provide some small motivation for anger at the reporter who was going to spotlight that story. But it has no evident connection that I can think of to Vespa or Keating. The third note about 'shell' just has me baffled. So everything there seems to be a dead end.

"But," Koesler continued, "I began thinking about the beginning of this thing—when you were investigating the disappearance of Father Keating. I went with you that one day. But I was not really collaborating with you. At that time, I was bound—so I thought—to keep a confessional secret. And that was about all I had on my mind. My main concern now is all that time we spent in the rectory at St. Waldo's. I don't know exactly what I might have done that I didn't do. I only know that I didn't do much of anything. So my question is: Do you think it would do any good to go back again?"

"Go back to the rectory and take another look?" Tully had been looking over reports waiting on his desk when he arrived just minutes before Koesler's call.

"Yes. This time without the restrictions of a secret I thought I had to keep."

Tully pondered the proposition. "Sounds good. Let's do it. I'll be right over to pick you up." As he put the phone down, Tully admitted to himself that he wasn't all that excited by Koesler's offer. But it was head and shoulders above anything else he could think of. After jotting some memos for members of his squad, he left.

*   *   *

Considering all the personnel had been through, Koesler was surprised at their reaction to his and Tully's arrival at St. Waldo's.

Just a couple of weeks ago, this place had been awash with police from various communities. Now there was merely one detective and one simple parish priest.

But no sooner had the two visitors emerged from their car than the janitor, with a startled expression, dropped his garden tools into the shrubbery he'd been working on and quickly disappeared around the corner of the rectory.

Tully rang the doorbell. They could hear people moving about inside. The curtain fluttered as someone peered through it. Finally, as Tully was about to ring again, the door was opened by the woman both knew was the secretary. "Yes?" She looked as if she was about to cry.

Tully reintroduced himself and Koesler. "We've come to look around again."

"I . . . I don't think I can permit that." She said it as if she might prefer being in purgatory than here just at this moment.

Tully was about to pull clout and scare her stiff, when Koesler spoke. "What is it, dear? Did someone tell you not to let anyone in?"

"Well . . . not anyone, Father. Only the police."

"The police!" Tully did manage to frighten her, though he didn't intend to. "How do you think we're going to conduct a—"

"Who was it told you?" Koesler asked.

"Father Mitchell." She hoped the spotlight would shift from herself to Mitchell.

"Fred?" Koesler said. "What in the world—? Where is Father Mitchell now? Can you get him?"

She nodded. "Would you mind waiting?"

"Outside?" Tully scared her again. He modulated his voice. "If this weren't such a nice day . . ." The quieter tone helped.

Slowly and carefully the door was closed, leaving Tully and Koesler standing awkwardly on the porch. While they waited, they kept their thoughts to themselves. It was several minutes before the door reopened. This time it was Father Fred Mitchell, obviously not in a receptive mood.

The first thing that caught his attention was the stark contrast of a white arm sling against Koesler's black suit. "God! I didn't expect to see you for a while. I read about what happened. How's the arm?"

"Don't ask," Koesler replied. "What's this about an embargo on the police?"

"Orders."

" 'Orders'? Who said?" Such an order, thought Koesler, would have been completely out of character for Detroit's archbishop, Cardinal Boyle. And of course St. Waldo's was pastorless.

"The parish council met two evenings ago," Mitchell explained.

"It was a regularly scheduled meeting. That's where the order originated. The council decided to put its trust in prayer and the eventual return of Father Keating. So they resolved to allow no more disruptions in the ordinary routine of parish life. They were explicit when it came to police poking around disturbing everyone."

"But . . . but whose idea was it to get the police involved in the first place?" Koesler was perplexed.

"It doesn't matter," Mitchell replied. "When the pastor first disappeared, the council—well, the council president—was worried that something terrible had happened to him. But now, they're convinced that he must be occupied in something very important—which, for his own good reasons, must be kept secret—and that he will return and explain in his own good time."

"Do you really believe that?" Koesler asked.

Mitchell hesitated. "Well, no. Between you and me it seems ridiculous. But what am I? An associate with not very clearly defined boundaries on what kind of authority I've got in this situation. And, need I remind you, this parish contains some pretty important movers and shakers."

Guido Vespa's "confession" with the concomitant information about Keating's murder had not been made public. Still, Tully found it incomprehensible that anyone still thought that Keating was alive.

"Father," Tully's tone was the soul of calm reason, "we've got a couple of ways to go at this point. You can step aside and let us look at whatever we need to look at . . . or"—he drew the word out—"I will go to the trouble of getting a warrant and come back with as many cops as I can rouse on short notice. One way or the other, we're going to go in here. Now, which will it be?" Tully was smiling benevolently.

Mitchell returned the smile and stepped aside. "You have just made me an offer I can understand. However, I'd better call the council president and tell him what's happening. Otherwise, I'm going to have to borrow your sling, Bob, for another part of my anatomy."

"You do whatever you think right, Father." Tully led the way into the rectory.

Koesler and Tully headed upstairs to Keating's suite. The conspicuous opulence of Keating's lifestyle still vaguely disturbed Tully. Yet the two men found no more than had been found before. Nor did any fresh insight occur to Koesler. He began to wonder if this were such a bright idea after all. With the doubt came the awareness of the dull ache in his shoulder. And with that ache came a renewed determination to get to the core of what had happened to Keating and Vespa and led to his being disabled.

Koesler looked again through drawers, closets, and files. Nothing. He shrugged, and he and Tully returned downstairs to scour Keating's office and den and whatever else they came across. Desperation was not far off, and both of them knew it.

Meanwhile, Mitchell had placed a call to Eric Dunstable.

One did not simply call Dunstable. One placed a call. Odds were that the caller would never reach the man. At best, one might speak to a distant assistant and, if lucky, get to leave a message.

Mitchell would have been more than happy to leave a message that would get lost somewhere in the muddle of bureaucracy. As for Koesler and Tully's searching the place, frankly, Mitchell didn't give a damn. He wasn't at all eager for Dunstable to get in on this and muck up something which, left alone, would probably just go away.

But as bad luck would have it, Dunstable had apparently given his staff instructions that any message coming from St. Waldo's should be red-flagged.

Thus Mitchell's call was expedited right through to the boss, who was not happy with the news.

Had this officer been informed of the council's decision, Dunstable demanded to know. Mitchell assured him that the council's vote to debar the police from parish property had been imparted.

Throughout this conversation, Mitchell continued mentally to thank God that he had handled this matter by the book. He had conducted everything strictly according to the council's instructions. Now, if they wanted to get angry at someone, that someone would not be Fred Mitchell. It would be Lieutenant Tully.

And as it turned out, Eric Dunstable was very angry. So angry that he did what he hardly ever did: He canceled all further appointments and commitments for the day. This would place a most serious burden on the staff, including assistants and various vice presidents. Dunstable of course couldn't have cared less. The phone calls, juggling of appointments and conferences, all were the underlings' problems. Dunstable's problem was to straighten out an uppity cop. He told Mitchell he was on his way. Mitchell could almost see the avenging knight galloping up Woodward Avenue on his white charger.

Since the door to Mitchell's office had been left ajar, the parish secretary could not help but overhear Mitchell's end of the phone conversation. That was sufficient for her to comprehend what was going on and, more to the point, what was about to happen.

Understandably, she was upset. Having no other shoulder on which to lean, she went to the kitchen and confided in the cook.

The cook reacted with alarm. What to do?

Nothing, the secretary suggested.

It was the cook's opinion that shortly all hell was going to bust loose. The secretary concurred, but counseled that was precisely why they should do nothing: stay out of the way and hope and pray that Vesuvius would blow in another direction.

But, the cook argued, so omnivorous was the council president's appetite when aroused, that the two women might be swallowed whole and regurgitated unemployed.

How could that be; they were no more than innocent bystanders, the secretary maintained.

They were also, countered the cook, replaceable—and the only ones in sight who were expendable. Dunstable could not fire, dismiss, or otherwise discipline a Detroit police officer—or either of the two priests. The janitor was off hiding somewhere. That, the cook concluded, "leaves you and me, dearie."

The secretary finally came around to the cook's evaluation of this mess. But what to do? What course of action could save them from the wrath of Dunstable?

After several moments of worried wondering, the cook thought she might have a solution. "Remember that nice reporter who was here that day that all the cops were swarming around?"

The secretary reflected. "A . . . DeVere? Lacy DeVere?"

"No, no, no!" the cook said irritably. "She was definitely not nice. The other one . . . the one I let in the back door. You remember; you and I talked with her while the cops searched."

"Oh." The light of recognition lit in the secretary's eyes. "Yes. That was . . . uh . . . Pringle, Pringle McSomething."

"Pringle McPhee!" the cook supplied. "Let's call her and see if she'll come over. Dunstable won't dare do anything to us if we've got a reporter as a witness."

"I don't know about that," said a worried secretary. "But it's worth a try."

*   *   *

"You remember me: I'm the cook at St. Waldo's. Remember?"

Pringle McPhee motioned Pat Lennon to pick up the extension phone.

"Yes, of course. What's up?"

"I . . . we . . . were wondering if you'd consider coming over here."

"Why?"

"Why?"

"We think Mr. Dunstable might fire us."

"What?"

"This is the secretary. Remember me?"

"Yes . . ."

"I'm on the extension phone. See, the parish council passed a resolution that no policemen be admitted to the rectory until Father Keating returns."

"They actually think—"

"Well, there's a police officer here now. He and that Father Koesler are rummaging through Father Keating's rooms in direct violation of the council's order."

Silently, for Lennon's benefit, Pringle formed the words: *This is crazy.* Aloud she said, "Wait! Who's there, and what are they doing?"

"Father Koesler and that Lieutenant Tully. It's the lieutenant that's got us in all this trouble. I wasn't supposed to let in any police. So I got Father Mitchell. But then the officer just barged right in anyway. Threatened to bring a whole bunch of policemen if Father Mitchell didn't let him in."

"So Father Mitchell let him in?"

"I guess he didn't have any choice."

"Well, what's this about Mr. Dunstable and getting fired?"

"Father Mitchell called Mr. Dunstable. And he's on his way here right now. He's president of the parish council. We're afraid he might fire us. We know that's not your concern. But we thought you might want to find out what's going on. You could come in the back door like before."

Pringle glanced at Pat, who winked and nodded.

"We'll be right over," Pringle said.

"*We?*"

"I'm going to bring another reporter with me."

*   *   *

"Fine!" said the secretary as she hung up. "The more the merrier."

"They're coming?" the cook asked.

"They're coming," the secretary affirmed.

"Then we're as ready as we ever will be."

"Not quite," the secretary said. "I'll just take some refreshments into Father Keating's office."

24

On the long, chauffeured drive to St. Waldo's, Eric Dunstable had time to cool off. He just didn't use it. Instead, he was more indignant than he'd been when Mitchell informed him that Waldo's rectory had been invaded.

Father Mitchell, in turn, was taken aback when Dunstable, after storming through the front entrance, proceeded to hold the associate pastor responsible.

Mitchell figured he had played it safe, gone by the book. Sure there was a police officer here in defiance of the parish council's order. And granted, Mitchell had admitted him. But that had been only to forestall Tully's threat to summon loads of cops. That latter state would have been much worse than the first. Besides, Tully had said he would return with not only a bunch of cops, but also a warrant. So any way this played out, Tully was going to get into the rectory and look around, parish council or no parish council. So how could Dunstable fault what Mitchell had done?

What Father Mitchell failed to comprehend was that Eric Dunstable did not deal in failure. His only frame of reference was success. In not tolerating checkmate, he had gone through countless employees, associates, friends, and even one wife.

Mitchell was well able to deal with occasional failure, projects that became doomed. He could understand that sometimes, despite one's best efforts and under circumstances beyond one's control, things simply didn't work out. And Tully's inevitable renewed investigation within St. Waldo's rectory was a case in point.

So there was a gap. Mitchell couldn't understand why Dunstable couldn't understand why blocking Tully had proved impossible. Dunstable couldn't understand why Mitchell hadn't carried out the council's order.

If it had been within Dunstable's jurisdiction, he would have dismissed the priest with extreme prejudice. As it was, Dunstable resolved to speak to the Cardinal about this undependable young man.

Having dealt with and diminished Mitchell, Dunstable turned to Tully.

The lieutenant had been studying Dunstable as he psychologically castrated the young priest. Tully judged Dunstable to be a bully— successful, but no more than a bully at the core. Tully's experience indicated that all bullies are essentially insecure. As long as one gave them room to intimidate, as Mitchell had, they would have their way, manipulating and trampling everyone in their path. Thus when Dunstable, now in a virtual convulsion of fury, turned to the lieutenant, Tully was ready for him.

Tully stood utterly relaxed, arms hanging loosely. He fixed his eyes intently on Dunstable's. It was a contest to match that of Ursus and the bull in *Quo Vadis*. Koesler found it a fascinating contest of wills.

Slowly Dunstable began to falter. He blinked nervously, and his eyes strayed from Tully's.

It was not so much what Tully said as his manner of presentation. Everything he said was true. But it wasn't the content that turned the tide but the calm authority with which Tully delivered the message. That was it: authority. There was a difference between genuine rooted authority and a facade built on the sands of bravado.

Two examples sprang to Koesler's mind. There were all those enemies of Christ who held immense power of religious domination over the people. The scribes and Pharisees appeared to have an authority above that of Jesus, who was, after all, no more than one of the people. But it was the people who saw the truth. As Mark noted, "The people were spellbound by his teaching because he taught with authority, and not like the scribes."

So it was with these two. Dunstable, successful, fulfilled, and wealthy beyond most people's dreams. But nothing more than a bully, a fraud. Tully, on the other hand, spoke with the quiet decisiveness that even a bully had to respect.

The other example that came to Koesler's mind indicated that true authority recognizes true authority. As in the case of the centurion in the Gospel whose favorite servant was at the point of death. Jesus agreed to come and cure. But the centurion said he was unworthy to host Jesus; he told him just to say the word and there would be healing. "Just give the order and my servant will be cured. I too am a man who knows the meaning of an order . . ."

In any case, Dunstable had been deflated. Yet Tully, in making certain that Dunstable had been neutralized, let him save a portion of face.

Grumbling all the way, Dunstable poured a cup of coffee and took a seat next to Koesler on the couch.

Even though the white sling cradling Koesler's arm had been obvious all along, only now for the first time did Dunstable express concern for Koesler's injury. Of course he was aware of how the priest had been wounded, so there was no need to go into that. It was easy to treat Koesler with a measure of respect. After all, he was a priest—and not a hairy young thing like Mitchell.

It was easy also for Koesler to start on a friendly basis with Dunstable. It was a play on the "tough cop, nice cop" routine. Even though Koesler was by no means a cop, he and Tully had somehow created a professional relationship in this case. And if Tully had civilly but firmly told Dunstable where to get off, Koesler was the station Dunstable landed on.

Meanwhile, Mitchell had retreated out of the line of fire to one corner of the room. He'd been confused and humiliated. He would not recover, at least for the duration of his stay at St. Waldo's.

Tully turned to Mitchell. "I suppose all that's left is to take a look at the books."

"Books?" Dunstable emerged warily from his protective cocoon. "What books?"

"Ledgers, financial records."

"See here, Lieutenant," Dunstable reverted to form, "this is something else entirely! These are sensitive records. Why, an audit hasn't even been ordered by the archdiocese yet!"

"This is not an audit, Mr. Dunstable. We don't even know what we're looking for. We don't know whether we've seen what we're looking for and didn't recognize it. We're in the dark. Humor us."

Again Koesler was deeply impressed with Tully's handling of himself, the situation, and particularly Dunstable. It was the manner, the tone, the self-assurance. However he accomplished it, the lieutenant had Dunstable on a string.

"Father Mitchell," Tully said, "where are the financial records kept, please?" By his respectful treatment, Tully attempted to restore some of the young priest's dignity.

Mitchell hesitated, glanced at Dunstable, then back at Tully. "In the safe behind his desk."

"Locked?"

"Not usually," Mitchell replied.

"He had nothing to hide," Dunstable snapped.

Mitchell crossed to the safe and tried the handle. It turned easily. He opened the door, reached in, removed several large, gray ledgers, and placed them on the desk.

Tully moved behind the desk, opened one of the books, and began paging through it almost aimlessly.

"I want to be on record that I protest your delving into the private records of this parish," Dunstable said firmly.

"Noted." Tully did not look up.

"I say it's an invasion of privacy . . ." Dunstable had been reduced to muttering.

"You might want to take a look at these," Tully said, as he glanced at Koesler.

Koesler walked to the desk and began looking through the ledgers. He had almost forgotten that he was indeed the prime cause of this "invasion" of St. Waldo's. However, like Tully, Koesler was going through this without direction, hoping that something strange, indicative, or suggestive would pop up and grab his attention. He felt like praying the old Catholic rhyme: "Dear St. Anthony, please come around/Something is lost and can't be found." Except that he didn't know what was lost.

"I say it's an insult—a gratuitous insult—to impugn the integrity of a man like Father Keating." Dunstable had risen to something more articulate than a mutter.

Neither Tully nor Koesler responded. Actually Koesler was the only one of the two paying any attention at all to Dunstable.

"You know, I've been over those books," Dunstable continued his monologue. "I know what I'm looking at when I've got a financial statement in front of me. There's nothing wrong with those books. All they show is that we have a generous parish, that the parish is well managed, and that we pay our bills on time. Our D and B, if we had one, would be impeccable."

"I'm sure you're right," Koesler said with little feeling.

"This is a waste of time. A waste of everyone's time. A waste of my time."

Koesler tended to agree. It was proving to be a monumental waste of time. Tully continued to page through the books. He was now practically up to date in the financial records. Koesler, losing interest in the books, turned his attention to the fuming executive on the couch. "You were close to Father Keating, weren't you?" he said kindly.

"I *am* close to Father Keating."

"Of course. You must be one of those who even vacationed with him."

Dunstable appreciated the friendly approach Koesler was extending. By God, these old-time priests appreciated his standing! He warmed to the memory of those vacations. "Yes, we were among those privileged to have the good father with us occasionally at home and on vacations as well."

In his imagination, Koesler had to grant that a Keating-Dunstable vacation undoubtedly was a lot more splendid than Florida with the good old boys.

"He was—uh, *is* —a very close friend. He has always been with me when I needed him."

Koesler thought the man might break down and cry.

"I don't think," Dunstable continued, "anyone could have been more helpful, concerned, or involved than Father Jack was when we went through that annulment process."

"You had an annulment?" Koesler was loath to go, unbidden, into anyone's private affairs. But Dunstable had brought up the subject and apparently wanted to proclaim Keating's solicitous care during what admittedly was a traumatic procedure.

"Yes. My first wife. Back in eighty-five."

"Followed by a convalidation?" Koesler diplomatically steered the exchange so that Dunstable did not have to admit specifically that after divorcing his first wife he had invalidly married his second wife and only later, after the declaration of nullity, married his second wife in the Church.

"Yes." Dunstable seemed uncomfortable that he'd brought up the subject. But in his effort to indicate what a kind pastor Keating had been, he had let the cat out of the bag. He hoped Tully had not been paying attention. In this hope he was fortunate. Mitchell may or may not have known that, for a time, Dunstable had "lived in sin" with his second wife. It was there in the records to which Mitchell had access. But Mitchell didn't matter. And Koesler seemed a nice sort.

Koesler was pleased. He was so proud of his priesthood, he took quite personally both the good and bad reports about other priests. Besides, sometime in the future Father Keating's body might turn up. In which case, there would be a funeral. It was at least possible that Koesler might be asked to deliver a eulogy. Learning as many good things as possible about Keating could be a practically rewarding enterprise.

Koesler did not want to delve into the reason Dunstable's first marriage had been ruled null from its inception—which would have to have been the case or the Church would never have granted a decree of nullity.

Had he been curious, it would have been simple for Koesler to discover that the first Mrs. Dunstable had been committed to a rather nice rest home for the mentally disturbed. And that she was there to this day. Koesler's assumption at that point would have been that her unbalanced condition was proved to have existed prior to her marriage to Dunstable. Otherwise, if he had married a sane woman who later became ill, the marriage could not have been declared null on those grounds. The marriage would have been found valid and there would have been no way the Church would recognize Dunstable's freedom to marry. Nor would the Church have convalidated Dunstable's civil second marriage.

These would have been Koesler's assumptions if he had been aware of the first Mrs. Dunstable's present whereabouts.

These assumptions would have been only partly incorrect.

The first Mrs. Dunstable had been quite sane, though not entirely wise, when she married. Years of psychological abuse, the never-ending demand for perfection, service, sacrifice, and dedication to Dunstable, along with his requirement that she perform in public as a loved and pampered spouse, drove the poor woman bonkers.

He divorced her when she slipped into a psychotic state, and he had her committed. But God did not will that Dunstable remain alone. At least that's the way he saw it. He married again. But his previous marriage prevented the second marriage from being valid in the eyes of the Church.

Dunstable was more than uncomfortable with this. It was common knowledge that he was Catholic—a pillar of the Church—and that, the second time around, he did not have benefit of clergy.

Enter Father Keating.

From experience and manipulation, Keating knew that one could find any number of psychotherapists—psychiatrists, psychologists—who could be counted on to categorize someone as sane or insane, depending upon which state was desired. And in conjunction with his search into the first Mrs. Dunstable's past, Keating was able to come up with several such therapists. Those who judged her to be quite sane at the time of her marriage were discarded. Those who found that her unfortunate condition had been alive and thriving as early as her teen years were the ones interviewed for the record.

Thus, with some expediting from a bishop or so, the nullity was granted and a quiet convalidation was witnessed by Father John Keating himself.

"Yes," Dunstable reaffirmed, "Father Jack was with me—with us—when we really needed him. I don't know what we'd have done without him."

Koesler was touched by the seeming sincerity of this tribute. "How did he help?"

Dunstable was most willing to go into some detail. "He just was . . . *there*. He opened the canonical procedure. He helped with the presentation of the case—even picked out the witnesses and arranged for them to testify. Just shepherded the whole thing through from beginning to end. Even had a bishop—a friend of his—smooth the way. But," he emphasized defensively, "that doesn't mean I got any special consideration because of my position. It's not that I *bought* this dispensation!"

"I understand," Koesler said. "I understand. Thank God the day is past when the Church can be accused of *selling* these decisions."

"That's right." Dunstable seemed gratified that Koesler understood. "Father Jack actually kept the cost to an absolute minimum."

Tully had been paying only cursory attention to the records that marched past his eyes. He had been paying even less attention to the conversation between Koesler and Dunstable. But he hadn't banked on silence. Like someone half asleep in front of a blaring television when someone turns it off: One is not prepared for silence, so one comes wide awake.

Dunstable had a similar reaction. Why hadn't Father Koesler replied? Their conversation had been running so smoothly. The priest should have said something to the effect of "Wasn't that thoughtful of Father Jack?" Instead, he said nothing.

The silence was electric.

"Excuse me, Mr. Dunstable," Koesler said quietly after a few moments, "did you say something about Father Keating keeping the cost of your nullity declaration to a minimum?"

Dunstable felt unsure of himself, an exceedingly rare state. What had been a casual conversation with Koesler, with no indication that either Mitchell or Tully was paying any mind, had suddenly taken on some undefined significance.

The aura of hauteur appeared to have dissolved. "Well, Father Jack explained how a case like mine would have to go to Rome. All the documents, all the testimony would have to be translated into Latin. Attorneys in Rome would have to be retained to argue the case.

"Really, gentlemen . . ." Dunstable addressed not only Koesler, but the others, since everyone now was paying rapt attention. ". . . he didn't have to go through all that. Don't you see: It's just one more example of how kind and thoughtful Father Jack was during my time of need.

"Of course," he added, "I understand that things cost money." He smiled—a we're-men-of-the-world smile. "We all have to live, after all. I presented a case that had to be worked on. Well, you pay for work. No one understands that better than I. Those lawyers in Rome have to eat! After all, I am well able to pay. Father Jack explained that if I were poor, there would be no charge. I think that rather thoughtful of the Church—not charging the indigent."

He smiled, smugly this time. "Really, gentlemen, I don't understand your concern with this. I just said that with all this in mind that Father Jack went out of his way to keep my costs at a minimum. All things considered, I think that a rather touching example of how special that very special priest was—is."

Koesler, Tully, and Mitchell merely looked at Dunstable.

Dunstable began to squirm a bit. Mitchell was beginning to get the point. Tully had no idea what was going on. But a sixth sense told him that something telling was happening and that this case had just taken a pivotal turn.

Without speaking, Koesler returned to the desk, alongside Tully.

After a few moments, he said, "I beg your pardon, Mr. Dunstable, but exactly how much was that charge for processing your case?"

"Well," Dunstable sputtered, "I don't see how that's here or there . . ."

"Answer him." Tully's quiet voice was incisive, commanding.

Dunstable licked his lips several times. Finally, he decided he was not on trial. He had done nothing wrong. Simply paid a bill. If they were so goddam curious about the cost of his dispensation, well, hell, he'd tell them. "The total cost was a mere five thousand dollars. And with all that was involved, I considered it a bargain. And I know the value of money," he added, as if daring anyone to argue the point.

Koesler gave the impression of being dumbstruck. Out of the corner of his eye, Tully glanced at him. "What is it?"

Without taking his eyes from Dunstable, Koesler said, "There is no charge for processing marriage cases. There hasn't been for a good number of years. The diocese absorbs the cost. Been doing so for almost fifteen years—well before Mr. Dunstable's case."

Koesler slumped into the chair behind the desk. He massaged his forehead as he tried to make sense of this peculiar revelation. "Mr. Dunstable," he said, "I assume you made this payment with a check."

Dunstable nodded.

"Then," Koesler continued, "who did you make the check out to?"

"Why . . . why . . ." Dunstable tried to recall. "I made it out to the parish, I believe. Yes . . ." He was more certain now. ". . . to St. Waldo's."

"Now that doesn't make much sense, does it?" Koesler asked of no one in particular.

"No, it doesn't." Mitchell picked up on the question. "If Keating charged five grand for a no-charge item, you'd think he'd have had the check made out to him."

"Now just a minute!" Dunstable objected. "There must be some explanation for this! You're insinuating—"

"I'm not insinuating anything, Mr. Dunstable," Koesler said. "We're trying to figure out what happened here. Any light you can shed on it?"

Dunstable was confused. But then, so was everyone else. "No," he said, "I have no idea. I told you just the way it happened. Just the way Father Keating helped. I don't know . . ." His voice trailed off.

"Mr. Dunstable," Tully said, "this seems like it would be a transaction with Rome. Why would you make out the check to this parish?"

"The question crossed my mind," Dunstable admitted. "But Father Jack explained that since all the paperwork would be originating from the parish, the payment also would come from the parish. I was, in a sense, compensating the parish in advance for costs that would come from the archdiocese as well as from Rome." He put on his contentious hat. "How can you even suggest that Father Jack would enrich himself from this transaction? If you knew him, you'd know that such a thought would never cross his mind. Besides, as Father Mitchell already said, if he were going to profit from this, why did he have me make the check out to the parish? Why didn't he have me make it out to him?"

No one had an answer. There was a prolonged period of silence and thought.

"Wait a minute," Koesler said suddenly. "I'm not sure of this, or how it fits, or if it fits, but . . . let's take another look at those books." He opened the current ledger. He ran his finger down the list of billings. "Something vaguely occurred to me earlier, when we were going through the books. Something . . . something . . . something . . . some of these accounts, some of these companies, some of these billings . . ."

"What?" Tully wanted to know.

"Well," Koesler said, "some of these billings are from companies or institutions I've never heard of."

"Is that odd?"

"In a sense, yes. See, I've been a pastor for twenty-two years. That's twenty-two years of running up bills and paying bills or at least being accountable for paying bills. Some might find it surprising, I suppose, that the billings are not all that different from one parish to the next.

"But, for example, there's a firm that sells and delivers Mass wine as well as, in some instances, table wine. The ad for that company has it that only Catholic Teamsters drive the trucks that deliver the wine."

Tully smiled.

"Okay," Koesler said, "it's hokey, but apparently it works. You'd be surprised how many parishes get their wine from this company. Then there's the matter of hosts."

"Hosts?" Tully had the impression that this case was on the brink of coming to a conclusion. He didn't want to risk being sidetracked by Catholic jargon.

"The altar breads that are used at Mass," Koesler clarified. "Communion wafers."

Tully nodded.

"Well, when it comes to providing hosts, there's a local convent whose nuns have virtually cornered the market. They're available almost anytime and they've always got a good supply. Say some Sunday the crowded late Masses are coming up, and you're running low on hosts. It could be time to panic—except for the good Sisters. They are especially at hand for that sort of emergency."

"And they deliver," Mitchell interjected.

"Like Domino's?" Tully asked.

"Not quite," Koesler said, "but you'll get the wafers as soon as the fastest cab driver can deliver them. And in a fix like that the priest will be happy to pay the cab fare. Besides, they *are* nuns."

"So," Tully said, "how about this parish? Does St. Waldo's buy from the Catholic Teamsters and the handy nuns?"

"Yes," Koesler looked again at the ledger, "they're both on the billing list. So are a number of other firms, companies, and services that I'm familiar with.

"But there are others that I've never heard of. I could swear I've never gotten any literature from them. I've never heard any of the guys mention doing business with any of them." He looked up from the books. "And we do talk about these things.

"As I said before," Koesler continued to look in a baffled way around the room at the other men, "I don't exactly know what this means. It's just that in the light of Mr. Dunstable's paying for a canonical process for which there is no charge, I thought that these completely unfamiliar billings were a bit peculiar. But I don't know where we go from here. I'd sure like to find out something about these companies."

"Well . . ." Dunstable stood, repossessed of his original aggressive manner. ". . . I know where we go from here." He stepped around to join Koesler and Tully behind the large desk. He took the ledger from Koesler, who winced as Dunstable inadvertently brushed against the injured shoulder. "Which of these billings are you questioning?"

"Well . . ." Koesler squeezed the sore arm with his left hand as he swallowed the pain. ". . . there's this one—Med Corp Roofing—and

Murray Athletic Supplies, and GOPITS, INC.—and these three down at the bottom of the page."

Dunstable shook his head. "I've seen these names any number of times when I went over the books with Father Jack. But I never suspected . . . not for an instant." He looked around the room. "Any one have any objection if I follow through on Father Koesler's hunch?"

Mitchell was intent only on maintaining an extremely low profile. Tully couldn't think of anyone he'd rather have check out businesses than Dunstable. And of course it was Koesler's lead that Dunstable was following. No objection. Koesler made his way back to the couch.

Dunstable picked up the phone, whose cord seemed to be near infinite, dialed, and began to pace about as he ticked off orders à la Jimmy Cagney in "One, Two, Three."

Koesler could imagine whoever Dunstable had called being up to his or her ears in work. Now that person would be expected to drop everything and respond to these new orders. In all probability, the poor soul would also be expected to finish the interrupted work by the end of the day.

Though Koesler was intensely interested in what Dunstable was saying, he could pick up only bits and snatches. Among these fragments were, "securities commission," "articles of incorporation," "names of directors and officers" and "copy of annual report." Then followed the names of the companies Koesler had indicated. And a forceful instruction to get this information back yesterday. Dunstable gave his employee St. Waldo's fax number and hung up.

There was nothing to do but wait.

Mitchell was resolved to stay in his corner and contemplate what possible future he had at this parish. It was a nice enough place, but he'd pretty well had enough of influential people who ran roughshod over others. Those who did this were only a small percentage of St. Waldo's parishioners, but they certainly made their presence felt. Chief among these, of course, was Eric Dunstable.

Maybe, Mitchell thought, he'd apply for a different parish. He was not immediately aware of an attractive opening, but there had to be one someplace. Besides, it was a buyer's market; he ought to be able to swing something worthwhile.

Dunstable continued to pace.

Inwardly, he was fuming. He would not explode. Not here. Not in the presence of Tully. The man had bested him once already; he would not give the lieutenant another opportunity. But someone in the near future would pay. That vice president had better come up with that information soon or he would be the victim du jour.

Dunstable well knew why some nameless serf would have to suffer. Because he could not get his hands on Father John Keating. Dunstable was now willing to admit that Keating was dead. And that was sad because it removed the opportunity of killing the priest himself.

He had been had. He, Eric Dunstable, grossly successful executive, had been taken. And by a parish priest!

It wasn't the five thousand dollars. Hell, five grand to him was twenty dollars to the ordinary stiff. No, it wasn't the money. It was that somebody—no, make that a nobody—had taken advantage of him. The shoe very definitely was on the wrong foot. Taking advantage of people was his game.

It was as if a youthful, inexperienced card player had dealt from the bottom of the deck to a riverboat gambler and gotten away with it.

The fire in his viscera burned when he recalled how touched he'd been when Keating had been so solicitous, had appeared to put himself out so that the petitioner had to do little more than sign his name to documents—and, of course, to that check.

Purgatory was too good for the bastard!

Sure, sure, sure, all the documents had to be translated, the Italian canonical lawyers had to eat, a little gratuity here and there with a well-positioned monsignor could help. Dunstable resolved he would have someone look into this and discover just how far his petition had had to travel before it was granted. Probably never even left the archdiocese of Detroit!

Somewhere in this there had to be an expense. Nothing that complicated could be complimentary. There was no such thing as a free undertaking in the Catholic Church. If the expense was swallowed by the Detroit archdiocese it had to be absorbed by the annual archdiocesan collection. Dunstable traditionally contributed most generously to that drive. In effect, then, he'd paid for his dispensation twice. Once in the annual drive, which, among other things, covered the costs incurred by the matrimonial court. And again to line the pockets of Keating's top-of-the-line black silk suit.

But five grand? Why five grand? Risking a comfortable career and total security for a measly five thousand dollars? Why? Unless Koesler's hunch gelled and there was something phony about those companies that were being checked out even as he paced.

Come to think of it, hell was too good for the bastard.

Dunstable, waiting for his answers, sat in Keating's oversize chair, opened the top ledger, and began feeding figures into the computer, while giving free rein to imaginative next-world punishments for his deceased former friend.

Mitchell pondered possible parishes to which he might flee.

Tully crossed to the couch and sat alongside a brooding Father Koesler. The two sat in silence for several minutes.

Without looking at him, Koesler said, finally, "You know, Lieutenant, I've been thinking . . ."

Tully waited.

"What if," Koesler spoke loudly enough for only Tully to hear, "what if it turns out that Father Keating was somehow profiting from one or more of these companies? I've been sitting here wondering, 'what if.' I've been trying to figure out why he'd do such a thing. But then, why would he have charged Dunstable five thousand dollars when he knew the whole thing was covered by the archdiocese? To help cover his gambling debts?

"It doesn't make much sense unless . . . unless I've been missing the point all along. Unless I've been just plain wrong."

Tully still said nothing. It was Koesler's ball game. If he'd been wrong before, perhaps now he'd be on target. Whatever was happening was happening in the priest's analytical mind. Tully wasn't as interested in the process as in the product.

"When I was telling you about John Keating's history, as well and as completely as I could," Koesler said, "I didn't tell you about how Jake once invested deeply in the stock market and lost a bundle. But it happened."

Tully nodded without comment. He would go along with Koesler's premises.

"From that I drew the conclusion that he was a poor gambler and that his tendency to gamble and lose eventually led to the gambling debts he built up recently. It was those debts, after all, that led to his murder at the hands of an assassin who had a contract to kill him.

"Well, maybe. But maybe not . . .

"I'm thinking now about that single instance when Jake in effect stole—dear God, I hate to even use that word—but, yes, stole five thousand dollars from Eric Dunstable. That was not a gamble. That was a sure thing. Well, what if Jake somehow profited from the use of these companies? Now we don't know that he did; all we have to go on at the moment is that they're unfamiliar to me.

"But what if he did profit from them? It wouldn't have been gambling. It would have been a sure thing."

Koesler fell silent again. He seemed to be weighing the conclusion he'd just reached.

"So," Tully said finally, "where are you going with this?"

"Oh . . ." It was as if he'd wakened Koesler. ". . . just this: If what I just suggested turns out to be true, then I drew exactly the wrong conclusion about his stock market experience. The loss he suffered there wasn't a symptom of an untreated disease he should have taken to Gamblers Anonymous. Rather it was a lesson he'd learned: Don't gamble. You're not good at it. Go for the sure thing."

Tully's brow was well knit. "But Vespa told you . . ."

"Yes, Vespa told me, in that pivotal confession . . . the confession that started all this. The confession that Vespa was paid to make."

"Yes, but—"

Koesler continued as if Tully had not spoken. "This new line of thought seems to be opening my memory. I mean my memory of what happened at Eastern Market the night Guido Vespa and I were shot."

"We've been over that." Indeed they had, and Tully felt they had milked it for all it was worth.

"I think," Koesler persisted, "I was so shocked that his confession had been faked that I lost the other things he said that night. The simulated confession seemed all that was important. Now, in the light of what I'm thinking, I can recall quite clearly what else he said. It wasn't much. He had just begun to tell me what he *really* wanted to confess when we were shot."

"Okay," Tully said, "this is important. Try to get it all."

"The first thing I told him was that I'd been at the church when they opened Clem Kern's coffin that day. And Guido wanted to know how Father Kern had looked."

Tully shook his head.

"I know it's inconsequential. I just mention that to show that my memory of what happened and what he said is quite clear now.

"After his question as to Clem's appearance, he told me about the confession having been a fake. That's the point at which my memory has pulled up short until now. But there was more.

"When he told me the confession was a fraud, I got angry and questioned whether he even had any sort of contract. He swore he did."

"Don't you sort of wonder now," Tully asked, "when Vespa was lying and when he was telling the truth?"

"No. Not then and not now. He seemed to know he was on borrowed time. He'd told whoever gave him this contract that he was going to make a clean breast of it to me. Lieutenant, what he said to me that night was as good as a deathbed confession."

"Okay, good enough."

"He charged himself with what his grandfather later complained of—getting too cute—in this case, by adding the fiction that he'd buried Keating's body with Clem Kern.

"But the most important thing he said, as it turns out now, was the last thing—the last words he spoke in this life." Koesler paused, either for effect or in an effort to get Vespa's last words exactly.

Tully said nothing.

"Vespa's last words to me were, 'And that ain't all—' And then the shots rang out and he was dead."

"'And that ain't all . . .' So what's it mean?" Tully asked.

"What was left?" Koesler answered with a question. "He had dissected everything he had originally told me in that bogus confession except one thing, the essence of the whole thing: the fact that he had actually killed Father Keating."

"What?"

"Grant you now that this whole premise rests on what we discover about those companies that are being checked out. But the way things would stand depending on those companies would be that Guido Vespa got a contract that called for nothing but the deceiving confession. That's it. No burial with another priest. And most of all—no murder."

"No murder!" A novel concept to Tully. "It might make sense if Keating stood to make a bundle and then blew the scene. It all seems to depend on—"

The phone sounded once; paper began to feed out of the fax machine.

Dunstable immediately stood and began a silent reading of what was being sent from his office. As he continued reading, his expression intensified to half smile, half sneer. "Well, Father Koesler," he said, "it seems your suspicions were right on target. Nothing, nothing, nothing: Each and every one of these companies you questioned never amounted to anything. Not only were they nothing when they were incorporated, but several years back they stopped sending in annual reports. As a result, their charters were canceled. They are now nonactive corporations."

"What does that mean?" Koesler asked.

"Anyone can incorporate. It's a legal process that sets up a company. The company doesn't necessarily have to do or accomplish anything or provide any sort of service. It's just a sort of legal fiction. They're also referred to as 'shells' . . ." He looked at Koesler and Tully in turn. ". . . empty shells."

Instantly, Tully and Koesler looked at each other. "Shells," Tully repeated. "Just what Salden had in his computer: 'shells! look into . . . trace down! could be key!' "

"Just so," said Koesler. "And the 'K' at the bottom of that note: *Keating*. We'll never know, since the poor man is gone, but probably that 'K' on the female Episcopal rector item did stand for the baseball designation of strikeout. But I'll bet the 'shells' belonged to Keating.

"But," Koesler looked at Dunstable, "did Father Keating profit from these shell companies?"

"Oh, I'd say so," Dunstable replied. "While we were waiting, I just did a little computing of what the parish paid these companies over the years. In excess of two million dollars! And since we don't really know how many more of these 'shell' companies there are on the parish books, it may go even higher. After all, we only checked the ones you questioned. There may be more."

"But did Father Keating have access to them?" Koesler asked.

Dunstable snorted. "I'd say so. A John Keating is listed as president and vice president of each of these companies."

"The only slight gamble he took," Tully said, "was that somebody might get suspicious and check into these companies. But that, especially since he was a priest, was really no gamble at all."

"That's right," Dunstable agreed. "And I can speak as the prime patsy. I don't know how many times I and the parish council and the finance committee checked these billings. It never occurred to any of us that we were paying bills of nonexistent companies. And he knew the books wouldn't be audited until he was transferred from this parish. They wouldn't be audited even now, even though he was missing, if it hadn't been for Father Koesler."

"Something else comes to mind," Koesler said. "I wonder if John would be content with nothing more than the money from these shell companies."

"There's more?" Tully asked.

"I was just thinking of the five thousand dollars he took from Mr. Dunstable. It seems to me his avarice was so insatiable, he would stop at nothing."

"What did you have in mind?"

"The collections. This is an extremely wealthy parish. I would guess the weekly collections would average about eighteen to twenty thousand dollars." He looked to Dunstable, who nodded and said, "That's in the ballpark."

"So," Koesler continued, "there was lots and lots of money to play with. You kept all the money in the parish account at the local bank?"

Again Dunstable nodded.

"The chancery doesn't like that," Koesler said. "They'd rather we banked with the chancery. But with a parish like St. Waldo's, they wouldn't insist. My thought is that he would give you full credit for what you gave in the collections, but he'd spread the money out wherever he wished and still have plenty to pay legitimate bills. John, I believe, handled the weekly collection pretty much by himself?"

Mitchell nodded.

"So," Koesler continued, "no one actually knew exactly how much money there was except John. He could write checks on accessing accounts without question." He pointed to an account listed in the ledger. "This, for instance: 'The Youth Apostolate Fund.' I've never heard of anything like that. My suspicion is that this and/or other funds might have been tampered with. John could put lots and lots of money pretty well anywhere he wanted."

Dunstable looked deflated. "He kept such good records. We professionals admired—*admired*—his financial professionalism. He was so good at using Treasury bills and commercial accounts. He was *good*, all right; he didn't even have the pressure a normal embezzler has.

"One thing seems certain, gentlemen: Father Keating is not lost, kidnapped, or harmed in any way. He is alive and well and very well off somewhere."

Only Fathers Koesler and Dunn, Inspector Koznicki, and Lieutenant Tully knew of Guido Vespa's "confession." Thus, everyone else, including Dunstable, had never operated under the "knowledge" that Keating had been killed. Thus it was somewhat easier for Dunstable to conclude that Keating was alive. By now, there wasn't much doubt in Koesler and Tully's minds either.

"Then," Koesler said, "the murders! Hal Salden and Guido Vespa! Keating?"

"Maybe." Tully's mind was now operating in leaps and bounds. "But that would be pretty tricky for him to pull off. There's always the chance of recognition. He got his picture in the papers and on TV often enough. Then there's the crime itself. Murder One is a long step from embezzlement. Maybe. But I'd like to find an accomplice. Somebody with as much to gain as Keating. But somebody who would go for the jugular."

"Well," Dunstable consulted the fax again, "here's a nominee . . . although I haven't the slightest idea who she is." He handed the sheet to Tully, pointing out the recurring name on the shell companies.

"Sally Dean," Tully read. "Each and every company lists as officers John Keating as president and vice president and Sally Dean as secretary and treasurer. Sally Dean." He looked at the others. "Who the hell is Sally Dean?"

It was evident no one in the room knew. But suddenly, there was a knock at the door. Mitchell opened it and four men were startled to address four women: a cook, a secretary, and two reporters—Pat Lennon and Pringle McPhee.

25

WHAT IN HELL—?!"

"You'd probably find out in time who Sally Dean is," Lennon said, "but we can save you a lot of that time and trouble."

"How in hell—?!" Tully was not having much luck in completing a sentence.

". . . did we get in? Pringle here makes one hell of a good impression," Lennon said. "She was in the kitchen here a while back when you gentlemen were investigating the disappearance of Father Keating. You may remember seeing her, Lieutenant, and"—she turned to nod at Koesler—"Father Koesler, when you were hurrying out the back door."

"Yes," Tully said, "oh, yes. But how in hell—?"

". . . did we know you were trying to find out who Sally Dean is?" Pat gestured toward the secretary, who suddenly seemed extremely uneasy. "Well, you see," the secretary fumbled, "when I brought refreshments in here just before you started your meeting, I must have—by accident—hit the intercom button, and . . ."

Dunstable glanced at the console. The tiny red light was lit. He nodded to the others: The intercom was on. The four women—of prime concern the two reporters—had heard everything. Well, not everything, but at least everything that had been said at or near the desk.

Had the women overheard, Koesler wondered, what he had said to Tully regarding Vespa's confession? It was most unlikely. No one else in the room could have heard that conversation. And they had been seated on the couch, a goodly distance from the intercom.

"Okay, okay," Tully said, "the damage is done. So who the hell is Sally Dean?"

"Sally Dean," Lennon said, "used to work in this town, but not very well. She left town and years later came back with a remade body but unfortunately the same mind. Now she writes under the name of Lacy DeVere."

"The gossip columnist?" Koesler said. He'd thought the name Sally Dean rang a bell; now he vaguely recalled her byline from the past.

"Lacy DeVere, the gossip columnist," Lennon affirmed. "This explains a lot, most of which you have no way of knowing."

"You gonna tell us?" Tully said.

"How about a bargain?" Lennon proposed. "Pringle and I get this story on a first-day exclusive, and you get some interesting details on Lacy DeVere."

"Done." It was both a good and a fair deal. All it involved was slightly delaying a press conference in return for promising details that these two reporters alone might have.

"Okay." Lennon began ticking off those details.

"One: Lacy's column contained the first intimation that Keating had been a victim of foul play and might be dead. She was first on that bandwagon because at the time there was no logical reason to suspect anything like that had happened to him. At the time, he was a missing person, nothing else. If he had turned up alive—and at the time, odds were that he would—she would have had a lot of crow to eat. But having him appear to be dead apparently is what they wanted. So he could run off with the money. And thanks to some clever planning, no one would be the wiser.

"Two: Hal Salden did discover the bones of what was about to happen. From what's been said in here today, that's what those notes in his basket were all about. Hal discovered the shell companies. This was even before Keating 'disappeared.' Hal could have blown the whole scheme out of the water. So he had to be killed. My guess is that Lacy did it.

"Three: This is the murky part. The wounding of Father Koesler here seems to have gotten you back on the case. So the wounding had to be a result of the investigation. My guess is that Guido Vespa somehow learned about the plot, maybe got involved in it, was going to tell the father about it—maybe to ease his conscience—and he was killed and Father was wounded. Again, my guess is Lacy did it.

"And four: Yesterday, just before you got to the *News* to look at Hal's CRT, Lacy was there for the same purpose. Why would she do that unless it was for the same purpose? She wanted to find out if Hal had entered anything about his investigation and suspicions."

"Then why didn't she kill the stuff about shell companies?" Tully asked.

"My guess is she would have but she never got the chance. Pringle didn't give her the password. And just after she started fooling with the machine, I came in and threw her out."

Tully counted this one of the best bargains he'd ever made, especially with anyone from the media. "Lemmee ask you: Why do you feel so strongly that the DeVere woman did the shootings?"

"Easy," Pat said. "She's notorious for doing anything—*anything*— to get what she wants."

"Even murder?"

"She could do it without blinking. And I think Keating blew this scene about the time he was reported missing. I think Keating found just the person to carry out the dirty end of the deal."

"For love or money?" Tully wondered. "Was theirs just a business arrangement—or more?" He scratched his chin. "Either way, for her to try to get into Salden's machine, they must have felt their world was falling apart."

"I think so," Pat agreed. "My guess, since the last we saw of DeVere was yesterday, is that she's long gone. Probably she and Keating are busy enjoying millions of bucks—somewhere—either together or separately."

"Yeah, somewhere. But where?"

After a moment, Koesler spoke. "I have a thought," he said tentatively.

Everyone looked at him with a mixture of hope and encouragement.

"Mr. Dunstable . . ."

"Eric," Dunstable insisted. He was really beginning to like Father Koesler.

"Very well then, Eric . . . when Father Keating used to accompany you on vacations, were there any places—was there any one place— that he seemed to prize more than the others?"

Dunstable gave that some thought. He chuckled ironically. "I can't think of a vacation he didn't enjoy to the hilt."

"Any one more than the others, though?"

Dunstable thought some more. "Maui, the French Riviera, Costa del Sol, a cruise to Bali, golf at St. Andrews, Troon, Pebble Beach . . .

there were so many. But I think I may be listing my favorites as well as his."

Another pause.

"Wait," Koesler said, "maybe I'm going at this the wrong way. Lieutenant, is there any way of finding out which countries have no extradition treaties with the U.S.?"

Tully brightened. "Of course! He had to figure that eventually his game would probably be uncovered. Possibly in the audit. Maybe a year or more away. He'd want to be somewhere where we couldn't get him back to stand trial. Wait a second."

Tully dialed a number, exchanged a few pro forma pleasantries, requested the information, and waited while drumming his fingers on the desk. The fax machine clicked. Tully scanned the incoming info, then grunted. "This doesn't look so good. I had no idea there were so many countries that have no extradition treaty with us. There are," he counted, "more than sixty countries on this list. Here . . ." He handed the list to Dunstable. ". . . see if any of these look good."

Dunstable scanned the list. "There are a lot, aren't there . . . I would never have guessed. Some of these countries are interesting, but mostly from an intellectual aspect—wait! Here's one . . . here's the one! It slipped my mind entirely. But of course: About five years ago we came across this fabulous resort. The climate that Father Ja—uh, Keating enjoyed. A bit pricey but worth every penny. So exclusive that practically no one knows about it. Father Jack"—he couldn't break himself of the habit of tacking the title onto Keating's name—"just loved it. I remember now. It seemed at the time that he was inordinately fond of the place. Now I know why: He was planning to retire there, safe and snug and beyond justice. Bahrain!"

Tully's brow was knit. "Where in hell's Bahrain?"

"The Persian Gulf," Dunstable said.

"The gulf!"

"I know it doesn't sound like much. But it's just off the coast of Saudi Arabia. And believe me, it's perfect. For Father Jack, it's more than perfect."

"But," Koesler cautioned, "it's still only a theory. How can we know for sure?"

"I'll be glad to go there now, at my own expense—today—and flush out the bastard," Dunstable offered.

"I don't think that's necessary—or even the quickest way to do this. I can ask the authorities there for verification. We may not be able to get Keating out of there, but at least we can locate him. And I'll run a LEIN on Lacy DeVere. We may just be able to sew this thing up. Maybe not to everybody's satisfaction . . . but not all endings are happy."

Tully got busy on the phone. Koesler, reminded again that his stamina wasn't what it had been before the shooting, dropped wearily to the couch. The cook and the secretary, having been admonished to keep mum on everything they'd heard, returned to their work with newfound confidence: Not only would they not be fired, but without Father Keating around they might just enjoy extended employment.

Dunstable and Father Mitchell, suddenly on a more congenial basis, huddled to arrange a speedy audit for St. Waldo of the Hills. Pringle McPhee and Pat Lennon quickly mapped their battle plan for last-minute interviews prior to filing this story under their joint byline.

If all this speculation became fact, Lacy DeVere would deservedly suffer an ultimate discreditation. That item linking Tully and Lennon would go down the tube along with the rest of DeVere's irresponsible gossip.

Lennon understood this outcome in the split second before she got busy pulling her side of the story together. And she realized that if they had not patched things up before, Tully and his Alice would be back together now.

As Tully himself had just remarked, not all endings are happy.

26

THE BRITISH Airways jetliner touched down faultlessly at Bahrain International Airport. It was 1:30 P.M. in Detroit where the meeting at St. Waldo's had just broken up. It was 8:30 P.M. in Bahrain.

In the first-class cabin, Lacy DeVere gathered up her carry-on luggage. No baggage claim delays for her. She had packed hurriedly, little more than the necessities. It didn't much matter. They had more money than they'd ever be able to spend.

Lacy was certain that fate had conspired against her back in Detroit. She'd held the fort above and beyond the agreement she'd made with Jack Keating. But yesterday when she tried to get into Hal Salden's basket, she began to see the handwriting on the wall. After Lennon in effect threw her out, she'd lingered outside the *News*. When she spotted Tully and Koesler entering, she knew it was time to leave.

That goddam priest! It had been Jack's idea to keep him out of the picture. She hadn't agreed at all. But Jack insisted. He had been certain that the police would call on Koesler to look into the disappearance. Koesler had built up an excellent track record in assisting the cops. And besides, Jack pointed out, in view of the fact that he and Koesler had been buddies once upon a time, Koesler might even be motivated to volunteer his expertise.

She still thought she'd been right. Koesler never would have caught on. The plan was too good. Keep it simple, she had argued. The more people involved, the more likely that excellent scheme would unravel.

But Jack had won out. After all, it was *his* money. Or rather, the money he'd embezzled.

In just a short while now, she'd remind Jack that he was the one who'd selected Guido Vespa. Even though she was the one who had negotiated the contract.

Vespa very definitely was the weak link. It might have worked had Vespa stuck to the contract and simply gone to Koesler and confessed murder. Though she still believed it had been unnecessary to "neutralize" the meddlesome priest, it would have worked if Vespa had just done what he contracted to do. Easiest money he ever earned. Nothing to do but tell a fable to a priest.

But no! He had to invent that cockamamy story of Jack's burial with another priest. It would have been ludicrous had it not led to the collapse of her house of cards.

As long as she lived she would never forget that phone call. When Vespa told her what he had "added" to the confession, she was speechless. When he told her he was going to meet Koesler and make a clean breast of the whole thing, she had the presence of mind to ascertain that the meeting would take place that evening.

It hadn't been difficult to park unobtrusively near Koesler's rectory to await Vespa's arrival. She assumed he would be armed; it was vital to take him by surprise. But instead of Vespa's arriving, Koesler had departed. It really hadn't been that challenging to follow him by car up Gratiot and then on foot into the Eastern Market. And it was no problem to stay in the shadows as she approached the two men.

Lacy wasn't sure whether love was better the second time around, but she discovered that killing was easier the second time around. Vespa hadn't had time to tell the priest the whole story before she fired. Still, she was relieved to see Koesler go down from one of the slugs she pumped into Vespa. If Koesler had not been knocked to the ground he might have been able to see and identify her and she would have had to kill him. No use multiplying murders needlessly.

It had been much harder to psych herself up to kill Hal Salden. But after a few of Salden's inquiring phone calls to St. Waldo's, Jack was certain the astute and perspicacious reporter was beginning to suspect the "imaginative bookkeeping" that was going on.

That's when Lacy learned that Jack was no good in an emergency. Oh, he was cool-headed enough when it came to setting up a scam, operating in the abstract. But present him with a crisis and he crumbled. So as usual, it was up to the little woman.

Still, it was difficult to kill for the first time. She'd had to tell herself over and over that it had to happen or she wouldn't get what she wanted.

Necessity being the mother of invention, she learned from research and investigation that the way to do this, she being no markswoman, was to get close, be part of the crowd—or, at Eastern Market, part of the shadows. If she set the machine pistol to fire in bursts, two simple trigger squeezes would be more than enough firepower. That's what the crackhead who sold her the pistol advised her to do. And his advice had been free as well as accurate.

But . . . that was the past.

Now she and Jack could reap the wealth, the comfort, the soft life they'd earned from all that planning, patience, and risk.

She would take a cab to that little piece of paradise they'd christened The Wheels after St. Waldo's—the mother of it all. No sense in renting a car; at last count there were three luxury autos stabled at The Wheels. And by the time she called Jack and he got here she could already be there.

Once the cab pulled away from the curb, she really started to unwind. She was headed toward retirement, many enjoyable years of all that a considerable fortune could guarantee.

Jack's brilliant inspiration to skim millions from the fat cats of St. Waldo's was equally matched by his selection of Bahrain as their golden hideaway. The little island had long ago abandoned oil as its most important product. Now the streets were lined with banks—banks and hotels. And a private patch of turf known to an intimate few as The Wheels.

Try as anyone might, there was nobody who could force them from their sanctuary. It was time to kick off her shoes. Lacy DeVere had arrived in The Promised Land.

She paid the cabbie, picked up her luggage, and paused before going up the steps. It was gorgeous to the point of being breathtaking. This—dusk settling in—was her favorite time of day, and this—The Wheels—was her dream come true.

Actually, it was well beyond her dreams. If, years ago, someone had told her she'd have a love affair with a Catholic priest, she'd have denied it out of hand. If anyone had told her that she and her lover would live out their lives in a never-never land where money was no object, she'd have laughed herself silly.

But here it was and here she was.

As she started up the marble steps, she felt as if her feet were hardly touching them. In the past couple of years, she and Jack had visited The Wheels on several occasions when he could absent himself from the parish for a few days. Sometimes when he had to hurry back she had stayed on to supervise construction. Thus she knew the mansion even better than he.

Now, never again would they have to take exquisite precautions not to be identified as being together. This was paradise, and no one, not even an avenging angel, would be able to drive them from it.

* * *

Upstairs, in the master bedroom of The Wheels, things were cooling down.

There was no mistaking the priorities of this room. The bed! Round, of Homeric size, it was mounted on a marble platform that could remind one of an altar. Except that instead of a baldachino, it was canopied by an overhead mirror of equally Homeric dimensions.

Then there was the imposing entertainment center, offering a large-screen TV with VCR, a compact disc player, and a short wave radio. But beyond doubt the bed was the undeniable focus of the room.

The bedding was mussed. The bed had been used recently and left disheveled. Its erstwhile occupants were now enjoying the Jacuzzi.

John Keating had all the servants he needed and then some. Soraya, a seductive Egyptian girl, was not an afterthought, but a confection he found irresistible. She would, he assured himself, make him young. And she wasn't doing badly. Just a few minutes earlier he had been as frisky as a man half his age or better. And now she ministered to him in the Jacuzzi where he could not think of being aroused again. Not for a while, anyway.

Keating, wearing nothing but a beatific smile and with an ample glass of fine wine within reach, looked about with deep appreciation. "Not bad for a simple parish priest," he commented aloud.

Soraya smiled broadly. Outside of a few words, and those often jumbled, she neither spoke nor understood English. Conversation, of course, was not why she'd been hired.

Keating's smile broadened. "Soraya, my dear," he said to her uncomprehending grin, "we could just as well be back in, say, 25 B.C. I could be a senator of imperial Rome. You know, 'Senatus Populusque Romanus.' And you could be . . . well . . . not a vestal virgin. Ah, yes, the Romans knew how to live. But before I'm done, I'll be able to teach them a thing or two."

He seemed pleased. She giggled.

He crooked a finger under her chin and lifted her head. Their eyes locked. He liked her. That was all that mattered.

"Well, m'dear," he said, "you are very definitely not Lacy and, God knows, she is not you. I've just got to figure out some place to stash you after she gets here. I haven't tested her jealousy threshhold. But I'll bet it's not very high. Anyway, whatever happens, you're going to be better off than you were. It is a far, far better thing I do . . ." He paused. "This is a rather extended monologue. I can't quite decide whether to teach you some English or not."

"Henglish?" she adapted happily.

"Henglish," he repeated. "No, on further thought, it's better this way. I'll have Lacy to talk to and physically satisfy from time to time. And you will be my love mate."

"Love!" she said with certainty.

"Yes, love. I ask you . . . no . . . I ask myself, what further need have we for words? Love will do nicely. But this is a big house—a very big house. There's got to be plenty of room for a couple of women who will scarcely if ever meet."

Soraya seemed to have lost interest in his as far as she was concerned incomprehensible babblings. She was concentrating on a segment of his anatomy.

"Well, I'll be . . ." he commented in wonder, "I didn't think I'd get up again for days. Soraya, you are a marvel!"

*   *   *

Lacy DeVere couldn't put her finger on it, but something was wrong. Perhaps it was intuition. But over the years she had learned to trust her sixth sense.

She dropped her luggage in the foyer. Quietly, deliberately, she ascended the winding staircase.

On the second floor landing she came upon Jack's black silk trousers. A little further on toward the bedroom, his favorite kimono had been discarded.

Had Jack been drinking? He had a history of that—just short of, he assured her, alcoholism. But usually his heaviest drinking occurred at times of stress. And God knows the pressure was off now. Lacy grew uneasy.

As she followed the trail of abandoned clothing, she came upon a lengthy and beautifully decorated width of watered silk. She recognized the sari Jack had given her. That was followed by female underclothing, a bra and panties of a size to fit a petite but well-endowed female.

Any lingering doubt was dispelled as she reached the bedroom doorway. She could clearly hear the sounds emanating from the Jacuzzi.

* * *

Rational thought surrendered to consuming anger as she advanced to the nightstand. She recalled how she had argued against keeping a weapon in the house. They had installed a state-of-the-art security system and they could hire as many security people as they wanted. But Jack had insisted on keeping the loaded gun at hand.

Now, recalling his insistence in the face of her objections, she smiled as she drew the weapon from the drawer.

Soundlessly she moved to the arched doorway and stood motionless there. The tan-skinned girl's shapely back was to the door, and Jack was too physically engaged to notice Lacy.

But something—possibly the hatred that flowed from Lacy's core—reached him. He looked up and saw her. And the gun in her hand. The sight dampened the excitement he had been enjoying. In the face of his manifest distraction, Soraya looked up, concerned she was doing something wrong. Seeing the fear in his eyes, she turned to look over her shoulder. At the sight of Lacy and the gun, she let out a small shriek and slipped, scrambled, and clambered out of the Jacuzzi.

Lacy had to give Jack credit. The girl seemed without physical flaw. And it was good; now she had a clean shot at him. The second killing had been easier than the first. The third was going to be pure pleasure.

"Lacy, no!" Jack held a hand up defensively in front of his face. "You don't know what you're doing! We've got it made. Finally got it made. Don't! This was nothing. I was lonesome for you, that's all. I can explain this whole thing. Don't ruin what we've got now."

Lacy slowly, methodically, raised the gun until it was aimed directly at the hand that shielded his face.

He knew her. He realized that nothing he could do or say would dissuade her. *"Oh, my God, I am heartily sorry . . ."* He began the traditional Catholic Act of Contrition.

Lacy, afraid his pronouncement of sorrow might work and save him from hell, pressed the trigger.

Nothing happened.

Taking that as divine reprieve, Jack cried out, "Lacy, give it up! It's God's will!"

She had forgotten the safety catch. She flipped the lever and fired.

The first slug tore through his extended hand to embed itself in the wall behind the Jacuzzi. The next four buried themselves in his head— or what was left of it. Jack Keating slumped and slid down into the rapidly reddening water.

Lacy DeVere lowered the gun as the police, weapons drawn, entered the room.

27

FATHER NICK DUNN was fond of calling it the Case of the Missing Pastor. Father Bob Koesler thought Father Dunn had seen too many Perry Mason programs.

Father Dunn wanted to have a party celebrating the closing of the Case of the Missing Pastor. Father Koesler could find nothing to celebrate. For him, the occasion marked the tragic end of a former friend and colleague.

In lieu of such a celebration, Koesler suggested that they accept Inspector Koznicki's invitation to Sunday dinner at his home. Koesler hoped this would satisfy Dunn's aspiration to meet and dine with important people. As for Koesler, dining with the Koznickis was old hat. He was confident that the inspector and his wife, Wanda, would make allowances for his less than exhilarated state.

The meal—pot roast, boiled potatoes, vegetables, and salad—was home cooked as usual, delicious if commonplace. Table talk revolved around pedestrian topics: Dunn's studies, Koesler's attempts to build his congregation from the neighboring apartments and condos, Koznicki's departmental budgetary problems, Wanda's recounting of the triumphs and mishaps of their children.

After dinner, they continued to sit around the dining table while Wanda served coffee and cake.

Conversation quite naturally turned to the star-crossed rise and fall of Father Keating.

"Without a doubt," Koznicki said, "that must have been the most unusual contract ever offered to anyone in the mob."

"I'll say," Wanda agreed. "Five thousand dollars just to pretend to go to confession. Many more deals like that and you'll be busy from sunup to sundown."

They chuckled.

"Yes," Koesler said, "but in the good old days—which weren't all that long ago—you'd have thought Catholics were being paid to go to confession. I can remember very well the days before Christmas and Easter—before St. Joseph's feast if you were in an Italian parish—it was wall-to-wall penitents. And yes, Wanda, from about sunup to sundown."

"Now that we're well past it," Dunn said, "and we know it was not a real confession—"

"And," Koesler interrupted, "we also know that no one else can ever know about that confession."

"Yes, yes, of course." Dunn was a bit tired of being reminded of this. "But something's been nagging at me all this time: What did you give Guido for a penance? I mean, that wouldn't be violating anything, any kind of secret, if you told. And outside of this crazy experience, I've never had anybody confess murder."

Koesler smiled and spread his hands on the table. "What sort of penance can you give? It's the ultimate crime and well up there in the moral order. We aren't back in the early centuries of the Church when penances could be lengthy, public, and humiliating—like being obliged to beg for the poor for a number of years. You know that."

"Sure," Dunn said, "but although I could hear him, I couldn't hear you. So what did you give him?"

"I'm not stalling. It's just that I'm a little embarrassed at Guido's penance.

"We have to remember," Koesler said, mostly for the benefit of the Koznickis, who hadn't had his theological training, "that there is no way we—any of us—can really repay the debt of sin. If we have wronged another—stolen something, say—we can at least try to take responsibility and repay him. But we cannot make up to God what we have done in violating any of His commands. Now, with that in mind, Guido not only confessed murder, he also identified who it was he'd killed.

"If it had been, for instance, a man with a family, he would have had the responsibility to supply what the family had lost. The income, at very least. But Guido claimed he'd killed a priest. No family; no one dependent on the victim. So I considered that part of his possible debt was nonexistent.

"But, as in all sin, we Christians have to fall back on the sacrifice of Christ. That's why we say Christ died for our sins. The God-man offered His life to His Father for us, for our sins.

"So whatever penance a priest gives—or assigns—is merely a token.

We usually assign a certain number of Our Fathers or Hail Marys, or maybe the Rosary." The others nodded in understanding.

"According to Guido, however, he wasn't familiar with any of the ordinary prayers Catholics routinely know." Here Koesler almost blushed. "The way it turned out, Guido suggested his own penance—which action is not unique in the annals of the Sacrament of Penance."

"*What?*" The explanation was much more than Dunn needed to know.

"Guido said he had a record at home of Sinatra singing The Lord's Prayer. And that he'd go home and listen to that."

After a moment of startled silence, they all laughed.

"If only Frank Sinatra knew!" Wanda said through her laughter.

"But," Koesler said, "he never will."

"Of course," Koznicki said, after the laughter died down, "we keep coming back to that little gem that Vespa added."

"The part," Dunn supplied, "about burying Keating with Monsignor Kern. A very active imagination, that Vespa had."

"Yes," Koznicki agreed, "but it was that compulsion to invent colorful details that proved his undoing. The department had given up on the case. Then Monsignor Kern was exhumed. Then things started happening."

"Yes," Koesler said, "apparently, Guido felt the need to let me in on the whole thing. And God knows I was thoroughly confused at that point. I don't know why he called Lacy DeVere. Maybe it was some misplaced sense of honor; after all, he was about to violate the contract. And that mistake—if we can call it a mistake—proved fatal to Guido . . . and almost to me."

"Whatever," Koznicki said. "As a result, the Case of the Missing Pastor was reopened."

"See! I told you that was a great title!" Dunn exulted.

"What?" Koznicki was mystified.

"Nothing," Koesler assured the inspector. "Part of Father Dunn's course is mystery solving.

"And, speaking of solving mysteries," he added, "I didn't do too well this time out. All the guideposts were there. But I sure wasn't interpreting them correctly."

"Come now, Father . . ." Koznicki began.

"No," Koesler said resolutely, "one of the keys was Father Keating's upbringing. He had a comfortable, wealthy background. He was used to living very, very well. Things began to go bad for him—at least as far as he was concerned—when his inheritance turned out to be fairly modest. Now I think his parents were wise to do that. But I also think they should have prepared him for that.

"Instead, he must have been terribly shocked to receive so comparatively small an inheritance.

"Then there was the matter of his stock investment that went sour. I think that scarred him. At that point, his future was still not much different than that of the rest of us. Which, I think, is not all that bad. The Church, at least in this diocese, takes pretty adequate care of its retired priests.

"However, I'm sure Jack didn't see it that way. And I guess that's when he decided to take care of his future himself."

The inspector rose and refilled the coffee cups. Koesler, not for the first time, was vaguely puzzled that his friends consumed so much coffee. They never did when he played host.

"Probably," Koesler continued, "his plot hatched sometime after he was assigned to St. Waldo's."

"And a clever plot it was," Koznicki said. "Fortunately for him, he had a great deal of money to manipulate. And manipulate it he did. The creation of those shell companies was at the heart of his plan—although the recent parish audit shows that he was also skimming the regular donations."

"That at least he might not have been able to get away with some years back when all parochial banking was done with the archdiocese," Koesler noted. "Except"—he shook his head—"the poor man didn't live to enjoy the fruits of his embezzlement."

"Poor!" Father Dunn exclaimed. "He built the most luxurious palace I've ever heard of!"

"Yes . . ." Koesler partway agreed, ". . . but to do that, he surrendered his service to God and God's people."

"Indeed it was a short-lived triumph," Koznicki said. "It began for Father Keating the day he disappeared. As it turned out, he really did disappear. He left for Bahrain that day, leaving behind his partner-in-crime to tie up all the loose ends."

"That's something that puzzles me," Dunn said. "Why didn't the two of them just run off together? They had the money, and they'd built themselves a castle in a country that didn't have an extradition treaty with us."

"That way," Koznicki said, "they would have, as the expression has it, given away the farm. As long as Father Keating remained merely missing, the Detroit archdiocese was unlikely to order an audit of St. Waldo's financial records. In addition, even after a year or so and the ordering of the audit, it is by no means certain that the audit would have uncovered the embezzlement.

"It was an almost perfect plan. One would almost have to view with suspicion St. Waldo's finances in order to unearth the crime. And," Koznicki turned toward Koesler, "that is where my dear friend Father Koesler enters the case.

"Your disclaimer to the contrary notwithstanding, Father, it was you who brought us back to St. Waldo's for one final look. And it was your suspicion that discovered what really was going on."

Koesler attempted to wave away the compliment. "Any priest in this archdiocese who handles marriage cases would know there's no charge for them anymore."

"True, my friend. But you brought us back to the scene. And, as I have told you many times, you have a good mind for this sort of thing."

Koesler chuckled. "Meaning I should have joined the police force?"

"Oh, no. If you had not become a priest, you would have missed your destiny. And we would have been the poorer for not having your expert contribution in some of these cases."

"Be that as it may," Koesler said, "and getting back to Father Dunn's question, Jack and Lacy DeVere certainly weren't looking for any sort of notoriety. They didn't want to become another Bonnie and Clyde. They wanted to live out their years in luxury and security. It was just possible, as the inspector said, that they might have gotten away with it for good and all. And even if, years later, they were discovered, well, time tends to soften a reaction—even to embezzlement."

"Excuse me," Dunn said, "this is just an honest question. But isn't there a statute of limitations? I mean couldn't Keating have spent his six or ten years or whatever in Bahrain and then been free to come and go here once the statute of limitations had expired?"

"There is, indeed, a statute of limitations on embezzlement," Koznicki replied, "but the person charged with embezzlement must spend those years in the jurisdiction where that crime was committed. In other words, when Father Keating left this country, the clock stopped ticking. In effect, he became a permanent expatriate. Although I doubt that this troubled him."

"Okay, so much for embezzlement . . ." Dunn continued his probe into every facet of what he hoped would be but his first of many homicide investigations. ". . . what about murder? They hadn't planned on murder, had they?"

"A moot question, Father," Koznicki said. "As far as Father Keating is concerned, probably not. But remember, the two of them had carved out their separate roles in this scheme. After their collaboration in setting up the shell companies, the actual manipulation of money was Father Keating's job. Keeping prying eyes away and patching up loose ends was Miss DeVere's responsibility.

"Remember that *before* Father Keating's 'disappearance,' the reporter, Mr. Salden, was on the trail of their scheme. Miss DeVere probably saw no way out but murder.

"Again, even though Father Keating was safely in Bahrain, Guido Vespa was about to disclose a vital ingredient of their scheme to Father Koesler. That would have robbed them of a scot-free getaway. And don't forget: She had already murdered once.

"But when things started closing in, she must've been fearful of being found out: She left the country in such haste that she neglected to dispose of her machine pistol. We found it in her apartment. It is the gun that killed both Salden and Vespa. And it is covered with her prints—and hers alone. She escaped us by a hairsbreadth. If she had been able to control her jealous rage when she found Father Keating with another woman . . ." Koznicki shrugged. The conclusion was obvious.

"What do you think will happen to her?" It seemed it had to be Father Dunn's final question.

Koznicki shrugged again. "The rules of evidence, presumption of innocence, and due process in Bahrain are certainly different from ours. If both the victim and the perpetrator were not U.S. citizens, I fear it would be capital punishment for a capital crime. As it is, my guess would be at least an extended prison sentence, perhaps life. And, might I add, I would not be surprised if their prison amenities are far less pleasant even than ours. In other words, a living hell.

"And . . ." Koznicki anticipated a corollary question from Dunn.

". . . should she be set free—live out her sentence, be paroled—she would always have to be looking over her shoulder. There are many well-placed local people who would dearly want her to pay for the crimes she committed here. If someday she were to be kidnapped and find herself dumped on the Wayne or Oakland County prosecutor's doorstep, she very surely would face trial for murder here.

"In other words, by one intemperate action, she went from paradise to despair."

"Oh . . . uh . . . one more thing . . ." This *had* to be Father Dunn's final question. ". . . the car."

"The car?" Koznicki repeated.

"Keating's car. How come it was found parked near Costello's house?"

"Truly bizarre," Koznicki commented, "but fitting neatly into place in this scheme. It was one more ploy to convince us that Father Keating was indeed dead and had been murdered.

"Late the same Friday night that Father left the country, Miss DeVere, wearing gloves, drove Father's car to where she parked it near the Costello home. After wiping the steering wheel clean of prints—another smokescreen—she walked two blocks to where the taxi she had arranged for was waiting.

"When we found the abandoned car—as inevitably we would—our suspicion of foul play would be confirmed. But we would not be able to link the car to the Costellos or to Remo Vespa because, on the one hand, they had nothing to do with it and, on the other, Guido assured her that his family would have alibis for the time frame. That he had determined without their knowledge."

Noting the furrow in Dunn's brow, Koznicki added, "Much of what we have discovered through our own investigation has been corroborated by statements Miss DeVere has made to the authorities in Bahrain. In her present situation, it is definitely in her own best interest that she be cooperative. She is bargaining now for her very life."

Father Koesler, who was developing almost a paternal solicitude toward Dunn, smiled. "Satisfied?"

The contented look on Dunn's face was response enough to Koesler's question. "Oh, yes. Both with the meal—thank you, Mrs. Koznicki—and the investigation—thank you, Bob Koesler."

Koesler smiled more broadly. "Look at all the stories you'll be able to tell your confreres in the Twin Cities about big bad Detroit."

"That's true . . . whenever I get back."

The smile faded. "What?"

"I've been thinking of renewing my enrollment in the university."

"What?"

"There's no end to what a person can learn about psychology. And there's lots more I can learn about police procedure and crime investigations."

Preliminary to my taking over from you, Dunn left unsaid.

Koesler understood the unspoken intention. "Listen, Nick, I know what you're thinking. Now you're welcome to stay, but you're mistaken if you think I get involved in these investigations as some sort of avocation. You couldn't be more wrong. The most exciting thing that's going to happen at Old St. Joe's is going to be figuring out how we'll raise enough money to fix the church roof. I'd be willing to bet that I'll never be involved in another police investigation."

Koznicki kept a straight face, but he couldn't keep the amusement from his eyes. Dunn smiled outright. "I know Guido Vespa tried to teach us that gambling can be harmful to one's health," he said, "but, Bob, I'll just cover that bet."